A Magical Inheritance

THE
LADIES
OCCULT
SOCIETY

A Magical Inheritance

THE
LADIES
OCCULT
SOCIETY

KRISTA D. BALL

✤ Historian's Note ✤

I REFERENCE MONEY in two different ways in this book: written out (e.g. one pound) and numerical (e.g. £1). Sometimes, the pound sterling was written *l* (e.g. 8*l*). I do not use that style in this book. However, I thought you should know, especially if you find yourself looking up a term or item that is mentioned in the book.

d – This means penny or pence. It was abbreviated in the period with a *d* not *p*, as in a Roman *denarius* not p as in penny. In this book, you will find Miss Knight writing down 9*d* and then calling it nine pence. It takes twelve pence to make a shilling.

s – This means shilling. Four shillings is written *4s*. Twelve pence made a shilling. Twenty shillings made a pound.

Guinea – In 1810, the year that this book is based, a guinea was worth twenty-one shillings.

I hope that helps!

❧ Chapter 1 ❧

Bryden Rectory
March 14, 1810

MISS ELIZABETH KNIGHT obeyed the summons to join her father in his study. She would need to prune back the roses later that day, provided her father did not require a large task of her. Otherwise, she would face months of thorn scratches as she worked the vegetable garden. She brushed her hands on her apron before hanging both it and her pruning scissors on the wooden hooks just inside the back entrance.

"Papa?" Elizabeth called out as she walked toward the study. "John said you requested me."

"In here, my dear," her father called out.

As it happened, he was not in his study as their bailiff had said. Instead, he was across the hall in the main drawing room. Isabella was with him, as she was in all things. Elizabeth smiled at her newest stepmother. It had been over a year now, and time had begun its task of dulling Elizabeth's exasperation surrounding her father marrying one of his *younger* daughters' acquaintances.

However, one look at their concerned faces was all Elizabeth needed to know the purpose of her summons. "Is there word of Uncle Edward?"

Her father was standing next to his wife, near the window, and he held two letters. An opened one bore the ominous black wax seal of the worst of news. The other was not yet opened.

"These," he said, holding up the letters in front of him, "are from an attorney in London. I am sorry, but your uncle is dead."

She had been preparing herself for this news for many months now, but still required that silent moment that followed to gather her grief. Tears threatened, but she successfully maintained her composure. That would please her father, who disliked young ladies parading their emotions, as he called it. "Poor soul. Does the letter say if he suffered much at the end?"

Her father gestured at the opened letter. "The attorney says the final decline was swift and that Edward Leigh was unaware of his surroundings in the final hours. I pray that also includes his own pain. I am very sorry, my dear. The girls were always a favourite with him."

Elizabeth let the comment pass. Most of her sisters were not related to Uncle Edward, as he was the brother of *her* mother, and of her father's first marriage. That marriage had only produced two children —Elizabeth and Mary—and he forgot too often that his unmarried daughters were their own individual persons. Her other siblings—Charles, Cassandra, Theodosia, and Georgiana—were not related to Uncle Edward.

"The attorney says that this sealed letter is for you. There will apparently be more letters to come, as the estate and will are discharged accordingly, but your uncle had written this specifically for you before his death," her father said with a hint of curiosity in his voice.

Elizabeth heard the unspoken request for her to read it aloud, but she was not yet up to the task.

Isabella clearly read Elizabeth's heart. She said, "I assume Mr. David Leigh will get the London house, yes?"

"This Mr. Grant does not say, but I assume as much." Her father's face brightened. "Oh! It quite slipped my mind. The letter did say, however, that Elizabeth will inherit fourteen-hundred pounds! What a good addition to our household that will make. I was hoping to repair the back stairs this summer. The wood is rotting."

"Oh, Elizabeth! How kind of him," Isabella said.

"He was always a very good uncle," Elizabeth said quietly.

"It is such a relief that he left some of the girls money," her father said. "It is too bad, though, he did not leave them *all* a little something. Though, I suppose he had his favourites."

"Mary does not want for more money," Elizabeth said coldly, and far colder than she'd intended. However, she knew her father well enough that he was already calculating the pounds, shillings, and pence of her new inheritance—easily forty pounds interest per annum, perhaps even as much as fifty-six pounds depending upon circumstance and a little luck.

That would easily cover her income of twenty pounds per annum that her father provided, not including her room and board, of course. Which he reminded her of weekly. Yes, indeed. Mr. Knight would come out ahead in this. They all knew it, and he was no doubt feeling the relief from the burden of his unmarried daughter's tea and clothing expenses.

No wonder he struggled to maintain an appropriate level of solemnity.

"I believe your father meant for the young girls. Georgiana is not quite sixteen, after all," Isabella said, giving her husband a pointed look. "Isn't that correct, Mr. Knight?"

"Oh, of course, my dear Isabella, I was thinking of Thea and G. Still, you are very cold toward your sister, Mary. It's unlikely you'll marry at your age, and you will need Mary's assistance soon. She has her own children now. Surely you wouldn't wish her to spend my grandson's inheritance upon her unmarried sister once I am dead."

Elizabeth steadied her mind in an attempt to ignore her father's cutting words. Even now, in this moment of grieving a dead uncle who she looked up to as a second father, her own father took the opportunity to remind her of how little he valued her choices. Mary would always be superior in his estimation. She had married the much older, but wealthy, widower. She had married for a home and the comforts of a large income. She had born the man's children. She had done her Christian and womanly duty. Elizabeth could not compete with that in her father's eyes.

"Elizabeth?" Isabella asked in a louder tone than was strictly necessary for the small room. "Did you wish to read your letter in private?"

"Oh, she can read it aloud," Mr. Knight said. "I'm certain it's for all to hear."

Isabella gave Elizabeth an apologetic look, one that announced she was merely attempting to distract Mr. Knight. For her part, Elizabeth struggled not to resent the woman just that bit more. However, she knew her irritation was with her father, and not Isabella. It was her father who chose to remarry for the third time. Though she was the eldest and was happy to care for her younger siblings, her father still hoped that she would marry. He could not possibly raise young ladies on his own with all his duties as a rector. No, indeed. He had to marry and, if he were very, very lucky, his new wife would provide him with only sons to help expand the family fortunes.

And, of course, to look after Elizabeth who seemed determined to be an old maid.

Her uncle's gift would provide her with some independence now. She would not need to ask her father for four shillings to purchase a pair of gloves because her old ones were worn at the seams. She would not need to explain how Theodosia had stolen her boots for a prank and had accidentally ruined them in the process. She could purchase replacements herself and not need to suffer any further with the wet seeping into her stockings and causing endless chills that compromised her health, which only brought about her father's rebukes.

"Elizabeth, are you well?" Isabella asked in a gentle voice.

"The shock," Elizabeth whispered. She wanted nothing more than to read her letter privately. It had been written for her. From her friends, she knew that all other households honoured and respected that some letters were private, but her father did not believe that the *girls* could have anything to conceal.

"Read the letter aloud then, Isabella," her father said. "Since Elizabeth is unequal to the task."

Elizabeth's jaw trembled, but she kept her composure. She could not speak, for fear a storm of emotions would rush out of her. She was not in command of herself, and she would not debase herself by speaking.

"Mr. Knight." There was the slightest hint of censure in Isabella's voice. "This is Elizabeth's letter."

"We are all family here," Mr. Knight said, in a casual, dismissive tone that cut Elizabeth all the more because he did not see her grief. He only saw the inheritance that was about to ease his life.

Isabella flashed Elizabeth a final apologetic expression before accepting the sealed letter from her husband. She read it aloud.

My dearest niece,

Allow me to apologize for not inviting you to town last Christmas, and my role in convincing your aunt into visiting Bryden, as opposed to her offering her home as a respite from the gayeties of that season in the country. My health was unsuitable for company, and I wished your last memories of me would be happier than what I could have offered you these last months.

Now Mr. Grant informs me that I am rambling and that I should keep this letter as close to the point as possible. Mr. Grant has taken to writing this for me, as opposed to my own hand, as the sickness first struck me there and the unceasing trembling now makes letter writing impossible. Rest assured that Mr. Grant is my attorney, and a true, long-time friend from the Royal Occult Society in London. I trust him completely.

I have instructed Mr. Grant to deliver you this letter upon my death. As you are reading this, I fear God did not see fit to keep me upon this Earth. I will regret leaving behind little except your dearest and sweetest companionship.

I hope the thousand-odd pounds I have afforded you will assist you with a modest amount of independence. I would have given everything to you, but alas. You understand all too well the entailment on both of my estates but please know that whatever was in my power to give, I have given it all to you.

I must now tell you the unusual part of your inheritance. I wish to give you my personal occult library in its entirely. I regret that I cannot gift you the four thousand books in the library, as they are a part of my London estate, and therefore will become the property of Mr. David Leigh. And, as Mr. Grant just informed me, you likely do not have the space to store four thousand books. He is not confident your father's house has the space for what I am giving to you as it is, but that is a trifle. If necessary, you are welcome to take a small portion of the inheritance and merely ask your father to build you a library.

Mr. Grant now informs me that he is writing down all of our little arguments between us for your amusement. I want you to know he is the most odious man in all creation and irritates me greatly.

(Miss Knight, this is Mr. Grant writing. I shall spare you the acerbic wit of your uncle at this time. Rest assured his beratement of me is in his usual style, and know I shall miss it greatly when the end finally comes upon him.)

However, my dear Elizabeth, I want you to know that I have already spoken to Cassandra. She will house your new inheritance of the three hundred sixteen books that do not belong to the estate. Mr. Grant has given her the list for your records, to save your father the postage costs of receiving such a hefty letter.

Do with these books as your heart dictates. Some will not be to your liking. I doubt any young lady of good sense has any interest in old men discussing the occult's influences on modern farming practices. Please, feel no obligation to my memory to keep those books. In fact, my hope is that you will fetch a decent sum for them at the booksellers. I particularly recommend Mr. Osborne on Charles St., London.

Most importantly, I leave you the three volumes of autograph ghost books of female occultists. Do you remember when you asked me about them as a child, and I said you were too young? Well, my dear niece, you are more than capable to attempt this amazing journey now. To be honest, you have been capable for a great many years, but I could not let go of the little girl. But you are not one anymore, as Mr. Grant constantly reminds me. Therefore, the autograph books are now yours.

I am convinced those lady occultists' magic bound within the pages will only work with a female, and I cannot think of a young woman I trust more than yourself.

I must warn you that gentlemen (and I use that term lightly) might come sniffing about to bully you into selling the autograph books. Do not allow them to trick you in any way. Mr. Grant will assist you if you have questions, or if you need a gentleman who can be trusted in business affairs who will not act against your own best interest to line his own pockets, as we all know you are lacking in male support in that manner.

Further, my hope is that the little sum of money I have left you will prevent you from ever having the temptation to sell the books in moments of desperation and loneliness. I wish for you to continue your studies in peace, and not to be sold to assist those who do not have your best interests in their souls.

For now, the books will be moved to my sister's house, as she has the room and would love any excuse for you to come to London for an extended stay. There is no need for the exchange of letters; she awaits your arrival. I have also included a pound note with this letter to assist with your journey to London and any mourning clothes expenses you might incur. I would not wish you to spend all your time in *drab mourning clothes, but I know your familial pressures all too well. But, for my memory, I beg you to sport the ghastly black bombazine for as little as possible. Young women should be in colour at all times, not sad and dreary in black and grey.*

(Miss Knight, this is Mr. Grant again. I shall spare you your uncle's thoughts on mourning attire for young ladies, but know that he has strong opinions on the notion of you wearing mourning clothes beyond a fortnight.)

Mr Grant informs me that this letter must end at some juncture, so I shall send my farewell. I regret not living to see this new adventure that lays before you. Know that I will be looking down from Heaven upon you and that I have ever been proud to call you my niece. I have loved you like my own child. You are perfection itself.

Your devoted uncle,
E Leigh

"What a strange man Edward Leigh had always been," Mr. Knight said. "Elizabeth has more than enough male assistance amongst her family. She does not require this lawyer's help. Besides, what will the girls do with occult books? Of all the things!"

Elizabeth's teeth chattered as she held back the tears. Uncle Edward never spoke of the heart, and it hurt her that it took his death for her to finally hear the light in which she shined in his eyes. How stubbornness and propriety too often stopped people from expressing the feelings of their hearts. She would have wanted him to know that she saw him as a father, and that his kindness and affection had been more supportive than the father standing in front of her now.

Isabella folded the letter and handed it to her step-daughter. "My dear Mr. Knight, the books are for Elizabeth's use."

"But, Isabella, what are the girls going to do with that?" He considered. "Perhaps Mary will want them. I shall write to her."

"Mr. Knight! They are not Mary's books," Isabella insisted. "They are Elizabeth's, and hers alone."

"But what is Elizabeth going to do with occult books?"

"Mr. Leigh has well educated your daughter on the occult." At the confused look on her husband's face, Isabella said, "She has often spoken of it."

"She has?"

"Yes, Mr. Knight. *Frequently*. Besides, you must consider that Mary took no interest in the occult and was not close to Mr. Leigh. The other girls are not related to him and do not know him. It would make sense for him to leave Elizabeth and Elizabeth *alone* all of his books."

"But what of the girls?"

Mr. Knight was not going to let the subject drop. It took all of Elizabeth's command of herself not to correct her father, but she successfully kept her thoughts to herself. Instead, she said, "I shall write to my aunt and inform her of my impending arrival in London. Maria Thorne is leaving for London tomorrow, and I shall request a seat in her carriage."

"We have dinner with the Pooles tomorrow," her father said. "We shall find you alternate travel next week."

"I believe the Pooles will be very understanding, Mr. Knight, given the circumstances," Isabella said. In a warmer tone, she said, "Elizabeth, I shall make your apologies. Your aunt, no doubt, needs you. Mrs. Poole will be very sympathetic."

"What use will Elizabeth be to the likes of Cassandra Spencer?" Mr. Knight asked. "That woman is rich enough to afford any comforts she requires. Elizabeth would be of better use here, to help you with the girls."

Cassandra Spencer, the sister of Uncle Edward and her own dearly departed mother, indeed carried the noble name of Spencer. However, the man she married was from the poorer side of that great family, as opposed to the branch that rubbed shoulders with royalty.

Isabella said, in a pleading tone, "Mrs. Spencer is richer than us, indeed, but she is not so rich as to remove grief on the loss of a brother."

Elizabeth offered her step-mother a smile of gratitude. There were things that no amount of money could buy.

Elizabeth mustered her courage before her father could argue. "Papa, my aunt is alone in the world now."

"Oh, yes. I forgot," Mr. Knight said with the coldness that he displayed too often towards his former family. "Well, Isabella, what do you think? Should we allow Elizabeth to go?"

Elizabeth glanced at her twenty-three-year-old stepmother and awaited a response. She fought against the feelings of bitterness that attacked her spirit.

"My dear Mr. Knight, I believe it is Elizabeth's *Christian duty* to go to town with her aunt for at least a month. Perhaps even a two-month visit, depending upon Mrs. Spencer's well-being. We must consider how *useful* Elizabeth will be during this time of mourning." Isabella's eyes widened. "Oh, I shall have to look after mourning outfits for the girls. I will consult my mother about the appropriate mourning length, since Mr. Leigh was not their uncle. Perhaps a week, just out of respect. No matter, Eliza, with the details. I shall discuss this with you later, Mr. Knight. For now, we must think about Elizabeth and how supportive she will be to her aunt."

"Very well, if you say so, my dear. This is the domain of women," Mr. Knight said. He smiled at Elizabeth, his expression filled with excitement as opposed to the support one would expect from her own father. It made the ache in her heart worsen. "Fourteen hundred! What a good thing for the girls. My dear, Isabella, will you assist Elizabeth in packing? I must visit Mrs. Audbrey this morning. She is doing poorly. Oh, and we should ask Charles when he can accompany Elizabeth to London. That will be a great comfort to her, I'm sure."

"Maria Thorne is leaving for London tomorrow," Elizabeth said. "I shall walk over and ask if I might accompany her."

But her father had already left the room, off to visit one of his poor parishioners. Elizabeth closed her eyes and said, in a shaky voice, "Please, I do not want or need Charles' help. Maria is going, and I am certain she will assistant me with transport."

Isabella sat down on the settee. "I'm so sorry for your father's insensitivity."

"I am long used to it," Elizabeth said.

"What will you do with the books?" Isabella hesitated. She lowered her voice and said, "I would caution you from bringing home a large number. I fear they will make a tempting target."

Elizabeth made a sound that bordered on a snort. "Between my father and Mary, I am certain they will find their way to furnishing Mary's home. Or, shall I say the dear cozy cottage."

Isabella was silent. She had been Mary Knight's best friend since school. Mary Knight, the second eldest of the Knight children and the daughter of Mr. Knight's first wife, Lucy Leigh, had married very well, fetching the rich Mr. Fitzharding of neighbouring Ashbrook. Ashbrook House, their "cozy cottage" as Mary called it, was a centuries old manor house that brought Mr. Fitzharding ten thousand a year.

Mary wasn't happy with just that, of course. She wanted everything that was Elizabeth's.

"I make it a firm policy to not place myself between you and Mary in your ongoing dispute," Isabella said. She licked her lips. "However, in this circumstance, I do not believe Mary deserves the books, and I wish to hint that you not make them an enticing target for her notice. Nor, for your father's notice, either, since their sale at auction might prove a temptation depending upon Charles' financial needs." At Elizabeth's growing silence, Isabella said, "It was very kind of Mr. Leigh to leave you the money, and what a surprise about his library. Did you have any hint of it?"

"None. I believe I am still in shock, to be very honest. I know that I will do all within my power to keep the occult books. He taught me everything I know, even if it is not much, and I would like to preserve those memories."

"I always thought the occult was the province of men, along with Latin and Greek."

Elizabeth sat down, wishing to be anywhere but here, having polite conversation while her heart broke. Nevertheless, there were expectations of stoicism. Therefore, she would get them out of the way, to grieve later in isolation. "My uncle believed there used to be lady occult societies. In fact, the three books mentioned are supposedly the autographs of now dead female occultists who bound their own souls to their autographs. With the right combination of spells, one supposedly could unlock the autographs to speak to the ladies' ghosts. Of course, he never let me touch those books as a girl."

"Oh, to hear from women long past. What stories they could tell. What a magnificent gift!"

"I suppose he wishes me to carry on his work, attempting to unlock the spells. He had often wondered if the ghosts would only speak to female occultists, but he didn't know any of sufficient skill to make the attempt. I fear I will never be one, either."

"Still, it's very exciting. Think of their worth to the Royal Occult Society!"

"I will not sell the books, Isabella," Elizabeth said in a cold, unyielding tone. "I have made up my mind, and I will not be dissuaded."

"Of course not. I don't believe your father would do that without your permission. You have your own bedroom, and the items there are yours."

Elizabeth kept her own thoughts to herself, for her bedroom and its contents were not hers alone no matter what was said.

Isabella, for her part, could clearly see Elizabeth was keeping back her anger and said, "We can spread the books between your friends, when you are ready. I will speak to your father, when the time is right. This inheritance will allow you a degree of independence, and that includes being able to keep the books. Your uncle was very prudent to give you the money. Now, you need to speak with Mrs. Thorne, of course. Did you want a servant to deliver a note?"

"No. I welcome the walk and privacy."

"Of course."

Elizabeth left her home with both letters in her reticule to read them herself in private during the one and a half mile walk to her dearest friend's house. There she would find the support that did not exist in her own home.

ELIZABETH WAS NO stranger to walking unaccompanied now that she was older and Mary married, and she relished the privacy afforded by the trek to Vane Park, home of her dearest friend. Alone with the cows and chickens, the apple trees and the wheat, Elizabeth was finally granted the luxury of grieving her dearest uncle.

No sooner had the rectory passed from view did her tears arrive. She did not care if the women in the field saw her, nor the men. Most tipped their hats to her or pretended to not see her weeping, and she kept her pace brisk, not bothering to hold back her quaking sobs. It was not the first time the farmers and their wives had seen her sobbing in their fields over the years, nor would it be the last she feared.

There goes Miss Knight weeping again. She knew that would be the local gossip soon enough. She only hoped her equally gossipy younger sisters would spread the news of Uncle Edward's death first and head off the commentary.

For now, the gossip of farm wives did not concern her. She had to present a strong face once she arrived at Maria's home, so that the servants would not gossip and the word get back to her father through John, his bailiff. Her heart was not up to another lecture about decorum from her father.

Uncle Edward had always been kind to her, especially after the death of her mother—his sister. Her father never quite understood that impact on his eldest daughter. Mary was very young, and had a new stepmother replacement so soon that even she had admitted her memories from that time were all a blur. Elizabeth's, however, were not. She remembered keenly, even now, the brutalizing pain of her mother closing her eyes for the last time.

She also recalled the betrayal in that little girl's heart when her father remarried within eighteen months of her mother's death. She did not like Miss Augusta Leigh, the mother of four of her siblings, and third cousin of her mother. Augusta had not been kind to Elizabeth, either. She'd doted on Mary, of course, but Elizabeth was too much stuck in her own head, as Augusta would say. That was why she could not like her. It had been Elizabeth's fault, and her father had agreed.

Therefore, it had fallen to Aunt Cass and Uncle Edward to be the supportive parents she no longer had. Looking back,

Elizabeth was certain Aunt Cass had spies in the village, to report back whenever Augusta was unnecessarily neglectful of her charge. To her child's eyes, however, it seemed like her mother's siblings would swoop in whenever things were bad and take her to London for several weeks. Sometimes, two whole months. Augusta never cared, and her father barely noticed her missing with an ever-growing brood of children. To him, one girl was interchangeable with another. What was two months?

Aunt Cass's husband had passed away. Uncle Spencer, as she has always called Mr. George Spencer, had been a jolly man. He loved town life and lived there even when the physicians told him fresh country air would improve his lungs. He did not listen, and eventually he succumbed to the dirty air of town. And now the air had claimed Uncle Edward, too.

Elizabeth knew in her good sense at the air itself had not killed them, even if the grief kept saying such nonsense. Her childhood memories were all ending now. She had such an unhappy childhood: the loss of her mother, the introduction of a new mother, three different schools that she hated, and a failed, somewhat imprudent, courtship that could have taken her away from all this pain.

She grieved for the loss of her childhood, and the memories Uncle Edward had made for her. His time for her was endless, teaching her how to use his occult books, the proper care of them, and even teaching her rudimentary Latin so that she could read the title pages. Her father never knew he'd done that; Mr. Knight opposed any education for ladies that went beyond how to run a household. He barely supported women learning foreign languages, such as French and Italian; the notion of a woman learning Latin or Greek would have alarmed her father.

But Uncle Edward was horrified by the poor education Elizabeth was receiving at her various schools, and he would insist she spend the summer holidays with him and Aunt Cass whenever possible so that he could teach her what he called "useful" information. It had been their secret; the Leigh side of her family all knew, of course, as they believed in useful education for women: history, geography, languages, mathematics, basic sciences, extensive reading.

Looking back, she wondered if her father even knew that about her mother. Or did he see her dowry of four thousand pounds and her willingness to move to a retired country rectory?

No wonder her father was excited about her additional inheritance. The marriage articles were negligent with regards to Lucy Leigh's dowry upon her death, and Mr. Knight had used some of the money to prop up his son. The rest went to Mary's dowry. Since it was clear Elizabeth would not marry, she did not need the money. Her brother did, was the reasoning. He'd have to look after her. Therefore, he needed a profession. However, illness had caused Charles to leave Oxford before finishing his education. Dissipation and laziness had caused him not to return upon his recovery.

This new inheritance meant her father would not need to provide her pin money now. He complained enough about the cost of her upkeep within the household itself, and knew down to the shilling how much her annual expenses in food, tea, and clothing she cost him. No doubt Isabella was appealing to that side of his mind, explaining that Elizabeth's stay in London would save him several pounds and shillings.

A wave of despondency hit Elizabeth and she struggled to breathe. She was not the first unmarried daughter to be a burden to her family, but she wished hers was kinder. Or, barring that hope, simply aware that she was a living, breathing individual who had a mind of her own, with hopes, dreams, and feelings.

Vane Park came into view once Elizabeth crested the hill and she struggled to gather her composure. She could not arrive and make a scene. She had to be calm, lest the servants talk. Or, worst, call for Mr. Andrews, the local apothecary. Her father would certainly forbid her to travel, and she needed to go to London.

Elizabeth stumbled up to the garden, where she would take a quick cut across to the main doors. However, the more she struggled to calm herself, the stronger her weeping came, and she caught the attention of two of the maids beating carpets.

They took one look at her before dropping their tools. The youngest maid ran toward the house shouting, "Mrs. Thorne! Bentley! Bentley! Get Mrs. Thorne!"

The other rushed to Elizabeth's side. The grey-haired maid wrapped an arm around Elizabeth and almost carried her to a nearby chair. "There, there, Miss Knight."

From beyond, Elizabeth could clearly hear the younger maid shouting, "Miss Knight is here and she's in a state. Bentley! Get Mrs. Thorne!"

"Please, don't call Mr. Clarke," Elizabeth managed to choke out between her sobs.

"But…yes of course, miss. Ah, here is Mrs. Thorne. I see her now. Look," the maid said pointing through the window.

Maria walked out through the small door into the garden, took one look at Elizabeth, and asked, "Who died?"

"Uncle Edward," Elizabeth said, weeping.

"Oh, Eliza," Maria said. She approached her friend and wrapped strong, comforting arms around her shoulders. "Maggie? Miss Knight is in need of sustenance. Also get Bentley to fetch a bottle of Mr. Thorne's brandy, please. Bring it to the small drawing room. And have a fire lit, please."

"Shall I also fetch tea and coffee?" Maggie asked of her mistress, though she was looking at Elizabeth.

"Please," Elizabeth whispered.

"Yes miss." Maggie curtsied and ran indoors to relay her mistress' orders.

When the servants were away, Maria asked, "Was your father very insensitive?"

"Very," Elizabeth said through sobs.

"Oh, Eliza. I'm so very sorry," Maria said, squeezing her friend's hand. After a moment's pause, she asked, "Mrs. Spencer is still in London, yes?"

Elizabeth could only nod.

"Do you wish to travel with me tomorrow then? There is plenty of room, and Henry is already in town. It would just be us."

"Thank you. That is why I came. To beg. Father wants Charles to take me."

"You don't need to beg from me." Maria sighed. "And I'm not letting Charles anywhere near you when you are this fragile. Come inside and rest. Bentley will bring you a small glass of brandy, and it will help calm your nerves. Come, Eliza. I will look after you."

Elizabeth followed her friend, and finally felt like she was in the arms of a caring family, as her friend and servants hurried about to make her as comfortable as possible in her grief.

~ Chapter 2 ~

ELIZABETH AND MARIA Thorne, late Cuthbert, had been friends since near infancy. Their mothers had gone into their confinements within a week of each other. Both women emerged with healthy little girls who they determined would be the best of friends. When Elizabeth's own mother died, it had been Mrs. Cuthbert to share with Aunt Cass the care of both of the Knight girls in the early weeks of deep mourning.

Elizabeth sipped the glass of brandy provided by the butler and nibbled on a slice of caraway cake. After the refreshment blunted the edges of her grief, she could finally speak. Maria had read both letters Elizabeth had carried but had not really commented on them. She was content to drink her tea and wait.

"What am I going to do with three hundred books?"

"I am certain we will find room for them here in the house. They can go in one of the bedrooms upstairs. You know the one, with the horrid sloping ceiling? I am certain I can turn that closet into an excellent library storage," Maria said. She put her cup down on her saucer. "In fact, the only good thing about that room is the closet. I wager we could redo the shelves, to handle the weight of the books, and they could easily fit in there."

"I could not impose," Elizabeth said.

"Would you rather your father give them to Mary?"

Elizabeth rolled her eyes in a very unladylike manner.

"Then, allow me to install the shelves. I'm certain Henry will be fine with it. A home improvement that costs a couple of shillings will be a relief to him."

"Are you finally done reupholstering the dining room then?" Elizabeth asked. She was smiling, happy to find a topic that did not leave a gnawing sensation in the pit of her stomach.

It was Maria's turn to roll her eyes. "I regret ever bringing it up to him."

They chatted a little about the new scheme to reupholster the dining room chairs that were very elegant, if worn. It took Elizabeth's mind off her aching pain, which worked as well as the brandy.

Maria had been the luckiest girl in all of Bryden. Her grandfather had been a tradesman. He'd made his fortune very young, sold his businesses, and bought himself a lovely country estate with a good size of property. Then he married a rather elegant and upstanding widow, had one son, and lived a quiet, happy life as a country gentleman. That son eventually married and had one daughter. Maria Cuthbert had a comfortable, vibrant life as an only child of wealthy parents.

Then, a Mr. Thorne arrived in the neighbouring village of Woolerton. Mr. Thorne was the fifth son of a very wealthy man in the north of England, and the cousin of an earl. He was too far down the list to get any of the titles and any of the large estates, but there were plenty of small country cottages to hand out, and eventually Mr. Thorne inherited Wollerton's very lovely Vane Park from a dead relative.

And an annual income of four thousand a year.

Maria, with her dowry of ten thousand pounds, coupled with her wicked smile and womanly figure, was no match for young, newly independent Mr. Thorne. They married within a year.

"I told Henry that I would pay for the improvements myself if he was going to be so tight with money!" Maria exclaimed. "And he'd have more money if he'd stopped gambling with his wastrel friends in London every winter."

Elizabeth took the opportunity to take a sip of her brandy so that her friend would not see her smirk. Their marriage had not always been the happiest, but if two people loved to bicker, it was Mr. and Mrs. Thorne.

Finally, Maria sighed, having vented her spleen until her cheeks flushed, said, "I apologize, Eliza. I should not be complaining about my petty problems. Did you wish to spend the night here? I plan to leave very early in the morning. I am to dine with Lady Westley tomorrow night, and I wish to be rested. You remember me talking about her, from school?"

Elizabeth and Maria did not attend the same schools, of course. Elizabeth was sent to sensible schools to teach her how to make a small income go further. She was also sent away far earlier than Maria because the newly-arrived Augusta Leigh wanted her "difficult" stepdaughter out of the household once Charles arrived.

Maria was sent to the best school her father could find that wasn't more than a day's carriage ride away.

Maria misunderstood Elizabeth's silence. "If you need to leave later in the morning, I will send word that I will have to cancel. She will understand."

In truth, Elizabeth wanted Maria to complain and vent for hours more, since it helped take her mind off the pressure in her chest. However, she would not force Maria into doing that duty if her heart was not in it. "No, early is acceptable. I wish to get to my aunt's side as soon as possible. I have a mourning outfit already, so I shall change into that for the journey. I will not need to pack much beyond essentials, as most of my time will be in mourning clothes and not at dinner parties."

Elizabeth was a little relieved to be missing out on all the dinner invitations, balls, and card parties that would end up at her door with a visit to her aunt and with Maria in town. She would talk to her aunt about how long deep mourning would be appropriate, but as Elizabeth was so close to Uncle Edward, she would most likely mourn for the full three months alongside her aunt. That way, they could go into half mourning at the same time, allowing them to both accept dinner invitations toward the end of Elizabeth's stay in London. She was certain Aunt Cass would want it that way.

Uncle Edward's letter and wishes notwithstanding.

"If your father won't give you any money, simply let me know and I shall take you shopping for crepe if the weather is too warm," Maria said. "No arguments."

"I am independently wealthy now," Elizabeth said loftily. "I can afford my own mourning garment, thank you Mrs. Thorne."

That made the ladies laugh and they discussed the kindness of her uncle's endowment.

"Do you think you will study the occult, the way he asked?"

Elizabeth picked up a piece of cold ham and chewed as she thought. Finally, she said, "I do not know. It is hundreds of books, and I need to go through them. Some will be obviously sentimental, and I will not wish to part with those. My uncle mentions farming books that I will not want to keep. I might be able to sell those for a shilling or two each, which would be very welcome."

"Will you need any help? Henry and his friends will most likely be gambling until the wee early hours of the morning, as is their way, so I shall be alone in that miserable house of ours in town. I would love to be useful."

Elizabeth gave her friend a sad smile.

"Oh, do not pity me, Eliza. He always comes back to me, and never bets more than he can afford." She paused before amending, "Usually."

Elizabeth burst into laughter, quickly covered her face with her hand while trying to control herself. She knew laughter was the best medicine when in shock and grief, but it never felt completely right to her. Yet, as her father preached from the pulpit, they were called to stay upon the earth while others were called to heaven; it would be a sin to stop living, for that signaled that God had made an error in not calling you to heaven, too.

She said, "Oh, I wish I could write to my aunt to announce our arrival. It is very frustrating that I have not had the opportunity at all."

Maria waved over a footman. "Henry's valet is leaving for London this afternoon. His daughter had just come out of her confinement, and he wished to see his first grandson. He was planning to leave for London this afternoon, staying the night with his daughter along the way, before carrying on in the morning. He will be in London before any of us tomorrow, so we can send word with him."

"Oh, I would appreciate that, Maria."

"Mark, fetch Miss Knight paper. And please let Mr. Bell know about the letter."

My dearest aunt,

I have received the dreadful news by Mr. Grant's hand. I am most anxious to see you. Maria Thorne is leaving for London in the morning and I shall accompany her. She expects the journey to take twelve hours, as we are taking her carriage, so I will write to you when I arrive safely in London. Maria has extended her assistance with the books, if that is agreeable to you.

I am uncertain about the length of my visit, as my father had to be coaxed into allowing me to leave so suddenly. However, Isabella has promised to work on him and I hope to spend some weeks in London. If you wish me to remain at Maria's house, she wishes you to know that she would not be importuned at all. Both of us only wish for your comfort and to support you on Uncle Edward's sad departure.

All my love, etc

Elizabeth

MARIA SENT ELIZABETH home in the carriage before it became dark and worried her father. In her absence, Isabella had successfully worked her charms on Mr. Knight. He was now a strong supporter of Elizabeth's journey to London. He quoted the bible, from Matthew in particular, about how the grieving were blessed of the Lord, and he felt honoured that his unwed daughter could be of use in someone's time of need.

Isabella's neutral expression spoke of a sadness there, to Elizabeth's eyes, and a part of her was surprisingly sorry to leave her latest stepmother alone. She had not been away from home for more than a handful of days since her father's remarriage, and had been helping her sisters learn they had a new mother to obey now. However, the age difference between them was striking. Isabella was twenty-three. Her father was fifty-five. She was older than Isabella and had nothing to speak of to her father beyond the weather and the condition of the roads. What did Isabella have in common with her husband?

"Elizabeth, will you write to me? I will be very anxious for news."

Elizabeth could not deny her request and promised to be a faithful and prolific letter writer. For now, that was the best Elizabeth could offer.

She was disappointed to learn her father had already written to Mary to announce her uncle's death. She would have preferred to have done the task herself. Nevertheless, she excused herself from supper and cards, and asked to be permitted a four-hour wax candle in her room to write a letter to her sister, as well as others to excuse her from obligations about the village. She was granted the permission by Isabella. Elizabeth happily took to the quiet of her bedchamber.

March 14, 1810
Dear Mary,

I understand from our father that he has already written to you of Uncle Edward's death. However, I would have felt uneasy until you heard from my own pen, as well.

I leave for London tomorrow, so please direct any letters to our Aunt Cass's house. I will write as soon as I discuss the particulars of her desire for the mourning length.

Cassandra has offered her assistance in my absence if you need any help with the children.

I shall write more once I am settled in London.

Your devoted sister,
Elizabeth

Elizabeth re-read the letter three times before signing off. Her stomach tied itself into knots whenever she considered her sister. However, that must be set aside now, for they had more important things to consider. Mourning clothes. A change in social routines and expectations. Grief. Wills. Property. All of it.

And, she would be lying if she didn't admit to herself that she did not want to share her grief with her sister. Her grief was her own, and it galled her that Mary would no doubt exploit it to her own advantage. Either to dismiss it or to fully throw herself into it, whichever she would gain the better footing with in society.

Elizabeth folded and sealed the letter before she changed her mind. She wrote another twelve letters, all much easier and longer than the first. She spent nearly two hours on the task. Finally, she summoned her youngest sister, Georgiana. Elizabeth passed G the letters with the strictest of instructions to give them to Isabella. G rolled her eyes dramatically, prompting a scolding from the elder about unladylike behaviour. G pouted but promised to deliver the letters for the morrow's post, since Isabella had taken to her bed with a stomach pain.

With that, Elizabeth snuffed out the expensive candle and attempted, but failed, to sleep.

For the trip itself, the journey to London was uneventful. It only took eleven hours, as the roads were in excellent condition for nearly the entire journey, as it shockingly hadn't rained in three days. They also stopped for two hours at a roadside inn to rest the horses and take an excellent meal of boiled bacon and bread.

The ladies were not mere acquaintances and were able to exist quietly during the travel, which was a relief to Elizabeth's nerves. She had not a moment's peace after she left Maria's to return home and pack her trunk. Maria sensed this mental exhaustion, and asked Elizabeth's permission to nap during the journey. That left Elizabeth alone to gather her courage for the days ahead.

The servants at the town house had hot water and tea ready for the ladies. While the footmen hauled water upstairs for baths, Elizabeth had tea and cake in the drawing room. Soon, Elizabeth was summoned to her room by the maid, a young thing of about sixteen or seventeen. She helped Elizabeth out of her travel garments and carefully assisted her into the surprisingly warm bath. The maid excused herself to fetch a dressing gown from another closet, and Elizabeth soaked in the warmth of a private, personal bath.

At the rectory, bathing was a massive affair done every six weeks when the laundry women came from the village. After the clothes were all washed, the hired women would fill the half tub in the laundry room with hot water. Her father would take a bath, followed by Charles. Then, it would be the ladies to share the lukewarm water. Afterwards, they would empty and clean out the tub, and it was back to washing in their individual rooms every morning.

The maid returned to drop off a dressing gown, as well as soap. She organized the fire and said there would be more blankets arriving shortly. When Elizabeth asked about the need for the additional blankets, the maid said, "Mrs. Rundle says it's supposed to rain, Miss Knight, and she's never wrong. This side of the house gets extra cold in the damp, so she ordered me to bring you blankets and to get the fire going. She doesn't want you to catch cold on your first night in town, miss."

"I shall thank her when I see her," Elizabeth said of the housekeeper. "What is your name? I don't believe you were here last winter when I came to town."

"I'm Hannah, miss. I'm Mrs. Rundle's niece. I came to work in the spring, after Miss Scott decided to marry Sir Archibald's footman next door."

"Ah yes. How is Miss Scott, or Mrs…?"

"Mrs. Anderson, miss. She and Mr. Anderson are doing very well. Sir Archibald offered Mr. Anderson position at his country estate in Devon as an undergardener. So, they have moved and, the last I heard from Sir Archibald's chambermaid, was that they were settled very snug in a house in the village."

"That is very good news," Elizabeth said.

"Indeed, miss. Do you need assistance with washing your hair?"

"In a bit. I wish to soak a little longer, if I am not expected anywhere."

"No, miss. You are not."

After Hannah left the room, Elizabeth reflected that the last time she had a bath was at Aunt Cass' house. There, the servants doted on her so much that it was like being in the bath with her sisters gathered about.

Elizabeth chuckled thinking about when each of her sisters hit about twelve or thirteen and demanding to know why Charles got to go ahead of Elizabeth. She'd done the same at that age, too. Only her stepmother at the time refused to explain it to her. In fact, it was the laundry woman who did. The matronly woman of about forty waited until Augusta left little Elizabeth alone. Then, she explained to her how a woman's body worked and how fathers and brothers would not like to share that water. Elizabeth was horrified. And, in turn, each of her sisters were when the task fell to her to answer that question posed one by one over the years. Of course, each girl eventually learned to cope with womanhood. And Elizabeth ensured that her younger sisters were not left alone to the task, unlike her own experiences.

Sadness hit her. Aunt Cass and Uncle Edward had tried to always be there for her, too, so that she would never be alone in the trials of growing up without a mother. And now, Uncle Edward was gone.

After she regained her composure from a short cry, Elizabeth reached for the soap and cloth to begin cleaning half a day of sweat and dust off her neck. For March, it was shockingly dry outside. If the weather did not change, and change soon, the crops would be late.

The maid popped back in again and helped Elizabeth wash her hair. Then she was helped out of the bath, dried off, and then the maid helped dress her into one of the clean dresses that she laid out for her from the trunk. Her hair was still damp, so the maid braided and pinned her hair, then tucked it under a white cap. Elizabeth finally went downstairs to join Maria in the drawing room and was surprised to see Mr. Henry Thorne there.

"Good evening, Mr. Thorne!" Elizabeth said. "I am very glad to see you before I leave for my aunt's in the morning."

"And good evening to you, Miss Knight," Mr. Thorne said easily. "Maria tells me you inherited a tidy sum of money from your uncle. Congratulations."

"Henry, for the love of God! Her uncle just died," Maria scolded.

Mr. Thorne shrugged at his wife, though he gave Elizabeth a half-smile. "One thousand, and another four hundred on top of it. Why, that will help ease the grief, I'm sure. I might be writing to you soon for a loan."

"Elizabeth, I must apologize," Maria said. Glaring at her husband, she said, "It appears *someone* is in liquor tonight."

"Forgive me, Miss Knight," Mr. Thorne said, stretching out his arms to gesture at the room. "I had thought the house was my own until the morrow, and had been celebrating my bachelorhood."

Elizabeth looked away so that the couple could not see her grin. Then, to Mr. Thorne, she said, "Alas, I doubt my forty-odd pounds per annum will suffice your many needs, sir."

"Forty! Nonsense. I will be very surprised to see less than sixty pounds come from your inheritance. I am certain that is what your uncle had hoped."

Elizabeth sat down and accepted tea from an exasperated Maria. However, Elizabeth couldn't help but dig a little. "Let us find common ground and suppose I receive fifty pounds from the interest. Is that not your boot allowance in a year, Mr. Thorne?"

Maria coughed down a laugh.

"Oh, Miss Knight. No wonder you haven't caught a husband," Henry Thorne said in a delighted tone.

"Henry, *please*. We just arrived and Elizabeth is my guest," Maria pleaded.

"I am not offended, Maria, I promise you," Elizabeth said. She wasn't. Mr. Henry Thorne was always like this. He meant well, and from the flush upon his cheeks, had probably drank too much wine before their arrival. The fact that a tea cup was in his hand, as opposed to a wine glass, said he knew what was right and proper now that his wife and her guest was here. Still, Mr. Thorne was incapable of not teasing his own wife.

And Henry Thorne had frequently drawn out the ideal husband for Elizabeth in the past, teasing his wife that a true friend would have found this mythical man no matter if she had to travel to Rome to secure the gentleman. This was their little private joke.

"To answer your question, Mr. Thorne, there are a great many reasons why I have not caught a husband." She sighed, as her energy flagged. "However, I beg you to leave that argument for another evening, for my heart is not in it tonight, and you would certainly win."

Mr. Thorne turned serious; the laughter gone from his voice. "Then I greatly apologize, Miss Knight. I had supposed you needed distraction. I meant no offense. Please, forgive me."

And that was why Mr. Henry Thorne caught the very eligible, and very picky, Maria Cuthbert's eye. It wasn't just his fine looks or wicked grin. It was that, beneath all the fluff and foppery, Mr. Henry Thorne was a good man. Elizabeth could never be angry with him for long.

"I do forgive you, though there is no reason to feel that way, Mr. Thorne, I assure you. I am very tired this evening, and I still have to relocate again to my aunt's, as soon as she can have me." Elizabeth forced a smile. "I promise to let you tease me about my spinsterhood another day, and one very soon."

"Do I have your word upon it?"

"Henry…" Maria was pleading now.

"Of course, Mr. Thorne."

Henry Thorne tipped his cup to her in a salute. "Excellent."

"Oh, speaking of your aunt," Maria said. "Mrs. Spencer wrote. Now, where did I put it?"

"It is still on the mantle, dear," Mr. Thorne said absently. He was reaching across to the tea service that was near his chair.

"Oh, you're going to drop the pot," Maria said and snatched the teapot from his hand. She topped up his mug, leaving him to add his own sugar. She picked up the letter and passed it to Elizabeth.

Dear Mrs. Thorne,

I wish to thank you for your kindness toward my niece. Your servant arrived today with her own letter and the news of you conveying her in your own carriage. I cannot tell you the relief I felt over that. I had worried the business would be left to her father and brother.

I have been preparing Elizabeth's room, but please do not feel forced to hand over your guest upon arrival. If she needs clothes, please allow me to send my maid to fetch her the necessary fabrics.

Please send a note to let me know you have arrived in safety.

Mrs. G. Spencer

"You require a second dress," Maria stated as a fact that was not open to negotiation.

"I have packed my old lavender dress. The one with the faded flowers. Do you remember it? I shall pull it apart and dye it. It would be perfect for cool evenings and rainy days, since it has long sleeves."

"I doubt your aunt will allow you to do that," Maria said. "Besides, that thing is ancient. You can't wear that. It should be turned into rags."

Elizabeth gave her friend a patient look, and she hoped it did not come with too much of a rebuke. Maria could afford to turn her dresses into rags; Elizabeth could not. Her dresses would eventually become pelisse linings, undergarments, dresses for her younger siblings, and anything else useful, long before they became rags.

Even with her newfound wealth, she was a very long way from the kind of wealth that would allow her to be frivolous with a faded old dress.

She did not wish to quarrel, so she changed the subject. "If it is acceptable to you, Maria, I would like to remove to my aunt's tomorrow. I have a great deal of work ahead of me sorting through my uncle's books, and I would like to start the task immediately."

"If you require my assistance in any way, I am at your service," Henry Thorne said. "I happen to know three different booksellers who are all excellent men. They have been helping expand my library at Vane Park, and I believe I could fetch first-rate prices for any of the books you do not wish to keep."

"Thank you, Mr. Thorne. That is a great relief, if I could trespass on your kindness. My uncle recommended a Mr. Osborne, on Charles Street."

"Henry would be happy to help," Maria answered for her husband.

"Osborne was at the top of my list, in fact. Fine fellow." At the clock chiming nine, Henry vaulted from his chair. "Well, ladies, I am off to Sir Reynold's card table. I would have not accepted the invitation if I'd known you were coming today, Miss Knight."

"Will you be back tonight?" Maria asked.

"Do not expect me until tomorrow. William Boyd, the younger son of some Irish viscount, is in town and he has a watch that I am determined to win from him. I nearly got him to put it on the table last night, and I plan to get it from him tonight."

"Try not to bet my dowry," Maria said sourly.

"I would, but alas, your father was very thorough with the marriage articles. Good evening, ladies."

When Mr. Thorne left the room, Maria dismissed the servants. That left the two women completely alone. Elizabeth turned to her friend and asked, "Has his gambling gotten worse?"

Maria sipped at her tea. "He is upset that we remain childless."

"How does drinking and gambling correct the situation?"

"If anything, it ensures that we remain so."

"I am sorry. Truly."

"It isn't too bad. I had heard the stories of him as a young man, before we were married, I mean. He even told me, leading up to his proposal, the kind of life he once led."

"I remember you telling me that."

"So you know that I knew what I was getting into. As I understand it from his sister, his father only approved of our match because I came with enough independent money to keep Henry afloat." Maria blew out a breath. "His gambling debts are non-existent now. Why, I don't believe they have ever topped more than five hundred pounds in a winter. That has obviously been a great relief to his family. I have risen in their estimation. Or, as much as a woman whose grandfather was in trade can ever rise with the likes of those people."

Elizabeth used the excuse of serving herself another slice of cake to keep silent. Five hundred pounds of gambling debt. And that it was no bother for him to wipe out that debt at the end of every season. She was counting her pennies in her reticule to decide how much to tip the maids at Aunt Cass' house during her stay.

Maria didn't notice her friend's melancholy, which was for the best. Elizabeth prided herself on never comparing herself to her friend, and it was only her grief making her thoughts stray.

"Once the hot weather hits, he'll be back home, sobered up, paid off his debts of honour, and ready to manage the estate. We will be back to arguing over if we can afford to improve the dining room." Maria's smile said she looked forward to that argument. "For now, though, he feels that he should be in London with all of his family, even though they bring out the worst in him. Be thankful about your Mr. R. He's turned out the same way."

Elizabeth knew Maria wasn't meaning to be cruel, but she'd wished her friend did not bring up Mr. R: the man whose name hurt so much that they never used even his full surname. What was there to say when Maria was lost in disappointed spirits? Henry was a wonderful man, and a kind, attentive husband to Maria. However, amid discontentment, that would all be forgotten.

Elizabeth had no memories of her father and mother's marriage, and she thought her first stepmother's marriage to her father was contented enough. Likewise, Isabella's marriage with her father seemed, again, contented, if a little sad at times. Perhaps that was all women could hope for.

Oh, she just wished Mr. R hadn't come up. He might have protected her.

"Do you still wish to assist me with the books tomorrow?" Elizabeth asked, desperate for a change of topic. "Or will it be best that you wait for Mr. Thorne to return from his engagement?"

"Oh, nonsense. I promised my help and Henry won't mind. He'll be in no mood tomorrow morning for my presence. Most likely, he will lose all of his winnings that he'd gained over the last week and return home with a horrid headache and a very bitter spirit. I would rather miss that."

"And what if he wins heavily?"

Maria laughed. "Then he will hunt me down wherever I am to drag me back home to do my duty. I would rather miss that, too."

"Maria!" Elizabeth covered her mouth, both in shock and to hide her giggles.

"I believe this tea has been laced with spirits, and I shall blame it for me saying very inappropriate things. Now, tell me your plans for the books while I get Hannah to fetch us glasses to drink this bottle of wine Henry so kindly left us."

The ladies spent the evening talking about books, men, and how to marry Elizabeth off to an earl, since anyone higher in rank would be too full of themselves for Maria to respect properly. For her part, Elizabeth said she wanted a simple country gentleman, with an excellent vegetable garden for her to manage.

They did not mention Mr. R anymore, for which Elizabeth was grateful. Hopefully, she would not see him in town over the coming weeks, either.

"MY DEAREST GIRL!" Aunt Cass said, embracing Elizabeth as soon as she and Maria walked through the door. She gave Maria a curtsy while reaching out to clasp her hand. "And you, Mrs. Thorne. It is so good to see you girls at such a sad time."

Maria returned the curtsy. "And you, Mrs. Spencer. It is always good to see you. I am very sorry to hear of the loss of your brother."

"Thank you, my dear. You are very kind. Please, come in. Sally will take your things. Mrs. Thorne, can you possibly stay to tea?"

"I would love to," Maria said as she removed her hat and gloves, handing them to the servant.

"Aunt, with your permission, I have asked Maria to assist with the books. Will that be acceptable?"

"I do not wish to force myself upon you, Mrs. Spencer. If you need time to be alone with your niece, I will not be offended in the slightest."

"Having both of you here today will cheer me up greatly. Stay as long as you can."

Aunt Cass eyed Elizabeth's simple crepe dress. It was black, as was the mourning custom, with a plain ribbon about the bodice. It had a puff of gathered fabric at the shoulders, with long, slender detachable sleeves for warmth. She wore a black cotton neck scarf, edged with just a touch of lace.

"Is that the only gown you have, my dear?"

Elizabeth smiled at her aunt and said, "Yes. Maria has already threatened to buy me several yards of bombazine if it so much as threatens to rain."

Aunt Cass shook her head. She was wearing black, of course, thought her dress was a touch old-fashion by the fashion of the day. However, her aunt was a woman in her late forties and was allowed to wear whatever she wished. Within reason, of course. The mourning black looked good on Aunt Cass. It suited her darker complexion and black hair, and she looked robust as opposed to the sickly pallor that Elizabeth often got in dark dresses.

Most likely, she would insist Elizabeth not remain in full mourning as long as she would for her own brother. Elizabeth, though, saw her uncle as a second father and already felt conflicted over the appropriate length of mourning. No doubt, Mary would insist on the full length, provided there wasn't an important party or ball she wished to attend or host. In that case, Elizabeth would be expected to drop everything to switch out to grey or lavender with some black ribbon for a few weeks so that Mary could enjoy society.

In fact, Elizabeth awaited the letter asking for such an exception from her sister. There was no doubt in her mind that it would be arriving.

Aunt Cass lead them toward the back of the house, as opposed to the regular drawing room. "Say the word and Sally can make you up a dress within the week. The weather will turn poorly any day now and I fear that crepe may prove too chilly for a damp London spring."

"I do not wish to be an inconvenience, Aunt," Elizabeth said. In truth, she knew she needed a second dress, but she feared her father's reproach at her taking her aunt's charity. But, she also knew she only had one pound, two shillings to her name currently, and it would be some time before her uncle's inheritance was moved into her name. Even more time before it earned some interest and was paid out to her.

Her quarterly payment from her father of five pounds, however, should be doled out to her upon her return to Bryden. He normally paid toward the end of March typically, but if his own income was late, well...

No, she must be prudent.

"My uncle expressly noted in his final letter to me that he did not wish me in bombazine."

Aunt Cass made a dismissive sound. "Like Edward understood what it was like wearing a dress during a spring rain shower. Mrs. Thorne, might I rely upon your good taste to find my dear niece some appropriate fabric the next time you are at the shops? Place it on my account, do not worry in the slightest."

"I shall happily look after all the details, Mrs. Spencer. Do not fret in the slightest. I have already expressed my feelings about this dress to Eliza."

"More than once," Elizabeth said steadily.

"And, yet, my niece has not heeded you?" Aunt Cass said in a playful tone.

"Not at all, Mrs. Spencer. Your niece has always been a stubborn young woman."

That brought laughter from the three women, which abruptly stopped upon entering the dining room. The lovely dining table that she'd spent so many delightful meals at was pushed back against one wall. Elizabeth assumed it was to make room for all of the boxes underneath the table, and around it.

Elizabeth was horrified to see trunks upon trunks, boxes and more boxes everywhere. There even trunks stuffed underneath the table itself, and on top of all but one chair. Individual books were piled upon the table, leaving only the smallest path to a singular empty chair and the cramped space about it.

"I had not realized what three hundred books would look like," Elizabeth said, not bothering to hide her horror. "What was my uncle thinking?"

"This is double that amount!" Maria exclaimed. "Easily. Where did all of these books comes from?"

"I assume a letter did not arrive at Bryden before you left?" Aunt Cass asked. When Elizabeth said only that from her uncle's attorney, Aunt Cass said, "Ah. That explained your shock. Should I call for tea first? You may need it."

Tea was called for and the servants fetched chairs from another room for the ladies to sit upon in the midst of the makeshift library. A small, round table soon arrived for their tea things to rest upon.

"Are all these books mine?"

"Apparently," Aunt Cass said.

"I am no bookseller, but this must be six hundred books," Maria said.

"Currently, this is five hundred and sixty, or so, with more on the way."

"More?" Elizabeth and Maria exclaimed at the same time.

A knock echoed in the distance and the footsteps of the butler announced that it was their door.

"Ah, and that will be more again. Please come with me, ladies. You shall enjoy this."

Elizabeth mentally noted that her aunt used her annoyed tone for that last part. She and Maria put down their teacups and followed behind Aunt Cass.

"Cousin David!" Elizabeth exclaimed when her cousin, Mr. David Leigh, walked through the open door. She collected her manners and curtsied to the inheritor of her uncle's estate. "I had not expected to see you."

David Leigh wore a dark grey jacket with a black armband and a black cravat. He bowed deeply. His hair was annoyingly foppish, and his auburn sideburns desperately needed attention from a pair of very sharp scissors. "My dearest cousin! It is good to see you, though I wish it was not on such sad circumstances. How do you fare?"

"Very well, sir, under the circumstances. Thank you. I believe you remember my friend, Mrs. Thorne."

"Yes, of course. Mrs. Thorne, how do you do?" He gave a stiff bow.

Maria curtsied the bare minimum. "Very well, Mr. Leigh."

Elizabeth opened her mouth to form a question about David Leigh's health, but he interrupted by asking, "Have you informed Cousin Eliza of the current arrangement, Aunt?"

"You arrived just as our tea had. Would you like to join us? We can discuss the situation then."

David Leigh shook his head. "Alas, no. I only had enough time to drop off this load of books before I went to call upon Miss Reeves and her mother. Mrs. Reeves sent me a note, requesting that I join them for tea, or else I would, of course, offer my assistance and company."

"How disappointing," Aunt Cass said in a tone that made Elizabeth's mouth twitch. Aunt Cass and David Leigh never quite saw eye-to-eye on most topics, and both were no doubt relieved not to need to sit in each other's company for half of an hour in conversation.

"Indeed. I can assure you, my dear aunt, that the servants are moving as swiftly as humanly possible to empty the library. As it is, I arrive with two trunks of implements, and there will be a cart arriving later this morning with another one hundred and eleven books."

"One prays my floor is made of sturdy stuff," Aunt Cass muttered.

"Implements?" Elizabeth asked, very confused.

"Oh! And Aunt Cassandra? I heard from my cook that there is no decent meat at the market today, but they have an excellent catch of fish that just came in."

"Thank you, David. I will look for those books later." Two footmen arrived carrying a large trunk between them. "Oh, just put that in the dining hall, as before. Same with the other trunk."

"Very good, ma'am," one of the footmen said.

"We shall return the trunks as soon as we can," Aunt Cass said.

"I greatly appreciate it. I have been borrowing from my new neighbours!" David Leigh said with a wide smile. "They are delightful people."

Elizabeth was certain she had misunderstood her cousin. Nevertheless, she had to ask the question. "Have you moved into our uncle's house already?"

"It had not been my plan, but circumstances have changed in my life as of late to make a new abode rather convenient. I will, of course, be canceling my lease once I have completed the move. I have also brought on several new servants to assist with the transition. My uncle's failing health had made it difficult for him to look after the house in the manner I believe it deserved, so the new servants will help bring it up to appropriate standards for a gentleman in my position. Well, ladies, Aunt, I shall not keep you. Might I come back tomorrow to pay a proper visit, Aunt?"

"Of course, David," Aunt Cass said in a rather neutral term.

"Then I shall be off!" David said, tipping his hat and heading out the door. He could be heard through the open door saying to his coachmen, "No, no! I shall walk! The weather is very fine, and the men aren't done with the trunks yet."

The three ladies stood in the entrance. Aunt Cass said, without turning her head away from the scene, "I forgot to ask, Mrs. Thorne, how were the roads coming up from the countryside?"

"Very tolerable," Maria said without even a hint of hesitation. "The lane going into Bryden Rectory is always impossible this time of the year, but we got further than most years."

"I would have walked down to meet you, if I were strong enough to carry my own trunk," Elizabeth said to help push the conversation onward while David Leigh's servants were in the house. "It is very difficult to carry anything of size when one is not very tall."

"Perhaps we should find you a doctor here in town who can stretch your arms," Maria said.

The ladies offered up false laughter that sounded insipid to Elizabeth's ears.

"Ma'am, sorry to interrupt, but those are the trunks for this trip," the footman said. "Do we have your permission to return in about two hours with the cart?"

"Yes, of course. Thank you," Aunt Cass said. When the front door closed, she let out a long sigh and said, "My nephew is going to be the cause of my death."

"Aunt, what is happening?" Elizabeth asked. "Where are all these books coming from?"

"I told David to write to you, but you know him. David has ordered the servants to pull *every* occult book from Edward's library, including the ones added by previous generations. He's giving them all to you. Well, to be very precise, he is giving them all to *me*, and I am giving them to *you*. He has become very anti-occult in the last year and does not want any of the books in *his* new house."

"How many books are we talking about?" Elizabeth asked.

"Hundreds, dear. *Hundreds.* If this continues much longer, I shall need a new house to live in while this one is turned into an occult library. Another one hundred and eleven." Aunt Cass sighed as she accepted a book from the butler, James. He also handed her a pencil. She scribbled in the book. "With today's impending delivery, that will place us at six hundred and seventy-one books thus far. Pray his house burns to the ground."

"Aunt! You can't say such things."

"I absolutely can."

"Mr. Leigh is opposed to the occult?" Maria asked. "Whatever for? Is he a Methodist now?"

"As far as I understand, Methodists are not even opposed to the occult," Elizabeth said. "Though, I suppose every belief has its own pockets of personal interpretation."

"I do not know what has happened, but he has become very anti-occult. He and his uncle argued frequently. I do not know what has gotten into the man. And to move into the house with your uncle barely cold in his grave. And what was he talking about with the servants? Why does he need more servants? It's just him living in the house."

"How much did he inherit?" Maria asked.

Aunt Cass shrugged. She motioned for the ladies to walk back toward the dining room. "About six thousand or so. He got the London house, of course, and the estate in Suffolk. My brother leased that out, and David said he wished to honour the terms of that agreement. Something about the sea air not agreeing with him. With the lease, it would be a bit more than six thousand. Plus, his previous inheritances, of course. He's done very well for himself."

"Perhaps he felt that with greater income came greater expectations," Maria said.

"You mean he wished to show off to London society?" Aunt Cass asked.

That brought a laugh from Maria. "Something like that."

Elizabeth was only half listening to their conversation. The pile of books waiting for her there was massive.

"What on earth will I do with hundreds of books?" Elizabeth asked.

Aunt Cass and Maria, at the same time, said, "Sell them."

"I hope it is that easy. Are the books my uncle expressly left to me separated?" Elizabeth asked.

"Yes. The ones that could fit are in your old bedchamber. The rest are in my personal drawing room. Since I rarely bring any guests back there —you ladies will be the exception, of course—I felt it was the best place for the overflow. As I will not be hosting any large dinners for several weeks, with the mourning happening, I do not need a functioning dining room at present. Though, my dear, you might need to take your meals with your feet upon a trunk, unless we make some excellent progress today."

Maria smiled. "Well, Mrs. Spencer, I came to work. And my maid said she would be very happy to join us with an entire team of help, at a moment's notice I add, if we find the task too much for us."

Aunt Cass smiled, her eyes gleaming with tears. "I cannot tell you how happy I am to see you two girls. Grown ladies. How time goes by! I remember bringing both of you to London for Christmas when you stood no taller than my waist. Now look at you both. I could not have gotten through this loneliness without you. Now, Cook has promised to make those jam tarts you like so much, Elizabeth, but she says they need to set. So you are not allowed into her kitchen to try them like last time."

Elizabeth laughed, a warm, genuine expression that melted away some of her pain and reserve. "I truly only meant to sneak one. However, Aunt, they are so good."

"And were not ready for eating!" Aunt Cass said sternly, though she could not completely hide her smile. "Cook is still very cross with you."

"Perhaps I should go into the kitchen to apologize."

"Ha!" Aunt Cass said. "She will smack your hands with a paddle and send you to your room if you go anywhere near her tarts. And I will not intervene. Now, I suppose I should show you the upstairs books as well, for there shall be even more today."

"Oh, where is Mrs. Dover?" Elizabeth asked.

"She's gone to see her sister for a month. With me in mourning, I told her it would be an excellent time for her to visit. Her sister is doing poorly. They don't have much hope for a recovery," Aunt Cass said.

"I'm so sorry to hear that," Elizabeth said.

"Indeed. She wanted to wait for your arrival, but she received distressing news, and Mr. and Mrs. Callingwood were heading to that part of the country and agreed to take her. She's travelling with their servants. She'll receive excellent care with them on the journey. Oh, right. Let us go upstairs for you to see those books."

The three ladies walked up the staircase. Aunt Cass was slower upon the stairs than Elizabeth's natural stride, and she corrected herself instantly. Her aunt had aged in the past year. She was still clearly robust and healthy, but what were once fine lines about her mouth were now cracks of age. Her eyes were dark and a little watery, like she had been crying just moments ago. Elizabeth knew that feeling, and her heart ached for her aunt.

"Did Mrs. Dover take Miss Puss Puss with her?"

"No, no. She left her to help Mrs. Cook with the pies. Mrs. Dover was too afraid that cat would spook and never be found again."

"I wonder if she will grace me with her purrs this visit?"

Aunt Cass shrugged. "I've not seen that thing since Mrs. Dover left, so don't count on it. She's attached herself to Mrs. Cook now. Oh, now, your uncle was very keen that some of the books would fetch you excellent prices at the booksellers, especially for those that work with collectors. He said a few of his oldest books should fetch you a guinea *each*."

"For one book?" Maria declared. When Aunt Cass said it was so, Maria added, "The generosity continues to flow."

"Now, remember, all of the books from David are to me, and not you." Aunt Cass cleared her throat. "For when you write home, that is."

Elizabeth stared at her aunt. "I don't understand the need for all this subterfuge."

"If I happened to gift you a large number of books to dispose of at your leisure that happens to be worth upwards of one hundred pounds, that is my choice and your father cannot interfere."

"There is some deceit in that, Aunt," Elizabeth said.

"Necessary deceit. Do you want people knowing the likes of David Leigh gave you hundreds of pounds worth of books? Your father would force you to marry him the moment the rumor hit his ears."

Maria made a displeased sound.

"Then I shall divide the proceeds with you," Elizabeth said.

"Don't you dare," Aunt Cass said. "Getting these damnable things out of my home will be payment enough for my favourite niece."

"Aunt, you aren't supposed to have favourites," Elizabeth said.

"That's with your own children. Nieces and nephews exist solely to choose favourites from," Aunt Cass said. "I'm certain the bible says that."

"Perhaps you should ask your father," Maria added helpfully.

"My father only knows the parts of the bible that benefit him in society's good opinion," Elizabeth said. She winced when she realized the words had tumbled out of her mouth, as opposed to only being upon her thoughts. "I apologize."

"None needed in my presence," Aunt Cass said. "Now here is the room. You do as you need, my dear. Shall Mrs. Thorne and I return to the dining room to begin sorting?"

"If that is agreeable to you, Aunt. I do not wish to be alone if you require any company."

"That is what I am for!" Maria said.

"I will have the maid bring you some tea and light your fire. Please join us when you are ready." To Maria, Aunt Cass said, "Mrs. Thorne, what is your opinion concerning wine before dinner?"

"I believe it is an excellent choice," Maria said.

The two ladies begged Elizabeth to fetch them at any time, and then she was left alone with a room stacked full of her uncle's memories.

⚜ Chapter 3 ⚜

ELIZABETH SAT ON the edge of the guest bed and stared at the boxes, trunks, and crates of books. They were stacked on top of each other, shoved under the bed, stacked in the closet, pushed into the corners, and just generally everywhere.

She had prepared herself for the sight of familiar book spines. She had not prepared herself for journals, personal spell books, and letters. She wept at the sight of her uncle's handwriting. This was going to be harder on her than she had thought. However, these books were precious to her. They were worth more to her than the pounds, shillings, and pence she could fetch. These were her uncle's words and thoughts; his entire life's work in ink. Those she would hoard for herself, and never share.

Grief washed upon her in gentle waves. She cautiously moved the journals from their simple crate to her top bureau drawer, careful to keep her dripping tears away from the precious pages. She dabbed her eyes and blew her nose, and drew in several deep breathes, but she continued her task. She would look at those special books later. There was work to be done.

The majority of the first trunk's books were on fossils, minerals, and mining, topics that held no interest to Elizabeth. She decided to keep the large encyclopedia, *On the Magical Properties of Stones, Rocks, Minerals, and Precious Gems: A Thorough Investigation by the Country's Foremost Occultists,* published in 1798. The drawings were intricate, every detail painstakingly rendered in ink for the reader. She would keep that for her own enjoyment. The remainder of the books went into the wooden crate formerly occupied by the journals. When the trunk was full, she enlisted Sally's help. The crate was carried into the hallway outside of Elizabeth's room.

Elizabeth accepted the offer of another pot of tea. At first, she declined the offer of a small tray of delights, but Sally said Cook was worried. She accepted, to ease the good woman's concerns. She had little appetite but did manage to nibble at some pound cake. She continued her work, sorting through another trunk.

A box wrapped in a pale blue silk ribbon sat at the bottom of a trunk. She picked it up and discovered that, underneath it, was another with a yellow ribbon. She carefully opened the box and discovered letters in her mother's own hand.

She stared at them, unable to open any of the precious gifts. Uncle Edward had always been her link to her long-dead mother. Her father, for all his good qualities, had not been sensitive about his eldest daughter's pain at losing her mother.

Then her stepmother, Augusta, died in childbirth, just like her own mother, and now she had yet another stepmother. Isabella was good enough as a companion, but she was younger than Elizabeth, something that Aunt Cass bristled at when she thought Elizabeth was out of ear shot. Maria, too. Even the servants whispered about it when they supposed themselves alone: *How awful it must be for Miss Knight, having a young thing like Mrs. Isabella Knight be mistress of the house.*

Elizabeth bore it all with a quiet solemnity, knowing and accepting that it was her lot in life. Men married women, and they married women who could bear them sons. Isabella was still a young, healthy woman. If she could give him a few more sons, all the better. That was her lot in life, and Elizabeth's to accept it.

But through it all, her mother's brother and sister had been her anchor. Now, one of those supportive ropes had been cut and the boat was rockier than ever.

Except that now, she stared at letters. Old letters that threatened to stab a sword through the scars her soul carried. Her grief was already raw, and she knew there was much work ahead of her. However, she opened the first packet of letters, and read the first one.

August 30, 1782
Bryden Rectory

My dearest brother,

It has been raining for eight days straight now in Bryden and I fear I am going mad waiting for my confinement to begin. Mr. Knight left three days ago to attend a parishioner, who was first said to only be suffering from a sore throat but was discovered to have a putrid fever. For my sake, the midwife had instructed that he not return to the house. Therefore, he stays at Mr. Frank Black's house, who is a bachelor.

I have not received word from him in two days, and with this rain, and the midwife now gone to attend to another confinement—our dairy maid's sister—I find myself alone with the servants and the midwife's apprentice.

And no news, Edward! None whatsoever. How I wish our dear mother was alive, for I could, at least, depend upon her assistance. I had already written to Cassy, begging her to make the journey to our poor, retired part of the country, but I fear these storms will keep her snug in London. The post did not even arrive yesterday because the roads on this side of the fields were flooded.

Please write to me with any news, no matter how mundane. I will happily accept a letter from your housekeeper, if she has any news of her niece and her upcoming confinement. If the news is bad, pray ask her to lie to me until mine is over. I am daily more fearful of what the Lord has planned for me. I do not wish to leave this gentle creature alone in the world, as so many mothers have been called to Heaven already. However, I must trust in the Lord and my midwife, and hope all will be well.

I shall send news as soon as I can. In the meantime, please write and end this tedious boredom.

Your loving sister, etc etc

Elizabeth's broken sobs were so loud that Maria and Aunt Cass came thundering up the staircase. Both women dropped to the floor and wrapped their arms around her before even knowing the source of her grief. Aunt Cass pressed Elizabeth against her chest, as Maria rubbed her hands and arms. Finally, Maria took up the letter in Elizabeth's hand and glanced over it.

"Oh, Eliza." To Aunt Cass, Maria said, "It's from her mother."

"Oh, dearest," Aunt Cass whispered. "This is not the time to read those."

"I thought I was strong enough to read one," Elizabeth whispered through her pained sobs.

"It is not about strength, my child," Aunt Cass said, her voice now cracking. "You must not tax yourself."

The three women stayed on the floor, with Elizabeth in the middle of the embraces, warm and safe in the arms of those who truly loved her. A moment later, Sally draped a heavy blanket over Elizabeth's weary shoulders.

And, for those fleeting moments, she could almost feel her own mother's arms about her, too. A woman who feared dying in childbirth, but who did her duty with dignity and strength. Elizabeth wanted to be that woman, to be a woman her mother would have been proud to have known.

But, perhaps most of all, right now, Elizabeth felt like a little girl, seeing her mother in her bed, cold and unmoving, and not understanding why God would take away a little girl's mama.

AUNT CASS DECIDED that London dining rules and conventions be damned; her niece required nourishment. It appeared that Mrs.

Cook had the same notion, for when Aunt Cass went to speak to Cook, she informed her mistress that the barley turnip soup was done, and that the mutton had nearly finished boiling. Elizabeth overheard Aunt Cass ask Maria if she would be terribly offended by an informal dinner, with no place settings or any of the usual proprieties. Aunt Cass declared herself fatigued, and she worried for her niece's strength.

Maria readily agreed that a casual family dinner, set in the dining room, with no servants to attend them, was the best approach at such a time, and that she would not be offended in the slightest. And so, Cook was informed that she did not need to worry about formality tonight; Sally could bring out the food as it was ready.

They started with the barley soup, which was excellent. More importantly, it awakened Elizabeth's sluggish appetite and she had a few forkfuls of the boiled mutton and peas. There was still room for Cook's jam tarts, and the three ladies happily cleared the tray.

"We wouldn't want Cook to think they weren't enjoyed," Aunt Cass has said, encouraging Elizabeth to have a fourth tart.

The ladies lingered over dinner until Elizabeth finally announced she was strong enough to return to her task, while there was still daylight left. Maria and Aunt Cass offered to accompany her, but she insisted upon her solitude. The grief would not overwhelm her this time, she promised. It had only been the shock of seeing her mother's letter. Now that she knew they existed, she could place them out of her mind, knowing they would be there for when she was ready. She pushed off their concerns of fatigue; she wanted something to keep her mind busy.

And, in all honestly, she reveled in the solitude. She had so little of it at the rectory. Any relief from the noise was welcomed.

Aunt Cass had argued against it, asking Elizabeth to sit a little longer in the dining room. Elizabeth dutifully stayed, sipping sherry, while Maria and Aunt Cass explained their sorting system. In the time Elizabeth had been upstairs earlier in the day, Maria and Aunt Cass had managed to sort four entire crates of books by themes: agriculture and mining, child rearing and young ladies' decorum, theological and philosophical, and a final crate of hodgepodge. Anything that appeared remotely interesting was placed on the sideboard table for Elizabeth's final decision.

"At least, please, look through what we've set aside for you thus far, Elizabeth," Aunt Cass said, still clearly uncomfortable with her young niece's unwillingness for company.

Elizabeth thumbed through the crates. She agreed with the choices made; none of those books appealed to her in the slightest. From the sideboard, she determined to only keep three occult history books; everything else was deemed sellable.

"Only three?" Aunt Cass asked. She was still seated and nursing a cup of tea. "Why so few?"

"I must be practical," Elizabeth said. "It could be many years before I successfully read through everything I choose. Even if some of the books only gain me half a shilling, that is half a shilling I do not need to worry about. I must consider my father's age and my circumstances. I cannot expect anyone to accept me and my estate-sized library, now can I?"

"When your father dies, I shall happily take you in," Aunt Cass said sternly. "There was never any worry on that score, surely."

"Charles seems to have other plans for me," Elizabeth said of her brother.

"Pish," was all Aunt Cass said in reply. "That man would need to keep a thought in his mind for more than a week to have a plan."

Elizabeth did not admit aloud that she did often worry about where she would end up *when* her father died. Her brother would be tasked with her upkeep. Elizabeth could see Charles insisting Elizabeth move to his small establishment to act as housekeeper until he could convince some poor, foolish woman to marry him. If she refused, could he withhold her income? Where would the interest on her inheritance be sent? She did not know the answers to those questions, only that her father took care of such things. She knew her husband would, also, if she could find someone to take her on.

Unfortunately, with so little money to her name and no dowry beyond her new inheritance, she had nothing tangible to tempt a man of good sense and a decent income to overlook her age. No one would marry her now without a considerable fortune landing at her feet.

And what would become of poor Isabella? And her unmarried sisters? What an unhappy household if G and Thea ended up living with Isabella!

"Don't worry, my dear. Your father is still very healthy. Besides, if Charles tried to steal as much as a farthing of your money, I would send my solicitors to scare him into submission," Aunt Cass said.

"I would send Henry," Maria said. "Charles had hinted he wants the parsonage in the village when old Mr. Crawford finally dies. I believe his ambition would be greater than his need for controlling his sister." Maria paused. "Of course, Charles would have to return to Oxford."

"Surely Mr. Knight has convinced the boy to go back. I understood he'd fully recovered," Aunt Cass said.

Maria shrugged and said, "If necessary, I suppose we could bring Mr. Leigh into the mix."

"I appreciate that you are trying to solve a problem that does not yet exist, but I believe that Charles would need to be extraordinarily cruel for me to turn to David Leigh's assistance. He is unmarried still, let us not forget, and I believe society would have some interesting things to say about an unmarried cousin helping his unmarried cousin. Let us not even ponder bringing that upon my head."

"Then let me find you a husband before your father leaves this earth!" Maria said, with a laugh. "There must be one useful man in England!"

"I believe that is my cue to speak up for my sex."

Elizabeth spun around to see Henry Thorne standing in the foyer. James gave Aunt Cass an apologetic look and said, "Mr. Thorne to see you, ma'am."

"Mr. Thorne!" Aunt Cass said cheerfully. She curtsied and said, "We are attempting to find a useful man in England. Surely you know of one."

"My wife might argue otherwise, but I am occasionally known to be helpful to ladies," Henry said with a smile. His face sobered when he said, "I wished to offer my condolences in person. It is not that I did not trust my dear wife to do it, of course. I merely felt I should not leave the entire task to her."

"Henry, my dear, none of that. We are in need of a man," Maria said.

"What is needed?"

"A great many things. However, first, let us find a husband for my dear friend here."

Henry Thorne shook his head, a sad expression across his face. "Alas, Maria, I do not believe there is a man in England worthy enough in our dear Miss Knight's eyes. Ah! And there she glares at me with those eyes. Ah, yes! I am correct."

He laughed and accepted a cup of tea from Aunt Cass. He sat down in the chair provided by James. "Now, is there something else I can assist with? Good God. Where did all these books come from?"

Elizabeth was about to ask what his plans were to assist in the selling of her books, and beg his help, but Maria interrupted her.

"May we store some of Elizabeth's books in our house?"

"Of course!" Henry looked about the dining room. "I may have to knock down a wall to accommodate all of them, but I am certain we can find room."

"This is one room of three, currently," Elizabeth said with a wince. "My hope was that I could prevail upon someone's good will to help either send them to auction or to sell them individually to the booksellers."

"We discussed this already, Miss Knight. But…" He looked about the room. "Where did all of these books comes from?"

They explained the David Leigh situation to Henry Thorne. He laughed merrily at the social conventions they were attempting to skirt about with gifting them to the aunt and not the niece. He did so with a gentleness that seemed to only mildly irritate his wife.

Finally, he said, "With your permission, Mrs. Spencer, and yours, Miss Knight, I would like to take one of the volumes to Osborne, to get his opinion."

"We also have an inventory list that we've started today," Aunt Cass said. She passed him the sheets of paper. "This is only for what is sorted, of course."

"Please, Henry, do not lose the list," Maria said, wincing as her husband folded the sheets in half. "It is the only copy! Pray, take care!"

"I am certain, my darling, that I am capable of walking several sheets of paper through London and back unharmed."

Maria's expression clearly expressed her doubt. "Hmm."

Henry pulled out his pocket watch. "I believe Osborne's will be open for a few more hours. Goodness, ladies. You had dinner early today. You do realize you are in London, and not the country during the time of our grandparents, yes?"

Maria gave Henry a withering glance. "Mrs. Spencer is in mourning and should be allowed to eat whenever she sees fit without commentary from guests."

"I was only teasing, Maria," Henry said in a much softer tone. "Mrs. Spencer, forgive me. I did not mean any offensive."

"Oh, Mr. Thorne! There is nothing to forgive," Aunt Cass insisted.

"It was my fault," Elizabeth said. She bashfully looked down at her hands. "My uncle had saved letters from my mother. I did not know that, so you can imagine the pain of their discovery."

"Oh, Miss Knight. How dreadful for you." Henry Thorne took a long drink from his cup. "Ladies, with your permission, I shall be off. Hmm, may I also take one of the books? I believe Sir William Donsdale was looking for volumes on occult history, so if you have something of that nature...."

Elizabeth nodded her agreement. As she said before, a half shilling was still a half shilling. She thumbed through the appropriate crate and pulled out *The Occult in Wales: 1688 to Present.*

"Would this be acceptable? I have no interest in keeping it."

Henry nodded and placed the inventory list inside the book's cover. "I'll be off. Hopefully, I can make it there in time."

More tea was ordered, and Maria happily began sorting through the books on the dining room table. Her rational was solid: it gave them a space to place other books later. Plus, having a place to eat was never a bad thing. David Leigh's servants arrived with the promised one hundred and eleven books. There was no room for them in the dining room.

"Just put them in the drawing room. No, not the one upstairs. The one just over there. Yes, that one," Aunt Cass instructed.

After those boxes and crates were arranged to Aunt Cass' preference, they left and Aunt Cass returned to the foyer where the ladies watched the delivery unfold.

"Is that the end of the books?" Elizabeth asked.

Aunt Cass scowled. "They said there were at least four more crates to deliver tomorrow. I wish they would just get this agony over with."

They made their way back to the dining room, determined to make some headway in the work there. They had only just sat down and poured themselves tea when James walked in.

"Mr. Joseph Baxter and Sir Matthew Beaumont to see Miss Knight," the butler announced.

Aunt Cass threw her napkin upon the table and rose. "Oh for the love of the Saviour!"

Elizabeth put down her tea cup and said to her aunt, "Do you know these gentlemen?"

"Only two of the most odious men I've ever met who pretend to be gentlemen," Aunt Cass said. "Come ladies. I do not want them to see this room. Be on your guard. Sally! Close the doors behind us."

"Why?" Elizabeth asked, following her aunt.

"I suspect they are here to rob us."

☙ Chapter 4 ❧

"THEY ARE THE London branch of the Royal Occult Society. Be on your guard, Elizabeth. They might have lofty titles, but they are hooligans. I shall speak with them, but do not allow them to bully you or needle you into a reaction."

"I will not be goaded into anything beyond a ladylike response," Elizabeth promised.

The three ladies walked to the common drawing room and greeted the gentlemen. Once introductions were made, Mr. Baxter said, "Very good to meet you, Miss Knight. Might I extend my condolences upon the loss of your dear uncle. He was a...most unique individual."

"Thank you, sir, for your kind words to my niece," Aunt Cass said.

"He was a dear friend of ours in the Society. I fear it will be a long time before we find someone of his calibre to replace him with."

Elizabeth made no reply. She was surprised her aunt did not offer refreshment of any kind. Nor did she sit. Nor did she offer to allow the men to sit. Marie and Elizabeth flanked her, and they all stood awkwardly about.

"Gentlemen, might I ask the purpose of this visit? We are a house of mourning, after all, and are not prepared for visitors," Aunt Cas said in the frostiest of tones.

"Oh, of course. We mean no disrespect with our visit, of course, Mrs. Spencer. We would have written, but we were under the impression that time was of the essence."

Aunt Cass' face was so stoic that Elizabeth began to worry that it might be her aunt, and not herself, that was going to be goaded into something.

"In matter of fact, we have come to assist with Miss Knight's burdens. We have been led to believe she has inherited Mr. Leigh's occult library."

Elizabeth took her aunt's lead and remained perfectly silent. The sight of three silent women seemed to rattle this Mr. Baxter, for he began to speak faster to break up the silence.

"Well, we understand that Miss Knight lives in a retired country rectory with her father and several siblings. We wished to make an offer to purchase Miss Knight's books from her uncle."

After a moment of silence, Mr. Baxter said, "We would like to offer seventy pounds for the entire lot."

Seventy pounds! It was a shocking sum of money. She had no concept the collection's true worth in terms of a book collector's opinion, but what a tempting amount. She tempered her surprised emotions with the realities and truths of the situation. Beyond her uncle's wishes for her further scholarship, there were the intangibles, such as the letters from her mother. No doubt worthless to others, but they were worth fifty thousand pounds to her heart. And, in either case, she was not selling anything until she went through it all and made her own decisions.

"That sum would help save Miss Knight from the ordeal of having to sort through any of those dusty old things," Mr. Baxter said. "Young ladies have more important things to do with their time."

Elizabeth's mood soured promptly. "That is a very generous offer, sir, and I very much appreciate you coming here to make it. However, I have not made any decisions regarding the books, and I cannot possibly in good conscience make any such arrangement now. However, if there is a particular volume or perhaps an encyclopedia that you wish to purchase, I will look for it and place it aside if I feel it is something I can part with."

"Well, it would be much easier, Miss Knight, if you permitted us access to the books. A young lady's mind is not equipped to discern the nuances of occult manuscripts." Mr. Baxter pointed at the wooden crates in the corner of the drawing room. "If those are them, I will happily peruse them now."

"I do not wish to allow strangers access to my books when I myself have not yet had the opportunity to examine them all."

It was Sir Mathew's turn to speak. "We understand how difficult these tasks can be for a young lady, so we wish to take it away from you. Call it in honour of our dear friend's regard for you. Just allow Mr. Baxter here to settle with your aunt, and we shall be on our way."

"My niece is old enough to know her own mind," Aunt Cass said. "If she says no, then that is her choice and everyone in this room will respect her decision."

"I would be happy to look at a list of titles or subjects that interest you," Elizabeth said. "I will not be keeping all of the library, so I would be pleased to set aside any particular volumes for you, after I have evaluated them for myself, of course. Many of the books have great sentimental value to me and I wish not to part from them."

"Well, there are many books and items. Too many for us to think of without careful reflection," Mr. Baxter said.

"There are some old journals, mostly written in Latin, that I would particularly like to have," Sir Matthew said. "As well, there are three leather bound and gold embossed books with nothing more than an autograph on one page and a short biography afterwards no more than 3 pages long. They are pet projects your uncle and I worked on, and I would like to continue the work out of respect to him."

And there was the truth: they wanted the female occultist autograph books.

"I will offer you ten pounds, simply for those, if you have them in your possession," Sir Matthew. "Shall we shake hands upon the deal?"

Aunt Cass did not speak, signalling that Elizabeth was to carry the negotiations at this stage. She inhaled to ensure her voice was steady and asked, "May I inquire as to why you feel you should have it when they were given to me?"

"Well," Mr. Baxter said, clearing his throat. "As you know, women cannot do the occult to any useful purpose. Your minds are too delicate and underdeveloped for the rigorous learning necessary. Latin, Greek, astronomy, astrology, herbology, riddles, puzzles, mathematics, and mineralogy. Even some medicine on occasion. It is obviously too much for a young lady such as yourself."

"Indeed." Maria didn't even attempt to hide her scorn.

"As my colleague here has said, we will happily purchase those three volumes for ten pounds. Immediately." He reached into his jacket pocket to produce a leather wallet. He displayed a ten-pound note. "As we understand, your father's financial situation is delicate, with such a large family and...an unwed daughter of your age."

Elizabeth did not have the opportunity to speak because Aunt Cass butted in. "Gentlemen, I will not allow my niece to be insulted in my home. Not ever."

Ten pounds was an exceptional amount of money for some journals and three books, which immediately alerted Elizabeth to several interesting pieces of evidence. First, they did not know her uncle had given her money in his will, allowing her a very small independence from her father. Second, they did not know she had some education in the occult, enough for her to find the books and determine which of the others were important. Thirdly, they wanted the books her uncle quite clearly did not want them to have; after all, if he wanted them to have the book, he'd have just willed them to the Society.

"I appreciate the financial offer you have made me. I cannot accept at this time. However, I would be very happy to provide the Royal Occult Society a list of the books I will be sending to auction and those available for private collectors to purchase. Mr. Henry Thorne has graciously offered to assist me in that endeavour, so you may speak to him or his wife."

"But..." Mr. Baxter began.

"Otherwise, I cannot make any promises. My uncle left me the books and with clear instructions in his will. I plan to carry out his wishes as best as my abilities and good sense allow."

"But..." Mr. Baxter attempted to interject, but Aunt Cass cut him off.

"My niece feels duty-bound to abide by my brother's will and wishes. I will be assisting her in that task, as well Mr. and Mrs. Thorne, of Vane Park. If we require any specialized assistance, I will, of course, send a letter to the Royal Society requesting a specialist. Otherwise, gentlemen, I believe your business is concluded."

"Yes, of course. Thank you, Mrs. Spencer. It is always a pleasure to see you," Mr. Baxter said, and in a tone that announced he hoped to never speak to Cassandra Spencer ever again.

Sir Matthew was less gentlemanly. "I will seek out Mr. Thorne and see if he is more reasonable than the women in his life. I look forward to you doing the right thing, Miss Knight. For everyone's sake."

When the front door closed behind the men, Elizabeth asked, "Did Sir Matthew just threaten me?"

"I hate the very sight of Sir Matthew and his silly little lawyer! Indeed, that man was threatening you the moment he arrived. How dare he insult you. My dear, I wouldn't give that man a farthing, not even if he were begging naked and starving on the streets. I won't tell you that you cannot sell the books to him, but if it is because of the money, I will give you twelve pounds myself to keep the books."

"My dear aunt, I had no intention of giving that odious man anything beyond my name," Elizabeth said. "To think the nerve of him to come here and insult me, especially after my uncle specifically asked in his letter that I continue his work on the autograph book. Sir Matthew doesn't even think I am capable of understanding what an autograph book is, let alone the work involved."

Maria turned to Aunt Cass. "With your permission, Mrs. Spencer, I would like to send one of your servants to my house with a note. My maid will find Henry and warn him."

"Send Sally. She is very dependable." Aunt Cass turned to Elizabeth and said, "My dear, do you wish to quit for the day?"

"No, Aunt. If anything, I am motivated more than ever to complete the task."

AFTER MILD PROTESTS from her aunt and friend, Elizabeth returned to her bedchamber and continued sorting. *On the Forgotten History of Female Occultists* (1763) she put into the closet, on a shelf she'd set aside for the books she would make final decisions on later. Likewise, *First Forays into the Study of Occult Flora* (1803) went on the same shelf. She wasted no time deciding that *The Great Men of British Occultism* (1801) and *A Study of British Occultism* (1799) would go in the auction trunks.

Too quickly, however, the shelf she'd set aside in the closet was filled, and she moved on to the second shelf. She reminded herself that these would need to be purged and pruned as necessary once the first stage of the task was complete. Too many of the books had her uncle's handwriting on them, and therefore she could not, at present, part with them. Perhaps it would be easier once faced with several closets of books. For now, however, she could not part with even that tiny speck of him.

Then, she discovered the autograph books. They were inside a box, wrapped in cloth. The box was placed inside a trunk, that was filled with straw, as if it was holding a precious piece of pottery discovered at an archeological dig far away. One of the leatherbond books had a ribbon tied around it, holding down a note underneath. Carefully, she undid the bow. She recognized her uncle's handwriting immediately. It was not addressed to her, but she knew it was written with her in mind. The letter's address read:

Read this aloud when you are ready.

At first, she thought she was reading a poem, but soon recognized that it had the cadence of an incantation. She read to the end and looked about her expectantly. Nothing happened, except the sighing of wind outside the window.

She frowned and read the incantation again, just in case she had not read it properly the first time. The sigh of wind was louder the second time, and had an almost feminine tenor to it.

Disappointed, though not surprised, that she was unable to do even the basic magic that the incantation had expected of her, she opened the book and flipped the first page. It had been the only page she'd ever been allowed to see of the book when it was in Uncle Edward's possession. It read SARAH EGERTON. It was a typical autograph ghost mark, with the clear ink signature on one side and the staining reflection pressed into the other half of the paper.

Around the ink bleeds were several ovals drawn, lavishly decorated into various herbs: sprigs of rosemary, a cluster of thyme, and bay leaves of various sizes. One section was turned into several steams of roses. At the opposite end, a few of the ink botches had been turned into beans of some sort next to a cup and saucer. At the bottom of the page was Sarah Egerton's name, printed carefully and without embellishment.

Elizabeth glanced at the paper she held, shrugged, and read the incantation again. This time, the sigh was unmistakable for anything other than a woman's annoyance.

"Who's there?" Elizabeth asked.

Another sigh.

Elizabeth flipped the page on the book and skimmed the biography. Mrs. Egerton, it seems, was the last female occultist to have been added to the collection, even though she was at the front of the book. She died in 1746 and called herself the last of the true English female occultists. She feared that a movement of genteel lady occultists would take her place, where they would not be taught the proper skills and would exist solely as ornamentation.

"Then it is well enough that you did not live to today, Mrs. Egerton," Elizabeth said aloud to the book. "For you would have seen your prophecy come true."

Another annoyed sigh. And then a feminine voice said, "My dear child, stop playing around with incantations if you are not ready for the consequences."

Elizabeth yelped and fell backwards, hitting her back against the edge of the bed.

"Should I assume that you are not ready?" said the disembodied voice.

"Um…who is speaking?"

"Shall I assume that you are Miss Elizabeth Knight, niece of Edward Leigh?"

"Yes." Elizabeth squeaked.

"Excellent. Now, follow my instructions carefully. I am to be packed very carefully back into my box, with the other books. Pay special attention to the straw. And keep me away from the damp. I dislike the damp greatly."

"Yes, of course," Elizabeth said in a very small voice.

She dutifully packed the books back as she had found them, all the while her good sense and her physical senses warred with each other. Had grief finally tossed her over the cliff's edge? Would she need admitting to an asylum now? Had she really unlocked the ghost that inhabited the book, as her uncle had often said could happen?

When Elizabeth began to untie the leather strapping around one of the other autograph books, the voice snapped, "Miss Knight! Do not touch that one. You are clearly not ready for anything in this trunk yet. Clean out Mr. Leigh's occult farming books and come back when you are not in such a state. There is no point to summon me until you are ready."

A little spark of joy tickled Elizabeth's insides. Had she really summoned one of the female occultists?

"Pardon my question, ma'am, but how will I know when I am ready to speak with you?"

The book sighed dramatically. "When you don't ask questions like that. Now, kindly close the truck lid, child."

"Why?"

The voice sighed again. "The damp, girl!"

Elizabeth did as the book instructed, and then stared at the now-silent trunk and wondered if she'd finally descended into madness. She lifted the lid carefully. Perhaps the book could not see her, if it were all snug and put away.

"Are you deaf, girl? Close. The. Lid."

The trunk lid slipped from Elizabeth's fingers and banged shut.

"Carefully, if you please," the voice chided.

Elizabeth started for a minute or two longer before tiptoeing from the room. She made her way down the stairs, following the sounds of laughter. Maria and Aunt Cass were in the dining room. Each of them had empty wine glasses, and there was a decanter that was suspiciously very close to empty on the table.

"Oh, Elizabeth! Look what we found. *A Guide for Young Ladies on How to Get a Husband.*" Aunt Cass's cheeks were flushed.

"Your aunt has been reading passages. It is delightful!"

Aunt Cass cleared her throat, and held the book out in front of her. In a deep voice, she read:

> *Men do not desire wives who ponder upon grand subjects. They want dutiful, obedient wives. Young ladies who giggle, read newspapers, and bury themselves upon the pages of a novel will find themselves unmarried and alone. This volume, written by a man of sense who has been searching England far and wide for a wife, hopes to address this modern age of uncouth young ladies and how their revolt against the good and natural order of the world had caused many men of sense and education to be left desolate without a good woman to rely upon.*

"Sounds to me it is not the ladies who are the problem!" Maria said through her own titters. "After all, I have found a husband and I giggle with the best of them!"

"I have been known to read a newspaper now and again, even!" Aunt Cass said, joining in the laughter.

"How did you ever manage to marry, my good lady?"

"Perhaps my dear George was not a man of sense after all!" Aunt Cass declared, which sent Maria down another giggle path.

Elizabeth sighed.

"My dear!" Aunt Cass said, trying to bring calm into her wine-addled voice. "Are you well? Do you require us?"

Elizabeth did not want to ask the question, but it was necessary. "Please don't misunderstand what I am about to ask, but have any of the books spoken to you?"

"Are you ill?" Aunt Cass asked.

"No, I am not ill. I merely want to know if any of the magical texts have spoken or sighed, or perhaps complained about the dampness of the weather."

Maria glanced at Aunt Cass. "We haven't had that much wine, Eliza."

"Yet," Aunt Cass said, which sent the ladies back into giggles.

"I ask seriously. One of the autograph books those gentlemen requested spoke to me. Well, to be very specific, it was very saucy to me and told me to leave it alone."

"To think, Mrs. Thorne? There is a book in this house with your personality!"

"Mrs. Spencer!" Maria exclaimed in faux outrage. "I must meet this saucy book. Come ladies!"

"I was being serious. I did not imagine it, I promise you."

Elizabeth's words fell on unheeding ears, for wine had warned off the good sense of the ladies. She followed behind the giggling women and up the staircase, her agitation growing with each step. What would she do if the book's voice did appear? Or, perhaps a worse fate, that she had imagined the book speaking to her; that grief had transported her mind into a fanciful world. She did not wish to spend her remaining days locked away in a horrid asylum, and yet the possibility now seemed more and more likely.

The ladies waited laughing in the hallway for Elizabeth, who walked into her bedchamber. She lifted the trunk's top carefully and dug out the protective inner box from the straw. Then, she opened it.

"For the love of...did I not just tell you to put me away? Oh, you have fetched company. I do not wish to appear to company. Good bye, Miss Knight."

Elizabeth clearly heard the voice. She glanced nervously at her aunt and friend, who both stared gap-mouthed at the book.

"Well?" Elizabeth finally asked, unable to handle the suspense any longer.

Maria asked, in a very small voice, "Please tell me someone else heard the book speak."

Aunt Cass nodded. "It spoke."

"Oh, thank goodness." Maria looked relieved.

"Then, you both heard it? I did not imagine it speaking earlier. Correct?"

The book sighed disapprovingly. "I am a she."

"She," Elizabeth said, correcting herself. "You have both heard her, yes?" When both of her companions nodded their heads, Elizabeth blew out a breath. "I am all relief. I feared grief had overtaken me."

"For a terrifying moment, I thought the wine had finally done me in," Maria said.

"Why is the book talking?" Aunt Cass asked. "Do all occult books speak?"

"The damp, Miss Knight! Pay heed!"

"Yes, of course," Elizabeth said. She placed the book back in its home. She didn't bother to latch the inner box, but she pushed straw over it. Then she closed the trunk's lid. She stood back from the trunk and talking book. "My uncle's books never spoke to me, and I have never been certain that the stories he told were real or embellished to the point of absurdity. Thought, now I wonder if I had simply dismissed his stories out of ignorance."

"I understood he'd taught you the occult," Maria said.

"It was all theory. He never practiced any incantations around me, for Father has always been a skeptic."

"And your father does not support women in the occult," Aunt Cass said. At Elizabeth's expression of reproof, her aunt apologized. "I should have not spoken of things. I simply wish your dear mother were alive. She would know what to do."

Elizabeth sighed. She had long heard the arguments. Her memory of her mother and father arguing were long faded, though she did know the tales. Instead, it was the arguments between her uncle and her father that she remembered the most. Her uncle shouting at her father that he had no right to keep Elizabeth away from him. That the occult arts were a part of her bloodline and hiding her inheritance was barbaric mistreatment. How her father shouted back, saying that no daughter of his would be filling her mind with nonsense when she should be learning how to manage a house for her husband.

It had been Aunt Cass and a reluctant Augusta who had provided the feminine bridge necessary to convince her father to let her cross it. And, in the end, Augusta has managed to convince her father by emphasizing the financial relief of having a daughter of age oft staying with relations in town. Plus, Mrs. Spencer had promised to expose Elizabeth to all kinds of society. Augusta argued this was the best way to find bookish, boring, so-very-sensible Elizabeth a husband.

And for years, Elizabeth had sat in the front row of the balls in London and at Bath, where the more desirable single ladies sat to be picked for dances: the ripest of the fruit in handy reach. She had endured being moved to the back row of chairs, too, when she was no longer considered the freshest face of the crop. Until, finally, she'd given up being seated at all and moved to assist with chaperoning and occasionally being asked to make a fourth at the card tables.

But by then, Augusta was gone and her father had grown accustomed to the financial relief of his wealthy relations taking his eldest, unmarried daughter off his hands for a few weeks at a time.

"Elizabeth? Are you well?" Maria asked, reaching out a hand to touch her friend.

Tears filled her eyes, but she gulped down the grief. She looked at her aunt and said, "I should have insisted upon coming to London for Christmas."

"Oh, child no. My brother did not want you to see him in his state. He knew he was dying by then, and he did not want your last memories of him to be tending to his failing body. No, he made us all promise to keep you away. On that head, your father was doing our wishes by insisting you stay in Bryden. I am sorry he did not explain himself properly, or have that his new wife of his to do it, but know that was your uncle's request."

"Was uncle alone? At the end, I mean."

"No, indeed not. I personally saw to the hiring of three nurses and two new girls to care for him 'round the clock. He always had the usual servants, plus the additional help so that no one was inconvenienced. Mr. Grant visited every day. And I was always about. All of his society fellows visited. And all the neighbours. Your uncle wanted for no company at all. Indeed, he made several comments about how he did not know the number of friends he possessed."

"I only met him a couple of times, but from what I remember," Maria said with a soft smile, "he must have said many disparaging remarks about the company not allowing him to sleep."

Aunt Cass laughed, even if her own eyes glistened with tears. "Yes."

"Thank you," Elizabeth whispered. Her soul wept for her uncle, but she knew to bear the pain with dignity. She took in several breaths until the crushing weight on her chest relented enough for her form sentences.

"What do you wish to do, Eliza?" Maria asked. Gone were the wine giggles now.

"I confess this task is too difficult for me at present. Might I assist with the farming books in the dining room and in the second drawing room?"

"Your company would be most welcome," Aunt Cass said. "Come ladies. I believe the next batch of jam tarts are finally ready. And there is still the second opened bottle of wine that we have yet to finish."

"I might pass on the wine, if you don't mind, Aunt," Elizabeth said.

"More for us, then!" Maria said.

The three women embraced at that, all laughing amongst themselves, and, together, they walked back to the dining room. There, one of the footmen had already begun the task of setting out supper on two small tables brought in from the drawing room. Jam tarts, cake, cold ham, bacon, and bread awaited them. They switched from wine to tea, and it wasn't until they burned through the second four-hour candle that Aunt Cass announced it was time for sleep.

⋘ Chapter 5 ⋙

THE AUTOGRAPH BOOK left Elizabeth alone for the remainder of the evening, and into the next morning. She dressed, with Sally's help, and headed downstairs to breakfast. Aunt Cass was already up, sipping at her tea and reading an old newspaper.

"There you are, my dear! Did you sleep well?"

"I confess I tossed and turned. I kept dreaming of Uncle Edward." Elizabeth smiled. "They were good dreams, at least."

"That is a blessing, then. Come sit. I am attempting to catch up on my current events. I am woefully behind. Does your father still get The Times from Mary?"

Elizabeth glanced at the gathering pile of newspapers and nodded. "Mr. Fitzharding is a Tory, so he sends over his copies once or twice a month to us. Mr. Thorne subscribes to the Morning Chronicle and The Morning Post, so he sends those to my father, too."

"Whig and Tory influences at the rectory. My, how progressive."

Elizabeth picked up her plate and inspected the food on offer. "As we've discovered, Isabella is a voracious newspaper reader. Once that got out in the village, everyone sends their papers to the rectory. I am permitted to read the papers, of course, as Isabella has insisted to my father that well-read women can attract husbands."

"I'm surprised at the new Mrs. Knight for saying that."

"As I am, being that I do not remember ever seeing a book in that girl's hand her entire life!" Elizabeth covered her mouth with her hand. "Oh dear, I should not have said that."

"I have said much worse! Now, do try the rolls. It is exceptional."

Elizabeth filled her plate with two hot rolls, and Mrs. Cook's special plum cake, the recipe straight from that lady's Scottish relations. She dropped a boiled egg in its cup. She also poured herself a cup of chocolate and remarked on the excellence of the morning meal. Her aunt proudly stated that Mrs. Cook had been determined to give Miss Knight an excellent welcome to London, and that she planned to prepare all of her favourites.

"Now, Cook says there was no decent meat at the market. However, she did procure some smoked kippers for tomorrow. Will that be agreeable?"

"Very much so!" Elizabeth said between bites of her breakfast. The hot rolls were delicious, but she resisted taking a third. "We rarely get fish of any kind at Bryden this time of the year."

"She expected as much. Excellent. She'll be happy to hear that." Aunt Cass motioned to Sally, who had entered the room to see if the ladies wanted for anything. "Bring me the parcel from this morning. Thank you, Sally. Now, Eliza, I went to the shops this morning while you were still asleep. I found an excellent lavender muslin and I think that we can have that made up into a dress for you."

"Aunt, I cannot think of that now," Elizabeth said.

"Nonsense! I will not allow you to be in that dreary black for three months. Edward would have been horrified to know you planned to sit around moping."

"It is not moping," Elizabeth protested. "I am in mourning, as is only proper."

"Be that as it may, I would like you to consider having Sally to make you up a dress. Now, if you prefer, Sally's cousin is a seamstress and she can do the more fashionable styles. I prefer

Sally's simpler style myself, but perhaps you feel the need to catch the eye of a young man."

"Please," Elizabeth muttered. "Sally, will you have the time to assist with a dress? I do not wish to take you from your duties."

Sally eyed the fabric. "It's excellent quality, miss. If my mistress approves, I will ask Martha, my cousin, if she can assist with the dress. This should be made in something fashionable. If I may offer my opinion, ma'am, of course."

"Whatever you think is best, Sally," Aunt Cass said. "I have never been a great seamstress myself. Shirts for Edward and my dear husband was about all I could manage."

"I shall pay your cousin," Elizabeth insisted.

"None of that," Aunt Cass said. To her servant, she said, "Arrange for Martha whenever she is free. Perhaps I should pick up some fabric myself. If she is to make the trip here to measure Eliza…"

"I can stay here, Aunt. You head back to the shops."

"I cannot abandon you!"

"Nonsense. I wish to have six full trunks ready for Mr. Thorne to arrange for an auction, or whatever he sees fit, and his note to Maria last night said he plans to be here at one o'clock sharp." Elizabeth glanced up at the old clock. "It's half past ten now, so that does not leave me as much time as I'd like."

"Then I shall stay," Aunt Cass said.

"Most of what is left is sorting the books I had wished to take a second glance at. I think I will do that faster alone. And it will please me to know you are out, getting fresh air."

"I live in London, dear," Aunt Cass said deadpan. "There is no such thing as fresh air."

They had a good chuckle at that, and Aunt Cass finally relented, but only after Elizabeth suggested that Aunt Cass search for a pair of warm gloves. Elizabeth's were terribly worn; she had planned to use some of the book proceeds to purchase her own but giving Aunt Cass that task seemed to spur her forward. Within thirty minutes, her aunt had called for a chair and was out the door.

Ink and paper were procured for her, as was a small, portable writing desk from the drawing room. Elizabeth folded the paper into quarters and cut it into squares carefully. She then labeled them in a flowing, elegant hand:

Keep
Consider
Sell
Royal Occult Society

Despite their annoying visit, Elizabeth did feel there was some obligation in offering them the pick of the unique or special edition books, especially those from Mr. Leigh's newly-inherited collection.

Armed with scissors, Elizabeth returned to her bedroom and faced her closet of books.

She placed the KEEP sign under a book on the top shelf. These would become the volumes she absolutely wanted to keep. The other shelves had books upon them, so she pushed them over as best as possible and adding the signs to the other three shelves. Then, she began to sort. First, with what was in the closet. Then, one trunk at a time.

Elizabeth was decisive and thorough with her pruning. Aunt Cass and Maria would have insisted Elizabeth keep most of these books, but she knew that the pence and shillings each book could bring her was to be weighed against its ownership. Some decisions were easy. She discovered she possessed three different versions of *First Forays into the Study of Occult Flora*, publication dates 1802, 1803, and 1805. She decided to keep the 1805 version, as it contained erratum in the front. The 1802 went on the Sell shelf for first edition collectors, and 1803 went to the Royal Occult Society shelf.

She struggled with the choice between *Magical Heirs* (1799) and *The True Heirs of Magic* (1799) as they seemed to have been published at the same time to spite the other's author. While they seemed interesting, she could not justify their existence on her shelf. Both went to the sell shelf.

She was uncertain which of the botanical books to choose, and was wondering aloud when a feminine voice said, "The 1742 volume by Anonymous is the best choice."

Elizabeth jumped from fright. When she was capable of speech, she said, "Is that the book?"

"You failed to lock my lid, thereby not protecting me from the damp."

"I apologize, madam. I shall do so at once."

The book sighed dramatically. "Since you have already kept me awake all of these hours by saying the incantation three times, you might as well enlist my assistance."

"If it would not be too great of inconvenience."

"I am dead, girl. How much more can I be inconvenienced? Now, what is your current system?"

Elizabeth pulled the book from the trunk. "First, what may I call you? *Book* seems unbearably rude."

"You may call me Mrs. Egerton. Now, the system, if you please."

Elizabeth explained her sorting system to Mrs. Egerton, who made interested sounds throughout. Finally, Elizabeth said, "I do not have room for many books. Maria—um, Mrs. Thorne—and Aunt Cass have offered me space, of course, but I wish to be practical above all things. I would rather ten excellent books that I will read for the rest of my life than a thousand that will collect dust."

Mrs. Egerton sighed. "Why you don't have a husband is beyond me. What a waste."

Unsure of how to address that particular comment, Elizabeth ignored it completely. "I am unclear which of the general knowledge books are the best option for me. I would prefer to do as my uncle bid and study the occult, of course, but I confess I am overwhelmed by choice at the moment. I do not possess the knowledge to know which of these books will best teach me. And now, with my cousin's books offered into the mix…"

"That is because Mr. Leigh is, as ever, a complete waste of a lady's time."

Elizabeth opened her mouth to argue with the book, but then shut it. She was not going to lower herself to argue with a book and its disembodied voice. Even if it spoke a rather improper truth.

Mrs. Egerton's sigh was tinged with annoyance. "Shall we get started then, or do you plan to spend the day dawdling?"

With that, Elizabeth got to work, with the book's ghostly assistance. Mrs. Egerton had several choice and insulting words for the Royal Occult Society, but Elizabeth would not be dissuaded from her shelf offering them first pick. Mrs. Egerton begrudgingly suggested the best books to go there; most were tailored to highly specialized interests within the occult.

To Elizabeth's surprise, and soon amusement, Mrs. Sarah Egerton had very strong feelings about any religious texts:

Decorum and Grace for Young Ladies From Occult Families (1766): "Throw it upon the fire."

A Gentleman's Guide to Attracting a Wife (1792): "The only thing that will lead young ladies to is the company of more ladies.

A Lady's Guide to Attracting a Husband (1723): "My parents made my sister read that one. She went to Scotland a month later.

Mrs. Egerton approved of Elizabeth's choices for her personal collection, and informed her that all of the books written by Mr. Arthur Sherry were, in fact, written by women.

"Indeed?"

"It is true. Mr. Arthur Sherry was the name my own occult group decided upon. We wrote our own books and then we hired a gentleman to be Mr. Arthur Sherry. He then hired a lawyer and all of the funds went into an account. From there, the money was distributed between us, after a generous fee was paid to the gentlemen, of course. I wonder if anyone ever found my box."

"Box?"

"I buried it in a wall. It contains coins, jewelry, and a few pieces of silver. There are some bank notes, but as I've never trusted paper notes, as a general rule, I converted nearly everything I owned into coinage. Gold is eternal."

"It must have been a rather large box you left behind." When no reply came, Elizabeth asked, "Mrs. Egerton?"

"I was considering if the new occupants of my old house have discovered the box yet," Mrs. Egerton said. "Your uncle sent his lawyer to sniff about and investigate. Apparently, there is a large family living in the home. I suspect they could use a little money. Alas."

"Should I write to them?" Elizabeth asked.

Mrs. Egerton laughed. "My dear. If they are too stupid to find a heavy trunk filled with gold and silver themselves, then they have no business spending the money inside it. No, I left it so that fate could do with my disposable life's worth as it pleased."

"That sounds very sad," Elizabeth said. "Did you not have anyone to leave the money to? A favourite niece?"

"Oh, for those things, such as my dowry and my jewels, those were all disposed of properly. However, a lady who earns royalties must have somewhere to hide that cash from a horrid husband."

"Did you have a horrid husband?"

Mrs. Egerton made a thoughtful sound. "Thankfully, he dropped dead before he became truly horrid."

"Mrs. Egerton! That is your husband you speak of."

That brought out a laugh from Mrs. Egerton that bordered upon a cackle. "Now, child, I need you to remember to read the incantation out every morning, but only if you wish to summon me for a day. Because you read it out several times, I am here for a bit."

"That seems simple enough," Elizabeth said. She pondered the book in her hands. "Will *Reflections on the Occult in England (1801)* be of any use for me?"

"There is nothing of note in that one. You are better off with Hendricks' book from 1793 on the topic. To address your comment, no, the incantation to make my voice appear is not simple. Because, that incantation will require more permanent spell craft to keep me active, and you have enough worries at present, I think. Your uncle worked diligently to fill the book with, how shall I explain it? It is like he placed magical firewood within my pages of my book. As long as the fire remains low, the fire will last a long time. However, if the fire is stoked raging hot, then the wood will be gone overnight and then you are left with nothing."

"Oh," Elizabeth said, not hiding the disappointment in her voice. "I am not certain I am ready for magical pursuits."

"I concur, that is why I have not assisted you in advancing my summoning."

"Oh," Elizabeth said. Again, more disappointment.

"Well, girl? You brought me back for another day, so let us finish the task at hand. No point wasting a day of spell craft."

Elizabeth acquiesced, and went back to her book organization. Once the closet was organized, she brought Mrs. Egerton's autograph book to the dining room with her. Together, they sorted through the books that were placed on the sideboard for her personal opinion. Sally fetched ink and paper and Elizabeth made the same signs again for four wooden crates. She filled them completely, and Andrews, the footman, and Tom, the household boy and runner, brought the "to keep" books upstairs to her closet, unpacking them on the appropriate shelf. Overall, it took two hours for the books to be sorted, but Elizabeth was left with several crates of potential income, which greatly pleased her.

The room was still overflowing with books, but at least now there was some order. Elizabeth's goal was to have the drawing room books from the previous day cleared completely. Then, the dining room's books sorted. That included the books upon the chairs, and underneath the table. She knew, of course, that as soon as it was properly assorted, more books from other parts of the house would eventually join these and the table would be is disarray. However, for now, there was progress.

"Well, Mrs. Egerton? I believe we deserve a cup of tea before visitors descend upon us."

A disgusted sound. "Doesn't anyone respect mourning customs anymore?"

Elizabeth chuckled. "This is an age of excess, Mrs. Egerton."

Chapter 6

When are you coming home? Cassandra says I'm supposed to write only news and the condition of the roads to you, and not to demand anything, but this is intolerable!!! First, Thea wore my blue hat — you know the one? With the blue and white ribbons? You helped me make that one just after Mama died. And she took it — without asking! You can surely guess the rest. It is completely and utterly and totally destroyed!!!

I know you are going to tell me to speak to Isabella, which I did, and she said that Thea and I need to stop playing pranks on one another and this was the outcome she had warned us against.

Can you imagine the nerve of her? I have played no pranks lately and this was simply because Thea wanted to wear a hat to impress Mr. Kingsley's nephew who's in the village for a while. I don't remember his name, that's how boring he is. And now my hat is ruined.

You must come home quickly or Thea might actually burn the place to the ground in one of her fits.

Your sister who loves you and wants you very much to come home before everything she owns is ruined,

G

I am back, as there is a great more that has happened since the above.

Elizabeth chuckled at the letter. When Aunt Cass gave her a quizzical eye, she handed it over. "It seems that Georgiana does not appreciate the disrespect of her items."

"What fifteen-year-old girl does?" Aunt Cass asked, chuckling at the letter. "Good heavens! It continues on the back. And…it crosses the previous lines!"

Elizabeth flipped over the page and, sure enough, the second page was not just the linear lines across, but she could turn the page once and several more paragraphs were written across the first paragraphs.

"Goodness, she wrote diagonally across the page, too! Not just cross wise!" Elizabeth said, laughing.

"Two sheets of paper, completely filled." Aunt Cass shook her head. "How many complaints could a girl of her age possibly have?"

"A great many, by the looks of it. I'll have to write to Isabella and Cassandra, I suppose. I had already sent letters to all of them, but it appears that there is disharmony preventing some of them from writing."

Aunt Cass had returned from the shops with several bundles of fabric for Sally's cousin to sew. She included more black, for a new mourning gown since she despaired that her current one was fraying about the seams. She also bought a smart tan fabric, and also striped satin of dark blues and purples. She also purchased eleven yards of a light brown fabric with a tiny rosebud pattern that she said Elizabeth "absolutely" needed.

In truth, Elizabeth adored the brown fabric and its rosebuds, though was shocked to discover the price.

"Dearest Aunt! Ten shillings a yard? And you bought eleven yards?"

"Well, you will need a dress! And the fabric is perfect for everyday. And then I thought that perhaps Cassandra would like a spencer made out of it, since the fabric is extraordinarily pretty, and would make a lovely summer covering. Then, I added a little extra in case the younger girls wanted a little something, too, or if you wished sleeves on your gown."

"I always desire sleeves, Aunt."

"Then there you have it. The extra yardage is already taken into account."

"It is a very kind gift," Elizabeth said.

"What is the point to have all this money if I cannot spend it on you?" Aunt Cass said. "It was so much easier when you were little! You never complained about prices back then. Now, what does Mrs. Knight have to say in her letter?"

I believe your youngest sisters have entered a pact to see which can drive me from this house the first. I apologize for having to do this, but I must beg your assistance with Theodosia. She's a darling child, when she is not attempting to rile up your sister. I do not know what to do with those two!

And, now, after Thea enraged G, Thea accidentally broke Cassandra's pearl necklace that was left to her by her grandmother. It is the Mary situation all over again here today. Cassandra is devastated. I attempted to restring and repair the necklace, but I do not have the necessary materials for a permanent mending. I have included a list. Would you be so kind to be on the look out for me when you visit the shops next? I am very sorry to ask this, but Cassandra so rarely gets attached to an item, and she has been weeping all morning. Your father attempted to offer helpful words about the sin of worldly possessions, but that only upset her more.

I am stuffing this into G's impossibly long letter to help save you the postage. Please write soon.

Isabella

"Oh, dear," Aunt Cass said.

"The girls aren't taking well to Isabella. It's been over a year now, but I think they have only grown bolder as Isabella grows stronger in her new role. I should write to them."

"Tom? Fetch Miss Knight writing materials please."

March 17, 1810

My dearest G,

Thank you for your letter. I have arrived in safety and am very glad to hear that you are doing well, despite the troubles at home. I promise to write to Thea to once again discuss this destructive feud the two of you have. However, my dearest sister, I would be remiss as the neutral party here that you yourself destroyed your sister's stockings not a month ago. They were her favourite.

I can hear you now, of course. But Eliza! They weren't from my mother! No, that is true, but they were from me. I stitched the embroidery into them myself and they were Thea's favourite. I hope you realize that this back and forth will do no one any use whatsoever and, to be very honest, I fear that it will one day result in the rectory burning to the ground. Surely, that is not what you want: we ladies homeless in the hedgerow foraging for our suppers.

Now, tell me all about this boring nephew. I see you've only invested three paragraphs about him and all were dedicated to his dullness. Have you met him at a dinner? Or perhaps in the village? At the Pooles'? Surely you have more to offer me than the knowledge that he is boring. After all, if you say that Thea is interested in this young gentleman, then perhaps he is not so very dull after all.

How are Father and Isabella? Have you begun planting the vegetable garden yet?

Would you like something brought back from London? Something small, G, and not fifty yards of silk if you please.

We are very busy here with my books, so I do not have much time to write. However, I look forward to more letters from you.

Your devoted sister,
E

Her second youngest sister got a very different letter.

Dearest Theodosia,

You must know severity of the contents of this letter, since I address you by your Christian name. I have received a letter from Isabella. I know your temper well and my spies are numerous, so I will know if you do anything to punish your stepmother for this letter.

My dear sister, you are tasked with feeding the poultry in the mornings. That is your job and you must do it. Refusing to feed those creatures who rely solely upon us is a grave torture to God's creatures. They were placed in our care until they are needed to nourish our bodies, and it is our duty to ensure we meet our obligations to them. One of those obligations is to do our daily chores and feed them.

Punishing Cassandra for reminding you of your chores is unacceptable, and you will apologize immediately for breaking her necklace. Cassandra has so few possessions that are solely hers, and that necklace was very precious to her. Now, because of your tantrum, I have been tasked with purchasing repair materials, when my time would be better spent helping my aunt grieve the loss of her brother. Please, for everyone's sake including your own, heed your manners. Control your temper. Use your reasoning.

I trust there will be no more issues with the chickens or the turkeys, or the ducks or the geese, and that they will all receive their morning breakfast. And before you receive yours, I might add.

Also, I pray you cease telling Isabella that your mother said you did not have to obey anyone beyond Papa. Even if Augusta said such a thing at the end, it is simply not practical. We all obey. We obey the laws of God and the laws of England. We obey the laws of society and fashion, of culture and expectation. We obey the wishes of our families, of our husbands, fathers, and brothers. We were put on this earth to obey, my dearest sister, and obey we must.

I am no stranger to the objection of the heart and I hope I would never press you into violating a covenant with yourself and God. However, disrespect towards your stepmother is willful obstinance. My dearest sister, I truly understand what you are feeling. Recall that I, too, have been through this and at a much younger age than yourself. I am very sympathetic to your plight, for I know the grief and sorrow you feel.

However, my dearest, sweetest sister, you must control your impulses. Isabella needs our support and just because I am not home does not mean you can run wild. If Isabella tells you to behave, then you must obey. That is simply what is good and right. If you are frustrated by her, pick up a pen and write it in a diary or even write a letter to me. Do not explode your frustrations upon someone who has done nothing to deserve them.

Faithfully,
E

A rap came at the front door. Aunt Cass sighed and complained about how people simply did not respect mourners anymore. Back in her youth, people had the good sense to stay away for a couple of weeks unless in possession of a written invitation.

"Nowadays, people just show up! And to think they believe they are welcomed." Aunt Cass tutted. She rose and motioned to be followed into the regular drawing room. "James, would you be so kind as to hang a plague sign upon the door?"

James was crossing the main entry to answer the door when Aunt Cass had spoke. He spoke loud enough to be heard. "I fear, ma'am, that will just encourage politicians and officials to show up."

"Too true," Aunt Cass said sullenly.

Elizabeth accepted her letters back from her aunt, who'd been reading them, and quickly stuffed them into the back of the autograph book.

The book sighed. "Take care lest you smudge my ink."

"Did you say something dear?" Aunt Cass asked. She stopped to check her hair and cap in a mirror in the foyer.

"Nothing, aunt."

Elizabeth removed the letter from the book. Once in the drawing room, she shoved the letters and book underneath the sofa she sat upon.

"Mr. David Leigh!" The butler announced.

"Ugh!" Mrs. Egerton audibly said.

Elizabeth kicked the book further under the sofa with the heel of her shoe, all the while Aunt Cass gave her a disapproving look.

"My apologies, Aunt. The book had caught on the foot of the sofa. It was not against my cousin."

Mr. Leigh strolled into the drawing room. A trail of servants carrying crates and trunks made their way across Aunt Cass's clean floors into the dining room. Even from where she stood, Elizabeth could see the muddy footprints. Sally was going to have a fit when she saw that.

"Excellent news, Aunt Cassandra! This is the final delivery."

"Wipe your feet! This isn't a barn!" Sally shouted somewhere deeper within the house. "Have you no sense? Take your boots off! All of you! Take them off this instant before Mrs. Cook sees this!"

"Thank you, Mr. Leigh," Elizabeth said, hoping to distract everyone from Sally's shouts from the dining room.

"That is good news, David," Aunt Cass said. "As you can hear, my maids, in particular, are growing annoyed by the trunks."

"No thanks needed! No thanks needed. I keenly feel how the entailment of your uncle's estate to me impacts your entire family, Cousin Elizabeth, but perhaps you most of all, as you are likely to remain single and in need of my charity."

Elizabeth kept her face serene. If David Leigh represented all that was left of the marriage market in England, then she would happily accept spinsterhood with dignity and relief.

"Now. Aunt Cassandra. Cousin Elizabeth. I must confess a grave sin of mine."

"Goodness, what did you do?" Aunt Cass asked.

"I must explain the full reason for my considerations toward my cousin, I must relate a situation that I find myself in at the moment, and that I must ask your permission and forgiveness."

Elizabeth found herself equal parts interested in this mortal sin, and also terrified that he was going to mention marriage. Particularly, his to her.

"Please, have a seat, David. What on earth do you think you've done that requires both bribing my niece and my own forgiveness?"

David Leigh stammered. "Aunt, well, I wouldn't call it bribery. Though, now that you say it, I suppose it is a just word."

Elizabeth sat upon the sofa and listened to her cousin talk in circles for a full minute about his particular fondness of his aunt and of herself, and his respect for his uncle, even if they did not always agree.

Sally appeared out of nowhere and closed the double doors to the drawing room. Then, Mrs. Cook's voice sounded, berating the Leigh household servants, shouting how she would make them scrub her floors on their hands and knees if they did not wipe their boots outside.

David Leigh cleared his throat. "Should I perchance send a gift to Mrs. Cook?"

"She is partial to Bath Buns," Aunt Cass said without hesitation.

Davide Leigh chuckled. "Well, aren't we all, but this is London. Perhaps some smoked kippers?"

Elizabeth allowed a small cough to escape her. In the most delicate manner possible, of course. "Mrs. Thorne informs me that there is a bakery shop just off Bond Street that sells them."

"That is excellent news, Eliza," Aunt Cass said. Turning back to her nephew without a trace of modesty nor rancor evident in her voice, she said, "Thank you for considering Mrs. Cook. She is an excellent servant."

"My mistress just lost her last living brother, you heathens! Wipe. Your. Boots. Pick that up! I saw that!"

David Leigh cleared his throat again in a nervous tick. "Indeed. I will fetch them personally."

"Now, about this grave sin," Aunt Cass said.

"Surely it cannot be that bad," Elizabeth said warmly. "After all, you have always been a good man, both in my eyes and in your reputation."

"Oh, Cousin Elizabeth. Now I feel even more guilt upon my actions." He sighed heavily, as if to confess to murder. "As you probably guessed, I have been spending more time than necessary at Miss Reeves' house, visiting her and her mother."

"I try not to pry into your private affairs, sir," Aunt Cass said. "After all, you are of age, and I feel that a young man needs to make his own choices in the world. That is the only way he will learn how to be a great man one day."

"Thank you, Aunt. It was always a comfort to know that you were there if I ever needed guidance."

Elizabeth noticed the genuine surprise that flickered across her aunt's face. She realized something in that moment: David Leigh truly did desire his aunt's good opinion. He was a silly, almost foolish man, and cared more about climbing society's ladder. That was true and obvious.

But he was also young, without any living parents. He knew he should be the head of the family name now, as the only living male, but Aunt Cass was the matriarch. No one would dare risk her wrath. Setting aside her own wealth and the desire of others to be in her will, Aunt Cass' temper was not something any of them wished to incur.

But as hot as her wit and tongue could be, her affection burned hotter. Elizabeth had been Aunt Cass', Uncle Edward's and

Uncle Spencer's favourite. Everyone knew. Her own father and Augusta attempted to exploit it whenever possible, for their own financial gain. Most likely, Elizabeth was in Aunt Cass' will. She'd never allowed her aunt to elaborate on the subject, of course, as she loved her aunt for herself and not her money. However, Aunt Cass was a rich woman. Rich enough that no one knew exactly how rich she was. And Elizabeth Knight was her favourite.

And, in that moment, Elizabeth found herself feeling a pity for Mr. David Leigh, for he struggled his entire life for his aunt's approval.

"You see, Aunt, the evening of my uncle's unfortunate death, I had made an offer to Miss Reeves. You must believe me, I did not know of my uncle's condition that day. Otherwise, I would have been immediately at his side. I had only seen Mr. Grant that morning and he believed Uncle Edward would tarry at least several more weeks."

Aunt Cass stared at him, her eyes wide. "Oh, David."

"As she is very diffident, she asked to be allowed a little time. I appreciate modesty and honesty in a woman, and both of those only succeeded in improving her charms to me. But, then, you had sent word that I was needed."

"That was why you were late," Aunt Cass whispered.

"Yes, Aunt. I felt hopeful in Miss Reeves' changing opinion, but I confess I was disappointed. I took to walking to clear my mind. It took the servants some time to find me."

"Oh."

"You must believe me, I came as soon as they discovered me. I need you to believe me, good Aunt."

"David, I believe you most heartily."

A warmth swelled in Elizabeth's heart. She did feel a little uncomfortable, for this was a private conversation. She interrupted her cousin, just as he paused to draw breath. "Cousin David. Aunt. Might I fetch Sally for some tea?"

"Indeed, no, cousin. I wish you to hear the rest."

She had already partially risen, so sat back down upon the sofa. "Then, pray, continue."

"With my uncle's death that night, I admit I pushed Miss Reeves out of my mind. There was much to be done, as I was assisting you and his lawyer with the details. And then, of course, the funeral, which I attended on the family's behalf."

"And I appreciate it. I attended my husband's funeral and it was odious. I did not wish to attend this one. I am so grateful that you took that task upon yourself."

"I am very glad, because I did so out of kindness toward you." He turned to Miss Knight. "And you, cousin. We wished to spare you the pain, as well. It was a small affair, as was your uncle's wish. However, Miss Reeves, I believe may have felt forgotten in the mix. Therefore, I decided to pay her visit."

"As was only right!" Elizabeth exclaimed. "That poor girl must have been so confused."

"I agree! She must have thought you cross with her for wanting not to rush into marriage," Aunt Cass said.

"Indeed. I explained to Miss Reeves what had happened, which she had thankfully already heard. She was not upset or feeling slighted in the least. Then, if I might be so bold to say, she hinted quite strongly that she would not be opposed to hearing the offer again. Which I made and was accepted."

Elizabeth glanced at her aunt, who looked rather shocked. They were all still in mourning! It was very bad form to be becoming engaged while the family still wore black!

Mr. Leigh must have sensed this, because he quickly added, "Rest assured, Aunt, Cousin Elizabeth, we have not made this known about town at all. In fact, only Mrs. Reeves knows at present, as I insisted that I be allowed to speak with you first. We will keep our engagement quiet for as long as you deem necessary, out of respect for you, of course. You have my word upon that."

Elizabeth's heart pounded. She was very confused by all of this. This lowered Miss Reeves in her estimation, quite honestly. If Miss Reeves wished to ensnare Mr. Leigh, then they should have sensibly kept the engagement completely secret! That was what people did, was it not? She was more offended that he had decided to come upon them in this manner and tell them this.

Aunt Cass' mouth twitched a few times before she managed to speak. "David. I appreciate you telling me. Obviously, I wish you joy and all happiness."

The interruption helped deflate Elizabeth's rising ire. Naturally, he had made the first offer without knowing Uncle Edward was upon his death bed. And, he'd had the assurance that day of his uncle's health. She could see David, in his own way, thinking that he could secure a gentlewoman as a wife to give his uncle comfort, knowing who the estate would go to upon his death.

"I am not up for company at present, but I hope that you will bring Miss Reeves, and her mother, to visit in a couple of weeks. Or so."

"What about two weeks from tomorrow?"

"Of course."

"But the books!" Elizabeth exclaimed. When both cousin and aunt turned to her, she felt the colour rise in her cheeks at her outburst. "I apologize, Cousin David, but goodness. Won't Miss Reeves be upset about the books?"

"Not at all! It was her idea! In fact, it was all her own doing. That was why I wished you to stay, to hear the story."

Elizabeth leaned forward, confused. "Surely I am mistaken. I do not know Miss Reeves, correct?"

"She knows of you, and briefly met you at a ball several years ago."

"I do not recall, I am sorry."

"She had no illusions of your remembrance. It is very difficult to recall such things when one is visiting town. However, she holds you in high esteem. She has many acquaintances about town who all speak very highly of you."

Elizabeth's cheeks heated again. "I do not know if I deserve such praise. I barely know anyone in town."

"Ah, but when people like the Thornes and Leighs, and Sir William next door, all know you, it is only natural that your reputation will be much talked about."

"I fear I shall disappoint your Miss Reeves."

"Not at all! Now, please! I have become distracted from the story. Miss Reeves had come up with the idea. She felt that donating them to Aunt Cassandra would then remove any uncomfortableness, or dare I say, potential expectation on your family's part regarding our relationship."

Elizabeth held her breath so that her face would not twitch in the slightest. She did not like where this conversation was headed.

"And I did wish to assist with your financial difficulties. Being unmarried at your age is going to be an increasing burden upon your relations—myself included—and I desperately wished to help now that I could. I have long been uncomfortable with the occult, as my dear aunt can inform you, but Miss Reeves is very much against it. She said, and I quote her now, 'I could not sleep in a house knowing those vile things were within, and I do not wish to count the pence and shillings and pounds they are worth for I fear their sin will rub off on my souls.'"

An annoyed sigh filled the silence in between the conversation.

Aunt Cass and Elizabeth both glanced at each other with accusing eyes, but then both realized it wasn't the other. Elizabeth then said, "I wonder, then, that Miss Reeves would make such a gift to me. Is she not worried about my soul? As the daughter of a clergyman, I can tell you that this is a topic very dear to my heart."

"Well," Mr. Leigh said, shifting in his chair. "I know little of the craft myself, but I am confident that a woman's own feminine mind would be less vulnerable to the corruptive nature of the occult. After all, a woman cannot even produce magic of note, so I suspect her natural charm and beauty protects her soul."

The sound of a cough echoed through the room. It was others' turn to look at Elizabeth with inquisitive eyes. Elizabeth gave them nothing.

"And does Miss Reeves share this belief?" Elizabeth asked.

"Very much so. In fact, she felt you were the proper inheritor of the collection. However, she was also very good about not wanting to mislead you in any form, Cousin, and she developed the plan to gift the books to our aunt."

Elizabeth's faux smile did not falter. "How kind of her."

"Yes, very," Aunt Cass said in the exact same tone, with the exact same smile.

"Well, Miss Reeves knows all too well, I think, the worries of being a burden upon one's family. She is twenty-four, though that only signifies to me that she has more sense than most. And, you will not know this, Cousin, but her mother is the widow of a clergyman. Nothing was set aside for them, though Miss Reeves did inherit eight thousand pounds six months ago. That was a great relief to her mother, I can assure you."

David Leigh rambled on for a couple of minutes about his engagement and his delightful dearest. A needle pricked her own heart at a remembrance of her near engagement, when Mr. R confided he had planned to propose in that meeting, but sadly could not. Then, he walked out of her life.

And she felt a little jealousy toward her cousin; he had found someone who changed her mind. Elizabeth did not have a suitor who renewed his attentions. He did not write upon the death of her uncle, hearing of her new good fortune. He was most likely in London. He would have heard. Anyone could have told him Aunt Cass' address. But he had not written. He had not followed her the way she had followed him.

No one was going to leave her eight thousand pounds anytime soon. Her aunt might, eventually, leave her a goodly sum, but Elizabeth would rather her aunt live another forty years than to take that good woman's money.

"Cousin, are you well?" David asked.

"I apologize," Elizabeth said automatically. She searched her brain for a reply. "I thought I saw a mouse off in the corner, but it was only the light."

David Leigh looked over his shoulder. "Ah, yes. Well it is supposed to rain the next several days. The mice should be running inside like the rest of us."

"I suppose the poor creatures need to get out of the damp as well as the rest of us," Elizabeth said with a smile. Back to her cousin she said, "I congratulate you, on your excellent choice. I look forward to meeting her."

"Oh, Cousin Elizabeth! I am so relieved to hear you say that. I worried…that is…"

Elizabeth stood abruptly. Her cousin struggled to his feet. She held out her hand and said, "Shall we shake hands on your good fortune?"

David Leigh gently took her fingers and gave them a slight squeeze. "Thank you, cousin. You are an extraordinary woman, and if I could find a wife, surely someone of your good sense might yet still find a sensible husband."

Elizabeth chuckled and took her seat upon the sofa once more. David Leigh sat back upon his chair. "I fear that Miss Reeves has made off with the last sensible man in England."

David Leigh laughed heartily with that. "You are too kind, cousin! Too kind!"

Desperate to change the subject away from her lack of marriage prospects and the very idea that the likes of David Leigh was the best she could hope for, she asked, "I apologize, cousin, but I must change the subject and inquire. How many books are you giving me? I have not finished the tally yet, and it appears you have delivered me more today!"

"Oh, of course! Eight hundred and thirty-seven by my count."

"My God," Aunt Cass whispered. "I will need a new house."

Elizabeth shook her head in astonishment. "Sir! That is too many. How can I accept such a gift?"

"On the contrary, I do believe I am following the spirit of our uncle's wishes. Setting aside my own feelings about the occult, I truly do believe Uncle Edward would have willed you the entire contents of the occult library if he thought he could. Not to mention the common silverware and all of his magical bowls. Oh, do you wish to have them? I was thinking about turning one of the silver bowls into a watering dish for my hounds, but I would be very happy to part with the others."

Aunt Cass made a thoughtful sound. "Did he leave behind the large silver serving bowl? If you are willing to part with that, Cook was saying just the other day that she did not like our current one, but she cannot find a suitable replacement in any of the shops."

"I will have it delivered tomorrow. Shall I send all of the magical items, too?"

"Why not?" Aunt Cass said. "The more the merrier."

"Allow me to share some of the proceeds of the auction with you," Elizabeth said.

"No, indeed. Miss Reeves would not wish for tainted money to come into our future home, I think, and my soul would feel better knowing that you will have the books your uncle wanted to give you. From there, perhaps the sale will help keep you settled for a great many years. All of my feelings aside regarding the occult, Uncle Edward cared for you like his own daughter and I feel keenly the insult of me inheriting over you. This is my way of correcting the balance."

"Thank you. I truly appreciate this generosity and consideration. It will never be forgotten." She smiled. "Would it be appropriate for me to purchase an engagement gift for Miss Reeves? Perhaps a new bonnet or pair of gloves? I am unsure of what is appropriate in this circumstance, but I feel compelled to do something."

"Nothing is needed, dear cousin! Nothing at all! You have done me a good turn, in fact. Miss Reeves and her mother would have never moved into my new abode if those books were present, so this will allow for a much swifter wedding. I am eager to become an old married man." He inclined his head to his aunt. "With your permission, always, of course. Oh, dear, look at the time. I must be off. I promised Miss Reeves that I would pop by after seeing you and giving you the happy news. Shall I inform Mrs. Reeves that my aunt approves?"

"Yes, of course, David. And I shall see her in a fortnight."

"Excellent!"

The ladies stood to say their good byes, and when Mr. Leigh left the house, Aunt Cass asked, "Is it unchristian to think so poorly of one's own nephew?"

Elizabeth collapsed back on the sofa. "That man is exhausting."

"How can anyone be so unaware of the words that exit his own mouth?" Aunt Cass asked. "I do not begrudge him the proposal. He did not know Edward was dying that night. But, all this dancing about. Lord. And could he have insulted you anymore? I thought I would need to stop him."

"Do you know this Miss Reeves?" Elizabeth asked.

"Not well," Aunt Cass said. "From what I've seen, she's pretty enough and she says all the correct words when called upon. She will make David an excellent ornament. But what was this of you wanting to give that girl a gift? You did hear him say she has a dowry of eight thousand, did you not?"

"I heard him say she was the reason he did not turn his affects towards me," Elizabeth said.

Aunt Cass let out a bark of laughter. "Perhaps I should leave that girl some money in my will!"

Sally entered then with tea and cakes. "I apologize, ma'am, that I did not come with them while Mr. Leigh was here. Cook is in a state."

"How bad is the mud?" Aunt Cass asked. "Tell me they didn't get it on the good carpet?"

Sally grimaced. "They also flicked some of the mud upon the furniture. Cook got Tom to run home to see if any of his sisters can be spared to help with the cleaning."

"I don't know what we'll do when Tom's sisters get full time positions of their own." Aunt Cass shook her head. She dismissed Sally and said to her niece, "Emily and Ellen are Tom's sisters and identical twins. Ten years old and you can't tell them apart just looking at them. They only do odd jobs for a few of us because they won't be apart, not even for a day. Most houses don't need to hire two girls. I don't even have one; I just have Tom and he's enough. But, I confess it's awfully good to call on them for these kinds of occasions. It would shock you to see them work, too. They work harder than most adults I've hired over the years. They'll do a good job cleaning the carpets. My neighbour, Sir William, even proposed we each hire one of the girls full time, and then share them between our households so that they are never parted. I've honestly been considering it. How is the situation at the rectory?"

They chatted a little about the struggle with servants at Bryden. Most came in from the village and didn't have any training or experience the way that London servants did. Aunt Cass said that simply made the London servants demanding; Elizabeth said she was certain Isabella wouldn't mind paying a little extra for a servant who knew their job. Aunt and niece good-naturedly debated the subject of servants over tea and cake when another knock came to the door. Thankfully, the happy sounds of Maria and Henry Thorne filled the air, and both ladies sat exhausted upon their seats until their company came into the room.

Elizabeth stood and embraced her friend. She shook Mr. Thorne's hand. Aunt Cass remained seated.

"My dear, Mrs. Thorne, Mr. Thorne, I would get up to greet you, but David Leigh just graced us with his presence. I do not have the will to stand."

"I did wonder at the black cloud outside your door," Henry Thorne said with a big smile.

That sent the ladies into a fit of laughter. "What brings you here today, Mr. Thorne? Was your trade successful?"

By way of reply, Henry pulled out the folded pages from his pocket, along with his pocket book. "The proceeds from yesterday's book sale, as well as offers for additional books."

He produced four, one-pound notes. Then, he dug in his pocket and said, "And three shillings."

"Goodness! I had only hoped for a pound, at most. Why so much?"

"Mr. Osborne has paid a pound as an advance to hold seven books on the list. A list which I did not lose, Maria."

His wife made a face before accepting a cup of tea from Aunt Cass and taking her seat.

"Now, Miss Knight, here is the original list. Now, you will notice I have added notes. See here? I have added his name and his offered prices to the titles he is interested in. Don't give me that look, Maria, my love. I am a capable bookkeeper when it is required. I did have excellent tutors as a boy. Mr. Rushworth of Rushworth Publishing and Books also paid a pound as a down-payment to have a first look at all books about the occult in ancient Greece published before 1775. He knows a private collector in Edinburgh who will want them, and you have at least one on the list already, so Mr. Rushworth is hopeful others will appear."

"An extraordinary sum," Elizabeth whispered.

She stared at the money in her hands. It was hers. Not hers given to her by her father. Not hers given to her by Aunt Cassandra. It was hers. She had conducted a business deal and had earned the money from her own property. She had never been allowed to do such a thing in her life. And, for that fleeting moment, it felt wonderful.

Of course, then she considered what her father would say. He did not approve of unmarried ladies engaging in commerce and business, nor did he approve of ladies of a certain position in life earning their own sources of income. He did not even agree with ladies in her rank of society becoming governesses. Hers was a precarious place, not quite wealthy enough to be a proper gentlewoman, but certainly too well educated, situated, and positioned to become a woman of trade or industry.

"The one book you gave me turned out to be a singular edition, whereby the author himself wrote in the margins! How your uncle ever managed to get that I will never know, but a Mr. Simmons was in Mr. Osborne's shop at that very moment and down slammed a pound note on counter then and there! And, finally, the final four shillings are from Mr. Osborne, for the farming book I took."

"If this good fortune continues, Eliza might be richer than all of us combined!" Maria said, a wide grin on her face. "Oh, thank you Henry for doing this."

He gave his wife a sly smile, before saying to Elizabeth, "It was my pleasure to be the only useful man in England. However, Mrs. Spencer, a Sir Brandon Langford, from Ireland, would like to pay a visit tomorrow, to peruse the books. He is looking specifically for occult geography and history."

"Tomorrow?" Aunt Cass shook her head. "Well, Elizabeth? What say you?"

Henry Thorne interruped Elizabeth before she could speak. "I informed Sir Brandon that this was a house of mourning, and he does not expect the ladies to wait upon him. He would be very content for me to assist him and conduct the business. He is heading to the north of England later this week, to visit relations, before returning to Ireland. Otherwise, he would have waited."

"Oh, I do not mind, Aunt, if you do not."

"What is this man's reputation, Mr. Thorne?" Aunt Cass asked.

"I inquired about his character to some of my discreet friends, and apparently there is not a better man in all of Ireland. Though, apparently, he does not like tea."

"I do not trust a man who dislikes tea," Aunt Cass said.

"That is his only fault. Apparently, he's quite rich, too."

"Wealth does not impress me as much as some," Aunt Cass said. She waved a hand. "As long as Elizabeth does not mind the worry."

"Not at all, aunt. I have been sorting all morning, and there is already a pile of books ready for sale. I do not mind working the rest of the day to clear out this drawing room and make it useable once more. Oh, and I could set aside the books for the gentlemen you mentioned. If it would be agreeable, Mr. Thorne, would you like to arrange for them to come see the books? Oh, aunt! We could use this drawing room for the purchasing. Any books in here will be sorted, so that we do not need to worry about anyone touching the books we haven't added to the inventory."

"That sounds like an excellent idea. Though, I fear we will need an army to help us."

"I would be honoured to assist, both in the sorting, the lifting, and even the commerce aspects." Henry Thorne said. "To be very truthful, this is the most fun I have had in London in years."

"If only I'd known," Maria said dryly. "You could have opened a book auction business."

"My father would have died of shock."

"From you going into trade?" Elizabeth asked.

"From me not being a useless wastrel!" Henry Thorne said with a laugh. "Now, Mrs. Spencer, I have cleared my day and I am yours completely and fully to order about and to assist you ladies with the book sorting. Though, my dear Maria tells me that I am not allowed to get in the way."

"We could always use the company of a man, Mr. Thorne," Aunt Cass said. "Right Elizabeth?"

"Very much. However, if no one objects, I would like to sit here a little longer, finish my tea, and hear some of the news," Elizabeth said. She looked down at the money still in her hand. "Though, I suppose I should do something with this."

She fetched the autograph book from under the sofa, along with her youngest sister's letter, and rushed up to her room. She did not know where to put the money; she would need to invest in a locking box and perhaps a small desk soon. For now, she placed it in her reticule.

"Mrs. Egerton," Elizabeth whispered. "Are you there?"

"You don't need to whisper, girl. There is no one about. What is it you want?"

"Would you prefer being left here in the trunk, or would you prefer to be brought downstairs to listen to the conversations?"

Mrs. Egerton was silent for a moment before answering. "Company would be amusing. Provided you take care not to injure my binding in any manner. And not to shove me under sofas again."

"I apologize, Mrs. Egerton. I did not want Mr. Leigh to inquire."

"Under the circumstances, it was acceptable. Perhaps we can find a useless book to hollow out the middle, so that I could rest within. Then, you would have a secret place for letters, and a little pin money, as you are now wealthy beyond all measure."

"Four pounds does not make me a rich woman, Mrs. Egerton."

"It is a start. Now, go. We have much work to do today, and I cannot speak to you around that Thorne fellow."

"He's a good man."

"I will be the judge of that. Now, go. They are waiting for you."

Elizabeth headed back downstairs, this time with her reticule and the autograph book. She placed both in her sewing basket next to the tea things. She'd brought her charity work with her to town, just in case. "What is the latest news about town?"

Henry's face stretched into a delighted smile. "The Royal Society is in an uproar the Mr. Edward Leigh donated his entire occult library to Miss Knight. I heard that it was a thousand books!"

"I heard it was nearly two thousand and that Miss Knight plans to move to London permanently with her aunt," Maria said.

"Elizabeth Knight! If you planned to move in with me, you could have least have told me yourself," Aunt Cass said with a wicked grin.

"Oh, Aunt Cass. You know I couldn't leave Isabella to my sisters. I am not that cruel. And, what strange rumor is that. None of it is even true!" Elizabeth exclaimed. "He left me a substantial collection, yes, but it was not him who dumped the entire library upon us."

"Oh, I realize that, Miss Knight, but that is not what society is saying. Apparently, your cousin has been spreading about the news that your uncle verbally expressed his wish for you to have the entire collection, so Mr. David Leigh wishes to honour that request. However, since it is such an extensive collection, he is moving to you over several days. He has already been approached four times with offers as high as two hundred pounds for the remaining books left in his possession, but Mr. Leigh refused, stating that he could not go against his uncle's will and wishes. He's been declared a man of principle by some, and a simpleton by those who had been sniffing about, waiting to get their hands on the collection themselves."

"Mr. Leigh has never made any sense to me," Maria said.

"On the contrary," Henry said, "he does enjoy being the hero. It is far more heroic, is it not, that he honour his dead uncle's bequeath than for him to ungratefully dump his library upon Miss Knight, with all of the work and inconvenience upon a grieving young lady from reduced circumstances."

"I would not call my circumstances reduced!" Elizabeth said in mock outrage.

Henry Thorne cocked an eyebrow. "My good neighbour, I know for a fact that you are wearing what used to be your blue dress, with the little rose print upon, and that you have dyed it specifically three months ago to avoid purchasing new mourning clothes."

Elizabeth shook her head.

"And I know, from a very reliable anonymous source, that you packed your lavender dress in hopes to purchase four shillings of dye and turn that into a black dress."

"If you are so bothered by my niece's outfits, feel free to make a donation to her clothing allowance. I'm sure her father would appreciate the financial burden lessened."

"Aunt…"

"I already gave her the four shillings for the dye."

"It would be very shocking for a married man to give a clothing allowance to an unrelated neighbour, Henry," Maria said.

"And besides, Eliza will not accept my money, so I have no expectation of her accepting yours."

"Maria…"

Elizabeth endured a few more minutes of gentle teasing before she finally stood up for herself. "I believe we have significant work to do today, and that cannot happen while you all are busy teasing me."

Plenty of protests said it was all harmless, but that made Elizabeth stick to her stern demeanor, even if she was smiling.

THAT EVENING, ELIZABETH was unable to sleep. They had worked hard sorting and categorizing well into the evening. Maria had made two additional copies of the book inventory list, which was made more annoying by how it continued to grow. However, she was determined not to allow her husband to leave the house with the original, as she did not trust him nearly as much as he trusted himself.

Mr. Thorne, for his part, took the insult with patience and a certain level of amusement, and spent the day writing to various booksellers with the particular titles he thought they would be interested in. He even wrote to the Royal Occult Society, acting as the representative of Miss Knight, offering up several gilded first edition volumes from the Tudor-era. Those, he insisted on the shocking price of six guineas each, arguing that there were rare collectors in America who he was certain would pay triple and was all too happy to send the books there, if necessary, for the best price.

Elizabeth and Aunt Cass managed to clear out several more stacks of books, organizing them into their various piles. For now, they kept the wooden crates, and had Andrews the footman returned emptied trunks to Mr. Leigh's house. A note was returned thanking his aunt and cousin for the thoughtful return of his neighbours' property in such a steady fashion.

They successfully filled part of Mr. Osborne's order and Henry Thorne drove those books to the bookseller's house himself. Henry returned with four pounds, ten shillings for the books. She was shocked by the handsome sum, though Mr.

Thorne was disappointed that he'd not managed to negotiate for a full five pounds.

Elizabeth stared at the money upon her bed. Disappointment over four pounds instead of five! What different lives she and her friend's husband lived.

Nine pounds and fifteen shillings. That was what was upon her quilt staring back at her. Her earnings and what was left of her pin money. Together, that was nearly half a year's money for her. And it was all hers.

She was placed in a horrid position now, however. If she told her father how much money she'd made from the sale of her books, one of several unpleasant outcomes would take place. He might demand the money to assist Charles and whatever over-expenditure he'd gotten himself into this time. He might declare her cut off from pin money for the next couple of years. He might even demand she repay back her room and board costs, which he had calculated to the halfpenny. He might offer to place the money into a bank and invest it into the four percents. He might offer to add it to her uncle's inheritance. Assuming that small amounts could even be added to the funds. For all she knew, it required thousands of pounds for an initial investment.

In any case, she did not trust her father with her money. She was ashamed of that thought; however, there was no denying it to herself, here in the firelight of her bedroom. Her father was most likely to demand most of the money himself, for the betterment of her brother. Or, he might insist she use the money to support her sisters.

She could not lie to him, though. There would be no possible way to hide the truth from him, as it would eventually come out. It always did. Setting aside the sin of the lie, she was not well practiced in the act itself, and she feared she would simply confess the entirety of her earnings to him.

"Why are you still up?"

Elizabeth glanced at the book on her nightstand. "Sorry, Mrs. Egerton. Am I keeping you awake?"

"I am a ghost, my dear. No, you are not keeping me awake. Though, I would appreciate it if you would settle down. You are going to give yourself a headache."

"I'm sorry, Mrs. Egerton. I will try for your sake."

The book sighed. In a much softer voice than her usual wit, she asked, "What is the matter, my dear?"

Elizabeth looked down at the bank notes and coins in front of her. "I do not know how to tell my father about this money."

"I do not understand."

"There will be more money, most likely," Elizabeth said. "What shall I tell him?"

"Should you not tell him truth?"

Elizabeth sighed. "My conscience says yes, but I know him. He will make me surrender it, one way or another. Most likely to my brother, Charles, who will waste it on yet another one of his schemes to make his fortune instead of simply working hard."

"Do you believe that of your own father? That he would steal your good fortune."

"He would call it as spreading the good fortune about the household."

"And would the good fortune of the son also be spread, in turn, to the daughters?"

Elizabeth was silent.

"Ah. You have that kind of father. Well, my dear, you can always lie."

"Mrs. Egerton, I cannot lie to my own father."

"I don't recommend it as a general rule, but if he is unreasonable, then I do not see any other course."

"He will know I did something with the books." Elizabeth began to stuff the money back into her reticule. "It was foolish to even think I could keep this money. Nothing is mine."

"Did you not get the inheritance? Mr. Leigh told me that he was giving you whatever of his own fortune not tied up in the entail."

"My father already has plans for that."

"Miss Knight. It is your inheritance, not his. Your uncle was clear."

"I suspect he will withdraw financial support from my younger sisters, thereby having them rely upon me for their general upkeep with the interest from what my uncle provided."

Mrs. Egerton made a disgusted sound. "I am appalled."

"And he will be very angry if the Royal Society offers him money, and then I pretend I sold it for less."

"Then, whatever the Royal Society offers him, keep slightly more aside. You can provide that sum to him. Keep the rest as hidden. If necessary, bring Mrs. Thorne into your confidence. She could hide the money at her estate."

"I do not wish to drag Maria into this."

"Then, I recommend you hide the money in one or two books there. She will never even think to look. The servants won't be going through the books."

"That is deceptive, Mrs. Egerton."

"Yes, it is. Young ladies such as yourself are so very vulnerable. Your survival will depend upon a kind father, and later, a kind brother. It is better to lie than to be destitute, my dear Miss Knight."

Elizabeth offered no argument. A heavy pit formed in her stomach. "I know it is the way of the world, Mrs. Egerton, but the reality of not controlling my own life does weigh upon me."

"I know. Get some sleep. Everything hurts more at night. No doubt, you will be hearing from the Royal Occult Society again tomorrow and you shall need your wits about you."

Mrs. Egerton was wrong; the Royal Occult Society did not visit. Instead, they sent someone to break into the house.

⚜ Chapter 7 ⚜

ELIZABETH HAD BLOWN out the candle but had not managed to drift off to sleep. She found herself recounting her uncle's occult journals. She loved his harsh, angled writing. She'd only glanced at the journals, for they brought out so much grief within her. Eventually, she would command her feelings enough to tackle the task. For now, she could only expose herself to the smallest of glimpses.

She would never allow anyone to take those books from her. She could promise herself that much. They were hers. Her uncle wished her to become an occultist. She did not believe she possessed the ability or talent to be as him, but he believed in her, and she wanted to try for the sake of his faith. She had always been interested in the occult. He was not asking anything odious of her. She would try.

It would have been easier if there was a society of ladies to join, however. Or, barring the challenges of geography, even women that she could correspond with on a regular basis. To Elizabeth's knowledge, the only formal lady occult society existed in London, and it was nothing more than a collection of wives who did no study whatsoever. Their only connection to the occult was through their husbands' membership in the Royal Occult Society.

Her uncle had told her there were pockets of women who studied in a much more informal and quiet manner than the Royal Occult Society's general style. Three sisters in Dublin. An elderly woman in Edinburgh. A pocket of occultists just outside Paris. He had attempted to correspond with them, but most did not wish to give up their identities, or the identities of their fellow ladies. On occasion, he had gotten Elizabeth to write to young women for him, who were rumored to practice the occult. Alas, they had all been rumours, but she'd enjoyed the letters from new acquaintances. It had been thrilling for her to send, and then receive, letters that were of more business than news.

Doubt gnawed at her in the darkness. What if she wasn't good enough? The Royal Occultists were educated men. Ancient languages. Sciences. Mathematics. What could her uncle possibly think she could offer the occult world that he could not? Why would he even think her father would allow her study? She was constantly being shipped off here and there, whenever her father wished to save a little money. Her room was small at home, and she did not trust her father with her books. Not after the Mary incident with the chair.

She knew Maria would take the books, but she hated to ask. Ditto her aunt. She longed for a place of her own. Why oh why couldn't she have inherited the London house as opposed to David Leigh? Elizabeth chuckled, even as tears flowed down her cheeks. She wouldn't have been allowed to live in the London house, even if she could have inherited it all. Even if it could have legally been entailed to her possession, which obviously it could not have been as a woman. No, she would have had to drag her entire family with her. Her problems would have followed her. Solving one problem would not have fixed them all.

At least her uncle provided her what money he could. She often worried that she would resort to becoming an unpaid governess at Mary's house when her father died. Or, if something were to happen to Mary, too, then Elizabeth might end up being forced to become a governess to support herself. The money from Uncle Edward would be more than her potential salary; she would not need to work. The relief in her soul was immeasurable.

And, for all his strange ways, David Leigh's book donation was turning out to provide a rather large sum of ready money. She did not know how to invest funds, nor how money was held in a bank. She would need her father or her brother to arrange that.

It seemed to her that Mrs. Egerton might be right: lying was the only option. She could use the money to buy herself essentials. And perhaps a frivolous thing or two. She would love a new pair of good boots. She could hide it in several places. At Maria's, for example. In her own books. In her reticule. In her private trunk. Even some at Aunt Cass's.

The sound of a metal something clattering to the floor startled Elizabeth. She listened, but no one responded. She knew the servants were all working late tonight to prepare the main drawing room for booksellers; Aunt Cass did not want them wandering about her house with their muddy boots. It couldn't have been the cat; Miss Puss Puss preferred to be down with the servants. Elizabeth hadn't even seen the shy creature since arriving.

Footsteps. A door creaked opened. A moment later, it creaked closed. More footsteps. Elizabeth carefully pushed herself up and swung her legs over the side of the bed.

Mrs. Egerton whispered, "Miss Knight? Take care."

"I agree," Elizabeth whispered back.

House-breaking was a hanging offense. To break into a lady's house, when there was no man at home, was such a vile violation of one's home and safety. How would any of them feel safe again, with a stranger's footfalls now coming outside her door. Her heart pounded in her chest. Were they to be murdered?

She thought to scream but feared that would only make the villain desperate. Instead, she pushed herself up from the bed. The bedposts creaked a little. The footsteps beyond stopped for a handful of heartbeats before beginning again.

Light illumined around the cracks in her door.

The fire poker was too far away.

The doorknob rattled.

She picked up one of her shoes from the floor.

The doorknob rattled more.

She positioned herself so that the shoe would hit an adult square in the face.

The door flung open.

She flung her shoe at him. Then she grabbed a book from her nightstand, aiming for his face. She did not recognize the intruder, but she could see his face plainly in the candlelight.

He was a dirty little child. No older than the twins, even taking into account his clear malnourishment. She stared at him, unable to figure out what to do next now that she was faced with a house-breaking child.

However, her appearance at the door startled the intruder. He threw his candle at her and ran away, back down the hallway from whence he came. The candle flame flicked to her nightgown. She shrieked in fear as the hem of the gown caught. Footsteps pounded from every direction in the house.

"Drop to the floor!" Mrs. Egerton shouted. "Roll! Miss Knight, you must roll to put out the flames!"

Panicked, Elizabeth attempted to follow Mrs. Egerton's instructions. She rubbed her legs against the carpets. Something crashed against her, but she paid no heed to it. Her skin grew hot and angry. She could not stop her screams and sobs, as they mingled together until her voice went hoarse.

Something was beating against her legs, and it took a moment for her to realize it was John, one of the footmen who'd been helping move the crates of books earlier. He'd stripped off his jacket and was beating out the fire, all the while shouting for someone to fetch the apothecary, Aunt Cass, the night watch, and anyone else he could think of.

The heat subsided and he collapsed to her side. "Miss Knight, oh speak to me. Are you injured badly? What did that brigand do to you? Are you hurt?"

Elizabeth was unable to speak or even to lift herself off the floor. She sobbed, exhausted by the strain of having nearly burned to death.

Mrs. Cook arrived and ordered candles. She inspected Elizabeth's legs and then said, "My dear. It isn't bad. The nightdress is ruined for sure now, but that is replaceable. You have cuts upon your feet and legs, but nothing serious. Hmm, you knocked over your water basin and table. Some blisters and burns, but they will fade."

Elizabeth did not remember knocking over a basin, let alone a table.

"You were very brave. You stood up to that fiend and got the fire out all yourself. What a good girl you are!" Mrs. Cook said, pride in her voice.

"Aunt Cass?" Elizabeth whispered. "Where is Aunt Cass?"

"She went next door, after you went to bed. She takes supper at Sir William's house every Saturday. He had a card party. You were also invited, but she did not wish to disturb you. You'd been working so hard all day and looked so very tired after dinner. Sally's gone to fetch her."

"Elizabeth!"

"There! She is back," Mrs. Cook said. "Would you like a glass of wine?"

"Please," Elizabeth said through her choking sobs.

Mrs. Cook stroked Elizabeth's arm. "John! Fetch Miss Knight a glass of wine."

"What happened?" a male voice demanded.

Elizabeth heard the footman recount the incident. A thief broke into the house. He happened upon Miss Knight, and she had defended herself against the brigand. He threw his candle upon her, and she nearly burned to death.

Elizabeth began sobbing once more. She attempted to tuck her legs under her gown's tattered hem for decency, but the dress was mostly missing from her knees down. However, the footman's coat covered her bare legs and saved her dignity.

"Oh Elizabeth!" Aunt Cass exclaimed. She collapsed to the floor next to her niece and gathered her up into her arms. "My dear, sweet girl."

"Mind the shards, ma'am!" John said. "We've not cleaned them up yet."

Elizabeth managed to find enough strength to say, "I am well, Aunt. I am well."

Sir William poked his head into the room. "Terrible business, Miss Knight! Terrible, indeed. Tell me, are those your shoes in the hallway?"

"Yes, Sir."

"Did you throw them at the intruder?"

"I believe so, Sir."

Sir William roared with laughter. "Good for you, Miss! You scared him off. He won't be back! Fearful of his life, no doubt now!"

That caused Elizabeth to laugh, and she broke into sobbing laughter, unable to find the middle ground between her terror and the absolute ridiculousness of her fending off a house-breaker with nothing more than a pair of shoes!

Mrs. Cook, however, was having none of it. "Sir William! Miss Elizabeth could have burned to death."

"A couple days in bed, Cook, and she'll be fully recovered," Sir William said, completely unbothered that one of the servants talked back to him.

Mrs. Cook gave Sir William a dubious look. "We'll need a salve for these burns."

"Your wine, Miss Knight," Sally said, returning to the room. "Sir William's butler has gone to alert the night watch. If we're lucky, they might catch the intruder. James is gone for the apothecary. Mrs. Spencer, he said he will take a chair when closer to that part of town so that they may hurry back faster."

"That's only sensible," Aunt Cass said. She lifted up the jacket to peer at Elizabeth's legs. "I believe Sir William is right, my dear. A few days and the only proof of this happening will be itchy legs. We'll soon be all right once more. Come, let's get you back into bed. Sir William! Gentlemen, out of the room while we move my niece."

Sir William and the male servants pointedly stepped out of the room and turned their backs, while her aunt, cook, and housemaid all moved Elizabeth into her bed. She pulled the blankets up over her burned legs.

"They hurt more than the injuries say they should," Elizabeth said, staring down at her legs.

"The shock, no doubt," Aunt Cass said.

"Carpet burns from putting out the fire, I suspect," Cook said. "How did you manage to think of putting out the fire yourself upon the carpet? You have a level head on you, girl."

Elizabeth did not see the ghost book on her nightstand. Panic rose in her. "Forgive me, but I must check on one of my uncle's books. I fear it might have been stolen. Sally, can you move the candle so I can see behind my stand?"

"Miss Elizabeth, they are only books," Sir William said as he re-entered the room. "And it appears only the basin took damage."

"Nevertheless, I will be uneasy until I see for myself."

"Sir William, may I offer you refreshment?" Cook asked.

"Brandy. Don't trouble, yourself, Mrs. Cook. I know where it is. Would you like me to send over Mrs. Reynolds to assist?"

"That would be very kind," Cook said.

Aunt Cass spoke up. "Sir William, might I ask Mrs. Reynolds myself?"

"Oh, of course, Mrs. Spencer, if you prefer."

Aunt Cass turned to her niece. "Elizabeth, do you mind if I step out? It will only be for a moment to arrange things with Sir William's housekeeper. She is an excellent woman."

"Of course not, Aunt."

"Then, I'll be back in just a moment."

With only Sally in the room now, as the others bustled about to do repairs, fetch brandy, and whatnot, Sally was able to relocate the book of autographs. It had fallen behind the bed, hidden in the shadows.

Elizabeth gingerly picked up the book of autographs. Whispering, she said, "I hope the brigand did not harm you."

The book opened its lid and closed it, in a wink. Elizabeth smiled.

"Miss Knight, was the book hurt?"

"It appears to be unharmed. Though, I will have to do an inventory in the morning once it is light. The fire was close to that stack of books in the corner. I'll inspect everything in the morning."

"I'm relieved, for your sake, miss. Mr. Edward Leigh was always a kind man to us girls. All the maids said so, and not just here. I don't know how they're all going to find work now, miss."

"Are some of them unemployed?" Elizabeth asked. "Didn't Mr. David Leigh take them?"

"No, miss. Sorry to gossip, miss. I know he's your cousin."

"I would like to know, please. Did he dismiss all my uncle's servants?"

"He kept Mrs. Stout, Mary-Anne, and Jimmy, but that was it. He brought his own servants because he said Mr. Leigh's old servants would just spy on him for the family." Sally cleared her throat. "Sorry, miss. That's only what I'd heard, on that last part."

"Did the others find employment?"

"The chambermaid has found work, yes, and the footman. Little Johnny Thatcher was hired by Sir William, but he was a casual worker so it wasn't hard for him. Old Mrs. Taylor hasn't found work. It's not likely she will, I suppose. She'd worked for the family her entire life. Your uncle left her an annuity, at least, though. But I don't think it's enough for her to support herself and her niece."

"She's supporting a niece?"

"Yes, miss. Her niece took ill and had to stop working. She used to work at the Royal Occult Society. She taught their daughters at the Society building itself. But when the coughing hit her, they hired another teacher. They're just living off whatever money your uncle left them, and a little both of them had saved. That's what I've heard from them."

Elizabeth squared her shoulders. "Are you telling me that Mrs. Taylor, who must be seventy by now, has been kicked out from under my cousin's protection and left to the wolves?"

Sally whispered, "Please don't tell on me. I will lose my position."

"You certainly will not," Elizabeth said harshly. "Where does Mrs. Taylor live now?"

At that point, there was bustling downstairs and Sally rushed off to lead Aunt Cass and Mrs. Reynolds up the stairs, insisting that Miss Elizabeth was mostly unharmed.

Sally curtsied to Aunt Cass and said, "Shall I wait for the apothecary?"

"Yes, go," Aunt Cass said.

Sally closed the door, leaving Elizabeth alone with her aunt and Mrs. Reynolds. The woman inspected Elizabeth's legs, nodding to herself as she poked and prodded.

"They aren't too serious, you are correct, but I will still feel better if the apothecary can offer his own opinion on the matter," Mrs. Reynolds said. "He might also have a salve to soothe the discomfort. If not, I can make one quite easily."

Mrs. Reynolds talked with Aunt Cass for a few more minutes, offering to spend the night in Elizabeth's room. Elizabeth insisted that was not necessary, as she did not wish to inconvenience the older woman in any capacity whatsoever. However, Mrs. Reynolds would not be easy until it was agreed that she would sleep in the guest bedroom across the hall from Elizabeth. Sally quickly went to make up the room, and that would allow Cook and the maids to continue their duties and ensure fires were made, all until a nurse could be found for Miss Knight, provided one was needed.

"I will not need a nurse," Elizabeth insisted to her aunt, once they were alone.

"It is best to allow people to fuss when they wish it," Aunt Cass said. "There are no children or even grandchildren amongst our little circle of friends here to fuss over and tend to. You must make allowances for people who need to fuss over the sick."

"Please, Aunt. If a nurse is hired for me, my father will insist I go back to Bryden. Then, he will see there is nothing the matter, and he will blame me for wasting everyone's money." Elizabeth fought back tears. "Please. I am well enough."

"You are beside yourself! You aren't thinking straight. Not that I blame you. You nearly just burned to death."

"The shock has faded. Now, I am mostly tired. All I wish is some sleep and a good meal in the morning."

"We have never had a break in before. This is most shocking. I might have to get Andrews and John sleeping next to the windows so that we can feel safe at night."

"No, Aunt. This wasn't a house picked at random."

"What do you mean by that? Are you saying they thought the house was full of riches?"

"I believe someone was trying to steal the books. He knew where my bedroom was, Aunt. I am convinced he came through the window down the hallway, which is incredibly difficult to open from the outside. I heard something fall to the floor. Is that not where the mahogany table is set up? With those little pewter statues Uncle Spencer loved?"

Aunt Cass silently thought on it for a moment and left the room, heading down the corridor. She returned a moment later. "You are correct, my dear. Several of the little things are upon the floor. Unharmed. That is a difficult window to climb through."

"Exactly! If he simply wished to steal the silverware, why not the main floor? You can clearly see that large silver vase with the dried flowers it in through the window from the street! Why wouldn't he have inspected the rooms between the window and here first? He could have stolen your jewelry if general theft was his goal."

"Indeed, the statues alone would have been worth something," Aunt Cass said. "I believe you might be right."

"I believe I am right in saying that boy had a very specific purpose. He avoided all of those rooms and made his way directly toward here. He opened the door across the corridor, realized he was turned around, and then came across to me."

"There are not that many people who know the layout of my upper rooms. And he certainly couldn't have stolen all of the books," Aunt Cass said.

Elizabeth looked at the book of autographs. "I get the feeling that my uncle had perhaps not informed me of the entire situation with the Occult Society."

Aunt Cass let out an annoyed sound. "I loved my brother, but he was a headache sometimes. All right, let's get you ready for the apothecary. And then I'll have Sally sleep in your bedroom tonight. And I'll have John sleep in the hallway. Oh, don't worry. We'll pull out the sofa from the spare bedroom. He'll be quite comfortable. Two of Sir William's dogs can come over and sleep with the men downstairs, too. Sir William insists. None of the maids are going to be alone tonight either, not even Cook. I shall ask her to sleep in my room. In fact, now that I considered it, I shall move everyone to this floor tonight. With the addition of the dogs at the front door, we will all know the other is safe. And, if necessary, we shall continue every night as long as there is a threat."

THE NEXT MORNING, the Thornes' arrival was loud and bustling, and entirely too early for propriety. Elizabeth was already awake and dressed, though her hair was under a white cap for both warmth and a general laziness about her appearance that morning. She preferred to be out of her cap whenever company arrived, but it was only Maria.

Maria demanded to know where Elizabeth was located and then scolded everyone for not calling for them as soon as the vicious assault had taken place. Elizabeth calmly, though unsuccessfully, explained that it was more of a shock than any true assault, but Maria was so riled up that she was ready to search through every gutter and alley in London to find the robber who attacked her friend.

"I am well," Elizabeth insisted. "Please, have a seat and join us for breakfast."

"Are you in much pain from the burns, Miss Knight?" Henry Thorne asked. "I heard they were excessive."

"It's ten in the morning, Mr. Thorne! What news could you have heard this early? Truly, I am very well. In fact, I believe the worst came from the cuts I received when I broke my basin!" Elizabeth chuckled. "I am to use a salve and silk stockings for the next few days, and then I am certain the blisters and redness will fade."

"Blisters," Maria whispered. "Good God."

"No one has ever died from a blister, Maria."

"Plenty of people have died of infected wounds, Miss Knight," Maria said in a rather irritated tone.

"I solemnly promise you that these blisters will be gone within a day and I shall fully recover." Elizabeth smiled. "To be very honest, there is one cut upon the bottom of my foot that is the most troublesome because that is where I put my weight when I take a step."

Mr. Thorne seemed mollified at that news, even if his wife did not. "Well, Maria and I have discussed the matter, and we would both feel significantly better if we could come stay in the house until we are certain you are safe here. Or, if you prefer, we can move everyone to our house and have some of the manservants stay here to look after the female servants. We can also make room to move your entire household to ours. Whatever you wish, Mrs. Spencer."

"Oh, it's not necessary," Elizabeth began to say.

Her aunt cut her off. "You are very kind, Mr. Thorne. I accept your offer to stay here with us."

"Aunt…"

"Eliza, listen to your aunt."

"But…"

Despite Elizabeth's protestations, it didn't take long for a deal to be struck: Henry and Maria would stay a full week with them, until the following Sunday. Elizabeth suspected it was for Aunt Cass' benefit more than her own, but she welcomed the company all the same.

"I suppose I must write to my father, so that he hears it from me first and not through gossip. No doubt, by the time it reaches him, it will be that I was burned alive in the street."

"If you wish, I can have it delivered to Bryden. Then, the horses can return tomorrow, and perhaps with news. We can even send back some books, if you wish."

"I couldn't possibly impose upon you, Mr. Thorne!"

But there was no arguing with Maria and Henry when they were being so very helpful. A writing desk was fetched.

March 18, 1810
London

Dear Isabella,

Please do not be alarmed by the sight of this letter's arrival. Rest assured; we are all well. The manner in which we are hurrying this letter to you is only to ensure that you can all hear the actual news of last night's events, without the taint of gossip.

Now, I realize upon reading that sentence, you are more alarmed. Please, comfort yourself. Everything is well. For, while the situation could have been dangerous, it was not, and I do not wish either of you to hear fanciful tales.

So allow me to tell you the entire story with my own pen and words.

Last night, there was an intruder in my aunt's home. A basin was broken. Uncle Spencer's metal army statues were knocked to the floor. A table was accidentally kicked. Nothing was stolen. No one was injured, beyond one of my gowns.

Now, Isabella, I must beg you to read this part slowly, as you might frighten yourself by allowing your imagination run away with you. A candle was knocked down and it caught the hem of my nightgown. I put the fire out quickly and all the injury I have to speak of is a couple of the tiniest blisters, as well as two insignificant cuts upon my foot where I had quite accidentally stepped upon some of the broken basin.

The apothecary was called, as was a physician. Both agreed I am in perfect health, and merely need to not wear shoes for a day, maybe two at the most, until the cuts heal over. Nothing of consequence at all!

My aunt's neighbour, Sir William Essex, has been very attentive to our needs. Also, Mr. and Mrs. Thorne will be staying with us until next Sunday, to assist with any of our needs. For my part, I shall be enjoying the quiet joy of being waited upon for a day. I shall pretend I am a duchess!

So, please, I beg all of you. Do not be alarmed. I write this only to get ahead of the rumors and gossip. I assure you; if this had happened at Bryden, we'd have not even called Mr. Clarke to come check on me. That is how insignificant my injuries are.

Give my love to everyone,
Elizabeth

"Will that do?" Elizabeth asked when she'd finished reading the letter aloud.

Aunt Cass shook her head. "Your father would not have called an apothecary unless you were dying. I'm certain the new Mrs. Knight will see through that."

"That isn't what I asked, Aunt Cass," Elizabeth said, with only a hint of rebuke in her voice. "Will it dispel their worries?"

"I believe it will. I don't know the new Mrs. Knight. Is she a sensible woman?"

Maria made an impolite sound. "I have seen worse, and I have seen better. Mostly, she is merely young."

"She will grow into the role," Elizabeth said.

"I thought you didn't like her," Maria asked.

"I have never had a complaint about her as a person. My issues are with my father choosing to remarry again. The girls are old enough that I could have taken on the role of mother and guardian. And the girls are at the age where a new stepmother is not an easy thing to understand. At least Mary and I were very young. Mary doesn't even remember our mother. Theodosia absolutely remembers her mother, and views Isabella as a usurper. Right or wrong."

"Why on earth would a man his age marry again?" Henry Thorne asked, shaking his head. "What foolishness."

"Some of us get lonely, Mr. Thorne," Aunt Cass said.

"Are we to be expecting some news, Mrs. Spencer?" Henry asked.

Aunt Cass snorted. "It would be news to me! No, my marriage days are done, I suspect. And good riddance, too. Men. What good are any of you?"

"I, madam, have been, on occasion, deemed *useful.*"

Aunt Cass laughed. "Indeed you have, Mr. Thorne! Alas, you are young enough to be my son."

"Nonsense! Any man worth the air he breathes would see that you are a woman of exceptional breeding and taste and would be honoured to have you upon their arm."

Maria sighed. "Now you all understand how I ended up married to this...this..."

"Useful man?" Henry offered hopefully.

"Fop," Maria said, finishing her thought.

"You wound me, my wife!"

Elizabeth watched the exchange and was surprised by the loneliness in her own heart. She couldn't help herself from thinking of her Mr. R.

No, he was not *her* Mr. R. He was someone else's. He had married the right woman, the one his family approved. The one that had the right dowry. That woman had twelve thousand pounds in her reticule. At the time, Elizabeth had a sweet smile and a rather pretty pale yellow dress. She had been naïve to think her charms were enough to sway a family of consequence.

"Eliza, are you well?"

Elizabeth jolted from her self-reflection to see everyone staring at her. Her aunt looked grave, and Marie concerned. Henry looked poised to rush for a physician.

"I did not eat enough at breakfast, I believe."

"I shall inform Cook immediately," Aunt Cass said. "Excuse me. Please, make yourselves at home."

When Aunt Cass left the room, Elizabeth said, "I need a favour, Mr. Thorne. I feel terrible for asking, but it is important."

"Of course. What do you need?"

"Two things. First, I really do wish you to stay about the house as much as possible. I suspect that we will be seeing the Royal Society today, or possibly tomorrow at the latest, and they shall be trying to use this situation to get my books. I believe they will respond better to a man in your position in the house. But I would also like someone to fetch my uncle's lawyer. A Mr. Grant. I would like him to be informed about the situation with the Royal Society. I have made enough money from my books to pay him for his time, if there is any concern on that score."

"I shall look after that aspect, Miss Knight. Have no fear."

"No, please. I wish to earn my way," Elizabeth said. She squared her shoulders. "I know that I am poor, but I am not destitute, Mr. Thorne. And, for now, I can afford to pay for the lawyer to spend the day here sipping tea, and I would like to do so. I may never have the opportunity again to feel so important and independent. Please respect my wish."

Henry glanced at his wife before saying, "As you say. What is the second thing you would like?"

"My uncle had a servant. A 'Mrs. Taylor'. Sally tells me she has been turned out by Mr. Leigh. Would you be able to discreetly find this servant? I would like to assist her."

"What is this about Mrs. Taylor?" Aunt Cass demanded. She was with Sally, who was carrying a tray of cold meats and buns.

Elizabeth had not wanted her aunt to hear of this, for she worried it would influence the aunt against the nephew. Also, she did not wish Sally to get in trouble.

"I learned from Sally last night that Cousin David dismissed some of Uncle Edward's servants, including Mrs. Taylor."

"What?" Aunt Cass exclaimed. "Sally, is this true?"

Sally nodded. "Yes, ma'am. I wasn't trying to gossip, ma'am. Miss Knight asked, and I felt it was proper to answer her, since she had known Mrs. Taylor all these years, ma'am."

"Of course it was proper. I only wished to have heard it directly from you and not in this manner. Where is Mrs. Taylor staying?"

Sally provided the address and both Henry and Aunt Cass gasped in shock. Maria and Elizabeth had not even heard of the street before. "She is there with her niece, who is very ill. Mrs. Taylor could only afford the smallest room there, and has called for Mr. Edward Leigh's apothecary twice. She says it was too expensive to bring him back for another visit. The gentleman told Mrs. Taylor that her niece, her name is Susan, needed fresh air, but they cannot afford a room with a window. And the air is so poor in that part of London that a window might not even help. So, Mrs. Taylor didn't see the use in another visit if she couldn't fix the air."

"Good God. Why did you not tell me? I would have had Cook send food."

Sally gulped. "Um, please do not be angry at Mrs. Cook, but she's had me take a little bit of supper to them every night. Please do not be angry. It was only what we'd eat ourselves, so it's only us that's going without. We were waiting for Mrs. Dover to return! We normally talk to her about these things and she decides if they need to come to you. But we did not wish to distress her by writing."

"The only person I am angry with at this moment is my nephew. Cook! Cook!" Aunt Cass called out. "Cook! Get in here! John, get Cook for me."

A moment later, Mrs. Cook came rushing into the room. "What is it? Is Miss Knight worse?"

"What do we have for ready food?"

"We have some bread, and the last of the pork. Boiled bacon and peas are for dinner. Sally is to go to market to see if she can find some fish, or anything edible for guests." Mrs. Cook glanced at Henry and Maria. "I was thinking to ask Tom if his eldest sister was available for the week. She could help in the kitchen while you have guests. Are we planning more dinner guests?"

"We must do something," Elizabeth said. "I've known her my entire life."

"I've known her since before I married," Aunt Cass said.

"What is appropriate help?" Elizabeth asked. "I have all these books and I'm willing to share my good fortune."

"Who?" Cook asked.

"Mrs. Taylor," Sally whispered.

Mrs. Cook gave Sally a stern look. "Sorry, ma'am. We didn't want to concern you with what Mr. Leigh had done."

"I understand you were protecting me from my nephew's true nature, but we must help this poor woman and her niece."

"May I offer a suggestion?" Henry asked. When Aunt Cass nodded, he said, "I believe that we could approach this from two different ways. First, we should send some food and bread these poor people. We have plenty at our house, especially with temporary relocation here. I shall have my coachman go with Sally here, to deliver food. That way, we will all know where they live. And, then my coachman can return with Sally, and then leave for Bryden with Miss Knight's letter."

"Oh! We should send Mrs. Rundle to assess!" Maria exclaimed. "Our housekeeper here in London is very sensible, Mrs. Spencer."

"Of course! We can send Mrs. Rundle with Sally. Then, she can determine what would be best to help. My wife is very correct. Mrs. Rundle is a sensible, practical woman."

"Very steady," Maria said. "You would approve of her, I am certain."

Henry Thorne nodded. "That will allow Mrs. Cook to do her duties here."

"I would like to set aside a little money from the book sales to pay for a physician to see Mrs. Taylor's niece as well."

"I don't believe that is necessary at present," Aunt Cass said.

"Nevertheless. We have Sir Brandon, I believe that was his name, visiting today. Correct, Mr. Thorne?"

"Indeed, though I had thought to inform him not to visit."

"No, I wish him to come. We will sell as many books as possible today, with what has been sorted. That will provide ready funds in case we need to call for another medical opinion."

"Then, I can write immediately and invite some individuals to the house to peruse. Are you certain, though, in your current situation?" Henry asked. "And you, Mrs. Spencer?"

"It is up to my niece."

"My uncle's death has affected these two poor women. I shall not abandon them because I had a few blisters and cuts," Elizabeth said. "When the physician says it is safe to visit Mrs. Taylor, I shall. Until then, I believe we should do everything possible to assist."

"Then, ladies and Mr. Thorne, we have a plan. Let us get to work," Aunt Cass said.

Chapter 8

FIRSTLY, MRS. RUNDLE reported back that she was grievously concerned about the situation of the two women living in West Alley Buildings. Mrs. Rundle took it upon herself to call for the Thorne's London physician to consult, as well as called back the apothecary to speak with them. All three agreed that the best course of action was to move the women from West Alley Buildings as soon as possible. However, Miss Susan's strength needed to rally a bit more before such an attempt should be made. As well, it would be best to wait for the rain to cease, for the damp air could be dangerous in her frail condition.

Her interviews with all concerned led her to conclude that the invalid required wholesome foods that were easy on the digestion. She presented her mistress with a menu for the week that would ensure the women would have the best possible hope of a full recovery.

"It is incumbent upon me, ma'am, Mrs. Spencer, to inform you that Mrs. Taylor has also taken ill. She is not nearly as ill as the niece and the physician believes there is no worry, but I am concerned nonetheless," Mrs. Rundle said. "As I understand the situation, Mrs. Taylor is about seventy. I believe caution must be exercised."

Elizabeth listened, worried as Mrs. Rundle related the details of the squalor of the housing situation. A tiny room, only big enough for a dirty, lumpy mattress upon the floor. Two chairs and a small table were tucked into a corner. The other corner a pile of trunks, containing the few possessions of the women. No means to cook or warm the room. No water pump within convenient walking distance. Noxious air. It was truly deplorable.

"Would it not be worth the risk to move them?" Elizabeth asked. "I will assist with the cost. I have a moral obligation to use my good fortune to assist my uncle's poor servant."

Mrs. Rundle shook her head. "My dear Miss Knight, if I believed that the niece would survive a move, I would have informed my mistress immediately. However, in my opinion, she is too grave to move. The aunt can, and should, but refuses to leave the girl. I cannot blame her. For now, if I might be so bold as to offer my opinion..."

Maria said, "We trust your opinion on this matter."

"We must get this girl's strength up. They are eating only what ready-made foods Mrs. Taylor can procure cheaply when Mrs. Cook is unable to provide them with charity."

"Cook, what should we do?" Elizabeth asked.

Mrs. Cook looked at her mistress, who nodded her consent.

"Well, Miss Knight, I believe a daily meal of bread soaked in pot liquor. I can procure the salt beef. That will help the girl's strength and be very easy on her digestion. Mr. Leigh swore by it, even toward his end."

"I agree with Mrs. Cook," Mrs. Rundle said. "With your permission, Mrs. Spencer and Mrs. Thorne, I believe I should undertake the meal, as Mrs. Cook has the added work of houseguests now."

"I am not afraid of hard work," Mrs. Cook insisted.

"Mrs. Rundle is right," Aunt Cass said. "Mrs. Thorne?"

"Yes, of course. Mrs. Rundle, may I entrust this to you?"

"I would be happy to help these poor creatures. I would appreciate Mrs. Cook's opinion on my menu of nutritious foods for the invalids, however, before I speak to our cook about it."

"Of course, Mrs. Rundle. Let me see."

Elizabeth read the list after Mrs. Cook, her aunt, and Maria were finished with it. A dish she'd frequently asked her own servants to make for the very poor in their village: rice, sugar, milk, and drippings baked together in a cooling bread oven. Boiled turnips, mashed with a little butter. Jam and bread. Bread soaked in pot liquor; the flavourful broth left over after boiling salt beef for hours.

"I would like to contribute," Elizabeth said. "Sally? Would you fetch my reticule from my nightstand please?"

Sally curtsied, but everyone else's objections stopped the young servant.

Finally, Aunt Cass said, "None of us expect you to assist in this, Elizabeth."

"Indeed," Maria said. "Henry and I can afford bread for these people."

"I am a clergyman's eldest daughter and I feel my obligation in this matter," Elizabeth said. "Mrs. Rundle, how best can I assist?"

"Eliza…" Maria started.

"I will not be deterred. Mrs. Rundle, if you please."

"Well, miss…since you asked…they are in need of wax candles. The rushlights are not helping Susan's lungs, and the apothecary said it was poisoning the air without windows. Perhaps a few would assist them. Also, they are in need of cheese and beer. They can afford neither. I also recommend molasses for the young miss. That on some bread to keep her strength up."

"What about butter?" Aunt Cass asked.

Mrs. Rundle shook her head. "It is too cold in their room to bother with making it spreadable, to be honest. Molasses or salt pork fat would be better."

"We are quite low on salt pork, to be very honest with you," Mrs. Cook said. "I've not been happy with what's been at the market as of late. But, if it's just for frying up to drain, the cheapest varieties should be fine."

"Sally, would a shilling be enough? I don't know London prices at all," Elizabeth asked.

"Not for the candles, miss, but for the food it would easily cover it. Would you like your reticule?" Sally asked.

"Please."

With the servant off to get her money purse, Maria said, "Please have Jenkins pick up wax candles for them. Put it on our account."

"Yes, ma'am," Mrs. Rundle said.

Elizabeth passed over two shillings for extra food items, and Mrs. Rundle promised to do the shopping herself, "to get the best prices."

With a plan in hand, Henry decided to write several of his bookseller and book collector friends to come by and see what books could be had.

"If I might be so bold, I believe you ladies should move to a different part of the house, so that you do not have to deal with the bickering of commerce," Henry said. "Also, two of you are in mourning. You should not have to endure your house being opened up like a shop."

"Anything to get rid of these crates!" Aunt Cass exclaimed. "Come, Elizabeth. Mrs. Thorne? Will you assist in moving my niece?"

Henry bowed deeply, but could not hide his wicked smile. "If I have Miss Knight's permission, I would be happy to carry her into the other drawing room."

Maria gave her husband a disgusted look. "Henry, the only thing you can carry is your winnings after a night of cards."

"You wound me!" Henry said. "Besides, I have given up the tables."

"Since when?"

"Since I heard of Miss Knight's assault. The tables are boring me, and I am more use here." Henry quirked a smile at his wife. "Besides, aren't you always wishing I was more helpful?"

Maria rolled her eyes. "Oh, Henry."

Elizabeth turned her head away, so that they would not see her smile. For all of their bickering and arguing, they had been a love match first and always. He did not have to marry the woman of dubious family background. And she did not have to marry the last son of a titled gentlemen who had little to give his youngest. But they'd married, and they'd not regretted it. Society could learn from their example.

"I do not need to be carried. Gracious," Elizabeth said. "All I wish for is a supportive arm so that I may walk upon my toes and avoid the cuts upon my heel."

Henry Thorne thrust his arm out, bringing laughter from Maria. While he helped Elizabeth from the sofa, he asked, "Shall we send word to Mr. David Leigh? About his servants, I mean."

"Please don't," Elizabeth said. "He will only be angry, and then…well…he might ask for the books back."

"He wouldn't dare!" Maria exclaimed.

"I don't think it is a point that we should push," Elizabeth said. "As inconvenient as this has been, I believe we are better positioned with the books than without. We can sell what is necessary, and then use the money to assist those my cousin harmed. But I cannot sit upon my good fortune by my uncle, knowing that his servants were tossed out with no support."

"Are you certain?"

"I shall have that word with him," Aunt Cass announced.

"Oh, aunt, please don't."

"Leave it to me, Eliza. Remember, that I know him better than any of you. I shall know when, where, and *how* to strike."

"Very well," Henry Thorne said. "So today, we shall continue sorting these books and engaging in exciting commerce?"

Elizabeth laughed. "Yes, indeed."

"Excellent. I should invite my family over to witness my utility," Henry Thorne declared.

"They would be shocked, indeed," Maria said deadpan.

That only made the other ladies and servants laugh harder. Even little Tom could be heard giggling in the other room.

AFTER ANOTHER HOUR of sorting her uncle's private books in Aunt Cass' preferred upper drawing room, an overwhelmed Elizabeth announced, "I believe we should ask Mrs. Egerton, the book, for help."

Aunt Cass was seated at a small table with a writing desk upon it, and was transcribing book titles and year of publication as Maria read them out to her. Then, Maria would either make an immediate decision about the book or place upon the sideboard for

Elizabeth's final decision. At least half the books went on the sideboard because Maria found half the books' titles interesting.

The system was working well, but Elizabeth was becoming overwhelmed by decisions. Each time she filled up the small trunk in the corner with possible books to keep, she would then vow to only keep half. Those would then go upstairs to her closet for later decisions. Only, Elizabeth couldn't decide anymore. She wavered between selling all of the books and selling none.

"I'm rather terrified of a talking book, if I am to be completely candid," Aunt Cass said.

"I understand, Aunt. However, one assumes a magical book would have thoughts on other magical books." Elizabeth looked at Maria and said, "Would you fetch my sewing basket from the other room? I accidentally left her in there. With my reticule."

Maria rolled her eyes at her friend, but dutifully disappeared. She returned a few moments later.

"Is that the book?" Aunt Cass asked. When Elizabeth nodded her head, she said, "I don't know about this, Eliza. Are we at risk of being led astray by this book?"

"While I'm not sure about all this occult business, I confess that the book probably does know more about occult books than the rest of us. However, I do not think we should let Henry know of this, for now."

"No, I don't think you should tell the man that I'm helping you," Mrs. Egerton said in a caustic voice.

The three ladies started and let out a series of surprised sounds. Mrs. Egerton let out a dramatic sigh as footsteps pounded across the house and heading toward them. When Henry and James arrived, demanding to know what had happened, it was Maria to tell the lie.

"A mouse came out of nowhere and caught us all by surprise."

Henry rolled his eyes. "For the love of God, Maria. It's just a mouse."

"As I said, Henry, it caught us by surprise."

Henry muttered under his breath about foolish women, but his wife's keen ears picked it up well enough.

"I heard that, Henry Thorne!"

An amused expression formed on his face, even as he tried to cover it up. "Mr. Osborne's assistant will be here at any moment. I shan't keep him waiting. If I see the elusive Miss Puss Puss, I shall direct her accordingly."

After Henry Thorne exited the room, Mrs. Egerton let out another dramatic sigh that now seemed to Elizabeth to be the ghost's preferred mode of expressing disappointment. "Ladies. I am not opposed to assisting my own sex with their tasks. I will, however, not work with a man until I deem him worth my time."

"Mr. Thorne is an exceptional man," Elizabeth said.

"I'll judge that for myself."

"Mrs. Egerton," Aunt Cass said. "Might I be so bold as to ask if you were spying upon our conversation?"

"Only long enough to hear you distrust me," the book said.

Aunt Cass flushed pink. "My dearest madam, pray forgive my manners. I...You must understand..."

"I understand that you are not acquainted with the occult and, therefore, can only say as your mind allows. I took no offence, dear woman."

Aunt Cass let out a relieved sound. "Thank you, Mrs. Egerton. You are too good."

"Being dead does help a lady avoid holding trivial grudges. At my time of existence, I prefer to save my dislike for those who truly deserve it. A minor slip of the tongue is hardly worth a generational grudge."

"You are very wise, Mrs. Egerton," Maria said. "I must confess I still struggle with that one."

"I have the benefit of death for my part. So, you wish me to help sort through this entire mess of books. Very well."

Mrs. Egerton's help turned out to be very useful, as she knew the rarity of many of the volumes. For instance, she knew that the second edition of *Conquering the Elements* (1740) was significantly more valuable than the first edition, as the second printing contained a letter from the author's wife detailing how he died failing to conquer the elements.

"I met the wife," Mrs. Egerton said absently. "Outstanding woman."

A rap came upon the door beyond, then the distant sound of men's voices.

"Oh, that is Mr. Osborne himself!" Maria said. "I would know his deep voice anywhere."

"Then I shall bring him these three rare books that Mrs. Egerton has pointed out. Perhaps I might make myself a guinea today!" Elizabeth said with a big grin.

"Try to be ladylike!" Aunt Cass called out, which made Elizabeth grin. Her aunt said that frequently when she was an excited girl.

Elizabeth carefully walked into the main drawing room. She took her time, as not to inflame her wounds. That meant Mr. Osborne and Henry Thorne were already in the drawing room heavily engaged in commerce upon her arrival.

She smiled up at the tall, black man who held two books in one hand, and their inventory list in the other. "Will you introduce me, Mr. Thorne?"

"Of course. Miss Knight, this is my good friend, and occasional gambling partner, Mr. Osborne."

Miss Knight curtsied and said, "Mr. Osborne. I have brought three more books which I think are rare editions. And, I confess, that I wished to meet the man with whom I am conducting business with."

"Thorne has spoken highly of you, Miss Knight. It is a great pleasure to meet you." Mr. Osborne gave her a wide smile of excellent teeth. Though, the smile faded immediately as a solemn tone entered his voice. "And, of course, my condolences and sorrow at the loss of your uncle. He was an excellent man. He's how I met your friend, Thorne, here."

"Mr. Thorne! You never told me that."

"I had forgotten it!"

"Well, Mr. Osborne, I do not wish to keep you from your trade. However, I did want to bring these three books out. Oh, and here is the most recent inventory list. We are still working on the list, but I made a line here, see? So that's where the new items began being added." She handed over the three volumes. "I have particular interest in this one, as the title is quite fetching. *The Society of London Occultists, Complete with Forays into Summoning the Ghosts of*

The Greatest Men and even Women of England: a primer on incantations, spells, and summoning. It has the publication date as 1603 and I believe it is a first printing. I was hoping the age and the quality of the book itself would fetch me a higher price. Perhaps, if I could be so bold, a guinea?"

Mr. Osborne accepted the list, but refused to accept the books, staring openly at them. "Miss Knight? Where did you get that book?"

"It was my uncle's."

Mr. Osborne's voice turned hushed, as though he were in the presence of a holy relic. "My dear lady, you cannot sell this."

"Why ever not?" Elizabeth asked.

"What's wrong with it?" Henry Thorne asked.

"There are only three copies left in England. Of this book." Mr. Osborne shook his head. "I cannot, in good conscience, buy this from you. I cannot afford it."

Elizabeth looked down at the rather plain, somewhat dusty book. "How much is it worth then? It has handwritten notes inside. Will that bring down the price?"

Mr. Osborne blinked. He motioned at James and requested his gloves. Once putting them back on, he reached out and asked, "May I touch it?"

A strange protective feeling hit Elizabeth, but she dutifully passed the book over. With his gloved hands, he carefully turned each page. When he stumbled upon the blank sections between chapters and volumes, his hands began to tremble.

"Osborne? Good God, man. Are you well?"

"Miss Knight." Mr. Osborne licked his lips. "Do not allow anyone to know of this book's existence that you do not trust with your own life."

"Osborne!" Mr. Thorne said. "Miss Knight is…"

"Holding a book worth almost as much as your income, Thorne."

Elizabeth whispered, "What?"

Mr. Osborne shakingly held the book out to her with both of his hands. Once she accepted it, he let out a breath. "Miss Knight. I consider myself a man of morals and principles, and I have the reputation of never having knowingly cheated a single person in my life. And, I confess to you now that, so that you understand what you possess, for a fleeting moment, even I considered lying to you by handing over a guinea for that book. If I may be so bold as to offer my advice to a young lady, squirrel that book away until you were certain you trusted the person responsible for that book's auction."

"Are you implying I should not tell my family?"

Mr. Osborne glanced at Mr. Thorne. "My friend here has told me a little of your family's situation. This book represents the kind of money that men have killed over. If I were you, I would keep it until you absolutely required the money. Then, I would give it to Mrs. Spencer for her to hire an attorney and a bookseller to arrange a full and public auction. And then, for her to put the money aside into an inheritance for you so that only you can touch it. That is my professional opinion."

Elizabeth struggled to breathe. "This book was a part of my uncle's private collection that he left me. Would he have known its worth?"

Mr. Osborne smiled. "My dear, he absolutely would have known that he was giving you a book that was worth at least three thousand pounds. That is my conservative estimate."

"I feel a little faint," Elizabeth said. A giggle escaped her. She stumbled and sat upon the piano's stool. "No one could afford a book worth that."

"The Royal Occult Society once bought a collection of books worth eight thousand pounds. The American Society of Occultists have representatives living in London and across Europe for the hope of procuring one of these rare books."

"Three thousand pounds," Elizabeth whispered.

"Maria will be thrilled for you!" Mr. Thorne said.

"No, Thorne. No. Miss Knight, for your own protection, please, keep this a secret for as long as possible. If necessary, tell Mrs. Spencer and her alone."

"I cannot keep a secret from Maria," Mr. Thorne said. "She is my wife, Osborne."

"Do you trust her with this?"

"Absolutely," Mr. Thorne said, with a conviction that warmed Elizabeth's heart. "I tease Maria and scold her far more than I know I should, but she is truly the best woman in England. And for all the worry and trouble I have given her, she would never think to do anything hurtful upon me in revenge. And, besides that, she would never harm Miss Knight."

Elizabeth smiled at her dearest friend's husband and asked, "Mr. Thorne. Have you ever considered telling Maria any of that?"

"Goodness, no." Henry laughed. "She might start liking me! We can't have that!"

"Then, Miss Knight," Mr. Osborne said. "My professional recommendation is that you tell only Mrs. Spencer when you can, knowing that Thorne here cannot keep secrets from his wife. And hide that book away. Guard it with your life."

"I will, Mr. Osborne. And, thank you for your honesty. There are a great many men in this world who would have taken advantage of me and my circumstances."

Mr. Osborne's cheeks darkened. He looked down at the floor and laughed awkwardly. "Well. How could I look Thorne in the eye again, knowing that I cheated a dear friend of his wife's? Now, I suppose I still need to buy some less expensive books! Miss Knight? Are you well?"

"I am…yes. Yes, I am well. I believe I shall hide this book. Mr. Thorne? Would you be so good as to wait for me to tell Maria?"

"If you wish," Mr. Thorne said. "You will tell her, though?"

"Yes. Just not yet. I need to consider a great many things."

"That is probably wise," Mr. Osborne said.

✢ Chapter 9 ✢

ONCE SUFFICIENTLY RECOVERED, Elizabeth carefully walked back to the dining room. Her feet stung a little from the pressure, but her euphoria blurred out most of the pain. Three thousand pounds. That was easily one hundred pounds per annum in interest. Together with the inheritance she already received from her uncle, she could make upwards of one hundred seventy-five pounds. Every. Year. For the rest of her life.

She could support her younger sisters, in the event of her father's death.

She could support Isabella, if needed.

She would not have to ask Charles for a single shilling.

Elizabeth leaned against the wall in the foyer. Her vision blurred and she felt the faintness come upon her again. She was saved.

She told herself to be calm. After all, there was no guarantee with an auction. She would require a great many trustworthy individuals to pull off such an event, and it would take time to arrange that. And she could not ask Aunt Cass to engage in that level of business when her last living brother was only lately put into the ground. No. She must be calm. She must exercise restraint.

Three thousand pounds.

Her heart skipped several beats while it leapt into her throat to regain its agitated state once more.

Three thousand pounds.

"Miss Knight?"

Elizabeth stared at Sally. "Yes?"

"Are you well?"

"Why…why do you ask?"

"You have been staring at that potted plant for several minutes."

Elizabeth blinked her eyes and took inventory of her surroundings and discovered that, indeed, she had been staring at a potted plant. "Oh. No. Sorry. I got distracted and needed to order my thoughts before I went back to…sorting the books. I apologize for worrying you."

Sally did not look convinced, but nodded and said, "Very well, miss. Did you need my help walking?"

"Yes, please, if it won't take away from your duties."

"No, miss."

Sally helped Elizabeth up the stairs to the drawing room where she faced her aunt and dear friend. She put on a warm smile for them, though she did attempt to bring herself down to the calm and even Elizabeth that they were expecting.

"Goodness, Eliza! You look out of sorts!"

"Did Mr. Osborne not want that book?" Aunt Cass asked. "We can put it in with the general auction books."

Elizabeth tightened her grip on the book. She did release it eventually, correcting her reflexive behaviour, but not in time for the others not to notice. At Aunt Cass' inquisitive expression, Elizabeth said, "I wish to keep this book. Please remove it from all of the lists."

"Is that not the book Mrs. Egerton thought would fetch a good price?" Maria asked.

"I wish to remove it from the lists," Elizabeth insisted.

"Of course, I'll do as you wish. But why?" Maria asked.

"Did Mr. Osborne say something to upset you?"

Elizabeth did not wish to lie, but she also knew both her aunt and friend well enough to know that asking them not to pry would only bring out more curiosity, not less. And, for now, she wished to keep this information to herself until she had an opportunity to think through the implications.

"I believe my uncle wished me to keep this one. Thus, it will not be for sale and I do not wish to experience any coercion to sell."

"If you feel that strongly, I shall strike it off the lists immediately," Maria said.

"Thank you, I shall put this upstairs before it becomes misplaced."

Elizabeth assured everyone that she could walk unassisted, and delighted in the several minutes of solitude. It helped order her thoughts and helped calm her excitement. After all, the worry of the book's sale began to settle in and she wondered if selling it for ten pounds might end up being the best option for her.

She placed the book in the trunk with the other autograph books. It was her trunk, left to her from her uncle, so there was no worry about it accidentally being returned to Mr. David Leigh. And this would allow her some time to figure out what to do.

Each time she considered her options, her heart began pounding loudly in her chest. The worry and uncertainty of attempting to sell such an item was so beyond her abilities, experiences, and indeed even her knowledge, that it completely overwhelmed her.

She told herself, rather sternly, that Mr. Thorne would assist her. Mr. Osborne, too, seemed a very trustworthy gentleman, who could have taken advantage of her ignorance and yet did not. Both her uncle and Mr. Thorne trusted Mr. Osborne. If her financial situation ever became dire, she could ask Henry Thorne to write to Mr. Osborne and request assistance.

Her heart began to settle back to its regular rhythm and she decided that it was not yet time to deal with the book. She would make decisions once she had sorted the library in its entirety. Then, and only then, would she address this apparently life-changing book.

Sense. Caution. Wits.

This was the proper path to a decision that she would not later regret. Caution must guide her. Greed must not.

Fortified with that decision, her anxieties mostly faded. Before her lay a path. Sorting. Selling. More sorting. More selling. Finding homes for what was left. And, finally, her eventual return to Bryden. Then, the knowledge of the book's existence might be all she needed to walk through life as an unmarried woman.

Elizabeth smiled. She could do this.

MR. OSBORNE SHOCKINGLY purchased three full crates of books. He had long been attempting to branch out more into occult materials for the general public and was very pleased by the diversity of Elizabeth's collection. He took half of the botany books, a quarter of the farming books, and several of the historical occult books. He even took two occult novels. He was uncertain if those would sell, but he felt it was worth the one-shilling risk.

All total, Elizabeth was presented later that day with eight pounds, nine shillings, and three pence.

At first, she vowed not to count the money, however, Maria insisted upon seeing the money laid out on the dining room table. Even Aunt Cass asked to see it.

She counted the coins and the bills and exclaimed, "My god! In total, including what I arrived in London with, I have over eighteen pounds!"

Aunt Cass gave her a hug and said, "I never thought I'd be so excited by trade."

"Indeed!" Maria said. "It is a bit like gambling."

Elizabeth let out a laugh. "Only more profitable!"

"Ladies, if I may interrupt the giggling," Henry Thorne said as he walked into the room. "With your permission, I must be off. I have received a letter from the Earl of Essex. He is in town, visiting a sick family member, and would like to see the book list."

"I thought he collected art," Aunt Cass said.

"Indeed, Mrs. Spencer. However, it says in his letter that he is looking for three specific books, and wished to know if we were in possession of them."

"And are we?" Elizabeth said.

"In fact, we are in possession of various editions." Henry glanced at the list and said, "Oh, excellent, Maria! You even noted the books with damage. Oh, you are a treasure."

"I aim to be thorough in all things," Maria said.

"That is why I married you, my dear!"

"I thought it was my rather large dowry?"

That brought a roar of laughter from Henry Thorne. "Well, that is why my family granted me permission!"

"Oh, Henry! Get out before Mrs. Spencer thinks ill of us."

Aunt Cass laughed. "My dear Mrs. Thorne, I come from a time when husband and wife did not even have to like each other to be married. I believe it was a full decade before I even liked my dear George, may God rest his soul."

"Aunt Cass! I know very well that you adored Uncle Spencer."

Aunt Cass tutted. "You young people and your notions. Be off with you, Mr. Thorne! We rely upon your bargaining skills to fetch my niece an excellent price."

Henry Thorne bowed deeply, as if he were addressing a duchess. "At your command, my dear woman."

"Get out, Henry," Maria chided.

Henry gave a final short bow and then waved to the ladies.

"Mrs. Thorne, I believe you are too hard on your husband."

A chuckle escaped Elizabeth, bringing a scowl from her friend. "I married a scoundrel, Mrs. Spencer. A handsome, affable, good-hearted scoundrel. One smile from that man and I lose all resolve. My only protection is for him to think he still has to win my entire affection."

"You married him. He already won, my dear Mrs. Thorne."

"Ah, but with Henry, that was only a battle." Maria lifted her chin. "I shall win the war."

Elizabeth shook her head, unable to hold back her laughter. "The two of you are impossibly stubborn."

"What has Henry said to you?"

"I do not break confidences, Maria Cuthbert Thorne, of which you know."

Mrs. Egerton sighed. "Ladies? Might we get back to work please? We currently have more books to sort through than what the king of England possesses."

"I believe that is an exaggeration, Mrs. Egerton," Elizabeth said, careful not to put any chiding or sternness in her voice.

For her part, Mrs. Egerton made a displeased sound, which was answer enough for Elizabeth. The ladies chatted as they sorted. Aunt Cass was feeling fatigued, so she took on the role of scribe, and continued the task of writing out the books that were sorted into each crate and trunk. It was a tedious task, but it was necessary work.

Elizabeth had spent too long upon her feet, and she began to feel the throbbing in her heel. She attempted to ignore it, but soon a limp formed, which set her aunt and friend into a whirl of worry. James promptly placed a chair next to the sideboard for Elizabeth's convenience, and assisted her into the chair.

"Thank you, James," Elizabeth said, feeling rather embarrassed by the scene.

"Would you like a glass of wine, Miss?" James asked.

"May I have tea instead? If it isn't any trouble, of course."

"I will inform Mrs. Cook," James said. To his mistress, he asked, "Ma'am?"

"Ask Cook if we can have a light tray of food."

"Nothing extravagant, please," Elizabeth insisted. "A bit of bread and butter would be very acceptable."

"Yes, miss. I'll let her know."

Food and tea was delivered and Aunt Cass asked James to close the door to the drawing room. He did so, and then they went back to work.

"Mrs. Egerton? I am feeling very overwhelmed by the choices before me. May I read out some of these titles for you to assist?"

"My dear girl, why else am I here?"

Elizabeth successfully covered a laugh with a cough, made more difficult by Maria making faces at Aunt Cass, and then her aunt attempting to swat Maria into silence.

The Adventures of An Irish Occultist, Interspersed with Whimsical Anecdotes of A Bottle (1744).

"Oh, put it in the sale pile. That will appeal to an older bachelor. Insipid book."

The History of a Young Lady, Who Was Ruined By Her Excessive Affection for The Occult. With notes by men of sense. (1797)

"This is why I believe there should be laws preventing the publication of this filth. Men of sense. Ha! They wished a woman would call them that."

The Amorous Adventures of the Famed Italian Occultist, an autobiography (1729).

"I am the lady in the red cap. That is the only faithful part of the tale."

"You are mentioned in this book about amorous adventures?" Aunt Cass asked.

"Indeed, Mrs. Spencer. Now, if you please, into the For Sale crate."

A twinkle formed in Aunt Cass' eye that Elizabeth knew well. "Niece, I shall give you a shilling for this book."

"Mrs. Spencer!" Mrs. Egerton said sternly.

"One shilling six," Maria said with a wink.

Mrs. Egerton sighed.

"Aunt, Maria, I believe Mrs. Egerton would prefer her privacy in this matter," Elizabeth said. "So, I shall place the book upon the top of the pile where I am certain neither of you will violate her wishes."

"I do not understand why you are not married," Mrs. Egerton said.

"No one is good enough for her," Maria said.

"That is unfair, Maria Thorne!" Elizabeth said sternly.

"Though accurate," Aunt Cass muttered. She offered her niece a smile when caught.

After a few more minutes of good-natured discussion, and a cup of tea, Elizabeth sighed and said, "This is going to take forever. There is still my bedchamber yet."

"Don't forget the dining room," Maria added helpfully.

"I forgot what my dining room looks like," Aunt Cass said.

Mrs. Egerton made a sound that seemed to announce she had come to a decision. "Miss Knight. Please open my book to my autograph. Now, turn the page. Good. Read the incantation out loud if you please."

Elizabeth followed the instructions, though first asked before reading aloud, "What will the spell do?"

"I will be released from the page and go about assisting you."

Elizabeth looked at Aunt Cass. "Should I?"

"Why are you asking her?" the book demanded. "I am right here, you know."

"It is my aunt's house, Mrs. Egerton. I wish to be a considerate guest."

Aunt Cass shrugged. "If there are problems, I'm sure we could call in the Royal Occult Society, as a favour, to help."

"Oh, please!" Mrs. Egerton scoffed. "That group of pompous old men would not know how to conjure the spirit of a dead pigeon. Now, hurry up. We have work to do."

Elizabeth glanced about, only to endure another wave of caustic commentary from Mrs. Egerton. Elizabeth braved up and read the incantation:

Spirit of Chocolate and Roses, Join Our Quest.

"That cannot be correct," Elizabeth said frowning down at the book. "What does that even mean? Oh!"

Elizabeth dropped the book. Mrs. Egerton stood in front of her, wearing a red riding habit from the previous century. She'd never seen such a masculine cut on a woman before, outside of paintings. A tricorne hat perched perfectly upon Mrs. Egerton's elaborate curls that somehow seemed real and not the work of a wig. Elegant blue satin shoes with heavy embroidery poked out from her hem.

Mrs. Egerton squared her shoulders. "Well now. That is better. Bring the book, if you please. Keep it safe and away from wet or fire. The incantation only works if the book is in view of me. Please remember that I am visible to anyone like this, and they can hear me. Therefore, exercise extreme caution. I also cannot go out of doors."

"Why not?" Maria asked in an awed voice. "Will the sunlight banish you?"

"Of course not, my dear Mrs. Thorne. This is *London*. I'd rather it not rain suddenly and dampen my hair. It will take hours of spellwork to fix the damage."

Elizabeth reached out to touch Mrs. Egerton's hair, but a fan slapped her hand hard enough to make it sting. "Do not touch a lady's hair."

Elizabeth rubbed at her stinging hand. "That hurt."

"It was meant to. Were you raised in a barn, child?"

"How are you able to do that?" Maria asked. "I thought ghosts were, well, *ghostly*."

It was apparent, however, that Mrs. Egerton did not wish to engage in a metaphysical discussion about ghosts manifesting. "Do you wish my assistance with the books, or do you desire a lecture on the nature of the occult? I can only do one of those tasks with the finite time granted to my existence."

"Finite time? What does that mean?" Elizabeth asked. "Mrs. Egerton, are you dying? I understand that you are a ghost, of course, but…can a ghost fade?"

"Indeed, Mrs. Egerton. I am now rather a little worried for you," Aunt Cass said.

"Is there a way we can help you?" Maria asked.

Mrs. Egerton sighed, though this sound was more weary than annoyed. A small smile came upon her face. "One of the pleasures of working with women is their consideration of others. I have been told that it is by habit, and not divine design, however, I do not know how to raise a man to have this habit."

Elizabeth smiled back at the ghost. "Perhaps the confinement of society is what makes us ladies consider the other ladies in this polite prison."

"Elizabeth!" Aunt Cass scolded. "Your life is not a prison. Surely, you do not mean that."

"Only some days, Aunt." Turning to Mrs. Egerton, who was silent for the exchange, Elizabeth said, "I would like you to tell us what you meant, if you are able, of course."

"Shall we have tea first?" Mrs. Egerton asked.

"Do you…can you drink tea?" Aunt Cass asked.

"Of course, I can drink tea," Mrs. Egerton said with disgust. "What am I? French?"

Elizabeth whispered, "My dear, Mrs. Egerton. I do believe the French also drink tea."

Mrs. Egerton's only answer was a snort of derision.

Aunt Cass leaned forward and whispered, "Where does it go?"

Mrs. Egerton rolled her eyes. "Are all ladies this curious? Goodness, how did men end up hiding you away from the occult if you are all so desperate for knowledge? If you must know, this body is formed by an incantation that gathers about the water and dust around me. If I were to drink tea, the small bits that I do not need go back out around me. Perhaps a little condensation will form on a window nearest me."

"That is amazing," Maria said.

"But, what is it that you need to tell us?" Elizabeth asked. Gracious, her aunt and friend were more curious about the ghost than she was!

"Thank you for bringing us back to the important information, Miss Knight. The incantation you used to summon me is limited. I will be available to appear as this for about a fortnight or so and then the spell will fade permanently. From there, Miss Knight will have to learn how to do the incantations herself to bring me forth."

"Surely, you could help, Mrs. Egerton," Elizabeth said.

"Only while in this form," the ghost said. "Once the magic that was stored in the book for your use is gone, it is gone. That means I will be once again locked away in slumber until you can unlock it. Therefore, I suggest that we sort through these books, set aside all that you will need, and then get to work assembling your team of occult experts."

Elizabeth blinked. "Team of occult experts? I need a team?"

"Indeed. You have no magical training, beyond your uncle's limited instruction. I assume you are not a master of magical botany, chemicals, medicine, Latin, or Greek? I leave off French and Italian, since all girls of decent upbringing know those languages."

"I do not, beyond what I have taught myself," Elizabeth said softly.

"Not even French?" Mrs. Egerton exclaimed. "Good God, child. What kind of country upbringing did you have?"

"My stepmother and father did not approve of girls learning languages. They preferred to teach more useful pursuits, such as sewing, accounts, and reading."

"How lucky we are that you can read a sentence, then," Mrs. Egerton's caustic voice said.

Elizabeth winced at the criticism. "I am sorry, ma'am, but I must defend my stepmother on this score. She was only doing what she felt was right. I am, after all, nothing but the penniless daughter of a country rector. At best, I would marry a country squire. I was sent to a school to help with the things I would need most in life. Accounts, sewing, reading. Those are useful skills for a wife, who will then have to teach her own children. I do not fault my stepmother and I kindly ask that no one criticize her in my hearing."

"Eliza…" Maria said with a lot of kindness in her voice. "Augusta Knight was awful to you."

"Nevertheless," Elizabeth said. "I must insist upon silence on this matter."

"Well," Mrs. Egerton said, interrupting the two friends. "In any case, there is no point to dwell on insufficient parents. We have work to do."

⁓⧼ Chapter 10 ⧽⁓

AND SO IT went the afternoon: the three real ladies worked with the ghostly assistance of a fourth. It eased Elizabeth's own grief to hear the ghost share outrageous stories of her uncle, things he always kept from his dear niece's ear. The tales also helped reinforce that her uncle was a powerful occultist in his own right, and Mrs. Egerton said he would not have chosen his niece as his successor if he doubted her intelligence. Finally, after what was clearly a tall tale, Aunt Cass had enough. "Mrs. Egerton. Ghostly being or not, I must insist you tell the truth to my niece about her uncle."

"I have uttered no falsehood, Mrs. Spencer, I can assure you. He was quite a character when he wished to be."

"He was my own brother, I already knew that," Aunt Cass said. "My objection is merely that I do not wish my niece to endure an altered perception of her uncle."

Mrs. Egerton made a dismissive sound, very unladylike. It was the one Elizabeth's first stepmother would make to her younger siblings when trying to herd them toward the weekly bathes. "Do you mean to tell me that Mr. Leigh never told you that he once sassed the king?"

Elizabeth giggled behind her hand. "I can believe it! I know the king visited the Royal Occult Society on occasion, and I knew he wasn't completely approving of the occult."

"Except when it benefited him, of course," Mrs. Egerton said.

"That's only to be expected," Aunt Cass said. "Royalty does as royalty must. Oh, that must be the new shipment. David said he was going to return with magical implements."

"Oh, excellent. We shall need those," Mrs. Egerton said. "Now, Miss Knight? Be a dear and read the incantation that is under the one you read to summon me. It will reduce me to my voice form, and that will use less of the stored magic. And I do not wish to appear before Mr. David Leigh."

Elizabeth readily agreed and picked up the book. She stared at the line and read it to herself. She gave Mrs. Egerton an exasperated look and said, "Roses faded, and chocolate consumed, the quest is now complete."

Mrs. Egerton's form dissolved before Elizabeth's eyes in a puff of dust and a cloud of water droplets.

"How extraordinary," Maria said.

"Get to the other drawing room, child," Mrs. Egerton's disembodied voice said.

Elizabeth walked behind Maria and her aunt toward the drawing room. It was still set up for the booksellers, but at least it was well organized and tidy. She carried the autograph book, along with several sheets of paper that were the ongoing book inventory list that Aunt Cass had copied.

Mr. David Leigh was still in the foyer, passing his hat to the butler. "Good day, ladies. I bring the final shipment of implements, including the silver bowl Mrs. Cook requested. I trust this has not been too inconvenient, Cousin."

Elizabeth smiled. "It has been a distraction, I must say."

"Good, good. Sometimes, the best cure for grief is a distraction. I was happy to have offered a small token of assistance."

"Will you stay for tea, David?" Aunt Cass asked.

"No, no. I must not. I only wished to drop by for a quarter of an hour to say I have completed the task of emptying the occult section of the library. I also wanted to let you know, in person, that my dear Miss Reeves must cancel her visit next week. She has taken with a terrible sore throat and now has a fever."

"Oh dear. That is terrible news," Aunt Cass said in a tone that suggested she didn't care in the slightest. "Do you know if it is an infectious condition, or was it because she caught cold?"

"The physician believes she overheated herself at the Campbells' ball the other night, and that it should pass soon enough. However, he is obviously cautious, so recommends she stay at home until the affliction has lifted."

"Then I wish her a steady recovery," Aunt Cass said. "Come. Elizabeth's foot is not yet healed from the break in, and I do not wish her standing for long periods of time."

Apparently, David Leigh had not heard of the event, and was most desirous of the minute details. By the time it was finished, he exclaimed, "Are you certain you are well?"

"Oh, yes! I am rather embarrassed to say that most of the damage that was done by my own hand!" Elizabeth said. "My foot is well wrapped, and the apothecary used a magnifying glass to ensure even the smallest of shards were pulled from under the skin. I am to soak my foot in warm, salted water every night, on the slightest chance that there would be infection."

"He also assured us that the warm soak would draw any remaining shards out," Aunt Cass said. "Though, I confess he was very thorough with cleaning the wound."

"And, of course, I will follow the instructions exactly. One must not argue with medical advice. But I must say that, even today, my foot is much improved. I believe a comforting soak before bed and a good night's rest, and I might be able to go without a bandage soon." Elizabeth smiled. "Honestly, I believe everyone else has been more terrified by this than myself."

"House-breaking." Mr. David Leigh shook his head gravely. "And in this part of town. What has become of the world?"

"No one was harmed beyond repair, which is all that I care about," Elizabeth said. "Now, would you like to hear about the books and what we have decided thus far?"

"Oh! Have you made decisions yet, Cousin Elizabeth? Miss Reeves is beside herself awaiting details!"

Elizabeth was relieved to change the subject away from the terrible event, so began explaining their current system of inventory and sorting. She happily told him of Mr. Osborne's recent visit and his purchases.

"How extraordinary! My Miss Reeves was hopeful you would earn upwards of one hundred pounds from the books. For myself, I confess I thought you would not make twenty guineas." He smiled, and it lit up his face. "It appears that my Miss Reeves is far better at business than I. I shall put her in charge of all major household decisions!"

"A sensible woman, David, is a blessing," Aunt Cass said without hiding her approval of Miss Reeves. "But a woman who understands how to turn a shilling into a pound is worth her weight in gold, for she will never lead her household into debt. I am very happy that you have chosen such a woman."

"Thank you, Aunt. Indeed, I am the happiest of men. I also confess that this eases so much of my guilt concerning the inheritance of both the estate and the townhouse." He smiled. "Indeed, this is excellent news."

Elizabeth struggled to reconcile the changeable nature of her cousin. She longed to point out his behaviour to his servant. However, Aunt Cass said she would handle it, and Elizabeth was determined to honour her word. No, she would keep her thoughts to herself. And she would share some of her newfound wealth with Mrs. Taylor and her niece, Susan.

"Oh! We have one empty crate and one small trunk that is yours, that we can return to you," Elizabeth said, interrupting the conversation between her aunt and cousin. "I apologize for interrupting, of course. However, if I do not tell you, then I worry I shall forget. They are in the corner behind the entrance door, just there."

"Oh, excellent! Those are Mr. Wilcox's. An excellent man. He is single, you know, Cousin Elizabeth."

Elizabeth forced a smile. "I have no thoughts of marriage at present, Cousin David."

"Oh, you young ladies always say you have no thoughts of marriage and then are swept off your feet when the first man comes along."

"I hate to disagree with anyone, especially not a relation, but I fear I must. After all, a young lady rarely marries the first man she falls in love with."

David Leigh shook his head, laughing. "My dear cousin! We shall never marry you off at this rate! Think of your family."

Desperate the change the subject again, she exclaimed, "I believe you know my uncle's lawyer, Mr. Grant? He wrote to Mr. Thorne earlier today that he knows of a bookseller in Manchester who is interested in occult history books. He thinks I might receive four guineas for one of the small collections I've arranged! Shall I have him forward you half the proceeds?"

"My dear cousin, I could not possibly take a farthing from you. No, indeed! It was my pleasure to provide you what I feel my uncle would have wished." Mr. Leigh puffed out his chest. "Indeed, I feel my uncle was trying to balance what was due by the law and what was right in Christian charity to a relation in your particular and unfortunate circumstance."

Elizabeth held her tongue and managed not to comment upon how she was diseased in her cousin's eyes.

"And, as I am personally affronted by the occult in my own home, I feel that this was the best way to carry out providing you with additional financial security all the while ensuring my conscience remains clear on two accounts. One, being free of the occult and all its evil influences, and two, being supportive of my dear, unmarried, poor cousin." He leaned forward. "And, of course, Miss Reeves is very much against the occult. It frightens her to her core. However, she is so forgiving and kind, that she understands you will need any source of income to help ease the burden of your relations, who will have to support you throughout your life. She is, indeed, an excellent woman."

"Indeed." Aunt Cass said. "Then, David, would you welcome Miss Knight donating some of the proceeds to help those in need?"

Elizabeth glanced at her aunt; she knew that intense look anywhere. Indeed, her aunt was about to launch an offensive that Lord Wellington himself would envy.

"In your name, of course, cousin," Elizabeth said, adding as much honey to her voice as possible.

"I would be honoured, my dearest cousin. Honoured, I tell you. You do your father proud. What an excellent young lady he has raised."

Elizabeth glanced at her aunt, who gave the slightest incline of her head. She was to lead the offensive. "Then, Cousin David, I have decided to seek out my uncle's servants and assist them in some small way. They were always so good to him, and I believe it is our Christian duty to look after servants well after their years of usefulness ends."

David Leigh's smile flickered, but he covered up the reaction quickly enough. "I think that is a splendid idea. Very genteel. Very proper. Now, Aunt Cassandra, I do hope I have not inconvenienced you too much?"

"No, it is the way of life. After all, you had to take possession of the house immediately. There was, no doubt, so much for you to look after that the library could not wait."

"You're quite right," Mr. Leigh said, not even noticing his aunt's tone of annoyance. "One cannot imagine the state of the papers, and the furniture! I will need to take most of my income this year to upholster all of the chairs, for they are in an abysmal condition. As it is, I had a mind to throw Uncle Edward's old chair upon the garbage heap myself!"

"If I may be so bold, cousin," Elizabeth asked. "Might I have it, before it ends up upon the heap in a pique of frustration? I have very fond memories of him reading to me from that chair. If it is possible at all, I would like to have it. I can have Charles arrange the details of transporting it back to Bryden."

David Leigh laughed again, only it was the nervous laugh that he was caught in an exaggeration. "Alas, my dearest cousin, I was merely being my old self. I have given the chair to an old servant of my uncle's. She wished assistance furnishing her new apartments and requested if I had any old thing about the house. Therefore, I gave it to her. I thought it was a proper and good chair, and that it could remind her of the fond memories of working in the household. But, alas, I could not keep her in my employ. She insisted upon going to care for her sickly niece. So, the chair went with her."

"How kind of you," Elizabeth said in an even tone. She didn't believe it for a moment that Mrs. Taylor had requested the chair, or that he had provided it. In fact, she expected to hear from Maria's housekeeper in the next day or two that a furniture delivery would have been made to West Alley Buildings from a Mr. Leigh.

"Speaking of!" David Leigh made a show of looking at his pocket watch. "I apologize, Aunt, perhaps I should have taken you upon the offer of tea! The time, how it gets away from me! But I must tell you this before I forget. Some gentlemen from the Royal Occult Society came by my house yesterday to inquire about the books I gave you. They offered me a sum of twenty pounds if I could fetch a couple of the books from you. I have a list."

Elizabeth accepted the list from her cousin. It was the autograph books, and a couple of others she did not recognize.

"They were here, as well. However, they only offered me ten pounds," Elizabeth said.

"Well, it is a large sum of money for a young lady to have all at once," David Leigh said.

Aunt Cass' polite façade slipped. "David. Please do not enter negotiations with these people on any topic without first consulting me."

"I was merely attempting to reduce the stress of this difficult time and—"

"David Abraham Leigh. Do not, under any circumstances, engage with these gentlemen or that organization regarding anything to do with the books that are now located in this house. Have I made myself completely clear?"

"Aunt, as the man of the family, it is my duty—"

Elizabeth flinched. She knew what was coming.

"Your duty, *sir*, was to care for my brother's elderly servant, and not to kick her to the streets without a farthing to her name."

The room went silent. Aunt Cass did not raise her voice. She did not shout. She did not curse. In fact, if one could not see the sharpness of her expression, they might mistake the anger behind her words. It was a gift, Elizabeth supposed.

"I believe you have been misinformed, Aunt."

Elizabeth did not shake her head at her cousin, no matter how tempted she might have been. How could he continue to pretend they were in ignorance?

"Mrs. Thorne's housekeeper has been to visit them. My own servants have been bringing food to them, to keep them from starving." Aunt Cass lifted her chin. "Now, David, you shall do *exactly* as I say, or I will let all of London know what a black-hearted villain you truly are."

David's mouth widened in shock. He then began to speak, but he stumbled over his words.

"Do you take my meaning, nephew? I will not allow this kind of behaviour in my house," Aunt Cass continued. "And, do not forget that this house, and my considerable fortune—the only living person who truly knows the extent of which is my lawyer, who is paid very well to keep it a secret—are all mine to dispense with as I please upon my death. And, be warned, nephew, I am very happy to change my will."

Shock hit David, as it finally sunk into his head what his aunt was threatening. A little of the shock hit Elizabeth, too. What did her aunt mean by the comment about the extent of her fortune? Was it not common knowledge that Aunt Cass had an annual income of four thousand a year? Her aunt was very comfortable, but as far as Elizabeth knew, the London property was the only house her aunt owned. It wasn't as if her aunt could bring in more money. Could she?

There was no time for Elizabeth's wonderings about her aunt's financial situation, however, as David Leigh had finally discovered his sense God had given him, and was now making proper use of it.

"Yes, Aunt. Of course. I meant no offense. What do you wish me to do? Anything to please you, of course."

"Nothing," Aunt Cass said.

"Aunt?"

"Aunt Cass?" Elizabeth asked at the same time. The cousins shared a confused glance between them, before both turning to their aunt.

"David. I wish you to do nothing at present. We are fixing the situation with your servant, and we are doing it all under your name. We will use the proceeds from the book sales to provide her a proper retirement, befitting her long service to my brother, and in consideration for her current situation. Do you agree, Elizabeth?"

"Yes, Aunt. The books are from Cousin David, and I do believe funds from those books could, no indeed should, be used to assist those of our greater family."

Elizabeth had a fleeting moment of disappointment that she would not enjoy all the profits of the auctions, but she quickly, and most properly, chastised that from her mind. She was not the kind of young woman to delight in another's suffering if it profited her. No. Her aunt was very correct: the books had come from Uncle Edward's house. The books shall help elevate all those touched by Uncle Edward in life and now with his death.

"In fact, now that I consider upon it, perhaps that was Miss Reeves' expectation all along! Oh, of course, Cousin David! How could I have missed it?"

It was the nephew and aunt's turn to exchange a confused glance.

"Miss Reeves is, no doubt, a demure, quiet creature, if I understand her reputation correctly from how you have presented her. Most likely, she felt unequal to laying out a plan for assistance with the library book sales. And, she knew that you were so very busy with your relocation to deal with that added worry." Elizabeth faked a cough, in an attempt to figure out the rest of her fanciful tale of Miss Reeves. "Oh, of course! Miss Reeves is truly frightened by the occult. However, she is also a good Christian woman who would not want you, Cousin David, to have to choose between accommodating her wishes and your own duty as a master. Oh, I would very much like to meet your Miss Reeves."

Thankfully, David Leigh did not see his aunt roll her eyes. Instead, his face lit up. "I swear upon my honour, Cousin Elizabeth, you truly do think the best of every human being upon this soil, don't you? Now that you lay it out, it all makes perfect sense. I should have seen it before. Yes, indeed. Of course! Of course. Miss Reeves will be forcing me to be a better man than I have ever right to be."

He glanced at his aunt and deflated immediately. Elizabeth had bolstered the future Mrs. Leigh's reputation in her husband's eyes that, she hoped, would ensure some kindness from both in the future. After all, David Leigh had managed not to disinherit himself today and Elizabeth's father was not getting any younger; she might need her cousin's help in the future.

Aunt Cass, however, was not through with her nephew. "Now that we have established Miss Reeves to be a calculating woman of excellent character who will clearly be using her knowledge and insight for the good of humanity, there is still the matter of the Royal Occult Society."

"Yes, Aunt. Of course, Aunt. What else do you wish of me?"

"You will cease all contact with the Royal Occult Society and will not enter into any form of negotiation with those gentlemen on behave of myself or my niece."

"Yes, Aunt. I will do exactly as you wish. Shall I direct them to you personally or to Mr. Grant?"

"Follow your good sense on that matter. Or, if you are uncertain, consult your Miss Reeves. But myself and Mr. Grant are your only choices in this matter. Do you understand?"

"Completely, Aunt." David Leigh cleared his throat. "I am so very sorry to have caused offense, Aunt Cassandra. And to you, Cousin Elizabeth. I had not meant to insult you at all, and I heartily apologize for my actions. I was attempting to be useful."

"In the future, I recommend you ask how best to be useful, as opposed to making assumptions," Aunt Cass said. "Now, if I recall, you have an ill lady to visit, and I would hate to keep her waiting. And, please, extend my best wishes on her recovery. I find myself growing more curious of our introduction with each day."

"I will happily pass along your wishes, Aunt. She will be very pleased to hear you look forward to meeting her. Again, I apologize for the offense. Good day, ladies."

After the door closed, Mrs. Egerton's disembodied voice broke the shocked silence. "Oh, well done, Mrs. Spencer! Well done, indeed."

Elizabeth stared at her aunt. "You threatened his inheritance!"

"My dear niece. What is the point of having money if I cannot use it as a weapon?"

"What if you anger him?"

"Elizabeth, my dear girl. You *do* know how much I am worth, surely?"

Elizabeth tried not to scold her aunt, but a little hint of it crept into her voice. "Aunt. Four thousand pounds is a lot of money, yes, but you should not use it as a weapon, as you call it."

An amused look came across Aunt Cass' face. "Four thousand pounds, you say? Well. I believe I shall raise Mr. Grant's salary."

Elizabeth had no idea what her aunt meant. "I did not know Mr. Grant worked for you."

Her aunt made a dismissive sound as they walked back toward the staircase. They were about to ascend, when Sally gestured that Maria was in the drawing room. They walked in to greet her.

Aunt Cass continued speaking. "Since my husband's death, I have made it a game to hide my financial affairs from the world. It has been rather liberating."

"I hate to speak ill of anyone's relations that are not Henry's, but I hate that man," Maria said. "My dear Mrs. Spencer, I have never enjoyed a visit more in my life. The Lord forbid he hold off moving into his horrible, shabby home until we could conveniently get through the library there. And you, Elizabeth! What was *that* about Miss Reeves?"

Elizabeth accepted a cup of tea from Maria before sitting down near the sideboard and her books. "I do not know Miss Reeves, but I do feel that any woman who asks for time to make a decision concerning marrying Mr. Leigh is a woman of sense. No, do not snicker, Maria. Consider. She would have known that my uncle was ill, and that the townhouse would go to him. And he has already inherited from his father. And when Uncle Spencer died, he even left a little to Cousin David. And, while I pray to God that Aunt Cass will be with us until she is ninety, there is still her property to consider."

Aunt Cass made a derisive snort. "The Lord better not take that long to call me to my heavenly mansion. What are you attempting to dance around saying, Elizabeth?"

"That Mr. David Leigh will continue to grow in wealth and consequence throughout his life. No one would fault a woman for marrying a man like him and securing her future, for not just herself but also her widowed mother." Elizabeth eyed them. "She asked him to give her time to consider."

"I confess that was a risk. Many a man would have taken offense and stormed off," Maria said.

"It was a shocking gamble," Mrs. Egerton said. Then, after a contemplative sound, she added, "Though, a touch of the coquette. After all, there are men who enjoy the chase."

"And property does make a man look better in candlelight," Aunt Cass said.

"Very true," Maria said.

"That is only proper for a young lady about to make a decision that will affect her entire life," Mrs. Egerton interjected. "If a woman is to be shackled with a man for the rest of their days, the least she can do is ensure she will be in some comfort."

"How long were you married, Mrs. Egerton?" Elizabeth asked.

"The longest sixteen months of my life," Mrs. Egerton said with her signature sigh.

That brought laughter from the ladies who relaxed into chatter and gossip. Maria wondered aloud if Mr. David Leigh would get a carriage now that he was moving up in society by way of an improved address, and Aunt Cass said she truly hoped this Miss Reeves would talk him out of it.

"A carriage in town is pointless. There is nowhere useful to even keep the horses! We got rid of ours ages ago. The poor creatures suffered with almost no space to themselves. What a pointless expense to show off to one's neighbours," Aunt Cass said. "Simply call for a chair. Or hire a carriage for the day if one is desperate."

Maria attempted to argue for the convenience, though conceded that they were known to send their carriage back and forth to Vane Park, as their horses were often needed in the country. Either by their own farmers or others about the village. And, as Mr. Thorne truly did believe in being a positive and active landlord, he would rather order a chair in town than have his horses sitting in a back alley, in cramped conditions, doing nothing.

"Father considered getting a carriage a couple months ago, but Isabella talked him out of it," Elizabeth said.

"Does your father even make enough money to afford one?" Aunt Cass asked. "I understood he was only making about seven hundred pounds."

Elizabeth shrugged. "I believe he said it was closer to nine hundred now. Augusta's dowry went to her children, of course, but she did have a little of her own money, which she left to my father. Then, Isabella brought a little money to the marriage herself. And the farm is doing very well."

"A carriage will bankrupt your father," Aunt Cass said. She waved James down and told him to have Sally bring them refreshment.

"That was Isabella's opinion," Elizabeth said. "She said it would make it difficult to assist Charles when he was ready to return to Oxford to finish his studies. She said the money would be better spent hiring a curate until Charles got his ordination, and then hiring Charles as a curate."

Maria scoffed at that. "I will allow that Charles left Oxford due to his health, but he is healthy as a horse now. He should go back, instead of running about the countryside with his wastrel friends."

"Oh, forget Charles Knight. I cannot believe you asked for the chair, Eliza!" Aunt Cass said. "What on earth are you going to do with that?"

"Mary took mother's chair from my bedroom, so I have been without one," Elizabeth said simply. "I could use one, as a particular statement, and I would like one with fond memories if possible."

"I'd forgotten Mary took that chair," Aunt Cass said.

Maria sighed. "Don't bring up the chair."

"What is this about a chair?" Mrs. Egerton's voice echoed out.

"I do not wish to discuss my sister," Elizabeth said coolly.

However, Maria was already well into explaining to the ghost the entire story.

Elizabeth's sister, Mary, was now the very fashionable and wealthy Mrs. Fitzharding. She had snagged herself an older gentleman of extensive property and promptly forgot her spinster sister, except to request free childcare whenever Mary wished to travel to London for shopping and dancing. Upon her marriage,

Mary had taken everything from the rectory that was their mother's, leaving Elizabeth with only the smallest tokens. Their father had done nothing to stop Mary, even going so far as to chide Elizabeth for being upset.

But it was last Christmas when someone finally stood up to Mary. In point of fact, it was Isabella who'd said, "Mary. That is enough."

Mary, for her part, turned on her old friend and newest stepmother and said, "You will address me as Mrs. Fitzharding."

"*Mary,*" Isabella said in a stern tone. "Those items belong to your sister. You are stealing from her, and I will not allow it in my home."

Mary threw the jewelry and small tokens on the floor. A small strand of pearls that had once belonged to the first Mrs. Knight shattered. Isabella said nothing. She simply got upon her hands and knees and began the tedious task of picking up every single pearl that had fallen into all the floorboard cracks. The housemaid escorted a sobbing Elizabeth down to the kitchen for a glass of wine and a slice of spiced cake.

It had not been the same between the sisters, not since Mary stole their mother's chair upon her marriage, and that was the beginning of the end for their relationship. But then the necklace changed things. Elizabeth had yet to forgive her. She'd only written to Mary out of obligation. She worked to avoid every single visit to Ashbrook, and only went when her father forced her to go. Whenever possible, Elizabeth found some distant relation to visit or an old school fellow who required nursing whenever Mary came to Bryden for a couple of weeks.

There were even times that Elizabeth thought she'd rather marry the butcher's son who had a sweet smile for her than endure the thumb of her father who could force her to Mary's at a whim.

The sisters were permanently estranged. Elizabeth could not imagine any bridge that could withstand past hurts to allow them to find their way back to sisterly friendship.

"It is obvious to me that this Mrs. Fitzharding feels resentful toward Miss Knight and is determined to punish her," Mrs. Egerton said upon the conclusion of the long history.

"Mary is rich and comfortable. I am a poor spinster, ma'am. She is not resentful of anything," Elizabeth said.

"Perhaps she resents your freedom," Mrs. Egerton said. "She married the old, fat country gentlemen. She has laid upon the bed she has made, and bore children for it. She did her duty to her family, whereas you have lived freely and without consequence. Here you are, in London, gayly gossiping and sipping tea. She is locked in her estate, caring for children she did not want and dotting upon a husband she cannot stand."

Elizabeth stared at the book. For all of the ghost's experiences, she was completely wrong on that score. Mary was not jealous. And Elizabeth was certainly not free.

"And let us recall that you still have memories of your mother."

"They are very dim, Mrs. Egerton," Elizabeth said softly. "Many are nothing more than half-finished paintings."

"Yet, that is more than she has. No one, not even your sister, can steal those from you. Only time can do that," Mrs. Egerton said in a calm tone.

Elizabeth made a point of standing to pour herself a cup of tea. It was lukewarm now, but she did not care. She needed to clear her mind from Mary.

"Please, I do not wish to dwell upon Mary anymore."

"May we, therefore, discuss Mr. David Leigh?" Mrs. Egerton said. "Mr. Edward Leigh never liked him, and always wished he'd had sons so that they could have gotten his estate instead of his useless nephew, as he called him."

"My brother would have had to marry for that to have happened," Aunt Cass said.

"My dear Mrs. Spencer, surely you know that isn't strictly true," Mrs. Egerton said.

The ladies all gasped and laughed, and Aunt Cass slapped the book's front cover. "For shame, Mrs. Egerton!"

"Mrs. Egerton!" Elizabeth said, attempting to push the laughter from her voice. "I am the unmarried daughter of a clergyman! I must be protected from such talk."

"Pish," Mrs. Egerton said. "I am so relieved that Mr. Leigh turned his attentions elsewhere."

"Elsewhere from where?' Elizabeth asked idly.

"From you, dear child, of course."

The three ladies all shared a look. Aunt Cass was the one to speak. "Am I understanding you correctly? David had wanted to make addresses to Elizabeth?"

"Yes, indeed. He was busy chasing women well outside his class, when he should be going after an older woman longing for protection from her family and could provide him a sensible home and talk him out of stupidity," Mrs. Egerton said. "I'd once suggested Miss Knight here as a potential marriage partner, but your uncle very clearly stated that he'd rather you be an old maid than married to his useless nephew. That is why he'd previously discouraged your cousin from turning his attentions to you."

"So, Uncle Edward discouraged him? From attentions to me?" Elizabeth whispered.

"Indeed. He emphasised, *repeatedly*, that you were too poor to be of good use to a man of Mr. David Leigh's position, and that you were also interested in the occult, and would no doubt carry on your studies after your marriage." Mrs. Egerton's voice had an airy, almost jovial quality to it. "That turned him off immediately, which shows his poor taste. Miss Knight would make any man an excellent wife."

"Then why would he give Eliza the library?" Maria asked.

"I suspect he feels guilty for having taken his uncle's marriage advice. His eyes were first upon Miss Knight, and this Miss Reeves only became interesting when a distant relation died and left her money and no sense."

Elizabeth sighed the sigh of the prisoner who'd escaped the noose. She, too, would rather the dread of being labeled an old maid than to be shackled as Mrs. David Leigh for the rest of her life.

And how fortunate that he spoke to their uncle first, as opposed to her father. For she would have been cast out of the house, she was certain, if she declined such an offer of marriage.

Three thousand pounds.

Oh, this Miss Reeves turned out to be a blessing on all of their lives.

⋘ Chapter 11 ⋙

THE NEXT TWO days were completely uneventful. Elizabeth arose late in the morning. The maids had not pulled back her curtains, but they had lit her a fire and left clean water in her new basin, along with a clean chamberpot. She relieved herself, and set about the task of washing. She scrubbed her body, and applied the provided ointment for her legs, which were already looking greatly improved. Likewise, the worst of the cuts upon her heel had lost most of its angry redness overnight, though a bruise had formed. The apothecary had warned her that might happen and not to be alarmed.

After summoning the maid to help her dress, Elizabeth went downstairs to the dining room. Maria and Aunt Cass were already hard at work making lists of books and sorting accordingly. A light meal of rolls, cakes, tea, coffee, and chocolate was off to the side.

"Good morning, my dear. How are you feeling today?" Aunt Cass asked.

"I believe I am healing faster than expected," Elizabeth said.

"Excellent news. Now, I hope you don't mind, but Mrs. Thorne and I wished to get an early start this morning."

"Henry has a bookseller coming to visit today, to make a potential purchase, so we wanted as many books available as possible."

"Why didn't you wake me?" Elizabeth asked. She glanced at the time. It was ten in the morning. "Goodness. I seemed to have overslept."

"We wanted you to get your rest," Aunt Cass said. "Oh, letters arrived for you. Sit and eat. We'll keep working here."

Dearest Elizabeth,

Thank you for your letter announcing your safe arrival in London. Bryden has not been the same without you. Georgiana and Theodosia have been in a competition to see which can run me out of the house first.

Mary has written again, still in desperate need for Mr. Knight to send him one of her sisters. She did not ask for you by name, but your father has assumed that is her design. However, I thought Cassandra or even Theodosia would be better choices. As they are not in mourning – though they have all requested from your father for a week's mourning out of respect to you and Mary – they would be the properest to go. What are your thoughts?

I have been struggling with the new maid from the village. She does not know a thing about milking cows at all, and neither do I. We are a sorry pair and I am so relieved you are not here to see my folly.

There was a man from London who came down this morning. He said he was with the Royal Occult Society and was looking for you. He spoke with your father at length, and I write to put you upon your guard that this man attempted to get your father to sell him the books. Your father could not, as they are not here, but you must know that he might have been induced. The gentlemen offered £25 to take them right then and there. Your father sent him to Mrs. Spencer's home, so I must warn you that these men will be showing up.

Your father nearly agreed to the deal right there in the drawing room, until I gently reminded him that they were your inheritance and that he was not legally able to sell them. I have drawn some ire about that from Mr. Knight, but it will pass. I write this to tell you to harden yourself. He plans to write you to educate you upon the sin of sentimentality and how a young woman must yield to a father's judgement in such matters. He has also threatened to send Charles. For now, at least, Charles is too busy to go to town.

As you may need news to read aloud in this letter, I will say that the apple tree looks as though it is threatening to bud, so I look forward to the blossoms soon. Cassandra and I have prepared the vegetable garden for planting. I had thought we should do it now, but she said to consult you to ask what you think we should plant. Cassandra was concerned about planting more potatoes again, since the last crop was rather blighted. She had thought you might like cucumbers this year, since you didn't plant any the last two years, due to Augusta's death. Cassandra feels strongly that they should be planted this year and that the remembrance of her mother's love of them will be no hardship upon her feelings.

I believe Cassandra would like the cucumbers because they are a reminder of her mother. I did not commit to planting them, but I think it would mean much to her to have you wish for cucumbers and to mention her mother.

Mrs. Perry came by this morning for a visit, and she suggested trying our hand at building a small hothouse, but that seems rather too adventurous for our small rectory garden. What are your thoughts? Neither your mother nor Augusta attempted it, so I have no notion of expense nor work involved. And, I confess, I am terrible with plants.

Georgiana insists that we grow celery, which should be no great barrier, though Theodosia wishes for a pear tree. I don't know where it would even go, let alone who we could ask. Mary would be the likely choice, but she doesn't have any pear trees. Does Mrs. Thorne? Do you think her gardener would be willing to give us a cutting? I had no idea a vegetable garden would be so much fuss! Is it always like this?

Mrs. Rush came to bed last night, and brought forth a healthy baby boy. She is also doing well herself. I plan to call upon her in a few days, when she is feeling stronger.

Your sister demands my attention. Her dress has a hole in it and she requires my assistance repairing the damage. Please remember to purchase yourself new boots while in town. Theodosia says she is very sorry for ruining them and has learned her lesson.

All our love,
Isabella

Theodosia says to tell you she bought you a yellow ribbon as a peace offering. It's upon your dresser for when you return. I do not know where she has gotten the money, though, so perhaps you might want to see if any is missing from your drawer.

Dear Lizzybeth,

I need you to write to Isabella and tell her to please let me have my pear tree. Father says the garden is for us girls and that we can grow whatever we want in it, as he needs to pay attention to the farm animals and the crops. So I want a pear tree! Think of the tarts and pies and jams we could have if we owned our own pear tree! For now, whenever we want pears, we must buy them in the market and you know how expensive things can be. But if we had our own tree, then we could have pears all winter long. Surely this is sensible.

It's awfully dull here without you. There's a new gentleman in the village that everyone but me is in love with. He is terribly dull. If you were here, you would find him dull, too.

Isabella says I cannot write a long letter as there isn't enough room on the page, so I'll go now I suppose. Hurry home because there is a surprise for you in your bedroom!

Your favourite sister,
Thea

Elizabeth smiled at her sister's enthusiasm about the prospect of more fruit at the rectory.

"What is so funny?" Aunt Cass asked.

Elizabeth read out the section of the letter considering the garden and the pear tree. "The problem with the scheme, of course, is that Thea will do nothing to assist with the collection of said pears, nor of the organization of the preserves and winter storage, nor cleaning up the fallen pears. So, while the idea is sound, I fear it's more work for me and Isabella."

"Poor Theodosia. What a scatterbrain that girl is," Aunt Cass. "She was a sweet enough baby, but gracious she's turned into a terror."

"Oh, she's not that bad," Maria said.

"That's because she reminds you of yourself at that age," Elizabeth said with a grin.

"And look how well I turned out," Maria declared.

Dear Elizabeth,

Thank you for your letter concerning Uncle Edward's death. I did not know him as well as you, so I extend to you my prayers upon your loss.

I have received Isabella's letter only this morning, too, about how you are staying in town with Aunt Cass for her mourning period. I think that is best for at least a few days. I do want to ask Aunt Cass for her permission, though.

Would she be entirely offended if we go ahead with our ball on the 27th? I would not ask, except that we have sent out the invitations. However, I do not wish to offend her and we will postpone it, even if Cassie will be greatly disappointed. There is a new gentleman in Bryden that I planned to invite, and I think Cassie would pleased with that. However, only with our aunt's permission, of course.

Mary

"That letter is from Mary. I know that sour expression anywhere," Maria said.

"Yes, it is from Mary, but she's very civil," Elizabeth said. She managed not to make a personal commentary upon the rareness of the feat.

"Oh, before I forget. Our coachman dropped this off for you, before he took Henry." Maria reached into her apron's pocket and pulled out a letter. "It is from Bryden."

My dear daughter,

I have spoken with your stepmother, and we are of one mind: you must return to Bryden as soon as it can possibly be arranged. London is clearly too dangerous for a young, unmarried woman. Only think of the disgrace that could have been brought upon you if the intruder had baser plans. No, indeed, you must return to Bryden this moment. And be assured that Mrs. Knight agrees as strongly as I do.

I shall send Charles in a few days, if you would prefer his company. I cannot make the trip myself, of course. I am needed in the parish. However, it is clearly too savage in town for you to dwell any longer.

Mr. Knight

"And that one is from her father," Aunt Cass said. "I have gotten the same expression on more than one occasion."

Elizabeth was too cross to laugh at her aunt's teasing. "My father wishes me to return home immediately because he fears some man will force himself upon me and then shame be brought upon the family."

"That is an overreaction," Maria said.

Aunt Cass shook her head. "For a man who claims to be a messenger of God, he does not offer the comfort and support one would expect from that post. If you wish, I will write to him."

"Do you mind, Aunt?"

"Not at all. Mrs. Thorne? Hand me a new sheet of paper, and I shall begin my letter this instant."

"Be kind, Aunt," Elizabeth instructed.

Aunt Cass offered up a withering look. "You are not so old as to boss me about, young lady."

"Please?"

Aunt Cass smiled. "You write to your stepmother. I shall write to your father. He's always hoped to be mentioned in my will, so I shall use that to my advantage."

Elizabeth did not bother to argue, since she knew Aunt Cass was best suited to argue her case. "Then I shall write Mary. And then, Isabella."

Dear Mary,

> *Thank you for your letter and your kind words. Please go ahead with your ball. I have already spoken with Aunt Cass and she agrees that our uncle never stood upon ceremony and would not want us to now that he was gone. I think the ball would be a splendid thing, and Cassie needs to get out into society more. She is eighteen, and I know all too well how much home life begins to chafe at that age. Bryden has too few gentlemen there, and still fewer single ones.*

> *I also recommend she spend some time to help care for the little ones. She does love your children, and I'm sure you*

could use the help. I cannot leave my aunt's side at this time, and I fear my dear sister is being drawn into mediating Georgiana and Theodosia's squabbles more than is good for her.

All my best,
Elizabeth

Elizabeth's stomach clenched, but she managed to finish the letter without picking a fight with her younger sister. Mary's letter was direct and to the point; nothing like the chatty letters she was used to receiving from other women. She also doubted Mary's letters to Isabella were nothing but several pages of gossip and fun. Indeed, Elizabeth and Mary once had that relationship, where they sent each other long, fun letters whenever Elizabeth was away. Now, however, that relationship had soured.

It hurt Elizabeth, though she never told anyone that. Not even Maria, who hated Mary with the fervor of a true friend. No, Elizabeth kept it to herself as much as possible. Everyone knew however. Except her father, who seemed oblivious. Or, maybe he supposed acting like nothing had changed between his daughters would help them come around to their old selves. Or perhaps more accurately he simply did not care. Girls were of little consequence.

Elizabeth felt the divide started the night Mary accepted her husband's hand in marriage. Elizabeth had told her not to do it. Elizabeth said it was foolish to marry without love, and Mary said Elizabeth was jealous of her good fortune, to have a house and an income of her own. After that, they said several very unkind words until Augusta had shouted at them both to stop. Even her father's demands for obedience in his women went unheeded. They fought the way that only sisters could fight. By the end, they were screaming at each other in Elizabeth's bedchamber.

They had barely spoken since except to fight about possessions. Elizabeth's father had occasionally commanded her to Mary's to assist with this or that, but the visits never lasted for long. The silent treatment was only so useful and eventually, one of the children would ask why Momma didn't like Aunt Eliza, and then Elizabeth was packed back to her father's house.

Occasionally, Cassandra had asked could she go instead, using the excuse of a greater society. That was probably true, but Cassandra hated that her sisters were fighting.

It was too messy for the family of a country rector, but it was life.

Dear Isabella,

For your own sake, please plant whatever you think is best. Theodosia will not help in the garden at all, no matter how much she will protest she will this time. Likewise, Georgiana's help generally involves ruining so much food that she's kicked out of the garden patch and sent to practice her drawing. And I shall selfishly be spending as much time as possible in London with my aunt.

Which brings me to the point of this letter. I have received my father's letter recalling me home. He says you support him without reservation. I do not believe this to be the case, so I beg you to exercise any influence you might have to allow me to stay in London.

I need to be here for my aunt, and truly I was not injured in the break in. I know it is terrifying because you were not here, but I promise you that I am perfectly fine. And my father's worries about my virtue are unfounded. There are plenty of servants in the household at all times. Nothing of that nature was going to happen to me. I would not stay here if I felt my safety was compromised in any form.

As well, consider that Mr. and Mrs. Thorne are now staying with us! Surely my father would not think they would stay if it was so unsafe here.

As for the books, thank you. We have had a visit from the Royal Occult Society, and they have been most disagreeable. They have even hinted threats to me, and so I was well prepared for them to approach my father. Clearly they arrived before my letter did, so I am sorry that they caught you all off guard.

Mr. Thorne is assisting me with the selling of the books I do not wish to keep, and I am well looked after. Charles is simply not needed here.

I do not have time to write further this morning for we have a bookseller coming to see the collection, and I wish for this letter to go out in the post today. I promise a significantly longer letter as soon as time allows.

All my love,
Elizabeth

"I know one thing, if the Royal Occult Society appears today, I might write a sternly worded letter to them," Maria said.

"I suspect men like that are used to getting their own way. It must have come as a shock to have a young lady talk back to them," Elizabeth said.

"Well, I for one am tired of men thinking they can demand things of us," Maria said.

"This is why I prefer being a widow," Aunt Cass said. "Don't get me wrong, I loved my dear husband. However, there is a charm to being a wealthy widow that should not be underestimated."

"Are you ladies planning my death?"

Elizabeth smiled at Henry Thorne's entrance into the dining room. "Mr. Thorne! How excellent to see you in spirits this morning."

"I sincerely hope it is only spirits in the spiritual sense," Maria muttered.

"My dear wife! Even in my most debauched days, I did not partake of spirits before dinner. I was raised a gentleman, after all." He smiled. "Now, Mrs. Spencer, Miss Knight. I have a Mr. Rideout coming to pay a business call at twelve o'clock sharp today. He understands the house is in mourning and begs you not to put yourself out by greeting him, offering tea, or any of that rot. He will deal solely with me, if that if is your desire."

Elizabeth spoke up. "If there are no objections, I would like to go shopping today. I wish to purchase the necessary items to repair Cassandra's necklace. I can do that while Mr. Thorne turns the drawing room into a house of commerce."

"Oh! I should tell you. Word has reached my father and, I shall have to quote what he said to me." He puffed out his chest and lowered his voice. "Dear boy, I never thought I'd be pleased to see a son of mine engaged in base trade, and yet, your mother tells me all about your latest scheme in defence of your wife's friend. Very good showing, my boy. That wife of yours was worth it after all."

"Praise indeed!" Maria exclaimed. "I believe that is the first compliment your family has ever given me!"

"My mother nodded approvingly," Henry Thorne said. "I thought Old Roberts was going to faint. Our butler had never heard my father say one good word about me my entire life. He offered to shake my hand when I took my leave, Roberts did. He told me he always believed in me."

Elizabeth gave Mr. Thorne a kind smile. She knew all too well the aching desire of parental approval so infrequently bestowed, and the Thorne family was not welcoming of Maria. For them to compliment both Henry Thorne and Maria, and in the same sentence, showed they were proud of him at last. If the Thornes were anything like her father, the approval would soon be forgotten, but they had this moment to grasp in future conflicts. At least, for this one time, they had pleased those who were impossible to please.

A knock came at the door to interrupt their planning for the day's events. James announced Mr. Joseph Baxter and Sir Matthew Beaumont had returned.

Aunt Cass sighed, not even bothering to pretend politeness. "We shall all greet them in the common drawing room, with the books that are prepared for sale."

The ladies, and Mr. Thorne, filed into the drawing room according to rank and marriage, meaning Elizabeth brought up in the rear. Over the years, her position in the file had been falling and she did not look forward to the day when she pulled up in the rear in her own father's house.

She knew it was coming, though.

Three thousand pounds, Miss Knight. The book is worth three thousand pounds.

How many men would immediately find her improved in beauty and accomplishments with that addition to her name? Perhaps it was better to keep the book locked away safely until she was an old woman. That might be the only protection against a parade of foppish men wanting her to pay for their tailoring bills.

"Mr. Baxter. Sir Matthew. What can I do for you at such an early hour?" Aunt Cass asked. "This is London, gentlemen. *Not* the country."

"We understood a private book auction is happening here this afternoon, and wished to extend our offer once more," Mr. Baxter said.

"As you see, these books are available for purchase today. Mr. Thorne here is assisting us."

"Sir Matthew and I are acquainted," Henry Thorne said. "I believe I own three of his watches."

"Two now," Sir Matthew said coolly. "You were foolish with your last hand."

"Of course," Mr. Thorne said in an equally calculating voice that caught Elizabeth's attention. There was not friendship between these men. "What is your offer for the books in this room?"

"All we want are three journals, a couple of autograph books that no one will want, and some letters. They are nothing more than scraps of paper to anyone not a member of any occult society," Mr. Baxter said. "They will offer no value to any young lady."

"They are of great personal value to me," Elizabeth said. "However, in the meantime, we have produced my own list that we had planned to forward to the Royal Occult Society. Some of the books appear valuable, and I felt it was only proper to offer it to my uncle's hobby."

"I assure you, miss, that the Society is not a hobby," Sir Matthew said with a scowl.

"Oh, dear. I had understood from my uncle that he made no money from his occult studies. How extraordinary, therefore, that the two of you have made a career of it."

Sir Matthew turned an interesting shade of red.

"My dear Miss Knight," Mr. Baxter said with a faux smile. "We only are thinking of what is best for you. That is why we approached…"

"My father and attempted to enlist my own family into the theft of my personal property that was left to me in a legal will," Elizabeth said. Her heart pounded, but she kept her words as even-toned as possible. "I am rather surprised that gentlemen would behave in such a manner, but perhaps the gentlemen of town are not of the same calibre as those from the country."

"Now, listen here, Miss Knight. We will have those books one way or another," Sir Matthew said.

"Excuse me, but did you just threaten my niece?" Aunt Cass demanded.

"I will have those books, Cassandra Leigh." He sneered at her. "You know I get what I want, when I want it."

"You will call me Mrs. Spencer. If you could not intimidate me at seventeen, *Sir* Matthew, why would you think you could do so now?"

Elizabeth shifted her eyes to look at her aunt, who looked so angry that she might strike at the gentleman in front of her. Feeling that some calmness was needed, Elizabeth cleared her throat. "I have already considered your previous kind offer, but I cannot, in good conscience, sell any item that I have not thoroughly investigated for myself. However, I do have many books that I am eager to part with, having already gone through them and decided they are not of particular interest to my tastes. Any of those you are welcome to examine. Mr. Thorne is handling those negotiations on my behalf. As for letters and journals, I must be forthright with you, gentlemen. They are part of my family's words and history. I will not part with them, no matter the financial inducement to do otherwise."

"We are not interested in ladies' letters to your uncle about linens and babies," Mr. Baxter said. His calm demeanour slipped. "We don't care about useless things."

"The only letters I have seen are ones just before my mother's death. Some are concerning my younger sister, of which I must protect, for her benefit. I'm very sorry, gentlemen, to cause disagreement between us, but I must decline."

"Miss Knight, obstinance isn't attractive in a woman of any age, let alone one in your situation," Sir Matthew said.

Elizabeth did not reply.

"Neither of you are welcome in my home again," Aunt Cass finally said. "You have abused my brother's good name, and you have insulted my niece. You have stood here, in front of witnesses, and threatened my niece. You have attempted to steal from her, by way of her own family. You offend me, sirs, and I will inform my servants never to admit again."

"We are not leaving without the books, Cassandra," Sir Matthew said.

Mr. Thorne stepped in front of Aunt Cass and said, "I believe this is where I step in and say, good day, gentlemen."

"Sir Matthew, I believe we should leave," Mr. Baxter urged. Sir Matthew stepped toward Aunt Cass. Mr. Thorne remained an impassive barrier between them. Finally, he accepted that he would not get in Aunt Cass' personal space and said, "Cassandra Leigh, you are nothing more than an upstart little shrew."

"Better a shrew than a rat," Aunt Cass snarled. Then she sucked in a breath. "Get out of my home before I air your dirty laundry for all of London to laugh at."

Rage filled Sir Matthew's face and it took Mr. Baxter to grab his companion by the arm and bodily tug on him before the gentleman moved. For a terrifying moment, Elizabeth feared he might strike her aunt. However, Mr. Baxter proved capable enough to handle his friend and they left in relative silence.

Mr. Baxter did take the final opportunity to say, "Consider our offer, Miss Knight. Things will get ugly from here."

James slammed the door. Briefly, Elizabeth worried that Mr. Baxter's shoulder may have taken the brunt of the force. "Ma'am, I will inform the servants personally not to admit either of those men, no matter the circumstance."

"Thank you, James."

"With your permission, ma'am, I wish to return to cleaning Mr. Spencer's figurines. I fear Henry II's face was pitted during the break in, but it might only be a scratch that I can buff out."

Aunt Cass nodded and said, "Of course, James."

"Thank you, ma'am. Mr. Spencer sure loved those figurines. Happy to keep them in top condition."

When James was up the stairs and out of earshot, Henry Thorne said, "I believe James loves those little statues as much as the master of the house once did."

Elizabeth looked at her aunt, who looked aged and weary. When Elizabeth asked if she could get her aunt anything, Aunt Cass merely excused herself, proclaiming a headache, and asked her guests to carry on without her. A moment later, an upstairs door closed. Aunt Cass had gone to her bedchamber.

"What just happened?" Maria whispered, having crept into the foyer from the dining room.

"I have no idea," Elizabeth said.

"What was all that between her and Sir Matthew?" Henry Thorne asked.

"Truly, both of you, I know nothing. Until this very moment, I'd assumed their acquaintance was nothing more than the usual connections of living in town and being associated with the Royal Occult Society. That was an…extraordinary revelation."

"There goes my Monday cards invitation tonight," Henry Thorne said. At Maria's disgusted look, he said, "Just as well. It was a rather tedious evening there. Sir Matthew is a horrid loser. He does not believe in paying debts of honour. He believes in trickery and theft to get back what he's lost."

"Perhaps we should alert the servants, since you own his watches," Maria said.

"I believe we should all be on our guard," Mr. Thorne said. "Miss Knight? Are you still certain you wish to go shopping today?"

Elizabeth inclined her head. "Even more so, if Maria will accompany me."

"I would feel safer if you went, Maria," Mr. Thorne said. With a happier voice, he said, "And I do believe the rain was cleared for the day."

"Oh, I would never turn down an afternoon of shopping! Let us fetch our bonnets, Eliza."

ELIZABETH WISHED TO rest her feet before heading out for shopping—and she needed to change her outfit, in any case—so opted to take tea in her bedchamber. Maria took the carriage back to her house to speak with her housekeeper before they set off for the afternoon. She promised to have a servant procure Mrs. Taylor cheese, beer, a decent meat pie, if one could be found. Maria was doubtful any milk of tolerable quality could be found so late in the day, but it was worth investigating. Also, the scheme would give Mrs. Rundle an opportunity to report back on the ill niece's recovery.

Aunt Cass begged the forgiveness of her niece. Her headache had not abated and she only wished to spend the afternoon in her bedchamber, hoping the quiet rest would refresh her enough to rejoin the party for dinner. Elizabeth readily gave her consent, urging her aunt to take all the rest and care she needed. The Thornes agreed and both said they did not wish a fancy dinner. Mr. Thorne even offered to make toast and butter for the houseguests in the drawing room fireplace, and Maria said a bit of jam and cake would suit her just fine.

Once alone in her room, Elizabeth chatted with an unmanifested Mrs. Egerton as she prepared her hair. She quickly determined her dress was acceptable for shopping, provided the additional of gloves, a hat, and a thicker scarf about the neck than what she wore for modesty about the house.

She checked her feet and announced to Mrs. Egerton that they were rapidly healing. All of the cuts had scabbed over, and even the blisters upon her legs had begun drying out. All in all, excellent news.

Elizabeth decided to spend the time remaining waiting for Maria's return sorting some of the books in her closet. Her "keep" shelf had grown from one shelf to three wooden milk crates and a large flat-topped trunk. Another forty or so books were piled on the trunk's lid. This was definitely Maria's doing.

"Mrs. Egerton, would you be so kind as to assist with helping me control this mess?" Elizabeth asked. "If it is at all possible, I would like to leave London with only one shelf's worth of books. Notwithstanding your trunk, of course, Mrs. Egerton."

Mrs. Egerton made a thoughtful sound. "I believe it would be prudent for you to accept that you will not be leaving London without an entire closet full of books, Miss Knight."

It was Elizabeth's turn to sigh disapprovingly. "I truly do not have the room. May we agree upon two shelves?"

"It might be possible. We shall see."

Thankfully, it quickly became evident that Maria had not so much added new books, but rather various editions and copies. That allowed Elizabeth to ensure she kept the correct volume. In some cases, Elizabeth choose to keep a stained or lightly damaged book to sell the more pristine copy. A little water damage or a kitty's inky paw print on the cover did not injure her ability to read the book. However, it would financially injure her to attempt to sell it.

Besides, Mary wouldn't want a damaged book in her cozy cottage.

"Tell me, Miss Knight, is the mistreatment of servants typical amongst the gentry now?" Mrs. Egerton asked. "I cannot believe that your cousin would think so little of Mr. Leigh's servants that he would dismiss them without pension or support of any kind. Is there not legal redress for this Mrs. Taylor? Surely, he must owe her wages for her contract term, if nothing else."

"Aunt Cass will help sort this out, of that I am certain. I have never wished more for an establishment of my own, Mrs. Egerton. I would invite them to stay with me."

"Maybe that is why you cannot find a husband," Mrs. Egerton said without any malice. In fact, there was a touch of laughter in her voice.

"If left to my own devices, I would probably open up a poor house in my drawing room and have a dozen wayward girls and destitute old ladies living with me."

That brought laughter to Mrs. Egerton's voice, and her book cover clapped several times, as if clapping her hands together. "Now, let us see. You will need to find the herbology books, and

I do not think they were found in the drawing room yet. There should be a total of eleven, but the most important one you will need to help power my book is *A Complete and Thorough Introduction to Occult Uses of Plants Native to England, Ireland, Wales, and Scotland, but not the Isles.*"

"I do not believe I have seen that particular book. I am certain I would recall that title," Elizabeth said. "No, I do not see it on Maria's master inventory list. Do you know which trunk it is in?"

"Unfortunately, no. However, it has a brown leather cover, gold embossing, and several of the pages have a red wine stain on the corners."

Elizabeth opened one of the trunks and began digging through it. She found several books that Mrs. Egerton said were very advanced and that they weren't needed for years yet. Elizabeth decided to move those to the closet shelves, under KEEP, for now. Eventually, she would want to organize them by skill level.

She also found several beginner history books. Some Mrs. Egerton said weren't very useful to her on a practical sense, but their topics appealed to Elizabeth, so on the KEEP shelf they went for now. Perhaps she would change her mind later.

"This one is An Examination of the Sexes and the Occult. Publication date 1788."

"That one can be burned in the fireplace. That's about all good it will do."

"Why would you say that?"

"It argued that women's brains are not large enough to handle occultism and that it's evident by our smaller heads."

"Not all women's heads are smaller than men's. I have met many a small man in my lifetime, and many a large woman," Elizabeth said thoughtfully.

"Exactly!" Mrs. Egerton said. "Filth, I say."

"I shall add it to the auction trunk, then."

"I would need to be paid to bring that trash into my home, but this age is different from the ones before me. We wore more clothing, for one thing," Mrs. Egerton said, the book pages flapping to a drawing of herself.

Elizabeth glanced at the drawing of Mrs. Egerton. "You were a very fine young woman."

"Thank you, dear. I was the envy of all the young men. Of course, back then, we did not marry for foolishness. We married to adjoin property whenever possible, and to expand one's title when not."

"Little has changed," Elizabeth said with a laugh.

"Then why hasn't your father found you an acceptable gentleman farmer to wed you to?"

Elizabeth smiled. "Because I wish to marry for foolishness first and above all."

"Silly girl. Your uncle encouraged this behaviour, I have no doubt."

"Independence in a female might not be an attractive flaw to many, but my uncle did appreciate it in me," Elizabeth said.

"Like I said," Mrs. Egerton said. "Now, eventually, you will need an herbologist, as well as someone who writes and reads Latin, Italian, and French as a minimum. However, for now, we can probably survive with limited French and Latin skills."

Elizabeth pressed her lips together, considering the issue. "If pressed, we could ask Mr. Thorne for assistance with the Latin."

"No, only a woman," Mrs. Egerton insisted. "I have yet to form my opinion of this Mr. Thorne and, until I do, I shall not allow his assistance."

Elizabeth was afraid of that answer. "It will be very difficult to find a woman who can read Latin, Mrs. Egerton. It is not proper."

"Not proper?" Mrs. Egerton exclaimed. "If it was good enough for Queen Elizabeth, why is it not good for the rest of us?"

"I know not."

"At least you can read English. Did they teach you anything at school?"

"Needlework, sums, dancing, drawing, and piano. I taught myself a little French and Italian, but I am a very poor scholar beyond the simplest of sentences."

"Dancing," Mrs. Egerton said with scorn. "I will allow for drawing, as an occultist is often called upon to draft out designs for new incantations and the elements must be well balanced. However, dancing? You do not need school for that, girl."

"Didn't they have dancing instructors when you were a young lady?"

"Yes, of course. They came to town, your father booked an hour or two of their time, and then you hopefully escaped without one of them fondling you." Mrs. Egerton sighed, flipping several pages of her book, back to the pressed herbs. "Will you have enough money to purchase items?"

"I have a little of my own money that I brought with me to London, as well as Mr. Thorne's efforts selling the books. When I return home, I can grow whatever I need in our small vegetable plot behind the house, provided, of course, that it is also accepted to add some of the plants to our meats."

"Of course. The occult is nothing if not practical."

"Then I believe I shall be fine on that score. Once all of the books are sold, I will know better what kind of income I will have made. From there, I plan to invest the majority safely, if that is a path I can follow. I will need my father's assistance, so we shall see. Regardless, I hope to hold some back, privately, for my own security. And, I confess I will keep back a modest sum for gifts and necessities. And new boots, if possible."

A knock at the door. The footman arrived with letters. She thanked him and said to Mrs. Egerton, "Letter from Isabella, by express in fact."

Be assured we are all well.

I send you this brief note to alert you that Mary has arrived at your father's house, requesting your assistance. Her nurse-maid must travel to Hampshire to assist her sister, who is about to enter her confinement. It is her first child, and the nurse-maid is obviously worried. I explained to Mary the circumstances of your time in London, but she was adamant. Please prepare your aunt for a letter from your father and Mary; they are both writing to her as I try to sketch out this note.

They are bustling about, so I must end this letter. I hope this arrives before theirs. Please, stay in London as long as you can. Mary is in an uproar about you going, but I will

attempt to distract them both. If possible, I shall see if
Cassandra or possibly Thea can go in your place. No doubt
Thea and G could use a break from one another. The pranks
and bickering have reached a fevered pitch.

"Mary is always in an uproar about me going anywhere," Elizabeth muttered. She glanced at the dresser that contained a book worth so much money. She told the ghost about the book, and Mr. Osborne's belief in its worth.

"For my part, Mrs. Egerton, I confess that I do not believe any book is worth that much money."

Mrs. Egerton made a thoughtful sound. "Your uncle's particular volume hasn't been seen outside of a private collection in three generations. However, one of the other surviving volumes went for auction at the Vatican about a decade ago. It went for just short of three thousand guineas."

"Guineas?" Elizabeth whispered. When speaking about a pair of boots or even a horse, the shilling difference between a pound and a guinea was nothing. When speaking of money in the thousands, that was a very different matter all together.

"I am surprised your uncle did not leave you a note detailing the book's worth. I am certain I saw him write it." Mrs. Egerton's voice trailed off in thought. "Have you found the English journal yet?"

"I found the Latin journal."

"Look about, then. There is a journal in English, too. It should have a letter for you. I am certain that is where he placed it."

"Then I shall begin with the trunk that contains the letters and more personal items." Elizabeth swallowed, attempting to push down her fears concerning her grief overtaking her once more. "I shall be strong."

Elizabeth sat down on the floor next to the trunk that she had been avoiding. She opened the lid. It was full of priceless keepsakes. Letters. Journals. Random scrawled notes. She reminded herself that she needed to be methodical and sensible in this duty. There would be time later to weep and mourn. For now, there was a task ahead of her that only she could do.

She began with the bundles of letters. She could not read those. However, she could sort them by date. Some would be about her. Others would be about Mary. That she could do.

"Why does the Royal Occult Society wish the autograph books so badly? I would think the rare book would be more important."

"They do not know your uncle owned the other book. He inherited it from a friend. That horrid man Sir Matthew tore apart the friend's house while his body was still warm upon the bed. They have no idea where it went."

"Is that why Mr. Osborne told me to hide it and not to tell anyone?"

"Mr. Osborne knew of the book's existence, though I suspect he'd just assumed the book had been stolen, not given to you."

Elizabeth considered that for a moment before asking, "Why didn't you tell me the book was valuable?"

"I did."

"Mrs. Egerton, I hate to disagree with anyone, but I recall the conversation perfectly. You advised me to offer it to Mr. Osborne."

"Yes, for I knew he would know of the current pricing on the manuscript."

Elizabeth stopped her sorting to glare at the book upon her nightstand. "That has a degree of deceit to it."

"Arguable," Mrs. Egerton said.

Elizabeth wiped away the tears that dripped down her face at the sight of her mother's handwriting, but she continued the task. Mrs. Egerton remained silent.

"I must point out that you did not answer my question. Why does the Royal Occult Society wish the autograph books?"

"I will answer. First, though, will you answer one for me?"

"Of course, if it is an answer within my power to provide."

"Why does your voice change pitch with each mention of your brother Charles' name? Or, indeed, your father's."

Elizabeth sighed. She looked at her letters. How different her life might have been if her mother had lived. "My father is very strict about an unmarried woman's contact with the world. My uncles and aunts all disagreed with his methods, especially after my mother's death. His own sisters and brothers live too far away for me to visit, and my father was never close with them from what I understand. I do not know the circumstances. So there was only ever Uncle Edward, Uncle Spencer and Aunt Cass, and Uncle William, David Leigh's father. Uncle William was the eldest but he died several years ago. My cousin David inherited his estate. Uncle Spencer followed him a few years later. And now, Uncle Edward is gone. So, I only have my father's rule now."

"And you do not thrive under your father's house?"

"I believe my father has never quite forgiven me for, if I might be so bold as to say such a thing, remaining unmarried. I do not believe myself deficient, despite the world's constant reminders of the burden that I have become. It is just God's will, I suppose. Or my own stubbornness to wish to marry for affection, if not outright love. And as I grow older, I find myself wanting a companion in life more than anything else. A man who will treat me as his equal in marriage. I do not believe such a man exists."

Mrs. Egerton did not answer, and Elizabeth fell into silence.

"And, I must confess, I also blame Napoleon."

"What does that upstart have to do with it?"

Elizabeth smiled, even if Mrs. Egerton could not see it. "He killed off a great many single young men of rank."

Falling into silence, Elizabeth sorted several more letters before speaking once more. "My father sends my brother Charles to do things for me, even those that I can do myself. Please, do not misunderstand or consider me ungrateful. It is not that I don't appreciate the assistance, but rather Charles has no interest in helping me. He sees me as a future burden and nothing else, and frequently has said those words to me. He turned twenty last month and is more interested in being young and foolish than helping his sister. If I am to be completely honest with you, Mrs. Egerton in a manner that I would not to a single living soul, Mr.

Thorne has done more for me than any other man in my immediate family that yet lives."

"What payment has Mr. Thorne asked of you?"

"I do not understand the question."

In a lower voice, one laced with suspicion, Mrs. Egerton said, "Every living soul has a price, Miss Knight. Everyone, and every*thing*. I am curious what price Mr. Thorne has attempted to extract from you."

Elizabeth was worldly enough to understand Mrs. Egerton's meaning. She considered playing the role of the naïve country girl, but she was not one. "He has occasionally teased me about being unmarried, but only with my permission. And, if I am not in good spirits to handle such talk, he will not continue. It is hard when a man totally unrelated to me treats me with more kindness than my own family."

"Then he believes himself honour bond to your assistance, due to your relationship with his wife?"

"I…why, Mrs. Egerton, I never heard it put in such a manner." After a moment's consideration, she said, "But, yes. Indeed, I believe that is the source of his kindness. Beyond, of course, his own decent nature. He revels in proclaiming a reputation that he does not actually live."

"Ah," Mrs. Egerton said. "I believe my opinion of him has grown somewhat. Tell me, beyond this Charles, do you have other brothers?"

"No. And, unfortunately, when my sister married, she, too, began to treat me as a drain on the household, and began to encourage such talk. Upon the death of my uncle, my father…" Elizabeth sighed. "It does not signify me speaking of it. Let us simply say that I long to be treated as an intelligent and resourceful young lady with her own feelings and dreams."

"I am very sorry, Miss Knight," Mrs. Egerton said, her tone sombre. "I truly am."

Elizabeth chuckled. "Considering I just confessed to you more than I have to any living being, please. You may call me Elizabeth."

"Thank you, Elizabeth. You must call me Mrs. Egerton, since the spell is tied to that name."

Elizabeth inclined her head out of habit. "I respect that."

"It is not easy being a woman of sense and intelligence," Mrs. Egerton said.

"I suppose not," Elizabeth whispered.

They were quiet for a while before Mrs. Egerton asked, "You said you had a question. What was it?"

Elizabeth finished the letters and wrapped them with the ribbons. One would go to Mary. A sick feeling settled in Elizabeth's gut all the same. Even now, even here with her uncle's things, some of it was Mary's. Even now, she would have to part with her possessions for Mary. Elizabeth sighed at her uncharitable nature. She should not think such things, yet she seemed ill-equipped to control them.

"Why did my uncle leave me the autograph books?"

"Are you certain you are ready for this conversation?"

Elizabeth looked about her. She'd been crying off and on for at least half an hour. She had lost her appetite, and her legs itched from the healing blisters. Her foot itched and throbbed at the same time. She picked up the autograph book and read the incantation to summon Mrs. Egerton.

When Mrs. Egerton appeared before her, still wearing her red riding habit, Elizabeth said, "I have so little that I own, and most of that can be taken from me. Knowledge is something no man can steal from me. No matter what happens in life, I will always keep what I have learned. So, I wish to know why he gifted me you."

Mrs. Egerton blew out a breath. Flecks of dust danced in the air before slowly sinking toward the floor. "And that, sweet Elizabeth, is why your uncle believed you could practice the occult as well as any man. Now, to answer your question. I am Mrs. Egerton, the gatekeeper of the book of autographs. In the past, women were occultists. In fact, there were far more lady occultists than men. This book, and the others, contain generations of lady occultists, who agreed to bind their eternal souls to assist future occultists. However, as time passed, men overtook the occult practices of females and sought to wipe us from history."

"That is terrible," Elizabeth said. She pushed herself to her feet and placed the letter bundle for Mary in her drawer, along with the terrifyingly expensive book. "My uncle had suspected there were lady occultists, but I fear he was alone in that belief. How did you become the voice of the autograph books?"

"After the members of my own group died, I continued in solitary practice for some time. Even I, at the height of my abilities while alive, could not summon all of the ghosts in the three books. However, those that I could, I summoned, and they decided amongst themselves to name me as their gatekeeper when I eventually passed from life."

"What a responsibility," Elizabeth whispered.

That made Mrs. Egerton smile. "It amazes me how you are not married. I suppose no man is worthy of you. Indeed, it was a responsibility more than an honour. They believed that, as the youngest, I would speak the language of a changing society more than any of them. I observed men hide our work from the world, and so decided I would only appear to women, or to men who truly deserved our knowledge. Your uncle purchased these three autograph books from a book seller friend of his in Ireland. He tried to unlock its pages, and I refused to allow him the privilege to know he'd succeeded. Then, he brought you to his study, year after year, and I listened to him. Sometimes, he'd talk to my very book, and tell me he knew what we were, and that he was trying to find a worthy soul to bring us back into remembrance. Then, toward the end of his life, I decided to speak to him."

"What happened when you did?"

"He fell out of his chair and nearly died," Mrs. Egerton said with annoyance. "Apparently, he was not as skilled of an occultist as he and his friends thought they were. Over the next several months until his death, I worked with him to include incantations, spellwork, and other tools so that I could appear to you until you were able to work on the book of autographs yourself."

Elizabeth took her seat upon the floor once more and began pulling out the journals, one by one. "Do you know how long your ability to appear will last?"

"We had hoped for several weeks, however... Elizabeth, your uncle was very ill toward the end, and should not have been working. I sensed an unevenness in his spellwork, but he was too weak to have corrected it. I did not tell him the spells might fail."

She smiled. "You were on his mind until he was bedridden. And, even then, he made that Mr. Grant of his promise over and over that he would protect your inheritance from your father. He truly loved and believed in you."

"He was always a kind uncle." Elizabeth dabbed her eyes with her handkerchief. "What happens when you cannot appear anymore?"

"You will be on your own, until you learn the occultcraft and incantations yourself."

Elizabeth looked down at the journal resting in her lap. This one was in Latin. "I do not believe I know enough to do such a thing. I cannot imagine my father allowing me to work on study like this at home. He most likely will be sending me about the countryside to stay with relations to ease their child rearing burdens. It will be difficult to learn when I shall be caring for my own nephews and nieces, and sick relations."

"This is why I recommend you form a collective of women you can trust. That way, even if you are all pulled apart across Europe, you can continue your work independently and write to each other." Mrs. Egerton gave Elizabeth a smile, though it was sad. "The greatest sorrow of the male occultist societies is that they work alone. It is all about individual gain. That was never the purpose of the occult. It was always meant to be a collective of minds. Of knowledge before glory. These men have forgotten that, and it is why their studies have faltered. Subsequently, you will need ladies who will support your occult practices and who will help stand against your father's tyranny."

"I would not call him tyrannical," Elizabeth protested. "There are indeed true villains out there and I do not believe my father means to be one. I must defend him."

"If your father chooses not to see you as you are, then I have no opinion of him, nor of your latest mother who cannot stand up to him."

"Oh, now Mrs. Egerton I must defend Isabella. She is very young, and she has enough problems with the girls, but she will learn."

Mrs. Egerton narrowed her eyes. "How young?"

"She is three and twenty."

"And you are?"

Elizabeth licked her lips. She knew where this conversation was headed. "Eight and twenty."

"Your father married a woman younger than you?"

Elizabeth did not answer, though she suspected her expression gave away her thoughts on the subject.

"Why did he marry for a third time?"

"He needed a wife to raise the girls. Georgianna is the youngest; she is only fifteen. And, as he is only in his fifties and very robust still, he felt he might have more sons with a young wife, and thereby better provide for his unmarried daughter."

Elizabeth attempted to smile through her small speech, even if it was tinged with disappointment and regret. She was not what her father wanted; she knew that. He reminded her whenever possible. There had been a couple of men over the years whom her father felt she could have married, if she'd made more of an effort. However, she did not like those men, and it seemed wrong to marry a man for his house.

But then she looked about the room. She could have had a house that was hers. These books could have been housed there, and then she could have time to study the way her uncle would have wanted. She could have asked her husband to sell her expensive book and know that money would go toward improving their income.

The dream did not last. Soon, the idea of bliss and independence was replaced with the faces of non-existent, screaming babies, one after another in a rapid succession whereby she would be too worn out to even wish to study, provided she did not die. Her own mother and her first stepmother both died in childbirth. Perhaps that would have been her fate, as well.

"Stop it," Mrs. Egerton said crossly.

Elizabeth blinked and realized she'd been staring down at a journal written in English. "Oh, I believe this is the journal you wanted me to look for."

"Miss Knight. Heed my words."

"I beg your pardon?"

"Cease your brooding immediately. It is not the behaviour of a young occultist, married or otherwise," Mrs. Egerton said with

authority. "It is time you begin your studies. Your task today is—
"

"Mrs. Egerton, excuse me for interrupting, but I have not yet decided if I wish to be an occultist."

Mrs. Egerton's perpetually annoyed expression turned downright offended. "You would wish those men at the Royal Occult Society to hide me away in a damp cellar for the Lord only knows how long because they are afraid of the female mind?"

"Well…"

"You would go against your uncle's most desired wishes, which was for you to resurrect the female role in occultism?"

"Well…"

Mrs. Egerton continued, unwilling to let Elizabeth finish a thought. "You would stand by and allow your uncertainty to prevent you from seizing an opportunity to be independent? And not only in a merely financial way, but independent of society's restrictions upon your own mind."

"I…"

"You would throw away all of your choices, all of your talents, just because you are afraid of what a *man* might think of you? Even if that man is your father?"

"But…"

"And your poor uncle, who died believing you would carry on the family tradition, and you would toss that away…"

"Enough!" Elizabeth said. "Please, Mrs. Egerton, I beg you. Allow me to get a word in. I will answer, if you allow me the opportunity."

"Speak, then."

"I wish to honour my uncle's request. I am merely uncertain how to achieve it. I am not trained, nor highly educated."

"Again, that is why I suggest you find a society of ladies like you. That is your first task. Then, speak to your stepmother. If you can bring her to your side, you will be safe from your father."

"Her?"

"Yes, her. She is a married woman, and a wife can have more sway over her husband, than a daughter over her father."

"I don't even know her opinions on the occult."

Mrs. Egerton spread her gloved hands out, as if the answer was obvious. "Then I recommend you discover her opinions."

THANKFULLY, THE RAIN had not returned that afternoon. Unfortunately for Elizabeth, she stepped into a puddle upon exiting the carriage in front of the jeweler's shop and the water seeped in through the holes Thea had made. She sighed. When her foot was completely healed, she would be visiting a cobbler.

Elizabeth only had to wait five minutes before it was her turn to speak with the jeweler. She explained the situation of the necklace, and purchased the necessary repair materials, including a new string that he said would be stronger than the original one.

"So strong that not even jealous young ladies could destroy!"

Elizabeth gave him a knowing smile. "You have sisters, too, sir?"

"Eight," he said gravely, his eyes wide. "I am the only boy."

"My condolences to your mother," Elizabeth said in a conspiratorial tone.

That made him laugh heartily. Once she described the necklace's style, he cautioned her that the smallest pearls nearest the clasp were most likely to be lost forever. She also purchased four tiny pearls under his advice. They were from a previous necklace of her mother's era that had broken in a similar manner. Upon inspection, Elizabeth believed them to be the correct size.

"Five shillings and...no, let us make it five shillings even."

She opened her reticule's drawstring. Inside was several one-pound notes, and several coins. She fished out five shillings and placed it on the counter. "Oh, just put that on my account," Maria said. "Mr. Henry Thorne, of Vane Park."

The clerk stopped before putting the money away out of sight. He did not interrupt the ladies, though his look clearly said he preferred the direct payment.

"I get all of my jewelry here, and Henry settles our account twice a year, so it would have been fine."

The clerk's smile was polite for a man who needed the business of a much wealthier Maria Thorne. However, it was clear to Elizabeth that he also liked having some cash on hand instead of waiting a half year for payment.

"I am happy to settle my accounts today," Elizabeth said with a smile at the clerk. She noticed a perceptible release of tension in his shoulders.

They made a trip across the street to the drapers. There, Elizabeth purchased a shocking amount of ribbon for her sisters, as well as blue silk ribbon for Isabella. There was a garish pattern of cotton with a pineapple print, of all things, that Elizabeth knew Georgiana would love, and so picked up a yard of it. Anything more than that and she feared her sister would make herself an entire wardrobe based on the hideous cloth. All in all, her purchases cost the shocking sum of three pounds, twelve shillings, and two pence. For frivolities.

Still, she handed over four one-pound bank notes and accepted the change back, which she put into her reticule. She had worried about carrying so much money on her person, but as she was determined to spend her money like water, as Augusta was fond of saying, she should have brought it all.

As she waited for her purchases to be packaged, Maria asked, "Is there any other shop that interests you? Or have you finally spent all your money?"

Elizabeth knew her friend was teasing and laughed along. "My dear Maria! Consider that I have made nearly a full year's pin money since arriving in London. You must forgive me for a little extravagance."

"My dear, I would be honoured to help you spend the entire fortune here today, if that is your wish." She considered for a moment. "We should get you new boots."

Elizabeth's heart skipped a beat. Footwear would be expensive, though she absolutely needed them.

"Consider it an early Christmas gift," Maria said.

Elizabeth laughed. "It's March!"

"Then, an early gift in celebration of turning twenty-nine."

"That is not until September."

Maria shrugged. "It is closer than December. But, please allow me. I need new shoes in any case, and it would be no trouble at all to tack on your boots."

The friends joyfully bickered about the boots during the packaging and up to leaving the shop. As they were exiting, a female voice said, "Mrs. Thorne?"

The ladies turned around to see a tall, lean woman. Her dark brown hair was pulled back to the nape of her neck in a severe bun. Not even the tiniest wisp of hair escaped the well-pinned style. She wore glasses and was dressed in a faded brown and yellow striped dress. She wore a rather matronly hat for so young a woman.

"Miss Thorne?" Maria blinked her eyes. "It is you! I did not know you were in town."

Miss Thorne politely curtsied. "My brother's wife had been confined over Christmas, so is only well enough to come to town now. So here I am."

"Oh, Miss Thorne. This is my very good friend, Miss Knight, from Bryden. We grew up together. Elizabeth, this is Henry's cousin, Miss Thorne."

"Delighted," Miss Thorne said automatically. Then, her face lit up. "Miss *Elizabeth* Knight? Mrs. George Spencer's niece?"

"Yes, indeed!" Elizabeth said. "Have we previously met?"

Miss Thorne's eyes lit up. "Miss Knight, might I be so bold as to ask if you have any occult books in Latin? My particular interests are in minerals and geography, and ideally I would prefer them in Latin, since I am attempting to improve my skills in that language. However, I will also accept French, Italian, and English. Actually, I change my mind. I will also accept German or Spanish books as well if you are so kind as to provide me with a list. My skill at both those languages is deplorable, but I shan't improve without more practice. I will happily compensate you."

Elizabeth opened her mouth to offer an invitation for this Miss Thorne to visit the house, when she continued. "Now, Miss Knight, I understand from my brother that you are a poor young lady, so I will insist upon paying for the books and at the price you would charge a man. Now, I must confess I only have four shillings to my name upon my person currently, but you may have them if we are able to strike upon a deal. I am desperate, Miss Knight."

"It is lovely to meet—" Elizabeth began. Gracious! She would not take a farthing from this clearly impoverished member of the

Thorne family. However, she was unable to even broach the subject before Miss Thorne interrupted her.

"And, indeed, if the books cost more than that I will simply ask my terrible sister-in-law for more money and if she will not give it to me, I will sell a little of my jewelry here at the shops. It will be no fuss at all, I assure you. I simply must have some new books, I truly am the most desperate of creatures."

"Calm yourself, Alice," Maria said. "If the situation is that dire at home, I will purchase you some books myself."

"Miss Thorne," Elizabeth said, interrupting her new acquaintance before she could speak again. "It pains me to see you in distress. You may call upon me at my aunt's house, at any time, and I shall personally show you my book inventory. You may borrow as many as you need, for as long as you require them for your further studies."

"Oh, Miss Knight! You have no idea of the torture a lady in my situation endured being in the country all through the winter months, without even a short jaunt to town for gifts or books or anything. And the lending library is fine for novels, but I am in need of—"

"Excuse me for interrupting, Miss Thorne, but did you say Latin?" Elizabeth asked.

"Yes, indeed," Miss Thorne grew quiet. She looked down at the book in her hands. "It is most likely why I am still unwed. At least, that is what my family says. I hope this does not affect your opinion of me, Miss Knight and your so very kind offer to lend me a book."

"How good is your Latin, Miss Thorne?"

"Elizabeth?" Maria asked. Then, realization flashed on her face. "Oh, of course. Yes. Henry has said her Latin is better than his. And he went to Cambridge."

"Of course it is," Miss Thorne said in a shockingly confident tone. "I have been in continuous study."

Elizabeth's mouth twitch upward. She was not used to a young lady being an advocate of her own excellence. Mrs. Egerton was going to adore her.

"Miss Thorne," Elizabeth said. "May I be so bold as to write you a letter? I have a rather interesting situation that, I believe, requires a woman of your *unique* talents."

Miss Thorne dug in her reticule and said, "Here is my card. It has my brother's address on it. You are very welcome to visit, even. Indeed, I would very much appreciate any female company that is not my sister-in-law or her horrid friends."

"Miss Knight is still in mourning for her dear uncle, so she might not be up for visiting at present," Maria said in a warning tone.

"Oh, yes." Miss Thorne gave Elizabeth an appraising look. "I had forgot."

With her grey pelisse and lavender-trimmed hat, Elizabeth knew she did not look the part of a grieving relation. She gave Miss Thorne what she hoped was a disarming smile. "I forgot my mourning pelisse in the haste of packing for London. I realized too late that I did not have a suitable black hat made up for springtime. My aunt is very understanding and assures me my uncle would not have wished me to in mourning clothes."

"Alas, society," Maria said. She managed not to roll her eyes, even if Elizabeth could hear it in her voice.

Elizabeth was excited to meet a young woman who only had a couple of shillings to rub together; they would have much in common, no doubt. "It may be some days before I can make the journey to visit, for I have been feeling rather inconvenienced by a cut upon my foot that is very bothersome. I fear all this walking about in the shops today will have me done for this evening and perhaps even tomorrow. However, I will write to you about my particular problem, if you wish."

"I will look forward to it."

"Alice! Alice! Where are you, girl?" Called a voice further up the lane.

Miss Thorne's body went rigid. "Coming!"

"Alice! What are you doing harassing strangers upon the street? Surely...oh! Mrs. Thorne!"

Elizabeth watched as a very fashionable woman approached them. Hair the colour of straw. Pale skin without even the slightest mar or blemish. A pouty mouth the perfect hue of red. And a scowl that ruined it all.

"Mrs. Thorne, it is very good to see you. I called at your house yesterday, but the housekeeper said you were at the Spencer house. Alas, I do not know them, and so I did not call upon you. Is Alice bothering you? Oh, who is this?"

"Mrs. Cecil Thorne, allow me to introduce you to Miss Knight, of Bryden. She is here in town visiting her aunt, Mrs. George Spencer. Elizabeth, this is Henry's cousin by marriage."

Mrs. Cecil Thorne curtsied and asked, "Are you the unmarried girl who inherited her uncle's occult books?"

"I do not know if I am the only girl, but I am one of them for sure."

Miss Thorne's eyes went wide and she bit her lip to stop what was clearly a laugh bubbling up. Elizabeth, however, smiled sweetly as if they were chatting about the weather.

"Are you one of those useless bookish girls, like Alice here?"

Elizabeth spoke before Maria could get in one of her verbal cuts. "I do love a good book, Mrs. Thorne."

"Miss Knight asked if I would visit her," Miss Thorne said sweetly.

"You are very busy caring for the baby," Mrs. Thorne said sourly. "You do not have time to be galivanting about town."

Maria drew in a breath and said, "Oh dear, how awkward. I had already invited Miss Thorne over to Mrs. Spencer's for tea tomorrow. I did not think you would miss her, for I have often heard how much you wished she would get out in society more. My friend here is in dire need of company, and a young lady of exceptional reputation. Her father is a clergyman. My friend's mother was Mrs. Spencer's sister, did you know?"

Mrs. Cecil Thorne's mouth continued to pucker. Finally, she managed to say, "Well, Alice is useless as a nurse in any case, so I suppose she can visit this Miss Knight here, if she must."

"Oh, thank you," Miss Thorne said without a trace of mockery.

"Well, we must be off, Mrs. Thorne. I have a large amount of shopping to get done today. Alice, there are at least three more boxes inside. I need you to carry them for me. Come along."

Miss Thorne looked at the ladies and said, "Thank you. Miss Knight, I shall see you tomorrow. What is the direction?"

"Alice!" Mrs. Thorne was already well down the lane. "Hurry up!"

Elizabeth quickly provided the address and Miss Thorne ran off, only to be loudly scolded about running in public.

"How old is Miss Thorne?"

"Thirty, if I recall. Perhaps one and thirty now? She doesn't look it, does she?"

"Goodness. I wouldn't have put her a day over twenty-five. Younger, if she styled her hair more fashionably. Is she from the poor side of the Thorne family?"

Maria laughed as they walked back toward her carriage. "She has a dowry of twenty thousand pounds."

Elizabeth stopped walking. She stared at Maria, who triumphantly grinned. "Indeed, it's true, Eliza."

"Did you see the sorry state of her dress? I own better gowns!"

Maria's smile disappeared. She remained silent until they were both helped into the carriage and she instructed the driver to take them to a cobbler. "So, you want to know about Alice Thorne. Well, she has always been buried in a book. Henry used to help her with her Latin, until her father found out. He was enraged. He practically locked her up. Put her with Sophia and Cecil. She's been turned into a free governess for the youngest children." Maria gave her friend a sad look.

Elizabeth didn't reply. Mary would have Elizabeth living full-time with her and teaching her own children their letters and numbers if she could. There was already a risk of Cassandra being turned into the free female labourer of the family.

"Even still, with that kind of fortune, I am surprised there have been no offers of marriage. Or that they didn't take the arranging upon themselves. Is that not what rich parents do? She is a bit plain, perhaps, but most of that is by choice and not by design. I believe she has a very pretty face. And she appears quite kind and without any airs whatsoever."

"They tried, but she scared off both those matches. Then, they left it to her." Maria noticed Elizabeth's expression and quickly added, "Oh, she's as kind and good as ever you will meet. And she's had plenty of suitors over the years. None got very far. So, her father withholds as much money from her as he possibly can, in hopes of forcing her to accept someone. Anyone, I think, would do at this stage. Unfortunately for her family, she did not care about dresses and ribbons provided she had a book in her hand. And it is impossible to ban books from a young lady. She will always find a way. So, for several years now, she has been shuffling between family members, ever since her mother died. It's been very sad."

"Even if she cannot help with our Mrs. Egerton problem, I believe I would like to know her better."

Maria smiled. "I think you will both get along famously, and then I would finally have an excuse to invite her to Vane Park. I have hinted in the past, but it has always been immediately dismissed. But now? A relation and a friend in neighbouring villages? They would be forced to accept."

Elizabeth quietly listened to Maria's stories about Miss Thorne's hardships, and her kinship toward the young lady grew. They had much in common and Elizabeth knew enough of the world that the darkest days were still ahead for herself. And, indeed, for Miss Thorne, too. Her heart said to make friends with this lady, for there might come a time when they would both need all the friends they could find.

⚜ Chapter 12 ⚜

March 23, 1810

Dear Miss Knight,

    I am in receipt of your letter and it astounded me to such a pitch that I confess I tripped and fell down the stairs. Thankfully, only the servants saw. So, do not worry if you see me with a slight limp! I seem to have bruised myself in several locations. That is my punishment for reading and walking!

    First, I wish to assure you that I agree completely with your assertions for secrecy on this matter. Indeed, we must exercise the highest caution. I do not trust any male member of the occult—Society or otherwise—currently abiding in London. I have had frequent interactions with them and they have all been horrid and rude.

    Secondly, to think that you are in possession of an autograph book! I have heard rumors of it, of course, about London, and that you actually possess the book and, what's more, that you have actually unlocked the ghost! Oh, Miss Knight, I fear I shall faint from excitement.

Of course, I shall assist you in any way possible. Now, for as long as you are in London, it is easy enough. Sophia has hired a new governess, finally! She begins directly. I don't believe for a moment that my sister-in-law had any intentions, but a cousin to the Duchess of Montagu paid a visit and was quite shocked that Sophia had not hired a governess. Sophia instantly set about finding one and, as it happens, this one was available. So I am free! Well, I should correct myself, free to continue our visits.

Now that I finally know of your true intention for making my acquaintance—oh, do not worry yourself in any way that I feel used or unwelcomed. No, indeed, I can barely contain my excitement that you have trusted me enough to bring me into this secret circle of yours. It is quite invigorating.

Now, the point of this matter. With your permission, I would like to postpone our tea visit today so that I can go through my own occult books for information on autograph books.

I know a great deal already, as they have been a pet hobby of study of mine, but I never thought I'd actually have the opportunity to work with one. Oh, I am beside myself with excitement!

Oh, that is Sophia shouting for me. I shall go attend her. She has been quite vexed at having to hire the governess. And you should have heard her when she discovered it was assumed that, at her rank in society, she'd have to pay the governess at least thirty pounds per annum! You should have seen the look on my sister-in-law's face! I thought she was going to die right there and then. Of course, she is going to pay it since she cannot have society gossip about her, and it has been a glorious day.

In fact, earlier today I heard her tell my brother that she would have to pay the poor creature thirty-two pounds because that is what Mrs. Weston is paying hers and her household has less money than my brother's, so the gossip about town would be unbar—
She is coming up the stairs!

Miss A.T.

Elizabeth had been in London for over a week, and yet it seemed like a lifetime had passed by. Miss Thorne became a fast friend of Elizabeth's and had visited twice already.

And Mr. Thorne, of course, who continued to prove helpful. He successfully sold the majority of the books that had been sorted and available in the drawing room, leaving Elizabeth with the grand sum of sixty-eight pounds, eleven shillings, and seven pence. The dining room was partially usable as of breakfast that morning.

Elizabeth sat her new writing desk upon the small, round table in the corner of her room. She had bought both with the proceeds of her book sale. At first, she had considered purchasing both used, but Maria, Aunt Cass, Henry Thorne, Sally, Miss Thorne, Mrs. Cook, Mr. Osborne, James, and even little Tom told her to buy something beautiful that was hers and would always be hers because, to quote them all, "Mr. Leigh would have wanted you to do that."

She carefully opened the top of the desk, using the key in her reticule. The writing desk was a perfect rectangular box, complete with carrying handles. The table was ingenious, as it had hinges on the legs, allowing it to fold up perfectly, and to be carried like a basket. Together, both items cost her eight pounds, two shillings, and ninepence which was a shocking sum of money. She never owned anything so expensive in her life.

Oh, but to have a locked box, that was her property! That she purchased with her own inheritance and earnings. It had a tiny compartment for an ink pot, and the lockable drawer where she could put money, papers, even a leather-bound journal. She'd also purchased a very basic, much smaller, volume as a diary of accounts and the various day-to-day business. The journals were a significantly cheaper expenditure, at just seven shillings and nine pence, but it was still a luxury in her eyes. However, if she were to be serious about the occult, and assisting Mrs. Egerton, then she would begin a magical journal. Plus, she needed a new daily accounts book.

She laughed at the two piles of money on her desk. Sixty pounds was three years worth of her pin money for clothes, gifts, plays, presents, letters, her parcels, tips for servants at Mary's, all of it! Three years worth lay in just one pile of money. The other was nearly three-quarters of her annual sum.

And here it was, just sitting upon the desk!

She put the journal, and all her money, back into her drawer. It was a mixture of bill notes and coins. The bill notes would only be useful in London; none of the Bryden shops took bills from town banks. She would have to make a point to purchase as much as possible with the larger bills while in town, so that she would have more coinage.

Though, she considered that part of the reason her desk and table cost so much was because they did not have the exact change in their drawer to provide her. So there was no guarantee on that score, either.

She could ask Charles to come to town and put it into a bank account for her, but quickly decided that she would rather carry around a trunk of coins for the rest of her life than do that. As soon as he knew how much money she had on her person, he would find a way to steal it.

Panic hit her. He might even break her desk, just to get the money.

She took several breaths to calm the panic that rose in her. There was no purpose to be served in summoning up imaginary situations that had not yet happened. She would prepare herself, of course, but she would do so in a dignified, and sensible manner.

To the immediate problem. The guineas and most of the smaller coins were placed in her desk's hidden drawer. She placed a fifteen-pound note in there, too, though she had no idea if she'd ever be able to spend it. She had several two- and five-pound notes. Those went into her reticule pile still upon the desk. A few of the odd coins went in there, too. She split the one-pound notes between both sections of money. Finally, she counted everything twice.

On the first page of the smaller journal, she wrote:

March 23
Total in desk: £60
Pin money: £14 6s 6d

She was struck between panic over the fear of the money being stolen and her spending it all on frivolous, useless things. She rested a hand upon the desk. No, she would not allow her good sense to be scared away. The desk was perfect for her, and it was time she had one of her own, especially if she was to begin occult studies. Besides, she and her sister Cassandra shared a desk with Isabella, and the two youngest girls had a used writing desk that was very poor. Even her father lamented that he would need to purchase a new one soon.

Terror struck her at that thought. She did not want Isabella or Cassandra using her desk. They might risk finding the hidden drawer and the money beyond.

She would order a desk for Cassandra. Of course! Her sister turned eighteen the next month. A lovely writing desk would be the perfect gift on such a significant birthday. She would get Cassandra a style different from her own, so that there would be no mistaking them.

The pressing weight on her chest eased. She needed to concentrate on the important things. She had the money now. More than she'd ever seen before. She would be cautious with it, but she would also not hoard it. It was expected she would tip Sally upon her eventual quitting of London, and she would leave double what she normally could afford. Her aunt paid for her mourning dress before Elizabeth could even offer. Mr. Baldwin's entire cobbler shop came down with a horrid fever and had wrote to tell Maria that their footwear would all be delayed. Knowing Maria, that would mean Elizabeth's boots would end up on an account.

She simply needed to exercise caution and good sense.

A stack of letters on her bed caught her gaze and brought her back to her original task at hand. She had been remiss in her duty—as a sister, a niece, and as a daughter. And, if she did not write the letter that she most did not wish to pen, she would continue to be so.

March 23, 1810
London

My dear Mary,

    I have been a faulty writing companion over these last days. I hear from Isabella that the children are all healthy, and that you are finally over your bad cold. I trust no lingering affects have come from it, and that you are back to your usual duties and pursuits. I have misplaced the letter you sent in all of the packing and repacking of books. It had the date of the ball in it. Have you had it yet? I hope you were not too ill.

    Now, I must come to the point of this letter. Be assured that I am well, as is Aunt Cass. However, what I am about to tell you might be distressing. It was for me. Please only read further when you are able.

    As you have no doubt heard, my uncle left me several books. What isn't commonly known yet is that he also kept all of the letters from our dear mother. In particular, seventeen are from the days just before you were brought into this world. They include her wishes and dreams for your life, and her own worries and hopes. It also contains the last letter I believe she wrote to him.

    I feel very strongly that our uncle wished for you to have them, but did not have the strength to sort through them during his final days. Therefore, I have taken the task upon myself. Mr. Thorne's brother is heading to your part of the country, and has graciously offered to bring the entire package to you himself. The entire Thorne clan have been excellent people to me during this entire affair, as I was very uneasy about sending these letters through the post.

I must confess, Mary, that I have experienced a significant amount of guilt at not writing to you about the letters until now. I can make no apology, other than I have been dealing with a great many things since our uncle's death. I have found this task, and so many others, to be rather painful and quite fatiguing.

There are more letters, written before your birth. I do not know the best way to divide them between us. Aunt Cass had thought perhaps we could pick a date between my birth and our mother's death and split the letters accordingly. However, I confess myself too taxed to make that decision at present. I will bring all the remaining letters back to Bryden with me and will keep them safe until we make a decision between us.

Send my best wishes to Mr. Fitzharding, and the children for me. Please ask the children what they would like from London. Boiled sweets perhaps? Also, pray ask Miss Hattie if there is anything she requires in town and I shall procure it for her.

"Miss Knight? Mrs. Thorne and Mrs. Spencer said they are ready to leave now."

"Thank you, Sally. I shall be down directly."

"Yes, miss."

Elizabeth quickly ended her letter, adding the address and seal. She picked up the bundled letters, which were tightly wrapped in brown paper. She tucked the letter underneath the string on the parcel. She tugged on her wool spencer. It looked to be a fine day outside, so her heavy pelisse would probably be too warm with her new wool mourning dress. She tied her lavender bonnet ribbons into a pretty bow.

She gave herself an appraising look in the mirror. She had grown tired of the black gowns, if she was perfectly honest. However, she wished to mourn her uncle appropriately. She had not yet reached an agreement with her aunt about the appropriate date for her to transition to half mourning. If her aunt had her way, Elizabeth would already be wearing lavender and grey.

The new gown was quite comfortable, being both warm and soft to the touch. The neckline was lower than she preferred for during the day, so she tied her black gauze neck scarf to reduce the amount of bare skin at her throat.

"Elizabeth!" Aunt Cass called out from somewhere within the house.

Elizabeth grabbed the package and rushed down the stairs, to the disapproving looks of her aunt. She handed the parcel to the Thorne's coachman. He nodded and said he'd make sure it was delivered. He had a storage box underneath his seat, which he placed the bundle of letters. Oh, she hoped it didn't rain, or at least the box was watertight. They squeezed into the tiny cabin of the carriage that was designed for three's comfort. However, they travelled in jolly companionship and eventually arrived at their destination.

West Alley Buildings weren't the sort of place a person like Elizabeth would normally visit in London. For all his Christian duty, her father would never have permitted her to pay a visit upon the impoverished neighbourhood. However, her father was not here, and she also had Maria and Mr. Thorne, and her aunt, and a carriage's servants.

"Do you need my assistance within?" Mr. Thorne asked.

Aunt Cass waved him off. "This is not the first time I have come looking for a former servant in the slums. We shall only be a moment, in any case, to speak with the ladies inside."

"I shall await with the carriage. Send word if I am required," Mr. Thorne said.

"We will," Aunt Cass replied.

The street was barely wide enough to handle the Thornes' chaise and four. The steps of West Alley Buildings were littered with desperate people: mothers holding dirty babies, war wounded, the ill, the abandoned.

Elizabeth felt a pang to stop and assist them all, but Aunt Cass said, "Come along, Elizabeth."

Elizabeth was unable to meet the eyes of a small toddler, dirty-faced, next to her mother who held an even smaller babe. Once inside the damp, dark, and dirty corridor, Elizabeth said, "Aunt, should we not help them?"

The hallway was so narrow and dark that Elizabeth's eyes struggled to adjust to the limited light. Her aunt continued walking, stepping over a cluster of a sick woman and her children. Elizabeth glanced down at their outstretched hands, and her heart tore.

Aunt Cass stopped in her tracks. She turned to the woman who was sat upon the floor. As Elizabeth's eyes adjusted, she noticed the woman's face was badly bruised. Cut lip. Swollen eye. The woman's children held out their dirty hands.

"Are the children outside yours, too?" Aunt Cass asked the woman upon the floor.

The woman nodded. Her eyes were heavy and lidded, noticeable even in the dimmed light.

"Is your man still inside the room?"

"He kicked us out, he did. Said my momma was useless," the little boy of about eight said. "We're waiting for my aunt to come home so that we have somewhere to live."

"Hush," the boy's mother scolded. "Sorry, ma'am."

"And why aren't you out working to help your mama?" Aunt Cass asked severely. "The baby is outside working. Why aren't you?"

Elizabeth was shocked by her aunt's tone, as well as the knowledge that the baby outside was this poor woman's own child. Did she loan out the babe? And at what price?

"Forgive us, ma'am," the woman said in a hoarse, pained voice that cut through Elizabeth's soul. "My boy here is my youngest son, so he stays with me during the day. He runs errands for the ladies in the back two apartments, who take in laundry. I do any sewing and mending repairs for them, and he brings it back and forth. But my hand is hurt, ma'am, I'm very sorry."

Elizabeth looked down at the woman's outstretched hand. Even through the cloth and dimness of the corridor, she could clearly see the blisters. "Good god, what happened to you?"

The woman lowered her head. "Just hurt it, miss."

"Will your sister take you in?" Maria asked.

"She always does, ma'am. Thank you for caring, ma'am."

Tears welling up in her eyes now, Elizabeth was unable to control herself any longer. She tugged the strings on her reticule and pulled out a one-pound note. "Take it."

Aunt Cass and the woman exchange a knowing look. Aunt Cass gently pushed the paper note back toward her niece. Even as her niece protested, Maria was already handing over several small coins to the boy.

Aunt Cass did the same to the lady. "That should pay your sister for your room and board, while you recover."

"Oh, thank you, ma'am. Thank you." She looked at Elizabeth. "Is this your daughter, ma'am?"

Aunt Cass's smile was gentle. "My niece."

"She is a very good girl. So elegant." She blinked her eyes and seemed to notice the black dresses upon two of the ladies for the first time. "Very sorry for your loss, miss. Ma'am."

"Thank you. And my niece is the best girl alive," Aunt Cass said. She gave the injured lady a final nod. "Come, ladies. We have a servant to find."

"Ma'am, might I be so bold? I might know who you are looking for," the woman said.

"Mrs. Taylor, an elderly former servant, and a Miss Susan...I do not know the young lady's surname now that I think of it." Aunt Cass pondered for a moment. "No, it quite escapes me. Mrs. Taylor must be seventy or thereabouts, and her niece has been quite ill with a cough."

"She is upstairs, in one of the cheap rooms. Danny, show the ladies please."

Little Danny jumped to his feet and rushed ahead to show them to the staircase. The boy chatted Maria's ear off, who seemed content to let him. Elizabeth whispered to her aunt, "Why would you not allow me to help them?"

"Elizabeth, what would these people do with a bank note?" Aunt Cass asked. "Consider that the boy here is as likely to have lost it in the wind as it be stolen from him. And who would make them change for a bill note when buying a pound of cheese? Someone will see that, and they'll be robbed. Or, let's say they don't get robbed. Who has enough coins on them to make change? The markets down here aren't Bond Street, child."

Elizabeth nodded and said, "Sorry, Aunt. I was overcome."

"I know. But, you cannot help everyone. So, when you do help them, help in the way that is best for them and not for you," Aunt Cass said. "A handful of coins, which might add up close to a pound in any case, will be easier for them to manage. Remember that, the next time you come somewhere like West Alley Buildings."

Elizabeth nodded and fell silent. Eventually, she pulled out a handkerchief from her reticule to cover her nose and mouth, to prevent the inhalation of miasmic air. Aunt Cass and Maria soon joined her, especially upon the sound of a racking cough coming from an adjacent room. They made their way down the long, even darker corridor than the one down below.

Elizabeth's heart ached for all of these wretched people, and wondered how to help them all. Of course, there was no way that she could. It would take more than her money to help. Her father might not have taken the bible's teachings on charity seriously, but she absolutely did.

So, she tried to remind herself that they did help. They helped the woman in the corridor. They were walking to help Mrs. Taylor and her niece. She was helping. She was doing all that she could.

She simply wished she could do more.

It was just as well that Danny announced they were at the correct apartment, lest she begin to experience a stab of resentment toward her rich friend and aunt. It was their money to do with as they pleased, and she knew Maria did plenty in her own village to help relieve the poor's suffering.

She only wished to do so much herself, to help ease the suffering, and to make life a little easier for all.

"Oh, Mrs. Spencer! Miss Knight! Ma'am! What a surprise. I had not expected visitors."

"We are here to see how your niece does," Aunt Cass said.

"Oh, you wouldn't believe the improvement. Come in, if you please."

Mrs. Taylor opened the door and they entered the cramped room. It was the size of Elizabeth's bedroom at the rectory. A candle burned on a table, casting the only light in the room. There was no window. No fireplace. The ladies had a small bed upon the floor in one corner, with a pile of shabby blankets upon it. Two wooden chairs with blankets upon each were to one side. A small table between them, with the leavings of an earlier meal.

"Mrs. Taylor, this is Mrs. Thorne," Aunt Cass said.

"Oh ma'am, I cannot tell you what assistance your husband and your housekeeper have been," Mrs. Taylor said. "Your Mr. Thorne has been here every day to check upon us, and to bring us some wildly expensive thing from the market. Why, only yesterday? He brought Susan a bottle of milk! Milk!"

Maria smiled and a hint of a laugh crept into her voice. "Mr. Thorne never said a word."

"Oh dear! He even said it was to be our secret." Mrs. Taylor's old face creased with worry. "I'm very sorry, ma'am. In my excitement, I told a secret I was supposed to keep."

"I believe we shall keep this one under our bonnets then," Maria said. "Is that Miss Susan?"

Mrs. Taylor looked back at the pile of blankets and nodded. It was then that Elizabeth realized that there was a small body underneath all those tattered quilts. "She is asleep, I believe. I don't wish to wake her."

"I am awake, Aunt," came a small voice from under the blankets.

Elizabeth was surprised to see that Miss Susan was a rather thin woman of about her own age, or a little older. Her eyes were tired, and her hair was half out of its braid. Her shift was thin and Susan held a blanket against her chest, no doubt both for modesty and to protect against the drafts.

"Susan, you know Mrs. Spencer, of course. This is Mrs. Thorne, Mr. Thorne's wife, and her friend, Miss Knight. I don't believe you have ever met Miss Knight."

"No, indeed. I was always at the Royal Occult Society whenever Miss Knight was in town. I only know her by reputation. I am Miss Susan Markson. My pupils always called me Miss Susan, so I would not object if you did."

"You are a teacher?" Elizabeth exclaimed.

"Yes," Miss Susan said in a weak voice. "I suppose, I was, until my illness. I taught the very young children of the Royal Occult Society families whenever they were in town. On occasion, I have lived with the various families to help out their governesses with the small ones."

"I had no idea," Elizabeth said. "What did you teach?" Susan settled into a coughing fit, and Mrs. Taylor poured her a glass of beer.

"Oh, please do not answer if it will distress your body," Elizabeth said.

"Oh, no, the doctor said the cough may linger for quite some time. Once the fever broke two days ago, I have been feeling much stronger. Though, if you could avoid making me laugh, that would be a kindness."

Mrs. Taylor looked at the ladies. "Mr. Thorne is a wonderful man, but he is determined to make that girl laugh."

"That would be in his nature," Maria muttered.

Miss Susan smiled. "To answer your question, Miss Knight, I taught the children their colours and letters, and the usual things you teach young children. I also taught the slightly older ones some of the very basics about the occult."

"Oh, how interesting," Elizabeth said.

Aunt Cass began asking Mrs. Taylor about financials, while Elizabeth remained quiet. If Miss Susan was a teacher, indeed a governess at the Royal Occult Society, then she could assist with the Mrs. Egerton problem. If she could have Miss Susan removed to their home, as opposed to Maria's, then she could assist Elizabeth with the basics. And Miss Susan might know different subjects than Miss Alice Thorne…

"I was hoping that we might take on some work. Susan's eyes are better than mine, so I could care for some little ones while she does some sewing. But until then, ma'am, I have an annuity of five pounds per annum. And your brother left me a pension, as well, which is another three pounds. However, that hasn't been paid yet. Susan had a little money saved, and she was paid two pounds eight shillings upon her dismissal, so we've used that to pay for the weekly lease." Mrs. Taylor forced a smile. "We are making do."

Aunt Cass kept her tone even, but Elizabeth knew that look of anger. "My nephew is, of course, very distraught that he forgot to pay for the wages he owed you. He had become engaged, not knowing his uncle was upon his death bed. So, you can imagine the worry and distress that has caused him."

"Oh, indeed. That is so difficult, when what should be an excellent time is clouded by such sadness," Mrs. Taylor said.

Aunt Cass did not acknowledge the statement, and Elizabeth knew it was because her aunt would not have been able to hold back a sarcastic comment. They talked some more about how Mr. David Leigh had tasked Aunt Cass with passing along the forgotten wages, and a little extra as way of an apology for having been remiss. Mrs. Taylor was all gratitude.

"Aunt? Might I have a word with you in the corridor, if you do not object?" Elizabeth asked, a thought striking her.

"Can it not wait?"

"No, aunt. There is something particular I believe to have forgotten. Mrs. Taylor, would you mind terribly if I leave Maria to keep you company?"

Maria answered for Mrs. Taylor. "If you leave me alone with this woman, know I shall be interrogating her on every single bit of news about my husband, so that I might tease him later."

Outside in the corridor, Elizabeth asked, "May we move Miss Susan to your house?"

"Mine? Why?"

"Did you not hear? She knows of the occult, and has taught children inside the actual Royal Occult Society building. She could be of use to us."

"Your father would never allow you to associate with a servant." She glanced over her shoulder at the door. "I confess I am not keen on the idea myself."

"She is not a servant. She is a teacher. A governess. That is a very acceptable person for me to associate with."

Aunt Cass sighed. "She is the great-niece of my brother's *servant*."

Elizabeth gave her aunt an annoyed look. "Who will be the one to tell my father that part of her history?"

Aunt Cass said nothing.

"Let us not forget that Maria's own grandfather was a grazier before he went into trade."

"Maria Thorne is wife of a very wealthy and respectable gentleman," Aunt Cass said. She lowered her voice. "It is not the same thing."

Elizabeth took as much care as possible with her words, but she knew she was in the right on this matter. "*Aunt*. We must help. I will, if you will not. I am determined."

Aunt Cass's shoulders slumped enough to alert to Elizabeth that she had won the argument. She would not be able to push her aunt much more, but she had achieved a victory.

"I will need a pretense. Mrs. Taylor is a proud woman. You're too used to the country. In town, servants have their own class. They are proud of their positions and they want to work."

"She is an old woman," Elizabeth said.

"And prouder than a young servant," Aunt Cass said. She gestured at the door. "Come. Let me do this before I change my mind."

Elizabeth followed her aunt inside, to a laughing Maria and a coughing Susan. "Did you make her laugh?"

Maria gave her friend a guilty look. "Henry."

Aunt Cass rolled her eyes. "Mrs. Taylor, I realize that the original offer was for you and Miss Susan to move to Mrs. Thorne's home as soon as the doctor gave permission. However, I was wondering if you would both considering moving in with me for the time being?"

"Oh, but we are staying with Henry's father for the next week, so they can still move in as planned. And there is so much room that we wouldn't even notice them."

"That is true. However, my niece and I have decided that Mrs. Taylor could be of great company to Mrs. Cook while my housekeeper is away. And, to be very honest, I would welcome the addition of company as well." Aunt Cass's words died abruptly. Then, as the rest of the tale suddenly came to her, she continued. "Oh, and Elizabeth would like to make more of Miss Susan's acquaintance. She has a particular occult problem that she is in…in…"

Elizabeth glanced at her aunt and jumped in to rescue her. "I am in need of knowledgeable ladies who could help me with a rather unique occult problem. Obviously, Miss Susan's health is of paramount priority. However, I thought that...perhaps Miss Susan's spirits would improve with company and...seeing my new collection of occult books. And...erm...helping with my particular problem."

"Oh, I would love to see your collection, Miss Knight!"

"That is very kind, Mrs. Spencer, but I could not take any more charity from you. You have already been too generous to us," Mrs. Taylor glanced at her niece. "Truly, you have been very kind."

"I believe I have misrepresented my case, Mrs. Taylor. I am offering you a position in my house, as temporary housekeeper. There is plenty of room in the servant's quarters below, which are heated I might add. Even Sally has her own bedchamber, and she is just a chambermaid, and she has often commented on how dry her own quarters are. Every room has a fireplace. You would not be inconveniencing anyone. And, since we have a spare bedroom upstairs, Miss Susan is welcome to come and stay until she is able to go back teaching."

"Ma'am, I lost my position when I became ill," Miss Susan said. "When I am fully recovered, I shall have to inquire for another placement, but I fear it might be some time."

"When the time comes, I would be happy to offer my assistance. I have many friends in town of the first class of society," Aunt Cass said. "This is a perfect scheme. While you recover, your aunt can assist about my house, giving poor Mrs. Cook a break. She has been trying to look after houseguests and be housekeeper, and still keeping up with all the meals, and she is run ragged."

"I fear for Mrs. Cook's health," Maria interjected. She glanced at a confused Aunt Cass and said, "I did not wish to pry, but she isn't as young as she used to be, Mrs. Spencer. And Sally can't help her, because of all of the books from Mr. Edward Leigh, and Mr. David Leigh. The poor woman."

"Oh," Mrs. Taylor said. "I have always liked Mrs. Cook. I had not realized how tired she must be."

Elizabeth made an encouraging gesture at Miss Susan, who quickly got the hint of what was happening. "Oh, aunt. Are you up for assisting Mrs. Spencer? I would so love to go and...assist Miss Knight. But, of course, if you do not feel up to the task..."

"Nonsense girl, I'm not that old. I don't turn seventy-four until Christmas." Mrs. Taylor looked at her sick niece and nodded. "Well, Mrs. Spencer, I would be honoured to work for you, for as little or as long as you need me to."

"Excellent."

⚜ Chapter 13 ⚜

AFTER CONSULTING MR. Grant yesterday afternoon, it was settled that a sum of seven pounds would be appropriate compensation for Mrs. Taylor's lost wages at her dismissal. Mr. David Leigh had provided her with a final sum that, while legally correct, would have angered Mr. Edward Leigh greatly. So, in accordance with the former employer's personality and general disposition toward those in his service, Mr. Grant believed seven pounds would be proper. He would write to Mrs. Taylor in a day or two, announcing the settlement, and ask her for a meeting to present her with the funds.

Elizabeth dutifully gave Mr. Grant one five-pound note and two one-pound notes. She was not upset by giving away the money to assist Mrs. Taylor. Though, she did have a slight sadness about parting with the money, as she might never see so much actual wealth in her hands again. However, she was practical about it all. Mrs. Taylor lived in London, and she would have an easier time spending a bank note issued by a London bank than she could ever do in the country.

£7 to Mrs. Taylor (via Mr. Grant) for services
Total in desk: £53

Then she considered her pin money expenditures:

2s 14d for charity at West Alley Buildings
£2 19s 5p Writing Desk for Cassandra
2s Music Lesson book for Cassandra
2d boiled sweets for Mary's children
Total pin money: £11 1s 9p

She dutifully recorded the expenditure into her journal, and it was then she felt the sense of accomplishment. The boiled sweets were in the parcel with Mary's letters. Cassandra's desk was simpler than her own, but it was new and well-finished. She'd spent a little extra to have a small journal, and a writing set all included within the desk. She purchased the used book of music at Mr. Osborne's bookshop, and it was in excellent condition.

She smiled at the money she'd donated outside Mrs. Taylor's apartments. She handed out every single small coin she had in her reticule to those begging outside the apartment doors.

Fifty-three pounds was still more than double her annual pin money. If she did not share it with Mrs. Taylor, she was certain it would have felt too much like stealing from an elderly, loyal servant. She could not have enjoyed her money with that over her head. No, it was right and proper, and she was happy to provide that payment.

Elizabeth returned to the dining room where only Aunt Cass sat. She had her usual stack of newspapers that James picked up for her every morning. Then, she and Sir William would exchange their papers in the evening. It had been their tradition since Uncle Spencer first moved into the house, and Aunt Cass said she'd miss her evening paper exchange with the neighbours.

"Is there word of Miss Susan?" Elizabeth asked.

Miss Susan and Mrs. Taylor had moved into the house on Saturday, and Elizabeth could clearly see the younger woman's health had improved upon arrival.

She sat down and picked up a warm roll, smearing strawberry preserves on it. Miss Susan had taken ill in the middle of the night with a coughing fit, but she'd been silent for some time now.

"I called for Mr. Smith and he said there is no cause for alarm. The coughing will take several weeks to properly clear, but she is well past the infectious stage. He recommended a medicine to help her sleep, but she refused it on the account that it gave her terrible headaches. Therefore, Mr. Smith recommended a tall glass of warm brandy, and she has been asleep since." Aunt Cass snickered. "As would I be if I'd drank that much all in one sitting!"

"I am certain she needed the sleep."

"Oh, she did. Cook has put aside a plate for her, in case she wakes after the breakfast dishes are cleared. So, do not concern yourself. Eat whatever you need and read your letters."

Elizabeth picked up the pile of fat envelopes. "Goodness. Bryden is never this exciting when I am there."

> *Dear Elizabeth,*
>
> *Isabella told us all about how you nearly died and I'm so happy to hear that you are not dead. Mostly because there is so much happening in Bryden right now.*

Elizabeth burst out into laughter at Georgiana's letter. At Aunt Cass's questioning glance, she clarified, "G is happy I am not dead."

"Shall I assume it is because she has news. Or does she need you to purchase something in London?"

Elizabeth grinned. "So far, news. But I am not through the letter yet!"

Aunt Cass made a thoughtful sound. "A request will be at the end, no doubt."

Elizabeth continued to read her letter while sipping her breakfast chocolate. A few more paragraphs of news about this person and that, and then sure enough:

> *Isabella said I am not to ask this, and I wouldn't except that it is vitally important. There is no decent lace in the shop in the village. It is all too wide. I tried cutting it, but it frayed dreadfully. Isabella said to try folding it, but*

that did not work. Would you please send home some lace? I only need six yards. Oh, and if you are going to be at the shops and have a little money to spare, I would also like three yards of flannel. Pink flower print, if you can find it.

"Six yards of lace? What on earth is she doing with it?" Aunt Cass asked. "And three yards of flannel? What use would three yards be?"

"She might wish to line her spencer? To make it warmer for the spring?"

Aunt Cass seemed dubious about that answer. "But in pink flowers? Have you even seen such a print on flannel?"

Elizabeth sighed. "I swear that girl will drive us all into bankruptcy if we let her."

"She will need to marry a very wealthy man," Aunt Cass said.

"I am not sure there is a man in England wealthy enough for her. Pink flowers on flannel!"

My dear sister,

G and Thea are causing Isabella so much stress that I had to return from Mary's. Isabella's health has not been its usual robustness since you left. She has fainted three times! Some days she is too weak to get out of bed. G and Thea have been horrid to her and I fear there will not be a house left standing if this tarries on much longer.

"Oh dear. Isabella is ill."

"Is it serious?"

"She has fainted three times this week, and is unable to get out of bed," Elizabeth said. Then it dawned on her and her shoulders slumped. "I wonder if she is with child."

Aunt Cass looked at Elizabeth over her newspaper. "That does sound likely. She is quite young still."

A sickness hit Elizabeth's stomach. She had already lost a mother and a stepmother to childbirth. Oh, she did not wish to lose yet another.

"Try not to worry, my dear," Aunt Cass said. "Women do survive pregnancy."

"I know, but…Well, my experiences have not cast a positive light on the situation. I shall have to write to the girls and lecture them. I've not been here a fortnight!"

I am considering sending Thea to stay with Mary, just so that we can get some peace at Bryden.

"Poor Cassie. I wish Mary would simply hire someone for the children. It's not as thought she cannot afford it," Elizabeth said.

"Maybe Cassandra was happy to get away from your sisters," Aunt Cass mused.

Elizabeth made a thoughtful sound. "Possibly. Bryden has been so dull this winter. No one interesting came to the village, I swear. Aunt, are you planning to go to Bath this year? If you are, you might consider bringing Cassandra with you."

"I hadn't considered it, to be truthful. I had planned to stay in London with Edward. Though, I suppose with him gone, I could head there for a couple of months. Would you like to come with me? Bring Cassandra, too, obviously. Maybe we could marry her off, and then you would have a more reasonable sister to spend your time with."

"It would be a relief, that is for sure," Elizabeth said. She glanced at one of the letters. "This one was for you. I'd recognize Mary's handwriting anywhere."

Aunt Cass accepted it and read the letter aloud.

Dear Aunt Cassandra,

I hope all is well in London. My children are delights and look forward to the excellent cake at your table when we return to London. We are very attentive to the particular loss of your brother, and I'm sure the company of children's laughter will be a cure.

I write to you to request that you send my sister, Elizabeth, to Ashbrook as soon as is convenient. My father is, of course, very concerned about the notion of her socializing in London when she should be in deep mourning, especially with my uncle so recently deceased. Likewise, I am in desperate need of her services. There is no one to care for the children, and I am, of course, too busy running the household. Elizabeth has such a way with them and I need her assistance immediately. And I'm sure you could spare her.

Please write directly with the particulars of her arrival.

Mary

Aunt Cass rolled her eyes at Elizabeth and asked, "Would you like me to write Mary?"

"Please," Elizabeth said. "I have already written her since I've arrived in London."

"Augusta Leigh-Knight was a horrible influence on that girl. Every time she speaks, all I can hear is that shrill woman's voice."

Elizabeth gave her aunt a disapproving look.

"Oh, don't give me that look, Elizabeth Knight. I grew up around Augusta, do not forget." She gave the letter a final glance over before saying, "Mary is only upset because she cannot find an excuse to come to London to sniff around! I suppose I have to read the letter from your father now."

"I didn't know he wrote."

"He wrote yesterday."

"And you have not opened it yet?"

Aunt Cass shrugged. "I will open it now."

Dear Mrs. Spencer and sister,

I wish to extend my condolences upon the death of your brother. Death is always a difficult event for those of us who remain, but we must comfort ourselves that your dear brother is, hopefully, within the embrace of the Lord Almighty in heaven above.

"Hopefully!" Aunt Cass exclaimed, interrupting her own reading. "*Hopefully?* How dare your father behave like a...a...there are no words."

Elizabeth managed to keep her smirk to herself. "He has always been uncomfortable with the Church of England's ambivalent opinion on the occult."

"That is not a good enough reason to make such an accusation! The idea of my brother not going to heaven. The offense! But that is not all."

I have been very uncomfortable with my eldest daughter's association with the occult. Now, however, I hear that she has received a gift from Mr. David Leigh, a gift that might result in a hundred pounds or even more! This is very unacceptable for a single young lady to receive from a single man of Mr. Leigh's position, even though he is her cousin. I am shocked that you would allow this. Shall I count on you to intercede? Perhaps Mr. Leigh will consider marrying Elizabeth as to preserve her reputation.

"Good god!" Elizabeth slumped in her chair. "I am absolutely buying Miss Reeves an engagement gift, I do not care what is proper or required. I am buying that woman something expensive and singular."

Aunt Cass waved the letter in the air. "Now I will have to write to that detestable nephew of mine and tell him to speak to your father. Why do men say women do nothing but gossip, when it's clear your cousin has been gossiping all about town enough that your father has heard!"

I am also writing to call Elizabeth upon her family duties. She is needed at Ashbrook. Her sister Mary quite depends upon her assistance with the little ones, as Mary is very busy at present visiting the poor.

"Mary has never visited the poor," Elizabeth said bitterly.

"Unless it was to steal something from them!" Aunt Cass only laughed harder at Elizabeth's condemning stare.

I am certain Elizabeth is of no use to you in London, and I am sending Charles to escort her onwards.

Elizabeth sighed. "I am so sorry, Aunt. I will write to them to ask them to delay it. There is simply too much going on here for me to leave."

Aunt Cass frowned. "I confess, I have some news that I have not shared with you yet this morning. Charles is already in London and will be calling this morning."

"I beg your pardon?" Elizabeth couldn't believe her ears.

"I received said note from Charles this morning, announcing that he will be here at one o'clock sharp to take you back to Bryden."

"That is…no!" Elizabeth said. "I cannot leave, especially not today. I am not even packed. And the books have not all been sorted yet, let alone sold. And Miss Thorne is coming over this afternoon so that we can work on Mrs. Egerton's incantations. Why did you not tell me?"

"Because there was no point. It is not possible for you to leave today. You've barely been in London. Why on earth would you leave now? No. I will not permit it. Mary can find someone else." Aunt Cass sighed. "Do you think your brother will assume he is invited to dinner?"

"I believe he will expect the invitation, yes," Elizabeth said apologetically.

Aunt Cass made an undignified sound and left to speak with Mrs. Cook about the dinner menu. Elizabeth glanced at the clock and saw that she had nearly two hours before both her brother and her new friend arrived. She was not in the mood whatsoever to tolerate any of Charles' foolishness, and she was certainly not going back to Bryden.

Her trunks weren't even packed!

Three thousand pounds.

Elizabeth had to keep that to herself. She mentally scolded her own mind into promising that she would not let those words tumble out of her mouth no matter what Charles did to provoke her temper.

She spoke with Mrs. Taylor and, together, they decided that the drawing room trunks should be moved to the foyer, in the corner where currently the oak table and dried flowers sat. The table could be moved into the drawing room, and the trunks placed there. It would be a little cluttered, but at least Charles would have somewhere to sit when he visited. And, most importantly, he would not complain of the state of Aunt Cass's house to their father.

With Mrs. Taylor's guidance, the male servants moved the trunks into the discreet corner. Thankfully, the trunks stacked very neatly.

Another letter arrived, this time from Mr. Henry Thorne's servant. He'd successfully hand sold all her agricultural books, both occult and general, and included four pounds, two shillings, and sixpence with the letter. Elizabeth immediately went upstairs to her room and pulled out her journal.

Sale of agricultural books, £4 2s 6d
Total in desk: £57 2s 6d

She heard a knock down below, and locked her desk as quickly as possible. She dropped the keys back into her reticule and carried it, and Mrs. Egerton's book, downstairs with her. She could see her aunt walking toward the drawing room, and James waited to answer the door, allowing Elizabeth to rush across the foyer. She collapsed into a chair, took a deep breath, and began to calm herself.

The door opened.

Footsteps.

James bowed. "Mr. Charles Knight."

Charles marched into the room, bowed slightly to his aunt and said, "Father has sent me to bring you home this minute."

Elizabeth had not expected Charles' angry expression. Nor had she expected his curt tone. It spoiled her mood immediately. "And good day to you, Charles. Why, thank you, my health is well."

"Will you not sit?" Aunt Cass asked, motioning at a spare chair.

He ignored her. "I lost a full day to get here and by God you are coming home this minute, Elizabeth. He wants you away from this occult business immediately and for you to return to the rectory. He orders you to come home."

"Elizabeth is *not* some country curate for him to order about," Aunt Cass said.

"Stay out of this, madam."

"Charles!" Elizabeth said, shocked that her brother would speak to her aunt in that manner.

"Madam, I must insist upon speaking to my sister in private," Charles said.

"Aunt Cass can hear all that you have to say to me."

Charles, however, kept that angry expression on his face and said, "Obey me at once, sister."

Aunt Cass pushed herself to her feet. "Charles Knight. You are nobody to me, and I only afford you good manners because you are my dear niece's half brother. But do not think for a minute I will allow you to come into my home and make demands upon me and my guest."

"Charles, for the love of God. Sit down and be calm," Elizabeth instructed of her younger sibling.

"Listen to me, Elizabeth. When Father is dead, I will be in charge of our household. Now, I recommend you do as I say, or I promise that—"

"How dare you threaten me!" Elizabeth roared, in a voice she had not hear come out of her own mouth since she was a child. She pushed herself from the sofa and stepped closer to him. "How dare you!"

"Look what the occult has turned you into!"

"I remember helping raise you, Charles Augustus Knight. I have endured you stealing, time and time again, the money Papa has given you to pass along to me. I am sorry, Charles, that you have not a career to keep your mind occupied, but whose fault is that? You could be a clergyman. You could have joined the navy or the army. You could even go into the law. I'm sure Mary's husband has enough connections to assist you. Instead, you laze about the countryside, seducing young women because they are only servants and gambling away what little money our family has and thinking none of us know any better."

"If you were not my sister, I would strike you for that comment."

Aunt Cass began to berate him but Elizabeth held up her hand. "Now you listen to me very carefully, brother, because I shall only speak this once to you. I am in London to assist my aunt with my uncle's estate. My cousin David Leigh, likewise, is here and needs assistance with the estate and his library. My help is needed. I am not needed in Bryden or at Ashbrook or anywhere else as badly as I am required here. I do not know what you or anyone else told Papa to make him like this, but it was not from me."

The look on Charles' face announced the answer: he had been the source of the gossip.

"It was you, wasn't it? You told our father some gossip."

"That you accepted a shocking gift from your cousin? Yes, I did tell him that."

"He gave it to Aunt Cass!" Elizabeth said. She threw up her hands in exasperation. "Mr. David Leigh is secretly engaged. He did not want anyone to know because he became engaged the night our uncle died. Only, Mr. Leigh didn't know that our uncle was dying until after he had secured the lady's hand. The books were her idea! "

Charles' anger vanished for a moment, replaced with confusion at her words. But the arrogant sneer returned. "That is not how I heard it."

"And, yet, that is how it happened."

Elizabeth looked around her brother to see Maria and Henry Thorne standing there. Maria's rage was evident. Henry's expression was one of calm; the look of a man who had nothing to fear in life.

To Aunt Cass, Henry Thorne said, "Madam, I apologize that we are late. I was haggling on your behalf and am pleased to announce that I have sold eleven more books for you. I will provide Miss Knight the titles and she can assist with the packing once her guest has left."

Charles snorted. "Thorne, please. I know you are selling them for my sister. It's all over town."

Elizabeth cut him off before he could answer. "Charles! Mr. Thorne is helping with the auction of everyone's books in this house. Do you have any concept of the number of books Cousin David gave to my aunt, as well as the ones my uncle gave me directly in his will? We needed Mr. Thorne's help, and he has been more helpful than you are at the present time. Good God, Charles. You show up here and threaten me, and call me a liar, and suggest that my reputation is blemished somehow."

Charles hesitated. Her anger had stunned him into silence. She did not care in the slightest, for her rage was pent up over years and he would finally feel the brunt of it.

"So, why are you here? Tell me the truth."

Charles licked his lips and it was clear to her that he was forming a lie.

"Tell me this instant!"

Elizabeth shouted so loud that Charles flinched. No one moved. No one spoke. Her calm and rational sense told her to collect herself before she caused herself more distress, but her heart thudded louder and pushed away that part of her.

Finally, it was Maria that broke the silence. "Henry, I left my gloves in the dining room last evening. We should go look for them."

"I know where they are, Mrs. Thorne. I shall escort you," Aunt Cass said in a hushed tone. The chair squeaked as Aunt Cass pushed herself to her feet.

Elizabeth did not take her eyes off her brother. "Everyone, I beg you stay where you are. It appears my brother will only believe gossip and the word of a man, so I may require Mr. Thorne to verify my words. Now. Charles. Speak. Why are you here?"

"Father threatened to cut you off, and it was only Isabella who stopped him. They quarrelled horribly."

In a calmer voice, Elizabeth said, "Charles. *Charles*. So long as I have no husband, I am bound to depend upon you and our father. But I have my own money that legally no man can take from me as long as I remain single. Therefore, if you are here to fetch me back to have me locked into my bedchamber until I will hand over the books for father to sell for your own benefit, then you might as well return home now."

"It has nothing to do with money." His look, however, said it had everything to do with money.

"How much of the sale of *my* books did our father offer you?"

"I don't know what you are…"

"How much Charles?"

Charles scoffed. "It is unseemly for an unmarried woman to discuss money."

"How. Much."

He was silent.

"All of it. Didn't he? If you fetched me back with my books, he would sell them to the Royal Occult Society who came sniffing about the rectory. Then, he promised to give you the money to help you out of whatever hole you are in this time."

In a frustrated voice, Charles said, "Why does any of that matter? You are a spinster and you need to obey your father. I am your brother. I've been sent to fetch you. You will obey."

"No, Charles."

"It's these damned books. They've possessed you, they have. How much money have you made? It wasn't enough that your uncle left you fourteen hundred pounds. He left you all these books, too! I've heard the talk about town. How much money have you made?"

Mr. Thorne cleared his throat. "Miss Knight has made ten guineas, or thereabouts, so far. The bulk of what I have sold has been from the library of Mr. Edward Leigh, which was given to Mrs. Spencer by Mr. David Leigh for her to dispense with as she saw fit."

"And why would David Leigh give *her* his library? She's richer than he is," Charles said.

"Because his lady will not marry him until all of the occult books were gone!" Elizabeth said as she threw her hands in the air. "My cousin did not know which books should stay in the family or leave, so he gave them to Aunt Cass for us to decide."

"Why do *you* get to decide?"

"He was my uncle!" Elizabeth shouted. She drew in another sharp breath and struggled to bring her temper under control. In a calmer voice, she said, "Uncle Edward taught me everything I know about the occult. I knew what books were important to him better than Aunt Cass or Cousin David. This is not some grand conspiracy. It was all of us who are here in London attempting to deal with a horrible event alongside supporting my cousin's engagement to Miss Reeves, and us helping him honour her wishes."

"Oh." Charles grew silent for a moment. "I heard he didn't want any of the auction money. He wanted you to have it all."

Elizabeth's shoulders slumped. "So that I could buy my siblings a few gifts. And a new pair of boots because Thea ruined mine months ago. And to help out one of my uncle's servants. Because Miss Reeves trusted me to make the best decisions, and Mr. David Leigh felt guilty about inheriting nearly all of Uncle Edward's estate. It was his way of helping balance the scales."

"Oh." Charles looked down at his gloves. "Oh no."

Elizabeth sighed, the last of her energy draining out of her. "Aunt? Would you kindly help Maria find her gloves, please?"

Aunt Cass lingered until Elizabeth gave her a small nod. Elizabeth waited until Aunt Cass, Maria, and Henry Thorne left the drawing room. "Were you the one who told Papa all this?"

"No. Not really. I had heard some of it because I came to town last week, just after you arrived. I didn't want you to know I was here. I hadn't told Father. He thought I was at Vane Park, helping the steward with a drainage problem. But I went to London to gamble with some of my old school friends, you see."

"Ah." Elizabeth succeeded at keeping most of the disappointment out of her voice.

"But then I returned to Bryden, there were two gentlemen from the Royal Occult Society there. They said that you had accepted the books from your cousin, and that you were refusing to hand over items that they were supposed to have according to your uncle's will. Then, they said that you were holding out for even more money from them, so they came to Papa to see if he could be reasoned with."

"And you believed them." Elizabeth didn't bother hiding her disappointment.

"You had gotten all that money and I thought…"

"You were jealous of my fourteen hundred pounds."

Charles bowed his head. "You don't understand how difficult it is for me. I am the only son. I will inherit almost nothing from my father when he dies, and I will be left with you and Isabella…and the three girls, unless one of them marries."

"Your mother left you money, Charles," Elizabeth said. "And whatever money father has put aside, you will get it all. He has already told us that."

"That will get me what? A couple hundred a year? I cannot look after five women on that!"

"Then go back to Oxford and finish your ordination. You could work as a curate for a while and support yourself."

Charles made a frustrated sound. "Earning fifty pounds a year dashing between rectories and doing all the work, and living in some dingy house set aside for me. Yes, you've said that before."

"I've said it because it is a good plan for you. You would do well as a curate, and later you might come into a living. Vane Park. Ashbrook. A dozen others about our county. And you are nearly finished with your studies. You are well recovered from the illness. Oxford will accept you back, if that is your worry."

"But how am I supposed to look after you, Elizabeth? It could be years, even decades, before I get a parish or a rectory." A whiny tone entered her brother's words. "It isn't fair that you won't marry. You're just leaving me with the burden of supporting you."

Elizabeth sat back down upon the sofa. For a moment, she was tempted to tell him about the book. But, no, it was not the right time. She did not know when that time would take place. For now, though, it was a secret.

"Charles, for pity's sake. Have some compassion on me. I won't be a burden. My uncle has seen to that. I will be making nearly as much in interest as you would as a curate."

A bitter sound escaped her brother and she knew instantly that was the wrong tactic. "Ah, yes. While I slave about the countryside for fifty pounds, you'll be sitting at home mending my stockings, living off your inheritance."

"What is it that you want, Charles?"

"I want someone to die and leave me money, all right? All of my friends, that's how they got their money. Someone died and left them some. And you? You did nothing, and now you got more than I will be able to make in my lifetime. And, what about when Mrs. Spencer dies, huh? How much of that money will come to you?"

She said nothing. Honestly, Elizabeth had no idea, and did not wish to presume.

"It's the only reason Father allows you to visit London so often. It was so that you could inherit something."

It hurt her to see her brother so full of jealousy and envy, that he would threaten his own sister this way. Still, she said nothing. She had nothing left to say. She had already debased herself with an emotional scene. She would not do so again.

"I know I am a great disappointment to you. I am only trying to make Papa happy. He said to stand up to you, so…I am sorry."

"Charles," Elizabeth said, with more compassion than her brother probably deserved in that moment. "You are the only son. No matter what you do, our father will always love and respect you far more than he will ever feel towards me. After all, are we not Charles and the girls? We don't even get our own names."

Charles lowered his head and sighed.

"Tell Papa that you believe I should be here another fortnight, while I attempt to finish organizing the last of the Leigh collection."

"Why would he believe me?"

She opened her reticule and pulled out the bank notes and coins. She passed it to Charles. "Here is a five pound bank note. And four shillings. Mr. Thorne will most likely have double that again by the time he's done. Tell our father I gave this to you to help support your time in London, and because you needed…whatever it is that you need."

"That is a lie, Elizabeth."

"You lied to him about helping with the drainage at Vane Park. You can lie about this," Elizabeth said. Normally, she felt guilt about lying, but there was only a coldness now. She could not trust any of the men in her family.

"What about the books?"

"I will bring back a very small selection when I return. The rest will be either sold or will remain in London, in Aunt Cass's collection."

He took the money from her and shoved it all into his breast pocket. "What about the Royal Occult Society?"

"The truth. Say that you have spoken with Mr. Thorne about it and he believes they were attempting to deceive us all. In fact, tell him that the Society gentlemen were attempting to steal what my uncle did not want them to have."

After a moment's consideration, he said, "I will do what you ask. But, Papa will not be pleased with you." Elizabeth said nothing. He stared at her for a moment longer, thinking she would speak. However, when it was clear she was dismissing him, he nodded and said, "Fine. I will tell him. Two weeks, Elizabeth. I doubt any of us can hold him off for longer."

"Two weeks, Charles."

The door was barely closed behind her brother when Miss Thorne walked into the room. "Miss Elizabeth, I am so sorry for having eavesdropped. The butler let me in and said you would wish to see me. I heard everything. I am so very sorry. Are you well? Would you like a glass of wine? I will ask the servant."

Elizabeth sucked in a breath and pushed down the rising terror in her soul. As horrid as that argument had just been, the one she was going to have in fourteen days would be so much worse. She tried to speak, but could not form the words.

"I will get Mrs. Spencer this instant. Oh, Mrs. Spencer! Elizabeth is done for."

Aunt Cass rushed into the room to wrap her arms around Elizabeth, who broke down into weeping sobs. "There, there, child. Mr. Thorne is off to chase your brother and bribe the worthless young man into submission."

That only made Elizabeth weep harder. Maybe she should just sell the damn book. Then maybe her father would leave her alone.

"I will go," Miss Thorne said.

"No."

Elizabeth pulled away from her aunt and wiped her eyes with the back of her sleeve. "No, Miss Thorne. You will stay. I have two weeks left in town and I am determined more than before that we shall figure out Mrs. Egerton's book incantation."

Given to Charles: £5 4s 0d
Total left in reticule: £5 17s 9d

~⚜ Chapter 14 ⚜~

ELIZABETH AND MISS Thorne sat down at the dining room table, while Maria and Aunt Cass puttered about. Miss Susan had woken up and insisted upon helping. Sally helped escort her downstairs, while Tom carried a blanket and a heavy shawl. Miss Susan was placed near the robust fire, then her legs and shoulders covered.

The ladies sat down to work, but Elizabeth's mind raced out of control. Her heart would not stop pounding, and her hands shook. She struggled to read her notes aloud, and her eyes welled with tears twice. Despite all her personal command, she could not will her body to behave proper according to society and custom.

She should not have raised her voice at her brother. She would pay the price for that in the future, and no doubt it would be a very high sum indeed. Shame and guilt flooded her for having behaved in such a manner. Fury at her brother and his horrid remarks.

"I am sorry, ladies, but I must speak up," Miss Thorne said after twenty minutes of Elizabeth struggling with the simplest of questions. "Miss Knight. You are in no condition to assist Mrs. Egerton if you are unable to even write your own name."

Elizabeth rubbed her forehead with the back of her hand. "I cannot just sit here and wait for Mrs. Egerton's spell to worsen. I only have a short period of time, and…"

"Miss Elizabeth Knight," Mrs. Egerton's voice said clearly into the silence that fell between the women. "Your friend is correct. You are of no use to anyone in this state. I suggest Miss Susan and Miss Thorne work together with me on the basics, while you, your aunt, and Mrs. Thorne continue the work of sorting and inventorying books for Mr. Thorne to foist upon the rich men of London."

"I wouldn't call it foisting," Elizabeth mumbled.

"I agree with Mrs. Egerton, Miss Knight," Miss Susan said. Her voice was stronger now that she'd had hot coffee with some bread and butter. "Miss Thorne and I can sit over here, and we'll bring Mrs. Egerton's book closer so that we can all speak quietly. Then, you can continue to work on the books. We are still missing several volumes that we require to do all of the necessary spellwork, and Mrs. Egerton is positive those books are somewhere in your collection. Perhaps the footman could bring in one of the unsorted trunks so that you can remain with us."

Elizabeth relented, but only because Miss Susan was in such a delicate place with her illness that she did not want to cause the young woman any distress. The footmen carried down one of the trunks from the upper drawing room as instructed, and Elizabeth began going through it.

Mrs. Egerton chattered on about the importance of focus and clarity of thought. Personal distractions could taint an incantation, even one that was previously created and deemed successful. There was an art to it, she explained. The occult was an exchange, just as at a shop. The occultist had to offer up something useful and then ghosts might decide to return a form of magic back upon the occultist in payment.

"What is most important is that there is not one spell, not one incantation. There is no such thing. A dozen different ones can be used to bring me back, for instance. What is important is the intent behind it."

"But your book has an incantation in it already," Elizabeth said.

Mrs. Egerton made an annoyed sound. "That was only because I feared the men of this age would be too stupid to figure out how to summon me and I'd be stuck in that book for a thousand years until women finally rose up and conquered them."

"Goodness," Aunt Cass said. "I do not know if I wish the present order of things be overturned in a revolution."

"Consider, Aunt. Roving bands of ladies, seducing the innocent young gentlemen and leaving them abandoned in their homes without reputation or a penny to their names."

"Hush. Your father would never speak to me again if he knew I let you speak such nonsense."

That made Elizabeth smile. When she considered what a roving band of ladies would look like, who behaved like men in a society with no consequences, she actually laughed at the shocking display that formed in her mind.

"Elizabeth Knight," Aunt Cass said in a very stern voice. "Stop thinking about whatever debauchery is in your head. It is unfit for a young lady to consider such things."

"Yes, indeed. Unless, of course, she wishes to use that knowledge to cast an incantation," Mrs. Egerton said.

"Mrs. Egerton!" It was Maria this time. "You will corrupt these young women."

There was silence. They turned to the book and waited for the sarcastic retort. Nothing came.

"Mrs. Egerton?" Elizabeth asked.

Nothing.

"Does the spell need resetting?" Miss Susan asked.

Elizabeth shook her head, unsure of what had happened. A sinking feeling settled into her belly. Perhaps they had finally used up the last of the ghost's stored magic. Elizabeth re-read the summoning spell, but nothing happened.

She sighed. "Well, ladies. It looks like we are now on our own."

THREE DAYS HAD passed since Mrs. Egerton's ghost disappeared. Aunt Cass wrote to Mrs. Cecil Thorne and introduced herself, asking if Miss Thorne could be spared.

> *Madam, I know this request contravenes propriety and the rules of society. Still, I hope with all my heart that you will grant my request. Miss Thorne has been a treasure to me in this difficult time. I have found my spirits in desperate need of youthful company, and it has been a relief to have Miss Thorne here. Might I trouble you to keep Miss Thorne for a full week, until the fifth of April? I find myself quite unable to live without the girl.*

Mrs. Cecil Thorne's reply came three hours later in the form of a carriage delivering Miss Thorne's packed trunks.

The ladies had managed to sort through all of Elizabeth's original magical inheritance. Once again, Mr. Henry Thorne was tasked with finding buyers. Elizabeth's bedroom closet was stuffed full of the books she wished to keep. Miss Thorne had gone through them, and then Miss Susan, and they both agreed that what was left should be kept. Elizabeth wished to dispose of another half again, but Aunt Cass was prevailed upon to step in, and Elizabeth relented.

While Henry Thorne was out harassing the local booksellers again, Elizabeth sat at the head of Aunt Cass' dining room table. Before her was Mrs. Egerton's autograph book, along with her own occult journal, and several reference books. There were crockery pots of rose petals, cocoa, thyme, rosemary, a silver bowl filled with water, a piece of red ribbon, and a drawing of Mrs. Egerton.

About the table were the other members of the small group. Aunt Cass was there, serving as the matronly chaperon. She had taken to the role rather quickly and jokingly announced she might stay in black attire to match the part.

Maria was there, in case anyone needed French translated. She was dressed smartly in a fashionable gown of light blue, along with a delightful cap and neck wrap.

Miss Susan was seated nearest the fire. Several botany books were laid out in front of her, along with her own occult journals purchased for her from Elizabeth's own money. Sally had organized the purchase, and had returned with several writing journals of various sizes. She'd haggled the prices down to eight shillings and sixpence and happily returned the correct change to Elizabeth. She spared Elizabeth the condescending remarks about how she was pitiful at haggling when carrying ready cash; those comments were left to Miss Thorne, who despaired of Elizabeth being near robbed by posted shop prices.

Miss Susan wore a simple gown that did not fit her properly, with a print that had been faded beyond recognition. The condition was made starker by the shawl she borrowed from Aunt Cass, with its intact lace, bright pattern, and the lack of holes. However, Miss Susan wasn't as pale as she'd been, and was strong enough to sit at the table for hours at a time now, provided her back was to the fire. She still struggled to eat a proper meal, but she was able to enjoy a small slice of cake or bun with cup of coffee. She preferred it to tea, so Mrs. Cook was constantly on her guard ready to have the drink available.

Miss Thorne was seated next to her in a striped yellow and brown dress. Her hair was pulled into a severe bun at the nape of her neck, and her spectacles kept falling down her nose. In front of her sat Uncle Edward's Latin writings, plus a stack of several Italian and German books. She had two of her own journals in front of her. One was new. The other was half-filled and worn with age.

The ladies nodded that they were ready to begin.

"Okay ladies. Shall we list the things we are uncertain about that could affect the summoning incantation? First, we do not know the amounts or weights. So those might have to be adjusted. We also do not know precisely the order of things, so we need to be methodical with how we approach that. And, finally, we do not know if there are any unknown elements that are interfering. Have I omitted anything?"

Miss Susan raised her hand slightly. "Miss Knight? I also wish to note that fresh and dried plants and herbs might have changeable effects. However, not all do, so that is another consideration."

Elizabeth added the note to her journal. When she finished, she noted the other ladies were adding to theirs, including even Maria. Elizabeth gave her friend a knowing smile.

"My dear Eliza, as the only official married woman involved in this scheme, I must learn my role fully. After all, I wouldn't want people to think that this was merely a way to catch a husband. With Mrs. Spencer's keen eye and my position in society, I hope to add some legitimacy to this group if it called upon."

"I doubt the Royal Occult Society cares about what a group of women are doing," Miss Susan said.

"Then more's the pity for them, for we shall do great things," Maria said.

"I do not know about great things, Maria, but I would be happy for Mrs. Egerton's sharp wit back in my life," Elizabeth said. She flipped her journal page back. "So, the things we do know. We know that we cannot have a man in the room at any time during the summoning because Mrs. Egerton will not appear to a man. I do not know if that also includes servants. Has anyone ever witnesses Mrs. Egerton speak around male servants?"

Everyone shook their heads. Even Sally spoke up. "She's never spoken with me in the room, miss."

Elizabeth considered that. "Then, to be prudent, let us assume that no new members or even servants. Would you all agree?"

The other women nodded. Sally curtsied and asked Aunt Cass, "Would you like me to stay outside and guard the door, ma'am? I can ensure you're not disturbed and can bring in the tea things or fetch anything else you need."

"I think that is an excellent notion, Sally. Also, please ask Mrs. Taylor to summon the twins for the next week, if they are available. We will be relying upon your assistance to fetch items from the shops, and whatever small tasks we need. You will require someone to take over your daily duties."

"Very good, ma'am. Do you wish the girls to stay here or return home?"

Aunt Cass considered. "Whatever their mother thinks is best. We have room for them in any case. I will summon you when we are ready for tea."

"Very good, ma'am." Sally left the room, careful not to swing open the door and allow the other servants to see inside.

"If I am remembering correctly, Mrs. Egerton said the autograph book was designed to provide all of the information on her summoning. However, she was unable to provide me with the specifics, as she said the entire purpose of the autograph book was that only those with sufficient magical ability could do the workings. Otherwise, someone might conjure up some ancient mystic and we would all end up cursed for having accidentally offended the ghost." Elizabeth glanced over at Miss Thorne for confirmation of that.

Miss Thorne nodded. "I have been reading Mr. Leigh's incantation and spell experiments. I believe I have found the spell that awoke Mrs. Egerton's voice, even if at the time he felt his working had failed."

"Indeed?" Elizabeth asked.

Miss Thorne nodded. "If I understood you correctly, Miss Knight, you said that you had read Mrs. Egerton's incantation, written by your uncle, and that she sighed several times in annoyance before speaking to you."

"Yes, that is how I remember it," Elizabeth said.

"So, making the assumption that Mrs. Egerton might have done the same to your uncle, I went back through his journals to find out the moment he wrote about hearing a sigh." She opened the journal to the page with a pink ribbon marker. At Elizabeth's smirk, she said, "I might have stolen the ribbon from my sister-in-law."

Maria laughed. "I've met her. She deserved it."

"Next time," Elizabeth said, "please ask one of us for assistance. I do not wish you to get into trouble at home."

"I fear they would need to notice me for me to get into trouble, as you say," Miss Thorne said with no trace of bitterness.

That astounded Elizabeth, and she admired Miss Thorne all the more for her fortitude with her situation. Still, if there was a small way that she could help ease Miss Thorne's life, she felt she would do it. Unmarried women had to stay together, after all.

"There is one incantation that your uncle did again and again, and each time, it caused a sigh. I believe he had successfully summoned her for years and she had merely refused to appear, but was listening to him."

"That would make sense," Elizabeth said. "She said that she appeared to him when it was obvious, to her, that he was dying.

Did he change the incantation in any form, or was it the same one?"

"He adjusted it several times. In actuality, he discussed the very things at this table that we have discussed. Therefore, I believe that the best course of action is to follow Mr. Leigh's path."

"We will no doubt fail," Miss Susan said, "and yet, if I might be so bold as to offer my opinion, I agree with Miss Thorne. This appears to be a proper course of action."

Elizabeth made notes in her journal. She looked up when silence filled the room. "Why is everyone looking at me?"

Miss Thorne looked at the other ladies before saying, "Miss Knight. You are the head of our group. We await your blessing to continue."

"Oh. I am not the leader of anything. I...I have no talent for such..."

"Miss Knight," Miss Thorne said in a rather stern, confident voice. "Might I speak freely to you, as a new acquaintance and, may I dare hope, a friend?"

Elizabeth looked about the room uncertain. "Yes, of course."

"There comes a point in every woman's life where she must accept if she is indeed the smartest person in the room or not. I have accepted that I am, present company excluded, of course, one of the most intelligent people in any room. And since that will never be acknowledged by the world, I refuse to hide my candle under a bushel, to use the holy words of the bible."

"Indeed, Miss Knight. I very much agree with Miss Thorne," Miss Susan said.

"Call me Alice, if I might be so bold," Miss Thorne said.

"I would be honoured, *Alice*. And you may call me Susan."

Miss Thorne inclined her head.

Elizabeth stared at the ladies. She did not know what to say. She had been taught from a very young age, that she was just a girl. Then a young lady. Then someone to be dismissed and complained about. Soon, she knew she would become the ridicule of the world: the old maid with a cat. A life of obscurity.

She looked down at her papers hoping to hide the fact that a lump unexpectedly formed in her throat. She did not know how to trust herself. And yet, here was Miss Thorne, who was far brasher than Elizabeth was accustomed to in an unmarried lady, who was abused and tormented by her family, who refused to hide her own talents from the world that she'd been born with.

And Miss Susan, who was discarded as soon as she was the least ill by powerful men who could have afforded to care for her, but who would rather see her living in squalor than lower themselves to help a poor governess.

"It is clear, to me, Miss Thorne—Alice— what your talents are. And you, Miss Susan. And indeed, Maria, yours is to light up a room and support. And you, Aunt Cass, to stand up for women who need that help." Elizabeth's voice grew feeble. "I have no such talents. I am nobody. That is why I need Mrs. Egerton, especially now that I am going back home soon."

"No," Aunt Cass said. All heads turned to look at her. "Ladies, I believe you need Mrs. Egerton only as a teacher. However, she desires pupils willing to trust their own abilities. Though I know little of her, I have known plenty of women with her personality. She will not tolerate wishy-washy, silly girls. And since none of you are, then I recommend you not act it when inside these walls."

"Very wise words, Mrs. Spencer," Maria said. "It is easy to forget that we must let our guard down on occasion."

"If acquaintance with the Royal Occult Society had taught me anything, self-doubt does not become a member of the *Ladies* Occult Society," Aunt Cass said sternly, though her eyes glittered with amusement.

"Ladies Occult Society?" Elizabeth asked.

"Well, are you not ladies, and is this not an occult society?" Aunt Cass asked.

"I had not considered," Elizabeth said. She thought on it some more as she looked about the room. She smiled. "I rather like the sound of that. The Ladies Occult Society."

"When I am feeling better, I will embroider us handkerchiefs."

"I look forward to mine!" Elizabeth said with a grin.

AFTER A FULL day of attempts, the ladies called it an end when Mrs. Cook announced dinner would arrive in an hour. They had not managed to summon Mrs. Egerton. However, they had made progress in narrowing down which of the incantations it was that Edward Leigh used. Unfortunately, he'd used six different slight variations on the same one that day, and they had run out of supplies.

"Sally, can you read and write?" When she bobbed her head and said she also could do accounts, Elizabeth said, "Good! Ladies, let's make a list of supplies that we need. Sally, some of them you might be able to find from an occult supply store first thing in the morning. Others, from the market."

Alice pressed her lips together. "The occult store on Bond Street will be significantly more expensive."

"Do you recommend we not go there?"

"I don't know. I can ask my brother for more money, I suppose," Alice said, in a tone that said her brother was not likely to give her a farthing of her own money.

Susan raised her hand. "May I speak?"

Elizabeth said, "Susan, if we are to use each other's Christian names, then surely you do not need to raise your hand."

"Sorry, miss. Elizabeth. A teacher in my position becomes accustomed to certain behaviours. If possible, I believe we should only purchase items from the occult store, for now. I have very limited experience with purification and cleansing spells, and we are very little time. If we succeed at keeping Mrs. Egerton's magic renewing, then it would be proper to start practicing simple spells then. For now, we must focus on her permanent incantation and hers alone."

"Very sensible," Elizabeth said. She looked down at her notes. "We have not tried the third incantation yet because we needed rosemary blessed by a priest. Does anyone here know a priest that supports the occult?"

Susan nodded. "I will add the directions to your list. Sally will be able to find it, but I do warn you. He will charge ten shillings for the first item that needs blessing, and five for each one after"

Elizabeth failed not to mentally calculate how much that would cost. "Lavender oil, purified rose water, cocoa and a spoonful of sugar. Why do we need chocolate again?"

Alice didn't look up from her book. She placed the ribbon and then flipped several pages. "Mr. Leigh says here that Mrs. Sarah

Egerton was…hmm…ah! Mrs. Egerton was known to love a mug of chocolate upon arriving in the dining room each morning during her short marriage. And…" Alice reached for the *Instructions in Autograph Ghost Creation, an Introduction*, "Yes! It says here that the ghosts need to be tethered with items they loved in life."

"Does my uncle say if he used prepared chocolate or not?"

Alice flipped back to the journal. She skimmed several pages before shaking her head. "No, he does not mention it that I can see, but I can continue to read. It has been several months since I have read anything of this nature in Latin and I fear my skills lack their usual sharpness. Mrs. Thorne? Would you be so good as to check the inventory list? I am looking for a very particular dictionary. I believe it is called, *A Primer on Latin to English Incantations for the Gentleman Occultist.*"

Maria handed Aunt Cass two pages of the inventory list while they both went through it. Elizabeth did not think it sounded familiar. However, they still were not through all of the sorting yet. A few minutes later, Aunt Cass declared it was not on her list. Ditto Maria.

"I shall continue to work to the best of my abilities, Elizabeth, you can be assured of that. Oh, dear, though. How I wish I could get my hands on that book! It is very vexing because I have gone to three different booksellers during my visit. Before I met you, in fact, my dear friend. And do you think that they would sell it to me? No, indeed! The occult shop actually refused. Refused my ready money! I had placed a guinea upon the counter to pass over to his possession and he refused to accept it."

"Why?" Susan asked.

"He thought I was purchasing it for my brother. Once he realized it was for me, he put the book back on the shelf and refused to let me have it. He said he could not, in good conscience, allow a young lady of breeding to see a book about Latin. I have not been back since."

Aunt Cass shook her head. "I swear, the shopkeepers of London must be very rich indeed if they can turn down ready money upon the counter."

"That was exactly what I said, Mrs. Spencer, you can be assured! The gall of the man."

Elizabeth considered that information for a moment. "Then ladies, I propose that we only frequent Mr. Osborne's shop. He sells new and used books, and he also owns the very small print publishing business next door. He has been an absolute gentleman throughout this entire process, and indeed I have direct knowledge that he is very honest and honourable and will not cheat a lady for his own profit, no matter the temptation."

"Indeed, Elizabeth? What happened?" Susan asked.

Elizabeth stopped speaking, realizing very quickly that she had nearly spilled the milk about her rare book. She did not wish to lie to the ladies; that would have been very wicked. So, instead, she engaged in a little misdirection.

"During this entire process, Mr. Osborne has offered very reasonable prices for all of the used books. There were some that Mrs. Egerton had mentioned were more prized editions. And, to his own reputation, Mr. Osborne would immediately point those out. Some were not appropriate for his own store, and yet he told me the price they should fetch somewhere else. He does not trade in the rare without a ready buyer, you see, but he wished me to know his estimated price of those books. And then Mr. Thorne was able to take that knowledge to ensure I was compensated appropriately."

"How honourable," Susan said.

"My brother never had a bad word to utter about Mr. Osborne," Aunt Cass supplied.

Alice nodded, seemingly pleased with this news. "Then, I agree, Elizabeth. We should only do business with this Mr. Osborne. May I have the directions to his shop? I shall pay him a visit tomorrow to set up an account."

A knock came to the door as Elizabeth was providing Alice the directions to Mr. Osborne's on Charles' Street. James introduced Mr. Henry Thorne, who practically ran into the dining room, red-faced and dewy.

"My apologies, ladies, for bursting in upon you. Mrs. Spencer. Miss Knight. You need to know that Mr. Baxter is returning with an attorney. Mr. Grant is on his way...ah! That must be him. James, would you please let him in. Quickly, now, before someone sees him on the street. Again, I apologize, Mrs. Spencer, for being so bold."

Aunt Cass was already getting to her feet and handed the book inventory list to Maria. "Under the circumstances, Mr. Thorne, I understand. Elizabeth, come with me. Ladies, please stay here for now."

"Would I be of assistance, Henry?"

Henry Thorne shook his head at his wife. "No, dear. They are here to attempt to threaten Miss Knight with legal action. Grant! Thank God you are here."

Mr. Grant was as red-faced as Mr. Thorne. He was puffing and huffing, and Elizabeth feared the portly man might drop of an apoplexy. "I came from Sir Gregory's as soon as I got your message. Am I too late?"

"Not at all, sir. Right on time."

"Now, if I understand from your valet, they are going to attempt to trick Miss Knight? Good, good. Let them think they have won." Another knock at the door. "Ah, good. That is Mr. Knight."

"My father?" Elizabeth asked, shocked.

Mr. Grant shook his head. "No, your brother. He was at Sir Gregory's as well. He went to Oxford with Sir Gregory's son. Ended up there for dinner."

Elizabeth's insides knotted.

"Oh, do not worry, Miss Knight. He has well been reined in," Mr. Grant said. To the foyer, he called out, "We'll be right out, my boy."

Elizabeth and Aunt Cass shared skeptical glances, but dutifully followed the men to the foyer. A rather sullen Charles stood there, head low. He did manage to say, "Good day, Mrs. Spencer. Elizabeth."

Mr. Grant motioned at Charles and said, "Now, young Mr. Knight here is our proof. He can say, quite truthfully without any subterfuge, that the elder Mr. Knight did not agree to sell anything of Miss Knight's property to the Royal Occult Society. Isn't that correct, Mr. Knight?"

Charles silently nodded his head.

"Will you do that, Knight?" Henry Thorne asked.

"Yes, Thorne." Charles glanced at his sister. "My father did not agree to sell the books. At first, he said aloud that maybe it would help Elizabeth not have to worry about doing it herself. Then, Isabella reminded him that the books were Elizabeth's and that her permission was necessary. He agreed, of course, and then said he would write to her, or perhaps wait until she returned home, to discuss the matter. At no point did I hear my father say he would force Elizabeth to sell the books."

"Good. Not that he could legally, as some were an inheritance and others were a gift from Mrs. Spencer. Oh, Mrs. Spencer, before I forget," Mr. Grant said. He handed her a rather large, though slender, leather book. "Please sign the bottom."

"What is this?" She asked as she opened it. She stared at the document inside.

At her shocked face, Elizabeth asked, "Aunt? What is it?"

"It appears Mr. Grant shall be getting a bonus beyond his standard fee," Aunt Cass said. "One moment, please. I shall sign this directly."

Elizabeth watched as her aunt, laughing to herself, walked into the drawing room. There, she knew was her own writing desk, as well as Aunt Cass's. She turned back to Mr. Grant. "Sir, I must ask what is happening."

"Indeed, Miss Knight. I apologize for going behind your back to deal with this, but there was so little time. I have drawn up a legal document between your cousin, Mr. David Leigh, and Mrs. Spencer. It is for the transfer of his occult library to Mrs. Spencer. For the sum of one guinea."

"You are in jest," Elizabeth said. "You made it legal?"

"As soon as Mrs. Spencer wrote to me about Mr. David Leigh's ill-planned scheme, I decided to take it upon myself to ensure that, at least that part of the book exchange, was protected. After all, Mrs. Spencer is a widow. No one can touch her." Mr. Grant said. He raised his hands in the air. "And if Mrs. Spencer, who is childless, decides to ask her unmarried niece to spend a month in London assisting her with the dispensation of said library and wishes to invest upon her any sum of money she so wishes, that is Mrs. Spencer's legal right."

Aunt Cass returned with the book, still open as she was blowing upon the ink for it to dry. "Done, Mr. Grant."

"Excellent, so now all we need is Mr. Knight here to speak when called up. Can you do that, sir?" Mr. Grant asked.

Charles lowered his head. "Yes, sir."

"Good."

Elizabeth glanced between the men. "Charles? I do not wish you to do something you do not want. Or, if this is a falsehood, I do not deserve you to lie on my behalf."

Charles sighed and glanced at Mr. Grant. "Do I have to tell her?"

Mr. Grant shrugged. "Sir, this is your sister, not mine."

Elizabeth stared at her brother. "Charles? Are you in trouble? What is happening?"

"I was not completely truthful with you," Charles said. His voice was rather subdued.

Henry Thorne scoffed.

"My father said he'd written you a letter demanding you return home with me."

Elizabeth nodded. "Yes, I received said letter the day you arrived in London."

"He had received some distressing news that he did not wish to tell you, so it had been Mary's idea to come across as a demand. However, after he'd sent the letter and had some time to reflect, he regretted the letter." Charles scowled. "I think Isabella had something to do with that."

"What distressing news? Charles, what is going on?" Elizabeth demanded.

Charles was silent for a moment before answering. "Isabella is with child, and there is a worry she is gravely ill."

Elizabeth stared at her brother in shock. The verification of the pregnancy was not a shock; the reported fainting and fatigue had tipped the ailment's arrival. However, the knowledge that Isabella was gravely ill, and here she was sitting about London, sipping chocolate in the mornings, all the while her youngest sisters were left to deal with a dying woman.

"Charles, I must know everything."

Her brother glanced at Mr. Grant, who nodded. "All right. Mr. Baxter isn't here yet, in any case. Isabella has known for about a month that she was with child, but your uncle died just as she realized that something was the matter. Eventually, she was unable to hide her situation and both the midwife and Mr. Clarke were called."

Elizabeth nodded. Isabella was not remotely close enough to be brought to bed and have a living child. To call the midwife? Her stomach twisted and knotted from fear.

"Both the apothecary and the midwife agreed. Isabella is much too large for her time. It's possible she has tumors. That's what the midwife said. She'd seen it before. The apothecary said, if that is the case, then it is very likely the baby will not survive. And it might also take Isabella."

The news struck Elizabeth hard. She blinked several times, failing to clear the fog from her thoughts. Eventually, a hand touched her arm and she was led to a chair. She glanced up to see James there. He gave her a small bow and went back to guarding the door.

After a moment of silence, she asked, "Why did no one tell me?"

Charles's expression said she would not like the answer. "At first, our father felt it wasn't the concern of an unmarried daughter. Mary agreed with him."

"Of course," Elizabeth said dryly.

"It did not matter what he wanted, however. The girls overheard the midwife and apothecary, so there was no keeping a secret for long. He instructed them not to tell you or give you a whiff of it until I could make it to London. But, by then, I was at Ashbrook, so we lost a couple of days with the back and forth."

"Why did Father not come himself?"

Charles shrugged. "I assume he wished to stay with his wife. Regardless, I was supposed to come to London and assist you with the book selling, so that you could return to Bryden."

"That was not what he said in his letter," Elizabeth said. She failed to hide all the bitterness. "I had the impression he did not like me being here."

"I do believe he has rather forgotten all that and only wants you to come home." Charles fiddled with his gloves, attempting to avoid meeting her gaze. Finally he looked up and said, "Isabella asked for you, and I think she wants the comfort of someone her age, with some experience."

"Why did no one send for Mary? She is closer!"

"Mary is at home with her." Charles sighed. "Eliza, you know how Mary gets when she is in one of her moods. She and Isabella have had tension since the necklace business at Christmas, and all Mary did was work Isabella up. Then the Royal Society fellows showed up and that only served to wind Mary up more. She and Isabella got into another row about how you should just sell them the damn books and come home, and... Well, you can imagine how desperate things have become."

"Oh no," Elizabeth muttered, burying her face in her hands. Her stays made it difficult to maintain the position for any length of time, though, and she sat back up to endure the agony of her family. "So Mary is upset with me because I'm busy with my books. Isabella is upset with Mary. Our father is upset about his wife. Cassandra is attempting to help Mary and Isabella. And the girls are still giving Isabella a hard time, since they are too young to truly understand the gravity of the situation, no doubt under Mary's advice."

Charles made a hopeless gesture. "A lot has been going on."

Elizabeth was shocked. She had no idea what her father or Isabella thought of her now. That Isabella was suffering and Elizabeth was still in town, as if nothing was the matter. What a cold-hearted daughter they must think her. While she did not care so much about Mary's good opinion, she did not wish for her own sister to think her a monster.

"Why would you do this to me?" Elizabeth pushed herself up from her chair and took several steps back toward her brother, who flinched away from her. "Why did you not simply tell me?"

"I am doing the right thing now."

"Tell her, or I will," Henry Thorne said.

"Or I," Mr. Grant said.

Elizabeth glanced between the three men. "What is happening here?"

Charles' shoulders slumped. "The Royal Occult Society offered me thirty pounds if I could convince you to hurry back to Bryden."

"If you had told me about Isabella, of course I would have hurried! I would have left the books here and asked my dear new friends to help with the task in my absence. But that does not answer the question of why?"

"They...they want three books that are yours now, and a journal of your uncle's. I don't know, it's all nonsense to me. But they said if you were scared into returning home, those would be the books you would carry back with you in your trunk."

She could not argue with that. In fact, they would most likely be in her lap the entire journey. "And?"

He did not look up at her. "You would be set upon by highwaymen who would steal the books from you."

She stared at him in horror. Her entire mind stopped thinking and all that it could do was repeat his words over and over, convinced that it had heard the words improperly. She stumbled back to the chair and collapsed into it.

"Highwaymen?" she whispered over and over.

Charles approached her to kneel and meet her eyes. "They assured me you would not have been injured in the slightest. All they care about are the books."

She looked at her brother with such pain. She had never been so weary in all of her life. That her safety, and indeed her very life, had a price. That was so low...how it stabbed her through the heart.

"Why do you hate me?" Elizabeth asked, her voice cracking.

"It has nothing to do with that."

She sniffled back tears. "No, it had to do with thirty pounds. That is all I am worth to you, apparently."

Charles grabbed her hands, and she pulled away so forcefully that her chair nearly toppled. She stood abruptly, causing her brother to fall back onto the floor. She paced back and forth across the foyer, tears dripping off her chin. She rubbed at her face with the back of her hand.

Finally, Charles said, "I have debts of honour. I needed the money."

Elizabeth ceased her pacing. "How much do you owe?"

"I have agreed to pay his debts—all of them—if he tells the truth in front of witnesses," Henry Thorne said.

Elizabeth glared. "Forgive me, but that was not what I asked, Mr. Thorne."

Henry Thorne lowered his eyes. "No, it was not."

To Charles, she demanded, "How much?"

"I owe seventy pounds here in town," Charles said.

Even if she gave him all of the money in her desk, it would not cover his debts. And they were not even debts to shopkeepers that could be paid back over the course of several years. Debts of honour! Her father...

"Does our father know you have gambling debts?"

"Of course not. I thought this would help settle some of my accounts." Charles said. Exasperated, he blurted, "Then, I would convince Father to sell your other books, then no one would have to know."

She could not look at him. It was bad enough that she supposed it was the Royal Occult Society who had sent the little boy to break into their house. Even if caught, his age would likely have spared the noose and instead transported him to Australia for a decade. Still, that was horrid enough. But a plan to set highwaymen upon her? What if the coachman shot at the highwaymen? What if a bullet missed and hit Maria or someone else? What if it hit her? What if they managed to stop the coach and she refused to hand over the books? Would they have murdered her?

"I was desperate, Elizabeth," Charles said in a subdued tone. "I have no way to pay any of that money back, and you know our father's opinion on gamesters."

"You were willing to risk your own sister's life for thirty pounds. How can I ever trust you again? With any of our lives, not just my own?" Elizabeth accepted Mr. Grant's handkerchief and dabbed at her eyes. "You could have asked me for the money."

"You don't have that kind of money," Charles said with a scoff. "If you did, father would only take it and then you'd still not be able to help me. I was trying to save myself."

Elizabeth considered the bank notes and coins locked up in her desk. It harmlessly sat upon the dining room table upon a cloth as to not scratch the smooth, finished surface. At times, she had considered sharing that money with her family. Slowly dolling it out, declaring she has been careful in her expenditures. However, it was clear that no one in her family could know the true nature of her financial situation.

If Charles knew there was money locked in that desk, he would most likely break the lock. She would need to purchase a small box that could be hidden in the back of the drawer to hide her money. Surely there was a secrecy box at the furniture shop where she'd purchased the desk and her table.

And she had to consider the safe keeping of the most precious of the books: Mrs. Egerton and her ghostly companions, and the rare book.

It hurt her that she was standing here, in front of these men, and realizing that she could not trust the men in her own family.

She would need to also purchase a false bottom for her trunk, to hide her books.

"Say something, Elizabeth. Yell at me, if you must. Don't just stand there, judging me."

The contempt in Charles' voice spurred her. For her entire life, she had been taught that the good fortune of one of them was the good fortune of all of them. She had abided by that principle. She had shared whatever little pittances of extras she had gained in her life. She had looked upon her fourteen-hundred-pound inheritance to help support herself and her sisters; it would ease her family's burden of supporting her.

She decided that she would still stick with that original decision. She would openly use that money to support any and all of them however they deemed necessary.

She would share the income of her uncle's books, save the one book. The *London Occultist Book* would remain hidden from the world. So long as she was under the thumb of a man, she would never tell them of the book. The next man who learned of the book from her own lips would either be one employed to assist her with its sale, or he would the man she would marry. And, she vowed that she would only marry a man who she trusted with that kind of money. If such a man did not exist, then she would simply wait. And, if her death were to come upon her, then the book would go to her new female companions. Together, they could sell the book and improve their own fortunes.

She would write a will when she returned to Bryden and place it in her journal. Until then, she would have to live with the knowledge that she was richer than anyone thought. She would live a life of deception. She would sin every day and risk her eternal soul.

Tears trickled down her cheeks once more and she squeezed her eyes shut. She silently prayed to God that he would understand and show her mercy. She asked for forgiveness, knowing she would not change her course. All she could do was hope that God understood the plight of a poor, oppressed unmarried woman who had to protect herself from her male relations. Jesus had a mother. Perhaps he would understand.

Charles sighed, which brought Elizabeth out of her prayers of remorse. "You don't know what it's like to be a poor man, Elizabeth. I'm the only son and I have nothing. All of my friends are wealthy and here I am unable to throw down even a handful of guineas on cards. I have to count every single farthing."

It was just as well that the expected knock came upon the door at that moment. Elizabeth glanced toward the dining room entrance, where the dark shadows of her friends and her aunt stretched out across the foyer's white tile floor. She didn't care that they heard. Let everyone witness her family's neglect.

Elizabeth stepped in front of the men and nodded at James to open the door. Mr. Baxter was there, of course, with two other men standing behind him. They were visibly shocked by the gathering waiting for them. The men bowed. Elizabeth did not curtsy nor offer any indicator that she acknowledged their presence.

By now, Elizabeth recognized Mr. Baxter's smile for the forgery that it was. She waited until Mr. Baxter opened his mouth to speak. She interrupted him before he uttered a word. "My aunt barred you from visiting her home."

Mr. Baxter had clearly expected a different greeting. He closed his mouth, considered, and then said, "I apologize for calling so near to dinner. May I speak with Mrs. Spencer?"

"No," Elizabeth said.

Mr. Baxter took a step to come inside the house and James blocked his path. Mr. Baxter forced a jovial sound, but his smile had turned sour. "Come now, Miss Knight. I understand that Sir Matthew upset everyone. However, I have business to discuss and I do not believe you wish to do that in the street like a fishmonger."

Elizabeth's eyes were still itchy and swollen from her crying, and she knew all too well that her face was as red as a strawberry. Nevertheless, the anger in her voice was unmistakable. "I know you are here to trick me into selling my books. I know someone from the Royal Occult Society attempted to bribe my brother to arrange a violent attack upon my very person when I depart for the country. So, no, sir. I will not be parting with my inheritance. So, therefore, you have no further business in my aunt's home."

Mr. Baxter looked over her shoulder. "Well, Mr. Knight. I suspect your father will be receiving a letter soon about your gambling debts. Or, did you forget to mention those to your dear sister here?"

Mr. Baxter's grin faded upon seeing Elizabeth's expression. He had honestly thought Charles would not have told her about the debts.

"I fear I have not been clear or forthright enough with you and Sir Matthew. It appears there is some confusion between us," Elizabeth said.

One of the men behind Mr. Baxter spoke. He was tall enough to loom over Mr. Baxter, despite being on a lower stair. "Excuse me, miss, I am—"

"I have no wish to make your acquaintance, sir," Elizabeth said. It had been the first time in her life she had cut someone, but she has seen Maria and Aunt Cass do it. She felt instantly guilty for her rudeness, but forced down her feminine graces. She would behave as a man in this conversation.

No. No, that was not correct. She would behave as the newly-minted heiress she actually was. She was in possession of fourteen hundred from her uncle. At least three thousand pounds sat in her drawer with her hose and stays. She was not as rich as many a young lady in England, but she was not penniless.

"It appears that I must set aside propriety for a moment and engage in a little trade and politics. Now, Mr. Baxter, I assume the two gentlemen with you are attorneys for the Royal Occult Society."

This time, the other lawyer spoke. He was an older gentleman, with grey whiskers. He leaned as to look around Mr. Baxter at her. "Yes, miss. As my colleague here wished to say, we are—"

"I also do not wish to make your acquaintance. My business is with Mr. Baxter."

Elizabeth's heart pounded at the shocked looks of the three gentlemen. They were not accustomed to young ladies speaking to them with such authority. Which was just as well, because she was also not accustomed to speaking to men in such a rude and undignified fashion. Nevertheless, she would persist in her present course. They had gone too far, and she was now fighting for her very life.

"Mr. Baxter, allow me to be clear in my words. You, sir, will not write my father. You, sir, will leave my brother alone and will never speak to him again. And in exchange…"

Mr. Baxter's face lit up. "You will give us the books?"

"In exchange, I will not report you to the nearest magistrate that you attempted to rob me. I am a young, unmarried woman, and the eldest daughter of a country rector. I suspect the papers will not take kindly upon a London occultist who threatens a lady with highwaymen because she refused to be swindled out of her inheritance."

Mr. Baxter's face flushed scarlet and he said, "Now see here, young lady!"

"I will be addressed as Miss Knight, as is fitting considering our acquaintance is in business only." She grew faint from the rapid pounding of her heart.

As she stared at Mr. Baxter's growing anger, she knew that one more lie was necessary to protect herself. For now, her only lies were those of omission. However, she hoped God would understand this next one.

"As for the journals you wish, they were destroyed in the housebreaking."

"That isn't what happened," Mr. Baxter blurted. Catching himself, he clarified. "I only mean, in terms of what I have heard about town. There was nothing destroyed."

"As the person who suffered burns and cuts, I can assure you plenty was destroyed as I attempted not to burn to death." She gulped down the lump in her throat. "Now, as for the letters you have repeatedly requested, many of those did survive and will be given to Mr. Fitzharding of Ashbrook. I would prefer not to write to my brother-in-law and beg his assistance in a legal matter, whereby I am being accosted to hand over his own wife's only tangible connection with her deceased mother."

Mr. Baxter took a step forward. He was significantly taller than her more modest feminine height, and she was certain he'd used it in the past to intimidate women. "Are you threatening me, girl?"

"Miss Knight," Elizabeth correct. "My name is Miss Knight. And, in point of fact, sir, the only person being threatened here is myself. Our unequal situations in life means that I will not be able to protect myself from your attacks. Therefore, I will use every method at my disposal to protect myself against powerful men as yourself."

"I could bring legal redress against you."

She did not flinch, nor did she pull away her gaze, no matter what her upbringing had told her to do. "Mr. Grant, may I beg your assistance please?"

Mr. Grant stepped next to her in the doorway. "I am very happy to be of service, Miss Knight. Mr. Baxter. Gentlemen. Good to see you all on this fine evening."

"Grant, what are you doing here?" Mr. Baxter demanded.

"Assisting my clients, of course. Now, as to the matter at hand. I have spoken with several of my legal colleagues throughout the city, and we are in unanimous agreement: Miss Knight's case is sound. The few books she does own, are hers by inheritance. Mr. Charles Knight can confirm their father did not give permission for the sale of the books. In fact, as Mr. Charles Knight tells it, Mr. Knight of Bryden wished to discuss the matter with his daughter himself. And, further, considering that his wife was suffering a grievous ailment at the time of your visit, it is rather ungentlemanly to have attempted to accost the poor man. In fact, I would consider it harassment, and if it were to continue, I might feel compelled to write a letter to The Times expressing my concerns."

"You wouldn't!" Mr. Baxter said. "You would risk your career over a penniless girl with no family of worth?"

"How dare you, sir!" Henry Thorne said, in a rather angry tone. "Miss Knight is the daughter of a respected country rector. She is the sister to Mrs. Fitzharding, a very wealthy wife of a country gentlemen. She has family, sir. And she has friends, sir. Wealthy, powerful friends."

The doorway was growing crowded, with her in the front, Mr. Grant to one side, and Henry Thorne practically breathing down her neck on the other side. Still, she was bolstered by their presence. She said nothing and waited for Mr. Baxter.

Finally, after some furtive glances with his companions, Mr. Baxter asked, "Will you give me your word that the books were destroyed?"

"I have given you more than I already wished to, sir. Is our business finally concluded, or will I have to endure more aggravation?"

Mr. Baxter stared at her long and hard, but when he glanced back at his lawyers, they both shook their heads. They had tried to trick her, threaten her, and steal from her. She had won.

"No. The Royal Occult Society rescinds its offer to purchase the books." He looked at Mr. Grant. "As for you, you are no longer welcome at the Royal Occult Society and we will be ceasing all business ties with you."

"I shall expect the return of my society fees by the end of the week," Mr. Grant said. "I would prefer it paid in Bank of England bank notes, if you please. I will inform my assistant you will be arriving."

"Good day, Mr. Baxter. Gentlemen." Elizabeth took a small step back. Mr. Grant and Henry Thorne quickly stepped out of her personal space. She nodded at James, who shut the door rather louder than was strictly necessary.

Elizabeth placed a hand on her torso and said, "I might faint."

"Miss Knight, you have more fortitude than some men I know," Mr. Grant said. He inclined his head to her and said, "I suspect it will be some time before they come knocking upon your door again."

"Oh, Mr. Grant. I must apologize that they have hurt your business. I had not wanted that. Is there anything I can do to assist?"

Mr. Grant waved a dismissive hand. "Oh, do not concern yourself with that. Honestly, the Royal Occult Society rarely pay their debts. I am happy to be rid of them."

"Did you really lose the books?" Charles asked.

She gave her brother a hard glare.

"You lied to those men, Elizabeth," Charles said. "Father will not be pleased with you."

"And how will he know, Charles?"

"God will know," Charles said in a smug, patronizing tone.

Elizabeth had enough guilt about lying. She did not need her own brother rubbing salt into the wound. "As I am certain God knows I lied to cover your lies. Perhaps you should concentrate on your own salvation, and I shall worry about mine. Mr. Grant, are you certain I am free of them?"

"For a time, yes. I suspect you will see them again if there is any financial trouble in the future, especially concerning your brother and debts." Mr. Grant gave Charles a side glance.

"I will try to lay off the cards, Elizabeth," Charles said. "Are you going to tell Papa?"

"Gentlemen? I would like to speak to my brother alone."

Mr. Grant and Henry Thorne walked to the dining room and James closed the large double doors. Elizabeth said to Charles, "It appears we both have secrets from our father that the other holds."

Charles nodded his head. "Shall we call a truce?"

She nodded. "I do not wish to quarrel."

"Neither do I. Elizabeth, I am so very sorry for the things I said to you. I cannot look at them without shame."

She wanted to yell at him. She wanted to scream and call him names and perhaps even throw a vase at him. Of course, she did none of those things. Instead, she nodded her head very slowly and said, "I know you regret your words."

"I wonder if Father still has the money set aside for me to return to Oxford?"

"If not, I am sure we can find a way. Perhaps you could go on a scholarship, and work at the university. That is how Papa paid for his time there."

"True enough," Charles said. He sighed. "I hated being poor there."

She reached out and touched his arm. "We are all as poor and as rich as what is in our hearts. People who judge you for being poor are not your true friends. I hope, one day, you will accept that. And, at least, you are a man. You have the opportunity to change your fate. I do not."

"You could marry a rich man," Charles said. The soft smile on his lips said he did not mean it harshly.

"Alas, the laws of England state that I still need the man's permission."

Charles nodded. "That is a hindrance, my dear sister. What shall we tell Papa?"

"I am not quite done in London, but I must head home. Is Isabella truly ill?"

"Yes," Charles said. "She did not want anyone to tell you, but she is in danger."

"Then, I must return home."

Elizabeth's shoulders slumped. She knew her duty, and she did truly wish to be by Isabella's side. Her younger sisters, still grieving their own mother's death, would be terrors to the poor woman. Now, to have in front of them that same situation all over again might prove too much for them. Georgiana could go either way: clinging to Isabella for dear life, or harshly abandoning her. Theodosia would, of course, turn to pranks and spite to hide her feelings and fears.

She was needed.

The dining room doors creaked open and footsteps sounded on the floor. "Elizabeth. Might I interrupt?"

Elizabeth turned to see not just her aunt, but also Mrs. Taylor and Susan. "Yes?"

"We have been discussing your delicate matter in the dining room. With your permission, Mrs. Taylor would like to go to Bryden to stay with Isabella until you are able to return."

"I am strong enough to not need a constant nurse, and I shall like to help you sort the remainder of the books. As well as our other tasks," Susan said.

Mrs. Taylor nodded. "And Mrs. Spencer has so kindly provided for my salary, that I would be very welcome to assist her in any way. I have never been to Bryden or even seen that part of the country in all my life. I would like to see it, and would not mind being a helper to your stepmother. She must need all of the help she can get."

"But…where would you stay? We have no servant quarters in the rectory because we hire from the village," Elizabeth said.

Charles cleared his throat. "She could stay in your room, while you are in London."

"Oh, I did not even think of that. Oh, but Mrs. Taylor, I could not ask that of you. No, I should go back. It is my duty."

Aunt Cass squared her shoulders, announcing that she was about to pull rank on her niece. "My dear girl. You are needed in two places at once. Mrs. Taylor, who is very experienced, will assist Mrs. Knight until you are finished here in London. Charles, do you see a problem with this scheme?"

"No, indeed, ma'am. In fact, I can escort Mrs. Taylor first thing in the morning."

"I can take you as far as the Hillsbury Inn in my carriage, and then you can switch to the coach," Mr. Thorne said from behind the ladies.

"Thank you, Thorne. That will make several hours of the journey more comfortable for Mrs. Taylor," Charles said.

"With your permission, ma'am, I shall pack immediately," Mrs. Taylor said.

Aunt Cass nodded. "Of course. And thank you, Mrs. Taylor. I shall have an advance on your wages directed to you at Bryden. Mr. Grant, will you assist?"

"In fact, Mrs. Spencer, if one of the footmen can escort me back to my office when our business here is concluded, I shall give him the advance immediately for her journey."

"That would be very agreeable."

Mrs. Taylor nodded and said, "Thank you sirs. I shall be ready in the morning for when you call."

The men agreed and Mrs. Taylor parted the company. Elizabeth was still very uneasy about the arrangement, and asked, "Won't Papa be upset?"

Charles pondered her question. "I can tell Papa that I was concerned about you knowing the particulars, so soon after the attack, that I did not immediately tell you the situation at home. However, when I was convinced you were indeed not injured in the slightest, I decided to speak with Mrs. Spencer first. And she felt…um…she felt…"

Aunt Cass helped with the chronicle of deception. "Since we have taken on an ill family friend, Miss Susan…Miss Susan…?"

"Miss Susan Markson," Susan reminded Aunt Cass.

"Yes, Miss Susan Markson, who is recovering from a terrible ailment and had lost her employment as a governess. Therefore, it was decided amongst us that Elizabeth would stay in town to finish the last of the book auctions and to care for Miss Susan. And, since Mrs. Taylor was no longer needed here to serve as nurse, due to Miss Susan's improving condition, she would be better served assisting Mrs. Knight, who needed the guiding hand of experience as opposed to an unmarried young woman."

Elizabeth gave her aunt a frustrated look. "Aunt, that is a deception."

"It is close enough to the truth," Charles said. "Then, we don't have to tell Father what I've done."

"This is why I do not approve of lying. The only way to get out of the lie is to tell more lies." Elizabeth sighed. "I will agree to this, but only this once. Charles, from now, I will not lie for you. Do you understand me? I promise faithfully that I will not tell our father about what has happened here, but I will never again lie for you."

"Yes, Elizabeth," Charles said with sullen frustration.

She did not believe for a moment that her brother learned his lesson. For as long as he continued to ally with men higher in rank than himself, Charles would struggle with his feelings of inadequacy. She wished with all her heart she could make him see that he would have an easier time in life if he took a profession. Mr. Fitzharding could assist him then. Henry Thorne could assist him. Even Aunt Cass could help him out. But it was impossible to help someone who refused to make the simplest of decisions.

"Then we are agreed?" Aunt Cass asked.

Elizabeth wanted to argue the point but relented. "Please tell Isabella and our father that I will be back as soon as I finish the book auction for my aunt, and when I am certain Miss Susan has recovered enough to not be a burden upon my aunt or any of the servants. Oh, Miss Susan, I apologize for how I phrased that. I am…quite fatigued."

"I was not offended, Elizabeth. Your aunt has been very kind to us, and I look forward to being able to go back to work as a teacher as soon as possible." Susan sighed. "Though, I suppose once it is known I have been staying here, my position at the Royal Occult Society school will be permanently rescinded."

That had not occurred to Elizabeth. "I had not even considered that. Please forgive me."

"Elizabeth," Aunt Cass said. "You take too much upon yourself. Allow me to shoulder some of the burden of my own brother's servant and her family, please. Now, I believe we should all gather back in the dining room and eat what Cook had spent all day preparing for us. Mr. Knight, you are welcome to join us."

"No, thank you Mrs. Spencer. I shall head back to my lodgings to pack. I have caused enough tension in this house already with my presence. Again, I am very sorry."

Aunt Cass inclined her head. Charles made a motion to hug his sister, but changed his mind and gently touched her arm. Then, he left the house.

Elizabeth closed her eyes and longed for a cup of tea.

❧ Chapter 15 ❧

Dearest Isabella,

I am shocked to have learned of your condition. I was grievously vexed with Charles until I learned of your situation. To enrage me further, Mr. Baxter of the Royal Occult Society attempted to trick both me and Charles, by lying about Papa's instructions! It has been a most trying time and I am so very sorry that I am not by your side.

Charles will, of course, fill you in with the details of last night's situation and why Mrs. Taylor has travelled to Bryden. However, I could not forgive myself without you hearing the story from my own pen.

Mrs. Taylor had worked for my uncle for many years. My Aunt Cass can confirm that she is the best of women, a hard worker, and a kind, compassionate nurse. I would have left everything behind in London. However, Aunt Cass, Charles, and indeed Mrs. Taylor all agreed that she could be of use to you with your ailment. Also, as Charles pointed out, the girls might be on their best behaviour with a new person in the house.

I am currently nursing Mrs. Taylor's niece, lately a governess to the Royal Occult Society. She is an excellent young woman. Her health has been improving daily. However, Mrs. Taylor felt that our ages made it better for me to stay and keep her company, while her experience with pregnancy would make her of more use to you. I cannot disagree with that, though I still hope I would have been of some use.

I shall be home as soon as possible. If you do need me, please write by express and I will come back as soon as possible. I will come by post, if necessary. Do not argue, Isabella. I am eight and twenty and have a younger sister who is already married. I can travel alone.

I have given Mrs. Taylor the handsome sum of three pounds, two shillings, and sixpence: some of the proceeds of my book auction enterprise. Please send the girls out to the village anytime you need peace and quiet. That should get them ribbon and other hat supplies and a bag of boiled sweets each from Jonas' shop every day for a fortnight. Do not be angry; I insist upon it. After all, the good that happens to one of us, happens to all of us.

All my love,
Elizabeth

A restless night's sleep did not help Elizabeth's worries, and neither did the letter. She believed quite strongly that omission of truth was still a lie, though admittedly it was a lesser sin in the eyes of most. She also found some of her guilt tempered by giving Mrs. Taylor an assortment of coins for the girls to spend.

She realized she'd forgotten to tally her latest income and her recent expenditures, so opened her journal to work.

£2 17s 4p Proceeds of book sale to Mr. Worth of Worth and Sons Bookshop

£3 2s 6d for the girls

£1 2s for Charles and Mrs. Taylor's coach fare, plus a hot meal each at the Carriage Inn

Total in desk: £56 17s 4d
Total in reticule: £3 17s 3d

Elizabeth stared at the journal for a full minute before she changed the entry:

Total in desk: £50
Total in reticule: £10 14s 7d

After she locked up her desk, she picked up Mrs. Egerton's autograph book and her reticule. She walked downstairs to the private drawing room, where Susan and Alice had their heads together as they poured over the books.

"I did not know you were both down here. Alice, when did you get back from shopping?"

"About twenty minutes ago. Sally had said she thought you went to bed to lay down, since you were up so early with your brother and Mrs. Taylor. I asked her not to disturb you."

Elizabeth glanced at their work. "Is that the official list of supplies we need?"

Susan nodded. "I believe we are on the cusp."

Elizabeth read the list aloud. "A Lady's Guide to Housemaking and the Occult?"

"It was written by Mrs. Egerton's occult group," Alice explained. "I wondered if her ghost might respond to us having sought out her own group's writings. I looked at the Arthur Sherry book you own. I hope you do not mind me poking about, Elizabeth, I simply had to see it. But, in any case, in the back of the book? There is a list of the other books by Arthur Sherry. And that one looked the most interesting, so I wondered if we could ask Mr. Osborne if he had a copy."

Elizabeth nodded. She was dressed for going out and had some items she wished to purchase in any case. "With my aunt's permission, I shall embark for Charles Street and gather these items."

"Would you like some company?" Alice asked.

Elizabeth looked at the very pale Susan. "Are you well enough to venture out?"

"Alas, no, not yet. However, I would be happy if you would both go and I shall continue making the final adjustments to the incantations while I wait. Alice has translated everything, so I can read it."

"There is nothing quite as invigorating as solving a linguistic puzzle, I assure you," Alice said.

Elizabeth gained her aunt's approval to go to Charles Street and the shops, and then James offered to call for a chair. However, the weather was fine and the walk quite short, and the ladies decided that they would have any purchases delivered if they were too awkward to carry.

The two young ladies set off. Elizabeth listened to Alice prattle on about her and Susan's latest breakthrough. Elizabeth always felt inadequate whenever Miss Alice Thorne spoke; she knew so little next to her. Even Susan, for she had been a teacher and a governess for most of her adult life. Elizabeth helped in the raising of her youngest siblings, but that was a far distance from being formally employed to educate someone's child.

At times, Elizabeth experienced the prick of envy, but she quickly quashed those thoughts. She genuinely appreciated the excellent friendships she had made in London, and she would do well to learn from them, as opposed to allowing petty jealousies to sour budding relationships.

It took Mr. Osborne's assistant some time, but he found the book. Elizabeth paid fourteen shillings for it, which Alice said was an exceptionally good price. Mr. Osborne's assistant accepted her bank note and made ready change for her, which greatly pleased her to have more coins in her reticule. However, it was growing heavy.

"I understand that you will have to return to the country soon, Miss Knight," Mr. Osborne said. "I will miss our trade."

Elizabeth smiled. "I am not yet done with the disposal of the library, so I hope to have more titles for your perusal."

"Then I look forward to a future meeting," Mr. Osborne said with a bow. "Good day, ladies."

They departed the bookstore and went next door to the occult store. Alice handed over the list to the assistant. He gave it a glance, nodded, and said, "Exact amounts or will pre-measured be acceptable?"

"Pre-measured will be fine," Alice said.

"Very good, miss. Will this be on your account?" he asked.

"No, I shall be paying for it," Elizabeth said.

As the assistant went back behind the curtains to look for the items, Alice asked, "Are you certain? I can have it added to my account."

Elizabeth shook her head. In a low whisper, she said, "Since my newfound wealth has come from the sale of the occult books, I think it is only fair that I use some of that money on our occult society. I think my uncle would have been rather humoured by that."

"Do you think so?"

"Three unwed ladies of near the same age, all gathered together studying the occult at his sister's house? Yes, he would have been very pleased with that." Elizabeth's eyes welled with tears, but she managed to smile them away. Her uncle would have truly loved this.

The shop assistant offered to deliver the items, but she and Alice decided to have their purchases split into two easy parcels for carrying. The assistant did as they requested, and he provided Elizabeth with the total: 6s 4d.

For a brief moment, Elizabeth considered handing over another bank note, but worried the seams on her reticule wouldn't take much more weight. She carefully doled out the coins and placed them on the counter. The assistant accepted the money and the owner thanked her for her business.

"Would you mind taking a trip to the furniture shop just there?" Elizabeth asked, pointing. "I was hoping to purchase a small wooden box to go in my desk."

A figure drew Elizabeth's attention in the crowd, and her attention to Alice faded.

"Oh, of course! I love that store. It has all of the most ingenious devices."

A flash of recognition washed over Elizabeth. No, it was her mind playing tricks on her. It had to be.

"Have you seen their puzzle secret boxes? They are wonderful. I would not be surprised if they have one that will fit your desk. Elizabeth? Miss Knight? Are you well?"

Miss Thorne's words were far away, echoing as if she were at the other end of the street. Elizabeth would have known those features anywhere: it was him.

"Oh, god help me," Elizabeth whispered.
"Elizabeth! What is the matter? Oh, that's Mr. Rutledge. Are you acquainted?"

Mr. R was walking toward her now. Black clawhammer coat. Fitted breeches. Expertly polished black riding boots. Tall, black hat. White gloves. White shirt. Perfect hair. Trimmed sideburns.

"Miss Knight? My god, is he the famous Mr. R?"

Elizabeth made a shushing sound. She gulped down her rising panic and the slight breathlessness of seeing him again, and focused on her posture and poise.

Mr. Rutledge bowed stiffly. "Good day, Miss Thorne. It is always excellent to see you. Might I be introduced to your companion?"

If Elizabeth was a younger, less experienced woman, she would have broke into heavy weeping there on the street. Instead, she worked to keep her shock and disappointment off her face.

"Oh, um, this is my friend, Miss Knight. Of Bryden. She is the eldest daughter of the rector there." Alice spoke slowly, either due to confusion or she was attempting to insult Mr. Rutledge. It was hard to tell with Alice. "Miss Knight, this is Mr. Rutledge."

"Miss Knight. Yes. I recall now. We met when we were quite young. I did not recognize you."

Elizabeth inclined her head slightly. "Mr. Rutledge. Are you in London with your wife?" She had not meant the harsh edge on that last word, but it was enough that even Alice noticed. She offered a sweet smile. "I heard she has an exquisite singing voice."

"Yes, indeed she does. Though, she does not perform now that she is married. And you, Miss Knight? Are you here with your family?"

She ignored the emphasis he placed on the title. "I am visiting my aunt."

They stared at each other and Elizabeth found herself a little disappointed by the sight of him. In her mind, he was the man who left her behind. Who married the woman his family predetermined. Who turned his back on an implied promise between them.

"How is your father's health?"

"Excellent. Your mother's?"

"Excellent."

Silence continued between them once more. Finally, Alice gained the courage to make a decision for her friend. "I am very sorry, Mr. Rutledge, but Miss Knight is needed at the furniture store. We are attempting to find a curiosity for her desk before she leaves for Bryden, and we cannot dawdle as we have a great many things to do today."

"Yes, of course. How long are you in London, Miss Knight?"

"Only so long as to pack my trunks," she said.

"Ah. Well, then I regret not being able to call upon you."

Elizabeth did not answer. She did not even make a sound of acknowledgment. For some unfathomable reason, a general dislike of the man was growing inside her chest. After years of building him up in her mind, he suddenly failed to pass the test.

"Good day, sir."

"Good day, Miss Thorne. Miss Knight."

Elizabeth grabbed Alice's arm for support. Together, they walked toward the shop in silence. When Mr. Rutledge was beyond hearing them, Alice asked, "What did I just witness?"

"What you witnessed was a man I thought I would one day marry pretend he didn't recognize me," Elizabeth said. She blew out a breath. "I have not spoken to him in years."

"Are you well?"

Elizabeth smiled. "Is it possible to feel both resentment and relief?"

Alice looked back down the street, toward Mr. Ruteledge's direction. "In such matters, I almost hope so. I have met his wife. She's ornamental."

Elizabeth chuckled. "Oh, Alice, you do not need to abuse his wife on my account. It's not the poor woman's fault that he did not marry me. Come. Let us find the perfect secret box. I will not settle for anything less worthy."

"Allow me to do the haggling. You are atrocious at shopping in London," Alice said.

The ladies laughed and, arm-in-arm, they entered the shop where Elizabeth purchased her writing desk. It took them an hour, but Elizabeth eventually did leave with the perfect secret box, designed to fit at the very back of her desk's secret drawer. It was lined with velvet, to muffle the sound of coins rubbing together, and it cost her a shocking six shillings and ninepence. She spent another one shilling and twopence for a false trunk liner for her journals.

And she felt no guilt whatsoever.

THE LADIES OCCULT Society gathered in Aunt Cass's dining room. They laid out the book and the items purchased from the occult store. Elizabeth was not going to show everyone her box, but Alice insisted on her putting it into the desk. Elizabeth was uncomfortable with the ladies seeing she had so much money in the drawer, but it was not like they didn't know what was wrapped up in a couple of handkerchiefs and ribbon. She carefully placed the box in the back of the drawer and it immediately stopped looking like a storage box. It locked into place and could not be moved or opened.

Elizabeth pressed a tiny button that appeared to be a decoration and there was an audible click. Then she could pick up the box, and open the cover.

"I thought I would put our money in there," Elizabeth said.

"Our?" Maria asked.

"I have been considering the matter and a Ladies Occult Society should not have to worry about money. So, I believe I shall set aside a little of the income from the books to ensure that we can all have the necessary supplies to continue our learning."

"Please do not set aside all of your money," Susan said. "I would be very vexed if I discovered you were going without to help me."

"Indeed, the same with me," Alice said. "If I become destitute, I shall tell my horrible relations that I intend to attract a husband. I shall get a small fortune for clothes, and then I shall spend it all on my hobbies. If I should happen to not attract a husband, well, at least I attempted to please my family."

"Alice, I believe even your family's best wishes for your future won't be fooled by that scheme." Elizabeth smiled at her friends. Indeed, these women were her friends and family. "I was thinking that, perhaps, we could restart the Arthur Sherry name, as we become better at the occult. We could ask Mr. Grant to serve as our attorney and agent, and we could pretend we are a descendant of the original Mr. Sherry. Perhaps a grandson or great-grandson?"

"But we have yet to summon Mrs. Egerton!" Susan said.

"Well, then we should get started," Alice declared. "I long to be an occult authoress."

The first summoning attempt was done in Latin. That was deemed by Alice as an embarrassment, and even Maria and Aunt Cass were snickering at their poor pronunciations and accents. Alice determined that it was impossible to use Latin incantations because she was the only one who knew the language and it would not work.

The second attempt caused a flicker of wind, but then it passed. Susan felt they were growing closer.

As they gathered for the third attempt, Elizabeth asked, "Why do we need incantations anyway?"

"What do you mean?" Alice asked.

"We have attempted my uncle's casting multiple times, correct? And we continue to fail. Is it because, perhaps, that incantation was written by him in a manner that reflected him? And would not us, being young women of difficult circumstances, call upon someone like Mrs. Egerton with a very different goal and purpose in mind?"

A breeze fluttered the pages of Alice's journal.

"Mrs. Egerton? Is that you toying with us?"

The breeze was slightly less forceful this time.

"I do not know how to simply develop incantations, Elizabeth," Alice said. "I only study the ones that have worked. I have never attempted anything until I met you."

"Indeed, my sole experience has been to study and teach the basics. I did not even know it was possible for ladies to participate in the occult, much less actively summon magic," Susan agreed.

"I made a candle flicker to life when I was a little girl, though I believe my uncle had a servant behind the curtain helping that spell along," Elizabeth said with a smile.

Something in her heart said that a woman like Mrs. Egerton, who had already appeared in the world and knew what society was like for women, wouldn't have as many rigid expectations for form and formality. She would demand strength of character, determination of purpose, and resolve.

"Mrs. Egerton. We have formed our own society. We are calling ourselves the Ladies Occult Society," Elizabeth said.

The breeze fluttered through the room.

"We have determined that us three ladies, with the assistance of Aunt Cass and Maria, will form a society that only admits ladies, and who will work to support today's lady occultists, and for those to come. We will not always be together in body, but we will continue our studies and projects apart, always only a letter away. And we will protect each other from the men who would try to steal the work of past lady occultists."

Susan smiled. "And, when we are ready, we would like your permission to carry on Arthur Sherry's work."

Alice nodded at the others. "We have many different skills, and we wish to learn everything that we can."

Elizabeth picked up the autograph book and read, "Spirit of Chocolate and Roses, Join Our Quest. It is not enough that we need your guidance, but rather that we wish your company and invite you to join our society."

And just like that, Mrs. Egerton appeared in a fashionably smart, pale-yellow muslin gown, trimmed with black embroidery. The sleeves were puffed slightly, and a gauzy scarf decorated her neck. Her hair was styled to the current fashion, and she wore a smart cap atop her head, befitting a widow.

"Well done, ladies!" Mrs. Egerton exclaimed.

Elizabeth nearly stabbed herself with her quill as Alice clutched her into an embrace. Even Aunt Cass and Maria were laughing and talking excitedly. Susan's own laughter fueled a coughing fit.

"Now, now, ladies. Let us not debase ourselves with *giggles*. Look what you have done to poor Miss Susan!"

Elizabeth covered her mouth with her hand, unable to stop the giggle fit that had washed over her. "We are celebrating, Mrs. Egerton. Surely, there is room for a break from decorum?"

"Not on my watch," Mrs. Egerton said sternly. Though, Elizabeth clearly saw the ghost's frown flicker as she struggled to keep her stern exterior. "What price have you paid for this?"

"Price?" Alice asked.

"There is a theory that incantations come with a cost," Susan said. "The Royal Occult Society hold debates on this, as there is much confusion over what constitutes a cost. Those who believe the theory seem to think it is a financial cost."

Mrs. Egerton sighed dramatically, and Elizabeth grinned. "Oh, how I have missed the sound of your disapproval."

Mrs. Egerton looked at her. "You were the one who paid the cost. What was it?"

Elizabeth considered for a moment before answering quietly. "My peace of mind. I have lied to my family, and I have decided I will continue in that lie."

"Ah." Mrs. Egerton said. "That explained why the incantations did not work. I felt them, and I attempted to stir, but something held me back. Now I know. You had to give up something important to you to begin this journey."

"Yes." Elizabeth frowned. "I suppose as the owner of the book, it fell to me to pay the price."

"That was last night, though. You made your decision to protect your brother from your father's disappointment. You could not have possibly known that was needed to summon Mrs. Egerton," Susan said.

Mrs. Egerton tapped her chin. "The magic itself sometimes has its own mind, especially when doing a complicated task as summoning. But, now that you have tapped into bringing me forth, I suspect we will be able to work on a shorthand to bring me back and forth as you see fit."

"What a wonderful way to end my time in London," Elizabeth said. She only laughed when Mrs. Egerton scolded her for crying.

⚜ Chapter 16 ⚜

MARY'S LETTER ARRIVED the day Elizabeth packed for Bryden. Maria insisted upon driving Elizabeth back home, as Henry Thorne decided to remain in London to assist with the book sales. He promised to take any books back to Vane Park that she wished to store and for as long as she wished. They waited in the foyer for Maria to arrive with the carriage.

Aunt Cass cried all morning, and it took both Alice and Susan's assurances that they would not leave her before she finally accepted that she would not be left alone.

"I have grown so used to having you girls around. How shall I part from you?"

"Mrs. Spencer, I am certain that my brother would be thrilled if you wrote to him and asked if I could remain here for some time as a companion. Thrilled would be the proper word for it, too," Alice said. "And I have never felt so free in my life as I have had these days."

Susan sniffled and wept quietly, which brought on a coughing fit. "I am very much at your disposal, Mrs. Spencer."

"Oh you girls!" Aunt Cass wrapped her arms around both of them, and motioned for Elizabeth to join them.

Elizabeth's trunks were packed on the back of the carriage. Her writing desk was neatly placed on the floor inside the carriage, and her little table neatly folded perfectly alongside it, out of the way.

Elizabeth had sent Sally out to purchase her a small, used trunk that was light enough for her to carry, but that could withstand the trials and tribulations of travel. Sally returned with a perfect little trunk that looked brand new for the surprisingly low cost of only a shilling.

It could fit on her lap inside the carriage, so she would not have it out of her sight, or even under her feet. She also moved her desk's secret wooden box, with her fifty pounds, into her new trunk. She did not trust that much money to sit on the back of the carriage.

Elizabeth gave Sally a one-pound note as a tip. Little Tom got two shillings. The twins, who'd moved into the house to assist with the two young ladies, got a shilling each. She had never been able to afford such extravagance before, having always despaired about how little she could leave the servants at Ashbrook whenever she went to stay with Mary. However, she could afford it this time, and so she would with no regrets.

"Ladies, I promise I will write as soon as I arrive. I suspect I will be needed some days to aid Isabella, but then I shall begin on my studies. If you would be so kind, Susan, would you write to me an outline of study? I must start somewhere. And Alice? Would you so kindly continue going through the library? I am so sorry to leave this house without having finished the task."

"I am desperate to finish the drawing room!" Alice exclaimed. "Susan has already offered to assist me with the inventory list and we will make copies, of course, just as Mrs. Spencer and Mrs. Thorne had done. And Mr. Thorne, of course, will continue to help with the sale of the books. I am certain it will all turn out well."

"Indeed, Elizabeth. Do not worry," Susan said. "We will take care of the rest of the business here in town."

"Thank you so much."

There was a knock at the door and the ladies all began their hurried goodbyes. Elizabeth hugged them all a final time, and then dashed for the carriage. Once inside, Elizabeth greeted Maria and placed her small trunk on the seat next to her. They made light chatter after the final waves of goodbye.

"What is that?" Maria asked. "Oh. A letter from Mary. I can tell by your expression."

"I have yet to read it. It came as I was packing."
"Well, might as well get on with it."

Elizabeth,

The children wish me to thank you for the sweets. Miss Hattie has been dolling them out for good behaviour.

Thank you for the letters. It was very kind of you to take some time out of your new occult studies to send me what you could. I have not read any of the letters. I do not know if I will. Still, it is comforting to know they exist if I ever wish to.

I believe I shall assist you with sorting the remainder when I return to Bryden later this summer, or Christmas if I cannot get away. As I understand from our father, your occult studies will make it difficult for you to find time for your many duties to your family, but Isabella says not to be cross with you, so I shall not.

Mary

"That was surprisingly cold, even for Mary," Maria said.

Elizabeth folded the letter carefully and placed it inside her trunk. "Mary does not remember our mother. Her only mother was Augusta. So, she struggles with the knowledge that another woman brought her into the world who was not Augusta. Now that I think on it, that is perhaps why Augusta did not like me. Mary called her Mama. I called her Mrs. Knight, until my father put an end to that."

"How did you ever get him to agree to you calling her Augusta?"

"My dear Maria, surely by now you have noticed I have the most displeasing of female traits. In some circles, it is called stubbornness." Elizabeth laughed. "I, however, prefer to call it conviction of purpose."

"That does sound nobler," Maria said.

They were outside of London before Maria finally said, "I know about Mr. R."

"Alice?" Elizabeth guessed.

"Henry was on Charles Street. He saw."

"Ah."

"How difficult was it?"

Elizabeth considered not answering her friend; Maria would understand. However, their friendship deserved the honesty. "At first, I felt the same rush of affection. But, there was a coldness about him that I never saw before. I do not know if I was blind to it, or if he had changed. The longer I stood there, the angrier I became at the very sight of him."

"That is only to be expected. You thought you were going to marry him."

"No, that was not the source of my anger. At least, it did not feel as though it came from there."

"Then where?"

"It was as though my heart was angry for ever having loved him." She smiled at Maria. "I believe whatever was in my heart for him is now gone forever. I am surprised by the relief that gives me."

ELIZABETH'S ARRIVAL HOME was not as joyous as it should have been. Cassandra grasped her in a grip of the suffering. Thea was sullen. G was loud and abrasive. Isabella looked pale and tired, but was in excellent spirits all the same. Mrs. Taylor stayed at the rectory for three more days, to allow Elizabeth the opportunity to settle in. Then, she accepted an invitation to return to London with Maria.

Her father was cold to her and avoided her company whenever possible. He frequently was away all day, and often did not return from his many visits about the parish until well into the evening. He was not at home for even one family dinner.

Charles, likewise, was nowhere to be seen. He left word that he and his father decided to travel to Ashbrook.

"Something about asking Mr. Fitzharding for assistance with Oxford," Isabella said.

Elizabeth was seated in the drawing room, in the small side chair. Isabella was propped up on pillows on the sofa. "My father is angry, isn't he?"

"No, I would not call it anger. It was more embarrassment that he and your brother were duped by those men. And that the person who saw through them…"

"Was me," Elizabeth finished.

"They will come around." Isabella looked about the room, ensuring they were alone. "Elizabeth, do not tell me how much money you made from your books."

"I…why not?"

Isabella chose her words carefully. "Most likely, we will have to hire a nurse to help care for me if my condition worsens. Charles wishes to return to Oxford. Cassandra is out in society now and we need to spend money on her clothes and dresses. And your father is leaning toward letting Thea and G as well, since that might be the only way to get any peace around here. So, more dresses and more hats, and all of that."

"Ah."

"Please take no offense in what I am about to say, but it is clear that you will not be marrying."

"I will not. Especially not at my age and with a much younger sisters."

Isabella nodded, still choosing her words carefully. "Charles may have let it slip that you will have made more money than any of us were expecting while in London. He said something about it being the talk of the town. Now, of course, we can dismiss most of that as idle gossip. But, you should know that there is an expectation that you will share."

Elizabeth blew out a breath. She had known this would happen. And she had prepared for it. "Mr. Thorne is selling the remainder of my books. I gave money to you, for the girls, and to Charles, to help him. I also purchased my desk and my table, as I wished something that was mine."

"Oh, Elizabeth, please do not think we want all your money. Not even your father said that. He simply…" Isabella sighed.

"You do not need to explain."

"Explain what?" Mr. Knight asked, strolling into the room.

"We were…um…" Isabella stammered.

Elizabeth smiled and said, "Discussing how best to distribute my good fortune from the sale of my books that I inherited from my uncle."

Mr. Knight's face brightened for the first time since she had arrived in Bryden. "Oh, indeed?"

"I am unsure of the total price, of course, since Mr. Thorne has not completed the task in London. And I gave Charles five pounds in London, to help with his expenses. And the three pounds to the girls. Then, I purchased myself my desk and table, as well as a small trunk. And the writing desk for Cassandra for her birthday, but please do not say anything. It's still in London. That leaves me with a little more than eight pounds."

"Oh, that is disappointing. Those occult fellows made it sound like it would be more."

"That is not all, though, Mr. Knight. There is still what is left in London," Isabella said. She glanced at Elizabeth. "How many books are left?"

Elizabeth did not lie when she said, "I have to think. We separated the library books from my inheritance. I believe my books are three of the trunks. I provided Mr. Thorne the list, so I do not remember precisely."

"Oh, so that should fetch us another pretty sum?" her father asked, brightened at the prospect of unexpected money.

"Yes, indeed. However, I cannot plan for that, since we do not know how long it will take to sell, or if they have to go to auction. We might not make as much that way. However, the eight pounds I have is ours to share. I simply did not know how best to distribute it, especially since I gave Charles more than the girls."

"It is only right and proper for Charles to have it. He has Oxford to consider."

"Is he going back?" Isabella asked.

"That is what he says. Mr. Fitzharding has agreed to cover his tuition for the final year, which is a great relief for us all." Mr.

Knight smiled at his daughter. "I must say, Elizabeth, Charles spoke rather highly of your behaviour in London."

"That is very kind of him," Elizabeth said.

Her father eyed her. "What happened in London? Charles was very much against going back to Oxford until he went to London. Now, he returns and begs for assistance."

"I had understood that was what you had wished for him," Elizabeth said.

She absolutely did not want to lie to her father's face. More importantly, she did not know if she could. He might see through her.

"Yes, Charles gaining his ordination has always been my wish. I think he will grow into the role. And he is still young enough to handle the rigors of a curacy, and has no wife or child to support." He did not break eye contact. "But not a day before he left for London, he'd said that he was not ready for Oxford. And yet, now he returns a changed man, with five pounds in his pocket."

"I gave him that, Papa."

"I know you did. Why?"

Elizabeth gulped and said, "There was no purpose. He was in town, and needed to stay some days. I had come into a little money, and felt it was better to share it with him than for him to write home and ask for more."

Her father was not convinced. It was obvious in his stare. "Was he gambling in London?"

"I did not see him gamble, or even play cards. As I understood it, he often ate at a Sir Gregory's house. Charles had gone to school with the gentleman's son."

"Are either of these men gamesters?"

Elizabeth shook her head. "Truly, I do not know. I have not met either. I only know Sir Gregory's name through my uncle's lawyer, Mr. Grant. He is also a friend of this Sir Gregory, so he is an acquaintance of Charles', too, I suppose."

"And this Mr. Grant. Do you trust him?"

"Me?" Elizabeth asked. Her father had never asked her opinion on anything in her entire life.

Her father drew in a deep breath, as if he were about to swallow a bee. He glanced at Isabella, who gave him a knowing look. He took another deep breath, preparing himself for whatever horrid thing he needed to say.

"Sometime, along the path of life, my eldest daughter turned into a rather intelligent, prudent, resourceful young woman. And, so, I find myself wondering if that daughter was able to do for my son what I could not."

Mr. Knight had never complimented Elizabeth in her entire life. Any compliment he issued was for all of his daughters, as one bunch of pretty flowers. He called Mary out by her name, of course. But never Elizabeth.

Until now.

"I did nothing but encourage him to follow what was in his heart." Elizabeth forced a smile. "So, whatever was there, you and Augusta had instilled it in him."

He gave Isabella a final look before his shoulders sagged. "Of course. All this worry is turning me into an old woman, fretting about the young people in the village. Eight pounds, did you say? That is after you gave away all of your money? I saw the ribbons you brought back from London, Miss Elizabeth Knight. There is enough there for us to open our own shop in the kitchen!"

Elizabeth let out the breath she was holding when her father turned to pour himself a cup of tea. She had managed not to tell an outright lie to her father. She thought of the book and her fifty pounds. Now both would need to remain a secret.

But, for now, she knew how Henry Thorne felt when his father told him well done. For she, too, would grasp at this compliment of her father's and hold it tight in the coming days. No doubt, she would need it.

~⚜ Author's Note ⚜~

MR. WILLIAM LEACH Osborne was a real person. He was the son of Ignatius Sancho, a British composer, writer, shopkeeper, and abolitionist. Sancho wrote poetry, plays, songs, minuets, and composed musical arrangements. He also had a wild streak and once lost his clothes gambling! The famous Thomas Gainsborough even painted his portrait. He was left a legacy by the Duchess of Montagu, which he used to set up a greengrocer shop. After Sancho's death, his son, William Osborne, inherited his father's shop on Charles Street and eventually turned it into a book shop and publishing house.

There's just a small problem with this: Mr. Osborne died in 1810, at the age of thirty-five. But, since this is fiction, I decided that this would not be a problem at all. And, since there was another London bookshop owner, another Mr. Osborne, who lived in the mid-eighteenth century, I decided to combine their careers somewhat.

Mr. *Thomas* Osborne was rather famous for buying up estate library collections, and then breaking them down into individual prices for each book. He even produced catalogues of his books. He died in 1767. This Mr. Osborne didn't have the best of reputations (there were plenty of comments about his abrasive personality), so I decided to use only his career exploits. After all, there are enough awful men in this book; I didn't need anymore inspirations.

So, while my Mr. William Osborne was a real person, his career exploits are fictional. Partially of my own making and partially reimagined from Mr. Thomas Osborne of half a century earlier.

IF YOU'D LIKE to read more about famous people from Georgian, Regency, and Victorian London, as well as the everyday lives for people like Miss Susan and Mrs. Taylor, I recommend you check out my non-fiction book, *Hustlers, Harlots, and Heroes: A Regency and Steampunk Field Guide*. It's available in ebook and print (and, just so you know, the print's layout is gorgeous and makes a lovely gift) .

About the Author

KRISTA D. BALL WAS BORN and raised in Deer Lake, Newfoundland, where she learned how to use a chainsaw, chop wood,and make raspberry jam. After obtaining a B.A. in British History from Mount Allison University, Krista moved to Edmonton, AB where she currently lives.

Somehow, she's picked up an engineer, two kids, six cats, and two very understanding corgis off ebay. Her credit card has been since taken away.

Like any good writer, Krista has had an eclectic array of jobs throughout her life, including strawberry picker, pub bathroom cleaner, oil spill cleaner upper and soupkitchen coordinator. These days, when Krista isn't software testing, she writes in her messy office.

 Also by Krista D. Ball

Tales of Tranquility Series
Spirit Caller Series
The Dark Abyss of Our Sins Series

Collaborator Series

Appropriately Aggressive

What Kings Ate and Wizards Drank
Hustlers, Harlots, and Heroes

www.ingramcontent.com/pod-product-compliance
Lightning Source LLC
Chambersburg PA
CBHW020604260626
47157CB00003B/859